MORNING JOURNEY

Books by James Hilton

LOST HORIZON
KNIGHT WITHOUT ARMOUR
RANDOM HARVEST
NOTHING SO STRANGE
SO WELL REMEMBERED

MORNING JOURNEY

BY

JAMES HILTON

MACMILLAN

First Edition 1951
Reprinted 1952, 1970

Published by
MACMILLAN AND CO LTD
London and Basingstoke
Associated companies in New York Toronto
Dublin Melbourne Johannesburg and Madras

Printed in Great Britain by
LOWE AND BRYDONE (PRINTERS) LTD
London

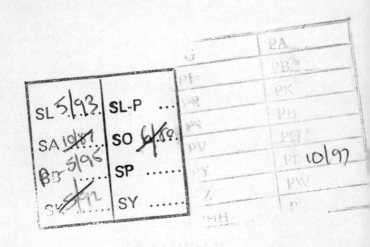

PROLOGUE

GEORGE HARE (of Hare, Briggs, Burton, and Kurtnitz) met Carey Arundel for the first time at the annual Critics' Dinner at Verino's. She was to receive a plaque for the best actress performance of the year, Greg Wilson was to get the actor's, and Paul Saffron the director's. These dinners were rather stuffy affairs, but the awards were worth getting; this year *Morning Journey* was the picture that had swept the board, all the winners having scored in it. George had seen the picture and thought it good, if a trifle tricky. He was far more concerned with his luck in being next to Carey at the dinner, for his own well-concealed importance in the movie world did not always receive such rewards. George had an eye for beauty which, combined with a somewhat cynical nose for fame, made him take special notice of her. Of course he had seen her on the stage as well as on the screen, but he thought she looked best of all in real life — which meant, even more remarkably, that she looked really alive at a party such as this, not merely brought to life by ambition or liquor.

George left her to her other neighbour for a while; he was lazy socially, content often to talk with those who would seek him out, which many people did, liking him personally and eager for any titbit of scandal that might slip from his legally acquired store. He never spilled anything worth much, but always seemed about to, and nobody realized that he picked up far more than he let drop. He was so shrewd in business that people thought his air of innocence could not possibly be real, but there was a sense in which it was, and thus he often fooled and foiled his adversaries. It was this innocence that had made him say, when introduced to Carey at the table: " You played in Boston once when I was at Harvard — I can't remember the play, but I couldn't forget *you*." She had laughed, and somebody who had overheard said later that nobody had ever pinned an age on an actress more securely (though that had not been George's intention at all). But now, turning to him again more than half-way through the meal, she said: " I think it must have been *Quality Street* you saw me in, Mr. Hare."

George was surprised she had even caught his name, and this was not modesty so much as an awareness that in a community where big names are a dime a dozen, some of the higher price tags are on the big nameless.

He said: " That's right, so it was."

" Because I don't believe I ever played in Boston in anything else. Not in those days."

" Not so very long ago," he commented gallantly.

" Twenty years."

He smiled. " What does it feel like to be a well-known actress all that time and then have people behave out here as if they'd discovered you ? "

She laughed. " It's funny."

" I hope you'll tell them that in your speech."

She seemed a little perturbed. " Oh, do I have to make a speech ? "

" I'm sure we all hope you will. But it needn't be a long one. Do speeches make you nervous ? "

" Other people's do, occasionally." He thought it was just a witticism till she added: " Paul's especially, Paul Saffron — the director. He can be so tactless." She went on hastily: " No, I'm not exactly scared to speak in public, but I find it much harder than acting. Perhaps that only means I find it hard to act the part of myself."

" Ethel Barrymore once told me practically the same thing." He proceeded to compliment her on *Morning Journey*, her first picture and such a success, and she thanked him with a genuine pleasure that lit her face like a girl's, but with life rather than mere youthfulness. George wondered (as one always must with an actress) whether the transfigurement was natural or a practised artifice; frankly he could

2

not judge, and admiringly he did not care — it was quite remarkable either way.

"Of course, you won't go back to the stage again," he said, and continued : " I say that because I hope you will."

" I might."

" But first, I suppose, another picture ? "

" No, I've no plans for that. I've no definite plans for anything, except perhaps a vacation in Ireland. . . . By the way, Mr. Hare, you're the lawyer, aren't you ? "

" *The* lawyer ? Let's settle for *a* lawyer."

" I wonder if you could help me."

" Of course. Trouble of some kind ? "

He guessed she must have some other lawyer or lawyers somewhere, together with the usual outfit of agents, business managers, tax-consultants, and so on ; he knew also how impulsively actors get themselves into a mess and how capriciously they can turn on those whom they pay to get them out. Maybe she was in a mood for such a change. He himself had tried to winnow down his clientele into those who were his personal friends and who, if they did get into trouble, would give him the pleasure as well as the task of extrication. He wondered if he would want Carey Arundel as such a client, even if she asked him. Possibly.

She was answering his question : " Oh, nothing very important. I just thought of sub-letting my apartment while I go to Ireland, but the lease says I can't."

George might well have replied that if the lease said she couldn't, then very probably she couldn't ; or he might have tactfully conveyed that he was a busy and expensive lawyer and that any financial advantage of sub-tenancy could easily turn out to be less than his fees if she got into trouble over it. But simply because he continued to like the look of her, and also the sound of her voice, he said instead : " Be glad to help you. Send — or better still — bring the lease along to my office and I'll see if anything can be done." The chairman was pounding his gavel for silence, so he hastened to add : " Any time. Tomorrow morning if you like."

" Thanks. Tomorrow morning, then," she said hurriedly,

fixing her face for the degree of attention that was appropriate in one about to be honoured.

The chairman made a very dull speech about the significance of motion pictures in the national life, and during the applause that followed George said: " Are you by any chance going on to the Fulton-Griffins' when this thing is over ? "

" Oh, I don't think so. I was asked, but I understand there's such a crowd always there, and I hate crowds."

" So do I, but a Fulton-Griffin party is something you ought to see if you haven't been to one before. I thought if you were going I'd have a chance to talk to you without all these interruptions."

" Oh yes, I'd like that, but I really think I ought to go home. I've been rather tired since the picture finished and—"

The chairman was introducing the next speaker, a local politician who would present the awards. He was her neighbour on the other side, so the mechanics of it would be simple. But he talked too long, though he was easier to listen to and told a few mildly amusing stories. Presently he veered his remarks in her direction and announced her as the winner of the actress award.

George applauded with more than his usual fervour when she accepted the plaque. Then she made a short but charming speech in which there was no discernible trace of nervousness at all. He wondered if it were concealed, or whether she had made a habit of telling people about it in advance and then surprising them. George, however, was not surprised. He had seen tricks like that before, and had sometimes practised them in court with much success. But he admired the total effect of her performance and was more than sincere in his whispered " Bravo " when she sat down. " You did very well," he commented.

" Did I ? Who's next ? Is it Greg ? "

It was Greg. He was a handsome fellow, invariably cast for heroic parts; not a great actor, not even in his own estimation. Sufficient that in a few ill-chosen sentences he could mumble thanks and work off a laboured gag about golf, which was his passion and pastime; any eloquence, even too much coherence, would have been almost disconcerting from such a source.

Then the director's award to Paul Saffron. For some reason Saffron was seated far down the table, and had to come forward to a microphone; as he did so George studied him with curiosity, chiefly because of Carey's remark that his speeches were apt to make her nervous. George wondered how many of them she had been forced to hear. Saffron was certainly a personality; his face large and jowly, the expression that of a man facing limitless challenge; there was a certain splendour, though, in the contour of cheeks and forehead, caprice in the waving wispy hair, something of a Pan-like sparkle in the small blue-grey eyes. George wondered if he had drunk too much; a few minutes later he was beginning to wonder what else could be the matter with the man.

For it was, by and large, the most deplorable exhibition George could remember. Saffron, in a strident staccato that would have been loud enough even without a microphone, began by telling the donors of the award that he considered their choice a bad one. At first some of the audience thought this must be a joke, but he glared them down and went on to state categorically that *Morning Journey* was the worst picture he had ever made. " Of course an artist gets used to being praised for all the wrong reasons — he's lucky to be praised at all — and in my own case I can boast that my best work was *never* praised, it was never even finished — they wouldn't allow me to finish it." (He didn't say who ' they ' were, but by this time it was abundantly clear that he was not cracking jokes.) " As for *Morning Journey*, I have this to say, and as an artist I must say it, that the picture you have so extravagantly praised and undeservedly honoured is a product of the gigantic factory that does for entertainment what Henry Ford has done for automobiles. A *competent* picture — oh yes. A *clever* picture — perhaps. But a *great* picture? . . . Oh dear no, let us save that word for some occasion when it might possibly be needed — even here. Because it *has* been needed here — in earlier days. Griffith could have claimed the word — and Chaplin — perhaps a few others whose names are less well known, perhaps a few whose names are by now completely forgotten. . . ."

George shared the general discomfort with which all this was received. It was not that he specially disagreed; he had no great opinion of Hollywood and all it stood for; to him it was a place to earn a living, a place also in which he had found friends. A few of Saffron's remarks he would not have disputed at all — for instance — " This place is full of craftsmen who might have been artists if only they'd stayed away." That, in a magazine article, might have been worth saying and quotable; on an occasion such as this it seemed merely graceless. There was, indeed, an appalling disregard of the feelings of others in the whole spectacle, and George, who considered manners more important than sincerity on many of the occasions of life, felt as if his mental well-being were being sandpapered. When, he speculated, does such an irritant make one get up and punch somebody on the nose? Then he chanced to catch Carey's face and saw in it a disturbance so extreme that his own indignation sharpened. By that time Saffron had abruptly finished; with the plaque in his hand, he had not even said thank-you.

There was perhaps as little applause as a speaker could ever receive without being actually booed or hissed; the chairman rose and, bore though he was, eased the situation and won a grateful laugh by saying: " I think, Mr. Saffron, we must all feel that you are a better maker of pictures than a judge of them."

The affair broke up very quickly after that, many showing an embarrassed eagerness to escape. Held in conversation with his other neighbour, George was presently aware that Carey had left the table without a sign or a good-night. As he mingled with the departing crowd, he caught sight of Randolph, the producer of *Morning Journey*. Randolph, whom he knew fairly well, was in consternation; all he

6

could mutter was : " What got into that guy ? Is he crazy ? You saw the press taking it all down — they loved it — I suppose that's what he's after — what *else* could he be after ? "

George thought it pathetic that Randolph should not even contemplate the possibility that Saffron, however nastily, had been actuated by a desire to tell what he believed to be the truth. One need not, of course, think of such a thing nine times out of ten, but it was foolish to deny that it could conceivably happen. All of which, however, George wisely kept to himself.

Suddenly voices upraised near the exit revealed the by now unmistakable element of Saffron's, his high-pitched tenor involved in an argument. " Of course she's an artist," he was shouting. " Not a supreme artist, I grant you, but——"

" What d'you mean ? " someone interrupted. " Are you talking like God, or just jealous of her success ? "

" I'm proud of her success. It was always my ambition——"

" So you take all the credit ? "

George was near enough now to recognize the other man as a young journalist named Hazelton who wrote movie criticism for one of the local papers.

" I take much of the credit," Saffron was retorting, " because I know she needs someone else to bring out what she has, which is quite enchanting in its own way——"

" Then how can you say she isn't a great artist ? "

" *Supreme* was the word I used."

" All right. *Supreme.* Maybe she isn't. Maybe she isn't even great. After your speech tonight we know how you feel about the word. But she's *good* — or do you deny that ? "

" Of course I don't, but *you* don't know *how* good she is. How could you ? Are you an actor ? Have you directed plays ? Do you know anything about acting and the theatre ? "

This was so brazen that it had to lead to either a fight or

laughter. Hazelton chose to laugh. " I won't argue that, Saffron, except to tell you I've seen her act when you had nothing to do with it."

" In what, may I ask ? "

Hazelton mentioned a Broadway comedy that had enjoyed a long run during the later years of the second world war.

Saffron snorted. " Rubbish."

" But *she* was good in it."

" No."

" Did you see her ? "

" My friend, I had the misfortune to spend that period of my life in an internment camp in France while you were gadding about to New York theatres—"

Hazelton laughed again. " I happened to be on leave from the Pacific, but let that pass. The point is — and take my word for it — she was *good* in that play."

" And take my word for it she was best of all as Desdemona, before you were born, and as Candida in the Shaw play, and as Mrs. Vincent in a play called *The Widow in the Forest* which was a great hit when you must have been in knee pants——"

" All of which, Saffron, by sheer coincidence you directed yourself ? "

" No coincidence at all. She's always best when I direct her."

" Ah — so now we know. She has to have you."

" Yes. And she knows it. She knows it better than anybody."

Hazelton moved away still laughing and Saffron completed his exit to the corridor. When he had gone, Hazelton spotted George, whom he knew, and walked over to him. " You heard all that ? What a guy ! What an evening ! Well, it's something to write about, anyhow. The most exciting thing at a show like this since DeMille called the Chinese Ambassador a Jap — remember that ? "

Randolph said : " I suppose it's no good asking you boys to play it down. A packet of bad publicity for the whole industry. . . ."

Of course it was no use. One might be able to buy a certain amount of good publicity space-wise, but the real news nuggets, the mishaps and misfires of the celebrated, were so precious that no paper could afford to let them go. By that reckoning a table brawl at Ciro's was always more important than the Nobel Peace Prize.

. . . . . .

George went on to the Fulton-Griffins', where the party was already in full swing and where every new arrival from the Critics' Dinner was being asked what had really happened. George took pleasure in lowering the temperature. " No," he kept on saying, " there were *no* blows traded — *nobody* got hurt — it wasn't half as exciting as you think. Saffron made a silly speech, that's all."

" But he insulted Miss Arundel, didn't he ? "

" No. All he said was that *Morning Journey* was the worst picture he'd ever made, which by implication of course wasn't so very kind to——"

" But didn't he say she was a bad actress and couldn't do a thing without him as director ? "

" That was afterwards — and anyhow, that wasn't what he said at all. As a matter of fact he defended her — he said she was enchanting—"

But George knew that rumour could never be overtaken by fact. He broke off with a shrug : " Ask someone else. I wasn't the only one there."

But he also knew that others who had been asked, or would be before the evening was out, were less trained than he in the reporting of evidence, as well as possibly less ethical. He edged away from the crowd and found his usual comfortable corner with a drink which he could make last a long time, and with enough people to enjoy talking to among those who would look for him. He kept thinking of Carey and wondering how soon the twists and exaggerations of what had happened would get to her ears. Several people he talked to mentioned her sympathetically ; during the short time she had been on the Coast she seemed to have made herself generally liked. Saffron, by contrast, was in the special dog-house reserved for those whose unpopularity has somehow not deprived them of stature. Diagnosis of him veered from the surly genius to the psychopathic charlatan; anecdotes in proof or disproof were in steady supply as argument grew livelier. An actor who had had a small part in *Morning Journey* remembered that Miss Arundel had once quarrelled bitterly with Saffron in one of the studio dressing-rooms during the making of the picture.

George acquired for a moment his court-room air. - " You heard this quarrel yourself ? "

" One of the prop men told me — seems it was the lunch time when nobody else was around. He said Saffron had a gun and was threatening her with it."

" Why didn't the prop man do something ? "

" Aw, why should he get mixed up in what wasn't his business ? That's what he said."

" Even if a man's threatening a woman with a gun ? "

" Apparently she wasn't hurt."

" And she didn't complain ? "

" I guess not."

" And they both went on with the picture after lunch as if nothing had happened ? "

" I know — it's hard to believe. But so was tonight hard to believe — unless you were there."

" But I *was* there. And already the whole thing's inflated out of all relation to the truth."

But again it was no use. George settled down to enjoying himself as a guest at a party; why work for nothing ?

Towards midnight someone brought him news which at first he could only think was another rumour — that Carey Arundel had actually arrived at the party. At that stage of the evening, with two or three hundred persons overflowing from a large house into flood-lit gardens, the presence or absence of any individual was not easy to determine outside the range of sight, and George recollected that he was probably the only person to whom Carey's intention of not coming to the Fulton-Griffin party had been definitely stated only a few hours before. So he doubted the report until he saw her approaching him.

The first thing he noticed was an almost astonishing radiance about her, as if she had given herself some central glow to match the exterior lighting of beauty. She had also changed into another dress much more startling than the one she had worn at the dinner; it had an austere simplicity of line that permitted a special drama of colour and texture. George would say afterwards " a sort of crimson velvet " and leave it at that.

" Hello, Mr. Hare," she said, smiling.

" Well, Miss Arundel, this *is* a surprise. You changed your mind ? "

" I often do."

" So we *can* finish our talk. That's good."

" Yes, but let's go outside. The gardens are lovely."

He led her through the French windows on to a terrace that stepped down to the swimming-pool where a fair-sized crowd had congregated. He found a side-path leading through a grove of eucalyptus trees.

" I felt I had to come," she said, " just to show I don't feel all the things people are thinking I feel."

" You're very wise," he answered, taking her arm. " What Saffron did say, as opposed to all the talk of what he said, wasn't really against *you*. Therefore there's nothing for you to be hurt or humiliated about."

" I'm so glad you think that."

" Just stupid of him and in bad taste."

" Oh yes, oh yes, I know it was."

" Rather odd — coming just after you'd told me his speeches sometimes made you nervous."

" Yes, wasn't it odd ? "

" You must have had a lot of experience of him."

She said quietly : " Well, we were married, once."

He could not conceal the measure of his surprise. " You *were* ? "

" Didn't you know ? '

" I didn't, and as everybody else here must, it's rather

astonishing nobody happened to mention it to me. I suppose they assumed I knew."

" So you've been talking about me to people ? "

" A few people have been talking about you to me."

" What do they say ? "

" They like you — and they don't like him."

" They don't have to couple us together any more."

" Except that you were in the picture together."

" Yes — for a special reason, but that's a long story — I might tell you some time, if you're interested."

Some men and girls were approaching.

" Maybe tomorrow ? Don't forget you have a date at my office. Make it eleven-thirty and I'll take you to lunch."

" Fine." And she added as they walked back towards the house : " He didn't show up here tonight, did he ? "

" No. I'm sure I'd have known if he had. Did you think he might ? "

" He's capable of it. If he'd been here I'd have wanted to leave — I couldn't stand any more."

" I don't blame you."

" I'm just about at the limit of what I can stand, to be frank."

" You probably need that holiday in Ireland you talked about. But why Ireland ? "

" I was born there. Where were you born ? "

" Vermont . . . on a farm."

" So was I. In County Kildare. The greenest fields, and my father rode the wildest and most beautiful horses. . . ." She paused as if some secret recollection had stolen her away ; George watched her, till she caught his look. She smiled embarrassedly. " Oh, I guess we all feel that about where we were born. Vermont is beautiful too."

" Yes, very. . . ." The people who were approaching had voices he recognized ; he said hastily : " There's just time for one more question before the mob finds you again . . . a rather personal question, so don't be startled. . . . Did Saffron ever — in a dressing-room at the studio while the picture was being made — did he ever quarrel with you and threaten you with a gun ? "

She looked amazed, then laughed. " Good heavens, no. Who on earth made that one up ? "

They separated inside the house, and soon afterwards George left ; it was already long past his usual bedtime. A few hours later (nine, to be exact) he was telling his secretary he would see Miss Arundel as soon as she arrived. But she did not arrive, and about noon he found out where she lived and telephoned. It was a fashionable apartment hotel and the desk informed him she was out. He thought she was probably on her way, but after a late lunch alone he was concerned enough to telephone Randolph at the studio. Randolph said she had not only not been there, but they had been trying for hours to find where she was and why she had broken an appointment to see some publicity people. It was not like her, Randolph said, to be either forgetful or unco-operative and already he was a little worried. " The hotel people were cagey at first about what time she got home, but finally they said it was about one o'clock."

" Sounds reasonable. I left the Fulton-Griffins' soon after midnight and she was still there. She had a date to see me at eleven-thirty this morning."

" I didn't know she was one of your clients."

" She wasn't — till last night."

" Was it important business — or I suppose you can't tell me that ? "

George Hare was a highly successful lawyer for a number of reasons, one of which was that he never kept a secret that didn't matter.

" Of course I'll tell you — she wanted to know if she could sub-let her apartment while she takes a vacation in Ireland. Hardly headline news, is it ? "

" Talking of headlines, what do you think of the Saffron thing ? "

" Been too busy to see the papers yet. Do they make much of it ? "

" You bet they do, and in some ways I'm glad they could

13

tie it all into one story. Sort of takes the edge off what he said when the police found him drunk."

" I don't — quite — get you, Randolph. How do the police come into it ? "

" You mean you don't know what happened after he left the dinner ? "

" I told you I hadn't seen the papers."

" Well, read 'em, they'll give you the details. Not that there's much to it if it hadn't been him, but he was a fool to talk back to the cops. That's probably why they took him along. Of course as a studio we're not interested — so far as he's concerned, we're through. But we don't like him upsetting *her*."

" Naturally. And from what she told me last night she's had enough of him to last a lifetime. By the way, how much of a lifetime *did* it last ? Her marriage, I mean ? "

" To Saffron ? Oh, that was all years ago."

" Did she never marry again ? "

" Sure, she's got a husband now — but they're supposed to be separating or separated. Millionaire banker, broker, something like that. New York. . . . The latest gossip links her with Greg Wilson."

Oh no, George thought in protest — not Greg Wilson. But then he realized what was behind the protest, and being skilled in self-diagnosis, he was astonished. For already he was aware of something quite unexampled in his experience. He liked women and had frequently thought he loved them, but never before had he been able to contemplate marriage. Now, quite suddenly, he was able. Not a desire, of course, just a pleasure in abstract thought. And it was absurd — after an hour or so of acquaintance and a few scraps of conversation. Yet it did not *seem* absurd, and that was what made it such an astonishment to him. He had not known he was capable of it.

Randolph was waiting, so he said lightly : " Sounds a little confusing, Randy."

" Did you ever know the life of an actress that wasn't ? Not that Greg Wilson seems to me her type."

14

"Maybe she doesn't have a type. She isn't one, why should she have one? Well, call me up later if you get more news."

George then sent out for the morning papers, and while they were coming he brushed aside the work on his desk and indulged in a daydream. He wondered if what she really sought from him was advice on matters more important than sub-letting an apartment — her marriage problem, maybe? Perhaps she wanted a divorce from the millionaire? George was an expert in getting divorces from (and for) millionaires. It would be exciting to be able to help her, to show off a little in doing so, to say in that calm, casual way that had reassured so many clients during their first professional interview: "Sure, we'll get what you want. Not a doubt of it. Just relax and don't worry. . . ."

The papers then arrived and he found the Saffron affair two-columned on the front page under the caption: "Abuses Hollywood, then Cops; Noted Director makes Morning Journey to Jail". There was the usual photograph through prison bars, and the story had been written up in that style of deadpan glee which, by long experience, has proved most effective in making the fall of the mighty pleasurable to the masses.

"Paul Saffron, director of the hit picture *Morning Journey*, gave Hollywood a straight punch to the jaw in his speech at the Critics' Dinner last night." (Then a technically indisputable but thoroughly tendentious summary of what Saffron had said.) "Unfortunately Mr. Saffron was just as mad with the police an hour later when they asked why he had bashed in the fenders of a parked car outside his apartment. . . ." Etc. etc.

George telephoned a few people who would know and found that the case, though trivial, would make further headlines if only because of Saffron's emphatic denials and generally truculent behaviour in court that morning. But as he had admitted a few drinks at the dinner and been unable to pass a sobriety test, he might just as well have pleaded guilty from the outset. On the whole he was lucky to get off with a fifty-dollar fine.

15

George was working late at the office that evening and about ten o'clock Randolph called him again. "Still missing, George, but a scrap more news. We finally got the hotel clerk to admit that she went out again about half an hour after checking in. She'd changed to street clothes and drove off in her car. Now where could she go alone at half-past one in the morning?"

"Ah," said George, beginning to chuckle because of the twinge of jealousy that made him catch his breath.

Randolph ignored the frivolity. "Well, it so happens we do know where she went, because the clerk eavesdropped on a phone call. You'd never guess."

"I probably wouldn't. Where was it?"

"The Observatory on Mount Wilson. She called up somebody there and asked if she could look at the stars."

"Any proof that she did?"

"Not yet, but someone's on his way there to find out. Have to tread carefully, we don't want the papers to make another sensation."

After Randolph hung up, George telephoned the Observatory. He wouldn't have been a good lawyer if he hadn't been able to ask a straight question without making it seem important. Within five minutes he was talking to a quiet-spoken man who said he was Professor Lingard and readily confirmed that Miss Arundel had indeed visited the Observatory the previous night. "Anything wrong?" asked the Professor.

"Not a thing," answered George. "She just didn't keep an appointment for lunch, but she often does things like that — she's a little haywire about times and places. We just wondered what she was up to during the small hours, that's all. 'We' is her studio and I'm her lawyer." And he laughed as if the whole thing was just part of some good-hearted fun he was having.

The Professor did not attempt to share the fun, but he explained with great seriousness how it had all come about. He said that about 1 A.M. Miss Arundel had telephoned to ask if it were a right time for coming up to look at the sky.

No, he didn't know her well, he had met her only once before, but they had talked about astronomy and he had invited her to visit the Observatory some suitable night. That night being one of the best, he had answered sure, come by all means. He himself was at work with his assistant, as always when weather conditions were thus favourable. She had reached the Observatory about two-thirty and he had been slightly surprised that she was alone — she hadn't mentioned anyone else, but somehow he had assumed she would have company on the rather lonely drive to the mountain-top. They had spent perhaps an hour at the big telescope; she had then said she must go. He and his assistant had taken her to her car about a quarter to four.

" Did she say she was going straight home ? "

" I imagined she was. We talked about it being sunrise before she'd get there."

" So she's probably asleep still. . . . Well, thanks, Professor, it's been very kind of you."

He was just about to hang up when the Professor added, with a blandness that George thought remarkable : " I suppose she never arrived home at all and you're looking for her ? I'm afraid I can't help you much about that. She was wide awake when she left and certainly able to drive a car. I myself drove down the mountain about half an hour later and there was no sign of any accident."

" Did you expect one ? " George asked sharply.

" There's a dangerous part of the road where several cars have gone over in recent months."

" And you wondered about it enough to follow her and make sure ? "

" Yes . . . for some reason I can't quite explain . . . I did."

" That's a strange thing."

" It is, isn't it ? But she was rather strange too. Behind a surface cheerfulness I'd have guessed her in acute distress of some kind."

" Look here, Professor, I think we ought to meet personally to talk about all this. . . ."

The Professor agreed, but before George could fix an appointment his secretary had entered with a typewritten message : " Randolph's been trying to phone you again. He said it's important — about Miss Arundel."

George got rid of the Professor as best he could and then called Randolph, who said simply : " She's gone off with Saffron. It'll be in the morning papers along with the drunk case. The real topper of toppers. Some paper up the Coast just spotted them together in a hotel. Calls it an elopement. I dare say this means we're through with her as well — I don't know what else we can do. If only these people would realize we don't give a damn what their morals are, provided they don't make trouble for *us* with 'em. . . . Personally, I can't understand it. Not only throwing away a career but for God's sake what on earth can she see in Saffron ? What on earth *did* she see ? Don't suppose we'll ever get the whole truth about that."

" Do you ever expect to get the whole truth about anything ? " George asked, with all his lawyer's experience. But behind the hardboiledness he felt a little sad. He was rather sure he would never meet another woman who would make him — even fleetingly — question the validity of his bachelorhood. He added : " She must have had an interesting life, Randy. Born in Ireland, she told me — on a farm. . . . I wonder how she ever . . ." But there were so many things he wondered.

PART ONE

AT the convent school just outside Dublin, Carey had nourished ambitions to be either a nun or an actress ; the nuns dissuaded her from the former, and her mother was equally against the latter. Mrs. Arundel, however, died when Carey was fifteen, and a year later, after a period of idleness at home, the girl managed to get a small part at the Abbey Theatre. It was in a bad play that lasted a week, and the sole press report that noticed her at all called her ' an interesting newcomer '. But whatever she had or lacked, she was both eager and popular, so that during later seasons she was given a number of even smaller parts in other plays. She read all the books she could get hold of about acting and theatrecraft, she studied plays and actors and tried to copy their tricks (some of which, at the Abbey, were among the neatest in the world), and occasionally she put into her lines a curious quality that riveted an audience's attention in the wrong place and made the director wrinkle his forehead in dismay.

She was a small girl, delicately featured, with a generous expressive mouth that twisted a little when she smiled, as if (a doctor admirer once said) she had once had a very slight attack of Bell's palsy and had only ninety-nine per cent recovered. Dark hair and grey-blue eyes added to a total that might have taken no first prize in a beauty contest, yet might well have drawn more glances than the winner. Her figure, slow to develop, was still boyish at a time when her voice had already acquired a richness rare even in a mature woman ; it was the most striking thing about her, this voice — low pitched, never shrill, yet capable of catching the random ear as colour catches the eye. (Much later, a critic said : " Whenever she speaks, her voice gives a command performance ", but ' command ' was not quite the word for a compulsion yielded to so happily. And another critic said, also much later : " She has a quality of womanhood so ample, and in a peculiar way so purposeless, that the nerves of the critic unclench and even his judgment is off guard ; for this reason she can often be over-praised, but never under-enjoyed ".) At school she had been a bright, gay, normal pupil, cleverer than the average, but no bluestocking. She liked horses, games, picnics. A ribald sense of humour had sometimes got her into scrapes, but never seriously ; she had many friends and no enemies, and when she recited Portia's speech at the school's annual concert the nuns applauded affectionately, not thinking she was specially good (and she wasn't), but beguiled by her voice into a vision they found vicariously satisfying — that of wifehood and motherhood in the well-tempered Catholic life.

Those years culminated in the period of the Sinn Fein ' troubles ' ; by the time she made her first stage appearance the treaty with England had been signed and the Free State, precariously born, was already fighting for its life against the Republican Army. At the height of the fratricide Rory O'Connor and his men were shelled in the Four Courts (within a few streets of the Abbey Theatre), and many a night the city echoed to sporadic roof-top shooting. One of the lively areas was the neighbourhood of the Portobello Bridge, which lay on a direct route between the theatre and the southern suburb of Terenure, where Carey lived with her stepfather. Several times, along with other passengers, she flattened herself on the floor of a tram as it crossed the bridge during a fusillade, and whenever she could arrange it she drove home with an actress friend named Ursula, who had a very ancient car ; they could then make long detours through safer districts. Sometimes, also, if there were shooting near the theatre, she would spend the night with another friend named Mona who lived in an apartment approachable by a sheltered route from the stage-door itself. Since the Terenure house had no telephone, her stepfather could not be notified, but she had always urged him not to worry or stay up for her return.

Often, though, when she got home late at night she found him still hard at work in the room which he called his study. He was learning Gaelic as an apt expression of his enthusiasm for the new Ireland, and perhaps as an aid to promotion in his job — he was an official in the Tax Department of the Dublin City Corporation. " How was it out tonight ? " he would ask, as about the weather.

" Ursula heard there was something going on in Rathmines, so we drove around by Donnybrook. It wasn't so bad that way."

" Ah, I *thought* I heard something — I wouldn't have been surprised if you'd stayed all night with Mona again. . . . Rathmines, eh ? Well, well, that's getting pretty close." His casualness was part of an English manner that many years in Ireland had not effaced and which, combined with short stature and a strutting walk, gave him an appearance which to Irish eyes was sometimes a little ridiculous. But he was a kindly man. " You know, Carey, you can always give it up if the journeys make you nervous."

" Oh, but I love the work — I wouldn't know what to do with my life if I didn't have it to think about."

" Well, well, so long as it doesn't get you down. These are certainly great days in the history of our country. And of course there's not much real danger — to you girls, I mean."

" Oh no." Which was true — statistically. " It's fun, in a way."

But this was not quite so true, for after the strain of a theatre performance all one wanted to do was to go home quickly and get to bed ; the effort to find a quiet route and the perhaps ten-thousand-to-one chance of stopping a stray bullet added no pleasurable thrills. " At least I'm getting to know much more about Dublin, finding all these different ways home." It was a cheerful way to look at it, and the colourful topography of Dublin and suburbs — such names as Crumlin, Dolphin's Barn, Harold's Cross, Beggarsbush, Drumnagh, Rathfarnham — became the symbols of her almost nightly ordeals.

One rainy morning about two o'clock, as she and Ursula detoured through Ballsbridge, a man, hatless and trench-coated and pointing a gun, stepped into the dark street in front of the car. When Ursula braked hard, he jumped into the back seat and gave curt orders. " Drive through Palmerston Park and towards Dundrum. Not too fast but don't slow down. Keep in the middle of the road. I'll tell you when to stop. And for your own sakes, no tricks."

Ursula panicked into silence, concentrated on the driving, but Carey was panicked into just the opposite. She began chattering and giggling for a reason she could not at first discover, but soon her nerves propelled her more and more surely into a pattern of behaviour; she felt the kind of unspeakable terror she sometimes felt on the stage, but which she could always with an effort control, and which sometimes seemed to help rather than hinder her perform-ance; and this too, she decided, must be a performance. So she fell into a rather broad and bawdy impersonation of a girl who had had too many drinks and was not particularly distressed at being kidnapped in the middle of the night by a forceful and handsome male. The man made no response. After a few miles there was a stretch of lonely country, and here he gave the order to stop; he then changed places with Ursula and took the wheel. Carey, sitting now beside him, kept her eyes on his stern profile and prayed that somehow, during the short interval of the drive to wherever they were bound for, she could talk herself and Ursula out of being raped, or even into being raped as a substitute for being murdered; maybe if she played up to him with all she had she could win him over. So she played. Actually the man was an exceptionally high-minded member of the Republican Army, burning with political zeal and puritanical to the point of primness. He had never even had a woman, much less raped one, and his only murders had been cold-blooded ones of men; on this occasion all he wanted was the car. Amidst empty moorland, where the climb began towards the Sally Gap, he brusquely ordered the two girls into the road, gave them a receipt for the commandeered vehicle (correct

I.R.A procedure), and drove off with scarcely concealed contempt for a couple of prostitutes.

Carey, indeed, had proved herself an effective actress, but her judgment had not been shrewd in her choice of the play. It was a combination that was to happen again in her life. The more immediate result, however, was a near collapse from the strain of the whole incident, for the two girls had to walk miles in the rain before they were picked up; they both caught bad chills. Furthermore, the theft of the car meant that from then on the problem of getting home from the theatre would be much more burdensome. " It's Ursula I'm really sorry for," Carey told her stepfather. " The car wasn't insured and she hadn't finished paying for it."

" She should keep the receipt," he answered judicially. " A truly independent Ireland has a responsibility in all such cases — I'm sure eventually it will realize that."

During her next non-acting spell Carey visited her great-uncle in Kingstown. He had been her childhood hero, and as he lived in a district where there had never been any ' trouble ' she could expect to relax more easily than at home. Captain Halloran (retired from the British Navy after a somewhat eccentric career) lived in a hillside house overlooking the harbour; he was seventy-odd, keen-eyed, loganberry red in countenance, with endearing qualities; he liked youngsters and animals, gave generously to the undeserving, and was a cheerful loser at Leopardstown races. Comfortably off, he kept a couple of horses which he galloped over the local countryside, or else hitched to a variety of two-wheeled vehicles that might well have been in a museum. Carey was driving one of these things on an August afternoon when she met Paul Saffron.

.   .   .   .   .   .

Paul was then twenty-nine, attractive in a slightly man-nered way that sometimes suggested the feminine but never the effeminate; a little plump, with wavy black hair, intense blue-grey eyes, and a long strong nose, he was striking

23

enough to be noticed in a crowd, and much more so on a quiet Irish road. Carey stared at him from some way off, and with growing apprehension, for he was hatless and wore a raincoat whose pockets bulged.

In truth the bulge on one side was from cigars, the other was from a rather conspicuous copy of the *New York Times*. The reason for this was that he wanted to be taken for an American before anyone could shoot him, and the reason he thought such a thing possible was that, being the kind of journalist as well as the kind of person he was, he thought anything possible. He had, in fact, just lately stepped down the gangway on to Irish soil with an almost conditioned reflex of naïveté, for he knew his job was to write something about Ireland that would be readable by those who were not really interested in Ireland at all. Somewhat to his carefully nurtured surprise there had been no ambush on the pier as the boat from Holyhead put in, so he had ignored the waiting train to Dublin and strolled inland through the first Irish streets he came to. It was often his luck to find things to write about thus casually — a dog or a child or a shop window or anything that met his eye. (One of his most successful pieces had been about a cat playing with a skein of wool in the ruins of an earthquake.) This time it was a girl, a girl driving a horse and some sort of a buggy along the road towards him, and he first noticed her because she was sitting on one leg in a way that looked uncomfortable. Now why? Or *was* it uncomfortable? Good enough for a start. . . . Then he glanced at her face, which did not seem to him beautiful so much as appealing and piquant ; it had a look that somehow complemented the question-mark of the posture. Maybe a talk with such a chance-met native would save him the effort of walking further, for he disliked walking ; so he stepped to the middle of the road in front of the cantering horse.

" Well ? " she said, before he could speak a word, and he caught then a quality in her voice that stirred him far more than anything in her looks. He did not guess that it was fear, and that she had not yet noticed his *Times*.

" Can you tell me where this road leads to ? " he asked.

" Just up in the hills."

" Ah, then I've lost my way. Are you driving into town ? Could you give me a lift back ? "

" Sure. Jump up."

She had been too scared not to invite him, and he took her readiness for affability. This made him pleased with her, for he liked people to like him, and when he thought they specially did so he paid them the supreme compliment of talking about himself. He did this then, as they clop-clopped through the peaceful downhill streets ; he told her who he was, of his recent arrival in Ireland, his mission to report on that disturbed country for an American magazine, his real ambition, which was quite different, and the extreme likelihood that he would one day be famous. He talked to her, indeed, as he could always do to anyone (whether celebrity or bell-hop) when he felt in the mood or thought it worth while — as if he had known and would continue to know them all his life, and as if neither his nor theirs could possibly have been complete before the meeting. It was a technique that had won him both friends and enemies, and would have perhaps worked out all right on balance if he had ever felt a need to discover who were which.

Carey, on her part, was warming to the relief of finding him not another gunman, and the warmth put her at odds with herself for having been so mistaken. She listened to his chatter in a daze, unwilling to try her voice lest there might still be too much tremor in it. By the time they reached the centre of the town she had said scarcely a word, and was already chagrined to find him so content with her silence. The looks she gave him were increasingly quizzical.

" Well, here we are," she said at length, pulling up at a corner.

" Already ? This is as far as you go ? Well, thanks. Very good of you. Can I get a street car from here into Dublin ? "

Street car ? " Oh yes, of course. They stop over there." She pointed.

" Much obliged for the lift," he said, climbing down with caution. She noticed he was not very agile. " It's a hot day," he added, mopping his forehead. " How about having a cup of tea somewhere ? "

" And what would I do with the horse ? " She half smiled, not so much to him as to herself about him. Maybe he thought a two-year-old would wait at the kerb like a car — a city fellow, evidently (she was wrong about that, for he came from Iowa, but she was basically right, since he had always been peculiarly inept at country ways). Paul Saffron. He had told her his name but had shown no curiosity about hers, and that too had rankled, giving her a sudden defensive pride in being Irish, and in the duality of Irish life that made nobody either countrified or citified to an absurd extent.

He was still mopping his forehead. " I wonder, then, is there a place I could get some ice-cold beer ? "

" Ice in Dunleary in the month of August ? " She shook her head at a rueful angle. . . . *Paul Saffron*. " And besides, the pubs aren't open yet."

" I see. Like the English. I thought you were free of them now."

" Sure, but they had us so long we learned all their bad habits."

He grinned. (More for his article. Irish counterpart of the New York taxi-driver — never at a loss for an answer.) " You said some name just then that I didn't quite catch ? "

" Dunleary ? It's the new name for Kingstown. Or rather the old name before our oppressors changed it. So we changed it back. It's spelt *Dun Laoghaire*. . . . And Dublin is *Baile Atha Cleath*."

" Tell me that again. How must I say it ? "

" Better not say it at all, or nobody'll know what you're talking about. It's a craze they have these days for turning everything into Gaelic. Dublin's still good enough for most people." She gave ' Dublin ' this time the caressing, almost Brooklynese vowels of the *patois*.

He looked as if the whole subject of place names and

pronunciations were infinitely beyond his comprehension, for he had heard again that peculiar note in her voice that set him listening without taking in the words. It made him, from the sidewalk, give her a slow upward scrutiny and then put the question that had been in his mind from the first. " What's the matter with your leg ? " For she was still sitting on it.

" 'Tis broke," she answered.

Her voice was so much in his ears that he didn't immediately show that he caught the joke ; and this, it seemed, was an extra joke at his expense, for after a few full seconds of relish she drove off laughing.

.   .   .   .   .   .

When she got back to the house on the hill, she could not stop thinking about the American, for he had told her, amongst so much else, that though his current task was journalism, he had directed plays in New York and the real love of his life was the theatre. Which would have been a natural cue for her to tell him about herself, but she had failed to do so, partly because she was still recovering from the initial shock of the meeting, but chiefly because his complete absorption in his own affairs had teased her to a more and more deliberate concealment of hers. She would not disclose anything that would interest him so much. Or would it ? As soon as the doubt prevailed she wished she had told him. Fortunately, it would be easy to let him know, since there were only three Dublin hotels at which he would be likely to stay.

Neither could Paul, on the tram, stop thinking of her, and for a reason that flattered them both : he already diagnosed what he called a histrionic personality. Not, of course, that it was specially rare ; many types in all walks of life were apt to be so equipped (auctioneers, athletes, and the clergy, for instance) ; besides which, one often met the unlikeliest people who made their personal or professional world a stage and their own lives a continuous play. To be an actor, a real actor, much more was needed than any kind of personality; nevertheless, to have the right kind was a good start.

By midnight of that August evening he was already blaming himself for the incredible stupidity of not having enquired even the girl's name — how on earth could he trace her, even if he should want to? For it might well become a whim to do so, as casual as her own voice answering him about her leg. " 'Tis broke." It was the way he would have liked her to say it if it had been a line in a play.

By that same late evening Carey was writing three identical notes addressed to Mr. Paul Saffron at the Gresham, the Shelbourne, and the Hibernian hotels. She wrote that since he had stressed so much his interest in the theatre, doubtless he would like to visit the famous one in Dublin, so she would leave a couple of tickets for next week's opening night for him to pick up at the box office in Middle Abbey Street. She signed herself 'Carey Arundel', but she still left it to him to discover, if and when he cared to, *what* she was.

.   .   .   .   .

He was not, as it happened, staying at any of the three hotels, but at a private house called Venton League, the home of a rich brewer whom he had met at a party in London, and who had promptly extended the invitation on learning of his Irish visit. Brewing, one of the more historic trades, has almost escaped the stigma of being a trade at all, and its distinguished dynasties rank high and are considerably international; Michael Rowden, in his late fifties, was a *fine fleur* of the culture, a Rothschild of his line, with family connections well scattered across England, Europe, and America, and financial interlockings from Milwaukee to Dortmund. Had he been a younger son he might have made an excellent diplomat, bishop, or even cardinal (for he was both a Catholic and a bachelor); as it was, he sold beer (with an inverted snobbery that made him thus describe his business), drank wine, collected French impressionist paintings, and found ample time to cultivate the habits of a gentleman-savant. Temperament and wealth insulated him from most of the troubles of life, even from the Irish 'troubles', for neither side wished to drive into exile a man so eminently taxable. The hotheads had once put Venton League on their list of large houses to be burned, but Rowden had let it be known that he didn't much care; its destruction would spare him the eventual problem of whether to demolish it for villa development or bequeath it to Holy Church for some institutional use. And there really was a sense in which he did not care; he would be quite happy, if he had to be, in London or Palm Beach or Capri. Yet Venton League did, for all that, give him a special sort of satisfaction; it was the house of his ancestors, as far back as four generations, and family pride, well tempered with cynicism about it, was strong in him. Moreover, since this was Dublin and not any other place in the world, there was a uniqueness in the kind of life he could live there — an eighteenth-century quality marvellously and miraculously preserved into the fabric of the twentieth. Leisurely elegance, half urban and half arcadian, part scholarly, part merely sophisticated, gave a ripeness even to anachronism; the kitchens were monstrous and old-fashioned, yet the bathrooms combined the luxuries of ancient Rome and modern America; the library windows offered a view of formal gardens backgrounded by green mountains, yet at the end of the half-mile carriage drive, and just outside the lodge gates, the threepenny tram started for the Pillar in O'Connell Street. All this suited him and immensely intrigued his constant succession of house guests. For as a suave Maecenas to young men of promise he performed a function all the more admirable because he took so much pleasure in it; at Venton League there was always apt to be some visiting painter, writer, musician, or even tennis champion, and the language at dinner was almost as often French or Italian as English. Rowden had not needed much acquaintance with Paul at that London party to decide that he would make an apt recruit, both culturally and racially, to the Venton League *ménage* — a young American with literary and theatrical connections . . . good . . . he could stay as long as he liked.

Paul, compared with all this, was brash; he had met American millionaires, and even American millionaire brewers, but they had not been in the least like Rowden. To that extent he was secretly baffled, but he gave Rowden the usual treatment of brilliant talk and affable self-display, hopeful though by no means sure that the man was being impressed. One evening wine unleashed his tongue to such vainglory that Rowden smiled and put his hand under the youth's arm as they walked into the library for coffee and cognac; Paul by that time was in the midst of a survey of all the grandiose theatrical ideas that had ever effervesced in his mind, one of which he had just thought of suddenly at the dining-table and which lifted him to a peak of excitement the more he enlarged upon it — *Othello* with an all-Negro cast, except for Othello himself, who should be white. Into a rare and breathless silence Rowden then managed to interject: " My dear young man, I admire your enthusiasms and I think it quite possible you are almost as wonderful as you say. But tell me . . . how are you going to *live* in this world ? "

" *Live?* "

" Yes. Make a living."

" You mean money ? Oh, I manage. I pick up a bit from journalism, and then I have a travelling fellowship — rather a juicy one — it's supposed to enable me to do ' creative writing ', whatever that means, but there's no problem, because if the worst comes to the worst I'll bundle some of my articles together and call 'em creative — who the hell can swear they aren't ? "

" You, of course, *know* that they aren't."

" Oh, sure. I'm not really a writer. I've got creativeness in me, but it's not that kind. . . . But don't worry — I'll get by. The fellowship's a racket, but it helps me around — they might renew it for another year. And sometimes I meet rich people who save me hotel bills."

Rowden was at first antagonized by what he took to be boorishness ; but then, beneath it, he caught other notes — frustration, ambition, cool self-criticism, and a sort of celestial you-be-damnedness. On the whole he was beginning to like Paul very much indeed.

Paul added, with a grin : " I'm only kidding. If you think I'd stay here just for that you don't know me. I'm really grateful to you. But it isn't all on one side, is it ? I'd have been worth my keep in the old days when artists had patrons. Then you could have built a theatre for me and I'd have made you famous."

" Quite a proposition."

" I'm still kidding. You must think I have a nerve."

" I do." Rowden smiled and continued : " Do you write as you talk ? "

" God, no. I wouldn't sell much if I did. I'm a sort of actor in print. I've created a fictional character that I call Myself, so I never write what *I* think, but what I think this character would think. The novelist does that all the time, but he does it honestly — he *labels* it fiction, but I pretend I really am the slightly ridiculous fellow I've invented."

Rowden eyed him critically, as if wondering how much of all this to suspect or discount. " Isn't it rather confusing at times ? "

" Sure, though of course it's nothing new — the public always tend to identify an actor with his part."

" Not the educated public ? "

" Yes, to some extent. Or else why would the man who plays Jesus in the Oberammergau Passion Play have to quit smoking and drinking ? "

" I didn't know that he did. Tell me, how did you launch yourself into this rather strange journalistic career ? "

" Ah, that's a story in itself."

He told it, but he didn't tell the whole truth about it, which was as follows. He had been in England just after the 1918 Armistice, awaiting the voyage home and demobilization. His war service had comprised a year in an Army office in London. The reason he had not been sent to fight was a pituitary condition which made him put on weight with alarming ease ; without proper dieting or treatment, he was at that time in danger of becoming almost comically fat.

31

(Back home as a civilian, a year later, he took medical advice, lost most of the excess poundage, and managed after that to remain merely stoutish.) It happened that during the early days of 1919 Mr. Lloyd George was to leave for the opening of the Peace Conference in Paris, and reporters were badgering him in vain for a scoop. In such circumstances one would have thought it sheerly ridiculous for Paul to seek an interview with the great man for an American small-town paper; and so it was, yet he succeeded. He simply sent a letter on U.S. Army notepaper and enclosed a photograph. " You will see from this ", he wrote, " the sort of fellow I am — I certainly carry a lot of weight around here, but it isn't the kind that helps. In fact, Mr. Lloyd George, I'm just a Yank without rank who'd be proud indeed to shake hands with you before I go home to Reedsville, Iowa." Perhaps the P.M. was seduced, or amused, or merely obliging; it is even possible that he practised the same mixture of innocence and guile, for he had never been unmindful of the value of American publicity. At any rate, Private Paul Saffron was invited to call at Number Ten Downing Street at four-thirty one January afternoon. Of course there was no political scoop, they didn't talk about politics or the war at all, but they did discuss America, England, Wales, tea, coffee, the beauties of nature, and choral singing; moreover Paul, who had a rather pleasing *bel canto* tenor, was able to demonstrate that a lament of the Seminole Indians was remarkably similar to a hymn tune popular among the slate miners of Blaenau Ffestiniog. Amidst these amenities half an hour passed, and then an hour, whereupon Mrs. Lloyd George joined them and Paul had to sing again. It was all very neighbourly, more like Iowa than London's West End — which, of course, was exactly the point that Paul made in the two-column piece he wrote. And the whole article, which was picked up by some of the big newspapers after its début in the *Reedsville Clarion*, proved something else too — that America was much more interested in a number of other things than in war and politics.

After this flash-in-the-pan success, Paul felt he had it in

him to earn a living from journalism if he had to, though he hoped he wouldn't, for his passionate leanings had already centred themselves elsewhere. But an editor named Merryweather had become interested in him and was shrewd enough to realize that while magazines and newspapers were full of stuff emanating from *informed* sources, the *uninformed* source, the fall guy who steps in where experts fear to tread, could be equally readable in a small corner of his own. (Later the technique was developed into one of the humaner and more profitable arts by Will Rogers and later still by Ernie Pyle.) It was the pose of having no pose — the trick of telling the public, in reporting a war, how scared one was, or of an international conference, how bored.

" I'm the Little Man," Paul said, gulping Rowden's brandy to give himself the right feeling about it. " I'm the world's hero because I'm not a hero — I'm Constant Reader, Pro Bono Publico, Worried Taxpayer, Average Citizen — I write as if writing's easy, unprofessional, no particular talent required, just a few pipes of tobacco and a sort of cute way of looking at things. . . . I'm Lowbrow and I'm human — my God, how human I am — when I did a piece about my dog's birthday I got over five hundred letters and a truckload of dog-food from readers. . . . Did that ever happen to Shakespeare ? . . . And I haven't got a dog, I don't smoke a pipe, and I think I'd loathe the fellow I pretend to be if ever I met him. One of these days, when I've made a big hit with a play, I'm going to lose all my public in one grand gesture — I shall confess that all the time I've been secretly enjoying Beethoven Quartets. . . . Only I'm afraid the editor wouldn't publish it, he wouldn't let me destroy my humble little Frankenstein midget, always on the watch for the Funny Side of Things, bless his tiny guts. . . . And finding it, too. My first article on Ireland — you'd never guess how I'll start it — nothing about the Free State, or Cosgrave, or the shooting — leave that to the regular writers. I'll do a piece about a girl — I met her just after I came ashore at Kingstown, Dunleary, whatever you call the place. I took a walk in the town and saw this girl driving a horse and buggy and she was sitting with one leg bent under her . . . the oddest thing . . . like this. . . ." He got up from the chair and reseated himself with his own leg clumsily imitating the posture. He was aware by then that he had drunk too much.

Rowden said : " Charming, I'm sure. Some more brandy ? No ? . . . But coming back to the stage . . . of course, you know about our own Abbey Theatre ? Maybe we should go one evening while you're here. . . ."

. . . . .

They went to the Abbey to see a new play called *Moon of the Galtees*, by a new Irish writer whom some of the critics had praised. It was typical of Rowden that he did not choose the opening night, that he bought seats in the third row, and that he took Paul to the city by tram. The chauffeur and Rolls-Royce would pick them up afterwards.

Paul was naturally astonished when he recognized Carey on the stage, as of course he did immediately, despite her part as a rather minor leprechaun. (It was that kind of play.) His desire to see her again revived and expanded, during the first act, into all kinds of agreeable expectations. At the interval he told Rowden excitedly that here was an amazing coincidence : that leprechaun was actually the girl at Kingstown, the one he intended to write about ! Perhaps they could go back-stage after the show ? But Rowden, at first vaguely assenting, then demurred. " I'm afraid it'll be rather hot and noisy — if you'd like to meet Barry Fitzgerald and Arthur Shields I can have them to dinner at the house some evening. I know them fairly well. Yes, that's quite an idea. Yeats, too — you *must* meet him — he's usually here, but I don't see him tonight. And perhaps Lennox Robinson and Dr. Starkie and A.E. . . . We have a genuine intelligentsia — just the people you'll enjoy meeting."

" But I'd like to see that girl."

" The *little* girl ? "

" Sure. The leprechaun. After meeting her the way I did it would be amusing——"

"I'd preserve my illusions, if I were you. The article might work out better."

"I wasn't thinking of the article."

"You like her acting, then?"

"Hell, no." He added hastily: "I mean, she's not good for the part, the part's not good, she seems to be untrained, or else badly trained, or something."

Rowden smiled. "It would be hard to make conversation then. Why don't you write your little friend a note? And I'll try to fix our party for next Sunday — that's always a good day."

So they didn't go backstage, but Paul left a scribbled message for delivery to her after the show, and the next day he sent flowers. He wasn't the kind of person who sent flowers to girls and he was rather surprised at himself for thinking of it.

She wrote back: "Thank you for the roses. I love roses, and everybody wondered who they were from. I didn't see you in the audience, but I'd half expected you on opening night, because I'd left tickets for you at the box-office. I'd written to you about that at three hotels. I never thought you'd be staying anywhere else. All this sounds complicated, I'll explain when we meet. You don't say if you liked the play. Tomorrow will do fine — say two-thirty at the Pillar."

The Pillar was the Nelson Pillar, stuck squarely and squatly astride the great width of O'Connell Street. Buildings on both sides had been destroyed in the 'sixteen rebellion, but the Pillar had escaped except for bullet nicks; it dominated the scene, providing a terminal point for tram routes, and a lofty monument to an Englishman whose public and private life made his memory a constantly delightful anachronism in the streets of Dublin. So Rowden had remarked to Paul, and it proved a good way to start a conversation when he met the girl, for he was unaccountably nervous at first. He had been late at the rendezvous owing to delay in getting away from Venton League after lunch, for he had not told Rowden he was going to meet the girl. He

35

had even wondered if she would wait when he did not arrive; the first thing he must do was to apologize. But he forgot all about that when he saw her, and as she did not mention it, the fact that she had been standing for half an hour amidst the scurrying crowd vanished for both of them as if it had never existed. She wore a blue dress and the kind of pert cloche hat that was in style in those days and happened to suit her; she came towards him smiling, having seen him first, a few anxious seconds first, for after leaving a taxi to cross the road he had nearly been run down by a tram whose driver gave him some picturesque language in passing. " I keep forgetting you keep to the left in this country," were his first breathless words of greeting.

" I know, I saw it," she said. " But there's terrible traffic here all the time. The Pillar gets in the way of everything."

Which led him to repeat Rowden's remark about it, and she too found the subject helpful to begin with; she told him how the City Corporation had considered moving the Pillar (as a traffic hazard, so as to dodge the political issue), but so far nothing had been done because it would cost too much.

"At least they could change the statue on the top," Paul said. " Why not some Irish hero ? "

"Ach, there mightn't be time. Before we could hoist him up there, somebody would have shot him as a traitor and half the country wouldn't think him a hero at all. That's what happened to Michael Collins."

" That's almost what happened to Lincoln."

" It's a curse on all of us, then. The English don't do things like that."

" They do as bad." He laughed. " Come now, don't say you're on *their* side."

" My stepfather's English. I wish there weren't any sides."

" Ah, then that accounts for it. He's the one that keeps you broad-minded."

" Not him — he's more Irish than some of the Irish. Spells his name S-e-a-n instead of John and it's pronounced ' Shawn '."

" Then I give up. This is a strange country."

" You can't give up if you've got to write about us."

" I shan't touch on politics much."

" No? . . . Perhaps that's sensible. But don't romanticize, whatever you do — none of the Killarney-blarney, broth of a boy, top o' the marnin' to ye — that's the stuff we can't stand."

When he reflected that this was the kind of article Merryweather would probably like, he almost blushed. " Maybe you'd rather be laughed at? I could do an amusing piece about those Gaelic changes you talked about."

" Why not, then? It's a good subject. The ancient tongue of Ireland that nobody speaks any more except a handful of peasants in the far west, so there have to be a handful of professors in Dublin to decide what the ancient Irish would have called a telephone if they'd ever seen one."

" If I wrote that way it would seem like an attack."

" And why not? 'Tis time someone attacked us in fun instead of seriously." She showed him the book under her arm. It was *Martin Chuzzlewit*, a library copy. " I've just been reading this. Dickens certainly didn't spare the Americans. And it wasn't all fun either."

" D'you know, I've never read *Chuzzlewit*."

" Why don't you? I'll lend you this — I've finished it."

" Thanks."

" It'll probably make you angry."

" I'll bet it won't. My family hadn't come to America when it was written, so why would I feel insulted? I'll tell you what I think when I've read it."

They went on talking, as vagrantly as that, while they skirted the quays past the burned-out Four Courts and entered Phoenix Park. It was windy on the upland there, with fast scudding clouds and a hint of rain. The view of mountains reminded him of a backdrop, grey-blue shapes as if cut in cardboard. He told her this, and it gave her the cue to remark that he still hadn't said how he liked the play.

" Oh, *that*? Well, it wasn't bad. In some ways it wasn't bad enough. You know when a play is really bad, anything good in it shows like a sort of outcropping. Take *Twelfth Night*—"

He wondered if the notion that a Shakespeare play could be called bad would shock her, and he had used the example chiefly to find out. But she seemed unconcerned. Or perhaps she had read Shaw. Or more likely still, her mind was anchored to the main issue, for she went on : " So you didn't like *Moon of the Galtees* ? Ach, nor did anybody. They're taking it off. . . . And I don't suppose you liked me in it either."

" It wasn't much of a part for you, was it ? "

She grimaced. " As good as I generally get. I try to believe it's because they think I'm too young."

" How old are you ? "

" Seventeen. Nearly eighteen."

" I'd have guessed you nearer twenty."

" I *feel* like twenty. And I dress to look older, but none of it seems to work. There's a fourteen-year-old part in a new play they're considering — I'll bet they offer it to me."

" Juliet was fourteen."

" Ah, now, if only I could have a chance like that ! "

" Would you take it ? "

" Who wouldn't ? Or is it absurd of me to be so ambitious ? Maybe I should stick to leprechauns ? "

" Leprechauns or Juliet — it's all acting."

" I know. And you haven't yet told me how — if — you *liked* my acting."

" You really want me to ? "

" Sure. I can bear it."

He said judicially after a pause : " I don't think you know *how* to act, but I think you have *something* — I don't quite know what — but it's something you'd be lucky to have as well, even if you did know how to act."

" All I have to do, then, is to learn ? "

" Yes. And *un*learn."

" Ah, I see."

The inflection he caught in her voice made him continue quickly : " Remember, that's only my opinion." The words

38

didn't sound like his, and he wondered how far the impulse to speak them could be identified as humility, truculence, or a simple desire to spare her feelings.

"It's what I asked for. Thank you."

"Yes, but — but——"

"But what?"

"Well, what I mean is, don't let *anybody's* opinion worry you. Because worrying wouldn't help. And unless the person who criticizes has something constructive to say—" He checked himself, aware of immense pitfalls.

She said musingly after a pause: "I expect you're right — that I've everything to learn and unlearn."

"I didn't say *everything*. You weren't at a dramatic school?"

"No. Is that what I need?"

"On the contrary, I rather thought you *had* been to some school." He laughed. "They teach a lot of the wrong things."

"Ah, now, Mr. Saffron, am I as bad as that?"

"My name's Paul, by the way. I wish you'd call me Paul."

"All right. *Paul.* And I don't know how to act, according to you. Maybe you think you could teach me?"

"Heavens, no. I'm not a teacher. I can't act myself — I haven't the vaguest idea how it's done." Again he knew that this was an attitude-cliché, with just enough truth in it for guile. "All I do — all I hope to do — is to . . . if I had to put it into a sentence . . . to . . . to communicate a sort of excitement." Well, that was true — fairly true, anyhow. "If you challenge me to say I could do that with you, then I'll say it — I'd try to, anyhow . . . I mean, if I were directing a play you were in."

"Excitement?"

"Of course there's much more to it than just that — there's style and technique and a hundred other things. But the essential thing is the kindling of emotion in the actor — in his mind, in his voice, in his movements."

"Emotional excitement?"

"Call it anything you like. Perhaps it's what Oscar

39

Wilde meant when he said he felt in a mood to pick his teeth with the spire of a cathedral."

" *He* said that ? "

He nodded, amused at what he guessed — that to her Catholic mind the name was necessarily a symbol of wickedness. " Are you surprised ? "

" Oh, no. But I'd never heard it before. It's a wonderful phrase."

" Wilde was one of the wittiest men who ever lived."

" I know. I've read his plays. Under the bedclothes with a flashlight." She caught his look and added : " That was at school. They were strict about the books we got, but we used to smuggle them in. I also read *De Profundis* and *The Ballad of Reading Gaol*."

" You were interested in Wilde at that age ? "

" Oh yes — and my great-uncle often talked about him — still does. He knew him. They were at T.C.D. together." Again she intercepted the look. " That's Trinity College, Dublin."

He gaped, a little enchanted by this strange Irish world in which there could be so much intimacy and innocence combined ; for of all the reasons for being concerned about Wilde, surely the fact that one's great-uncle had been at college with him was unmatchable.

She broke into his reverie by saying : " Did *you* ever have that feeling — that you could pick your teeth with the spire of a cathedral ? "

The answer that came to his mind (that he was enjoying such a sensation there and then) was too simple and astonishing to confess, so he said : " Well, on a first night when you know the play's a hit you feel pretty good." (He had never had this experience.)

She nodded, more with encouragement than assent, and he went on feverishly : " And sometimes also it happens at quieter moments — when you're alone or with just one other person . . . the heart suddenly beating a little faster, putting its private exclamation mark at the end of every thought."

"That's not a bad phrase either." (It was his own, but he had used it before in some article.) "You could be Irish, the way the words come."

He laughed. "A real playboy of the western world, with an American accent."

"Yes, and you ought to visit the West, by the way — *our* West — Kerry, Clare, Connemara. . . ."

"Perhaps I will when I've straightened out a few ideas about Ireland in general."

"Not too straight or they'll surely not be right. Remember we're a twisted people."

"And I'm a twisted man."

She said quietly : "What do you mean by that ? "

"Nothing, nothing. A joke. Can't I joke too ? But I *am* getting a feeling of this country and I think I *do* know what you mean when you call it twisted."

It was true that he was already aware of Ireland as an atmosphere — something at once garrulous and secretive, warm-hearted yet slightly mocking, as if after a thousand years of insolubility a problem could become itself a kind of dark inscrutable answer. So far he had been in Dublin a week and had written not a line ; all he had done was to sightsee, read newspapers, talk to everyone he met, hear a few shots in the distance, and go to the theatre. Yet deeper than such surface contacts was something that came to him by the same channel that it could pass from him to others — a communication of excitement, as he had called it, so that, had Dublin been a play, he would have been aching to put it on the stage. There was a symmetry in the emotion that the city gave him, and his meeting with Carey seemed part of it.

She on her side was equally aware that she had never met anyone who interested her so much as Paul. As he went on talking she was sure he must realize how comparatively ignorant she was, yet at the same time she knew how little it mattered ; she had wits to match his in the profound escapade which, at first, is every human relationship of consequence. Nor had she been really hurt by his telling her that she didn't know how to act, because she felt he would have been more polite if he had been less interested in her (though in that she was wrong) ; and, as the hours progressed till it was time to return to the streets, she passionately wanted to retain his interest, not only for its own sake, but for the strength she already felt she could draw from such a new thing in her life. For she alone knew how events during recent months had strained her nerve, had set up tensions that had kept her sleepless often till dawn, weakening even ambition, so that from the original ' I want to be a great actress ' that had kept her emotionally alive as a schoolgirl, she had caught herself lately in half-wistful clingings, as if the dream were becoming a prop instead of an urge. But suddenly, talking to Paul, she had felt the urge again.

When he took her hand outside the theatre he said he hoped it wasn't the last time they would see each other.

" Oh yes, I hope so too. When are you leaving ? "

" Don't know exactly. Depends on how soon I finish the job I'm here for." He smiled. " Maybe I won't hurry."

" Fine. So we really ought to meet again."

They waited, each for the other ; then he said, taking the plunge : " What about tomorrow ? "

" Oh dear, there's a matinée on Saturdays. But you could come for tea at Mona's afterwards. She has a little flat just round the corner — I always go there between shows on matinée days."

" Who's Mona ? "

" My best friend. She was Pegeen in the play, if you remember. . . . Can you come ? "

There wouldn't be much time, between the end of a theatre matinée and dinner at Venton League, but he made a note of the address and said he would be there.

.   .   .   .   .   .

All evening and the next morning and afternoon he had the recurrent feeling that to have made such an appointment was a mistake ; he wanted to see Carey again, but only alone ; to meet her with her friend was pointless, for he so often did not get along with strangers, especially girls, and he had a gloomy foreboding that Mona would prove to be one or another kind of bore. Up to five o'clock he was in mind not to go, but then it began to rain, the soft Irish rain that seemed to caress the air even more than sunshine. The rooms of Venton League darkened as the clouds rolled over, yet only the house was melancholy ; the rain tempted one out of doors into a luminous grey cheerfulness. He put on a mackintosh and walked down the drive, relishing the fragrance of lawns and shrubs. A tram was at the terminus outside the lodge gates ; boarding it he climbed to the upper deck where the rain lashed the windows soundlessly. He rubbed a clear space on the pane and stared down at the glistening pavements and bobbing umbrella-tops as the journey began. He tried to think what it was in Carey that so attracted him, something in her like a magnet to a compass needle, luring him into behaviour that was out of character — or perhaps only out of the character he had hitherto decided was his own. In this sense his discovery of her was a discovery of himself, and he was puzzled as well as fascinated. Was it merely her voice that did such things to him, or her slight, slanting smile, Mona Lisa among the leprechauns, or her face in quiet profile that was like the figurehead of a ship on a calm day ? An actress ? Yes, she had the makings of one in her. But the act that enticed him was that of her simple existence.

He left the tram at the Pillar and explored through the rain till he found the flat. A tall Regency house had been subdivided ; the flat was on the third floor. He climbed with his heart pounding only partly from the physical exertion, but when Carey opened the door all his tension vanished as if a switch had been pulled. The first exchange of looks confirmed the ease she could give him, instantly, so that he even forgot about Mona. Then when she was taking his dripping hat and mackintosh she mentioned that Mona was out.

" I don't mind," he said wryly.

" Oh, but you'll find her interesting — you could get at least an article out of her."

" About what ? "

" Irish legends — antiquities — old Dublin — she knows it all. This house, for instance, had quite a history before it came down in the world."

" I'd say that with you here it hasn't come down in the world at all."

He wasn't good at compliments, and this one sounded stilted and artificial. But she warmed it to life with her laughter. " Oh, what a sweet thing to say ! But it really was a grand house in the old days — it belonged to Lord Fitzhugh — the Catholic Fitzhughs. They were a wild, eccentric family — one of them fought with Wolfe Tone, and another was always called the holy man because he——"

" Are *you* a Catholic ? " he interrupted, brushing aside the Fitzhughs.

" Yes, but I'm not very holy."

" You mean religion doesn't matter much to you ? "

" Oh no, it matters a lot, but I'm just not conscious of it all the time. Like when you have a good digestion and you don't worry about what you eat."

" So you'd call a saint a fellow with a touch of spiritual indigestion ? "

" Ah, now, you're laughing at me."

" I'm never quite sure when you're joking."

" Neither am I. That's the trouble sometimes."

" Oh ? What trouble ? When ? "

" Well . . . during the worst of the street fighting recently nobody would believe how scared I really was."

" I think I'd be scared too."

" But you probably wouldn't laugh about it as I did."

" No, I'd just run — very seriously."

" But you can't, when you're in a panic. It transfixes you. Perhaps you've never known panic."

So the subject was panic, he thought, with the kind of acceptance that comes in a dream. He had a wild idea to

44

tell her about the panic he had indeed known, the secret panic that sprang from his ambition whenever he realized how time was passing and he was no nearer accomplishment, the rage that sometimes followed the panic, so that he said stupid, brutal things that were often held against him for ever. Panic — yes, he had felt it every birthday when he looked back on the year and reckoned his lack of advancement. Would she understand that if he tried to explain it ? Would her own ambitions give her any inkling ? He said gruffly : " I've never been shot at except by life, and that goes on all the time."

" Because you find battles everywhere, Paul . . . don't you ? "

" They *are* everywhere, except . . . a few moments . . . a few people . . . you, for instance." And saying that, in words so simple, even banal, gave him a comfort that was partly an immense laziness, so that he could relax the sinews of his spirit in her company and let come what might in either words or actions.

She exclaimed : " Oh, I'm so glad about that. I wondered if you'd ever want to see me again after yesterday."

" Why on earth shouldn't I ? "

" I'm not as clever as you. I don't know very much. I thought you were just trying to get material out of me for an article."

" Good heavens, do you think I'm always using people ? "

" I wouldn't blame you if you were. You're a writer — an artist. It's justified by the results."

" You really think it is, in my case ? "

And again the impulse overwhelmed him to tell her, of all things, the truth ; to confess it as she would doubtless confess to a priest. He could begin, at least, by admitting that all his boasts and brashness were to cover an almost complete lack of success in anything he had really wanted to do so far ; he could say that the articles he had the trick of writing were always trivial and sometimes contemptible, that he had had long spells of fruitless striving and agonized self-disgust, that he was still practically unknown on Broadway despite his poses and pretensions abroad, that he had directed only two plays in his entire life, both of them at an experimental theatre in a New York suburb ; that neither had attracted attention or been popular ; and that even these meagre achievements had taken place several years before, since when he had been unable to persuade anyone else to give him a third chance. All this he could tell her, and then, perhaps, could follow even other truths. . . .

He said : " Listen . . . you've been so kind, so . . . so friendly and . . . and sympathetic . . . I don't want you to get any wrong ideas about me. . . . Oh God, don't answer it — they'll call again if it's anything important . . . let it ring, let it ring. . . ."

But it wasn't the telephone, for the flat possessed none. Carey hesitated, but there was clearly nothing else she could do but admit Mona. Nervously effusive, devoured by curiosity, Mona was also maddeningly discreet in the way she had forborne to use her key.

Paul froze instantly, became glum, and soon got up to go. The fact that it was Mona's flat did not prevent him from regarding her as a complete intruder. Carey took him downstairs. They said nothing till they were in the hallway and could see out into the street. The rain had stopped and a watery sunlight glinted on the wet pavements. They were both aware of things unsaid that might never be said on any other occasion. She touched his arm and whispered : " Oh, Paul, I'm sorry."

" I'm sorry too, if I was rude, but I was just getting in a mood to talk — I mean, *really* talk."

" I know."

" I wonder if you do know."

She made no answer to that, but presently said : " We can meet again. Do you like the country — I mean, getting out of the city — mountains — scenery ? "

He didn't, but he rallied himself to give a grudging assent.

" We might go to Glendalough, if you have a day to spare, or even half a day. I could borrow Mona's car — it's terribly old and shabby, but it runs. There's the lake and

46

the famous Round Tower — might be something else for
one of your articles."

" Oh, damn the articles. I'd like to go, though, but
when ? "

" Yes, I know how busy you are——"

" Sunday's *your* best day, isn't it ? What about *this*
Sunday ? "

" Tomorrow ? *Again* tomorrow ? Oh yes, if I can get
the car. Do you mind if it rains ? It probably will . . .
this kind of weather . . . oh, it doesn't matter, does it ?
Would ten o'clock be too early to start ? I could pick you
up where you're staying. . . ."

" Venton League ? You know where that is ? "

" Of course — everyone knows Mr. Rowden's house.
It's less than a mile from where I live, and directly on our
way. . . . Tomorrow, then."

.   .   .   .   .   .

But they never did go to Glendalough. Late that evening,
when he mentioned the planned excursion, Rowden said
suavely : " But, my dear Paul, aren't you forgetting the
party *we* had planned ? A. E.'s coming, and even Yeats
promised — besides the Abbey crowd. . . ."

Paul had forgotten, but recovered himself enough, he
hoped, to conceal the fact. " I know — I'm looking forward
to it immensely, but if I start early I'll be back in plenty of
time for dinner."

" It happens to be a lunch party."

" *Lunch ?* I thought you said——"

" Several of them couldn't come in the evening — Yeats
in particular — and as I was anxious to have you meet our
leading lights — good material for a journalist apart from the
fun you might have."

Paul felt a sharp concern, realizing it wasn't Rowden's
fault, yet unwilling to accept at any price the cancellation
of his appointment with Carey.

" And you can go to Glendalough some other time,"
Rowden was continuing. " I won't accompany you, I've

been there so often, the place bores me a little. But *you* should go — it's worth seeing, touristically. You can have Roberts for the day." And after a pause : " Or had you other plans ? Perhaps you'd arranged to go with someone else ? "

" Well yes, I had, to be frank. . . ."

" Why don't you, then, by all means, take this — this someone else ? Roberts can drive you both — any time except tomorrow."

It seemed reasonable, even generous, though the thought of driving in state with a uniformed chauffeur at the wheel of Rowden's Rolls-Royce was completely unenticing. Besides, how did he know he would stay at Venton League as long as the following Sunday, and of course Sunday was her best day. He already wished he had been truculent enough to say at the outset : I'm sorry, I must go to Glendalough tomorrow, party or no party. But Rowden's conciliatoriness had outmanœuvred him, so that now he could only mutter : " Okay, I suppose that's what it'll have to be." Deprived of power to be adamant, he could only take refuge in ungraciousness.

It was too late to communicate with Carey that night to explain matters ; she would already have left the theatre and he did not know her home address. He would have to tell her when she arrived at Venton League in the morning, and though he guessed that she too would be disappointed, somehow that bothered him less than the thought of any possible meeting between her and Rowden, or even the chance that Rowden might see her driving up to the house in that ' terribly old and shabby ' car. A half-realized awkwardness in the whole situation kept him awake to wonder how he could circumvent it ; and in the morning, just before ten, he walked down the drive and past the lodge gates with the idea of intercepting her in the roadway outside. She was punctual, and immediately he told her what had happened. Because he was so chagrined he was rather testy and offhand, making almost no effort to seem blameless. She was not reproachful, assuring him that she fully understood and that naturally it would be impossible

48

for him to miss the lunch party. They did not talk long, and after separating (with no plans for any future meeting) he began to wonder whether she had been too disappointed or not disappointed enough. Whichever it was had put him in no mood for meeting celebrities.

They came, a little later, some by tram, others in cars far more ancient and battered than the one Carey had been driving. Dublin in those days was like that. And Paul, unhappy at first, was soon swept into a livelier mood by such exciting contacts ; once or twice during the lunch he felt a stab of regret that he was not where he had planned to be, but he killed it by self-derision — was it possible that he preferred naïve chatter with a girl of seventeen to an exchange of ideas with some of the brightest minds in such a captivating country ? If so, then what on earth had happened to him ? And all the discomforts of a long drive in a rattle-trap car with nothing but scenery at the end of it ? For Paul did not enjoy travel for its own sake ; art he loved, and a long way off and by no means next to it, nature. Moreover, he shared Dr. Johnson's attitude towards mountains, partly because of an aversion to most physical effort ; even the mountain view from Phoenix Park had impressed him only because he had seen it momentarily as a backdrop.

All this while he was listening to a very eminent poet recite some lines from one of his poems. Candidly, Paul did not think he recited very well, but since it was actually himself reciting himself, what more could one ask ? And then the almost equally famous Mr. So-and-so, who was opposite Paul, engaged him in talk that soon veered to a subject that was one of the few on which Paul had no ideas of his own — that of co-operative creameries, and for the next ten minutes there ensued a fascinating monologue to which Paul listened in growing wonderment coupled with the ghost of a feeling that he was missing something more interesting elsewhere. But presently Rowden suggested an adjournment to the garden, and once out there it was possible to escape from co-operative creameries and switch to another group who were discussing the theatre.

Paul was capricious in conversation ; his rare silences might indicate that he was either bored or entranced ; but so might his talkativeness, for if he were bored he would take quick refuge in the pleasure of his own voice, and if entranced, there would be generated in him sooner or later a terrific desire to entrance the entrancer. This latter occurred during the talk in the garden when Paul, having silently worshipped a well-known literary critic during the latter's eloquent opinion about the proper way to produce the plays of Synge, suddenly interrupted with an opinion of his own. It began modestly, soon acquired an eloquence fully equal to the critic's, and grew to a quite brilliant exegesis that attracted several listeners from another group.

And in the thick of it, without a nod or a word, the well-known literary critic walked off.

Paul finished his sentence and stopped. He felt himself flushing to the roots of his hair, and the aboriginal in him responded with a mental and almost muttered : Why, the son of a bitch. . . . He knew he had been snubbed, and though it was not the first time, the identity of the snubber made it perhaps the most devastating in his experience.

One of the group around him, an actor later to become world-famous, laughed and said : " Don't mind him, boy. He's just not used to being contradicted."

" But I wasn't contradicting him ! I was merely explaining—"

They all laughed then as if the whole incident had been a supreme joke climaxed by his own declaration of innocence. A tall, thin, youngish playwright whose white hair made effective contrast with his bead-black eyes, remarked : " I imagine you must have found Moscow very interesting, Mr. Saffron."

" Moscow ? I've never been to Moscow."

" Indeed ? I thought you must be a disciple of Stanislavski."

" Who ? "

The playwright looked as if the question could be damnation either way : the revelation of Paul as an ignoramus, or cover for his appropriation of another person's ideas.

Actually Paul had not caught the name, but the wine he had drunk increased the dismay he felt at having been snubbed by a man he admired and laughed at for a joke he couldn't share. He exclaimed hotly : " So I never heard of somebody ? . . . So what ? You guys never heard of me till today, did you ? "

Later it occurred to him that the name had been Stanislavski, and that he had behaved as if it were unknown to him. The gaucherie completed his mortification.

.   .   .   .

The party dispersed soon after that, and Paul, still troubled, found himself a couple of hours later in the library, staring at the Cézannes with his mind half elsewhere on a road that wandered disconcertingly between Moscow and Glendalough. The butler brought in a tray of tea-things, and Rowden entered soon afterwards. Paul noticed idly that he wore different clothes ; must have an enormous wardrobe, changed for every meal, a fad maybe . . . and he recollected something that Roberts had told him with evident pride during one of their drives : " Mr. Rowden, sir, is very particular. Clean sheets and pillow-slips every time he goes to bed — even when he takes his little nap in the afternoon. Very particular, he is." So he's probably been taking his little nap, Paul reflected.

Rowden attended to the tea-making, a ritual he always performed himself, because it involved bringing the water exactly to a boil over the spirit kettle, mixing the leaves from separate caddies, heating the silver pot with a swill of boiling water and then rinsing it into a bowl ; the result, no doubt, was an excellent brew, but Paul didn't like tea anyway and only drank it from politeness.

Rowden said, handing Paul a cup : " What on earth did you do to our latter-day Coleridge ? He went off in a considerable huff and somebody told me you'd insulted him."

" *I* insulted *him* ? All I did was to beg to differ from a few things he said. He'd been laying the law down — it was time someone else put in a word.'

" I'm afraid you upset him."

" I'm sorry if I did — I didn't mean to. But he was talking about the function of the stage director and I'm just as entitled to an opinion about that as he is about books."

" He directs plays too."

" Then I don't think he can be very good at it."

Rowden laughed. " Confidentially, I rather agree."

" Why confidentially ? "

" Because if you criticize him in this town it means you're agin the government, and as I'm not agin any government, provided it governs, I keep my mouth shut. I'm afraid you're too politically naïve to understand our local situation."

" Probably. That's why I was sent here to write about it."

" It might interest you, though, to note what happens to a writer when some accident of history makes him a cultural pontiff over a nationalist literature. The first result is that he ceases to produce any literature himself. The next thing is a tremendous inflation of his ego."

" I can see you don't like him much."

" Did you ? "

Paul hadn't liked him at all, yet he stirred uneasily at any sign of agreement with Rowden on such an issue. The important fact was that the literary critic, likeable or not, was indisputably an inhabitant of the world that Paul claimed as his own. He said : " I certainly didn't intend any disrespect and I'd hate to think he was so put out by anything I said that he wouldn't visit your house again. Maybe I should write him a note ? "

" I wouldn't bother. He'll be here again, don't worry. He's on so many committees he couldn't leave me alone for long. Whenever there's money to be raised for one thing or another these people change their tune."

Again Paul felt the uneasiness ; he could not allow Rowden to have that kind of last word. " If they do," he retorted, " maybe it's because they know so many tunes and changing them's so easy. Don't forget they have their opinion of you just as you have of them, and like you, they're

52

smart enough to keep it to themselves. When they ask for money you think they're humbling themselves, and they let you think it because they figure they get more that way, but actually there's something in them that your cheque-book couldn't buy, and secretly you resent that, so you give it a nasty name — you call it an inflated ego." Paul laughed to take away some of the sting. " Excuse me for being so personal. It's all because I enjoyed meeting the people you had here today. They're among the really important people in the world — a thousand times more so than all the politicians and gunmen——"

" Why don't you add ' and millionaires ' ? "

Paul laughed again. " That would be *too* personal, but it's not a bad idea for my article."

" I thought it was going to be about the little girl."

" Oh, I start with her, that's all. Then I work around to art and artists."

" From what you said about her acting I shouldn't have thought there was much connection."

Paul felt that in a rather dangerous way a core of antagonism between them had been found and now needed only to be exploited. He said lightly : " The way I write, there don't have to be connections. That's the trick — anything'll do that comes into my head."

" So long as you keep a *cool* head. Something I said just now seemed to rub you the wrong way."

" No, but it made me realize what side I'm on."

" Oh, come now, Paul, aren't you rather deliberately misunderstanding me ? You must know I'm not a philistine. I appreciate art and I respect artists as much as you do. If I don't take them quite as seriously as some of them take themselves, that's because I have a sense of humour."

" No, sir, that's because you have a million in the bank, or ten million, or whatever it is."

Rowden flushed. " Please don't call me ' sir '. And believe me when I say I was far more amused than shocked by your *gaffe* this afternoon. It *was* funny — one of the really important people in the world — by your own estimate, not mine — and you send him scurrying off like a — like a spanked puppy !"

" I've said I'm sorry. What else can I do ? "

" Not a thing — or you'd probably make it worse. . . . Some more tea ? "

" No, thanks."

" When are you going to write the article ? "

" Tomorrow, I think."

" Fine. You can have the library here to yourself and I'll tell Briggs you aren't to be interrupted. Would you like a secretary for the typing ? "

" Heavens, no — I do all that myself. What sort of life do you think I'm used to ? "

" I was really only trying to be of service."

Paul found himself suddenly touched. He was always sensitive to the hidden note in a voice, and in Rowden's last sentence there had been such a note, of humility, almost of self-abasement. But after being touched, he was disturbed ; the note came too uneasily from a man like Rowden and after such an argument. He knew then that what was happening between him and Rowden was a repetition of what had happened before in his life — the progress of a relationship to the point of chafing, as if there were something fundamentally raw in his personality that made friendship difficult and hostility almost welcome as a relief. He felt ashamed of his rudeness, yet at the same time he slightly resented having been out-generalled by Rowden's better manners, and he silently upbraided himself in words he remembered because he had once spoken them aloud, after a similar incident with someone else : " I shouldn't ever argue about art with people who aren't artists — I really ought to keep off the subject — I get a chip on my shoulder, I don't know why, I guess it's the way I'm made."

" Might I read the article before you send it off ? " Rowden was asking.

" Why, sure, but it won't be much in your line."

" Perhaps not, but I'm interested. . . . You see, I've done a little writing myself from time to time — though not commercially." He went to one of the library shelves and took down a small morocco-bound volume ; Paul was moving to inspect it when Rowden hastily put it back. " No, no — not now. There's another copy on the shelf by your bed — I thought you might have noticed it."

Paul said he hadn't. " If I'd known it was something of yours . . . but I haven't done much reading in bed while I've been here, I've been too sleepy. . . . I certainly won't miss it tonight, though." And then, with an effect of release from stress, he remembered the copy of *Martin Chuzzlewit* he had borrowed from Carey. He hadn't had time to look at that either.

Rowden's uneasiness had now reached a point of evident urgency. " Please don't take any trouble about it. I've inscribed the book to you — I would be happy for you to have it. Just a few verses I wrote years ago — trivial, one reviewer said — the only reviewer, in fact. Another word he used was ' unpleasant '."

" Unpleasant ? How did he make that out ? "

" Perhaps he was a little prim. Today that kind of attitude is rare among sophisticated people — almost as rare as scholarship. Some of the verses, by the way, are in Latin and Greek."

" Without a translation ? Not much good to me, then. I know Latin slightly, but no Greek at all."

" They have their uses, the classical tongues. One can sometimes put thoughts into them that are — shall I say ? — appropriately hidden from the casual reader. Gibbon, no doubt, did the same with his footnotes. . . . You've read Gibbon ? You should . . . a great stylist . . . but to get back to my own small foray into the literary arena — you've no idea how completely it was ignored — even by the few — the very few — who might have been expected to catch the mood of it."

" Classical scholars, you mean ? "

" Not entirely. . . . But I bear no grudge. The book's utter failure may have been merited. Certainly that one word ' unpleasant ' was the only ripple it stirred."

Paul was uncomfortable again; he felt that Rowden was trying to make some tortuous amends, to heal a rift that had developed between them, yet that in so doing he might soon be creating other stresses even less endurable.

Rowden went on : " I suppose you're surprised I should confess all this ? "

Paul laughed nervously. " No, because I think you're as proud of it in your own way as other people are proud of success."

" You're very shrewd. I — I admire your intelligence, Paul — in fact, I hope you'll always remember me as one of your earliest admirers."

" Well, thanks. I appreciate that. I'm sure you're a pretty good judge. I'll bet all those Picassos and Cézannes you have were bought at the beginning, before the prices went up."

" Some of them were, though I don't brag about it."

" I know you don't. I just guessed. And I also guess if you admire me it means I'll go sky-high too one of these days."

" I think you will, and you'll enjoy it, because you worship success far more than you should. . . . But tell me, Paul, what *is* the barrier between us ? I think there must be one — you seem unwilling to become as close a friend to me as I could be to you. To take a trivial example — absurdly trivial — I call you Paul, my own name's Michael, but you've never called me that . . . it's true you don't call me Mister Rowden — you never give me any name at all, I've noticed. I think it symbolizes that barrier. . . . And another thing — also absurdly trivial. You never told me you'd seen that little actress, had *met* her, I mean — the child who was the leprechaun in that rather dreadful play."

" Yes, I did meet her one afternoon. We took a walk in Phoenix Park. How did you know ? "

" Pure chance — Roberts happened to be driving through and saw you together. It's of no importance at all — except that it seems strange you didn't mention it."

" I didn't think you were interested in her."

56

" I'm not. But *you* evidently were. . . . Are you still ? "

Paul answered musingly : " Yes, in a sort of way. She's my kind if I had a kind."

" You mean if you were to have a girl ? "

" No . . . not exactly."

" Then I don't quite know what you mean by saying she's your kind if you had a kind."

" I don't quite know either. . . . And she's not a child, by the way. She's seventeen."

There followed a considerable silence which was broken (and Paul was glad of it) by the entrance of Briggs, carrying an envelope on a tray. " For you, Mr. Saffron. It just came."

Paul opened it : a cablegram from Boston as follows :

" PLEASE DROP IRISH ASSIGNMENT AND PROCEED LONDON AND ROME IMMEDIATELY STOP WOULD LIKE YOU TO INTERVIEW ITALIAN POLITICIAN NAMED BENITO MUSSOLINI SAID TO BE COMING MAN STOP AWAIT FURTHER INSTRUCTIONS BY CABLE AT LONDON OFFICE (SIGNED) MERRYWEATHER."

Paul read this with utter astonishment, then re-read it while a sharp pinpoint of relief transfixed him.

" Not bad news, I hope ? " Rowden was saying.

Paul called his thoughts to order. Now that he knew he could leave Venton League so soon and with such a valid excuse he felt at ease ; the pinpoint of relief expanded inside him rapidly. " Did I look as if it was bad news ? I'm sorry. . . . It'll seem pretty exciting when I've got over the first shock. . . . I expect the real reason I never called you Michael is the difference in our ages, but I will do from now on." He smiled and passed the cable over. " I never heard of this Mussolini fellow — he's probably a tough nut to crack, and since I don't speak Italian. . . . It beats me why I'm picked on for this kind of job. Just because I once had luck with Lloyd George is no guarantee I'll manage it again."

Rowden handed back the cable. " *Immediately* too."

" That's what it says. A hell of a life, isn't it ? "

"And just when you were beginning to feel at home here."

"Yes. . . . Too bad."

"I suppose — you don't think — you could ignore the instructions — and stay on a while ? "

"*What ?* " Paul laughed. "Ignore an editor ? That's not exactly the way to keep one's job."

"But you said you didn't like the job — that it was only a stopgap till you found a new play to direct ? "

Suddenly Paul wondered if Rowden would give or lend him a few thousand pounds to stage a play, say a Shakespeare production, in London or New York. Perhaps Rowden would enjoy a flutter of that kind, with all the patronly contacts it would involve. Certainly Paul had no qualms about taking money from a rich man and probably losing most of it. The idea tempted, fascinated, then grew suddenly sour ; and he heard his own voice, speaking as much to himself as to Rowden : "You bet I'd give up journalism if I could make a living in the theatre, but till I can — and I *will* — I have to do what the boss says."

"I see. The boss. This man Merryweather."

"Well, he pays me for writing the stuff."

Rowden nodded, lit a cigarette, and pressed the bell. "Then we must tell Briggs about your packing. You haven't time to catch the night boat, but there's another sails at eight in the morning. Leave here about seven — Roberts will drive you to Kingstown. If you'll excuse me, I won't get up to see you off, but we must certainly drink a good wine this evening — to celebrate your Roman holiday. Not champagne, I think — that is for cocottes . . . but I have a rather special Burgundy. . . ."

. . . .

Dinner was gay ; Rowden could be the most gracious of hosts, and Paul liked him almost feverishly now they were so soon to separate. Naturally much of their talk was of Rome and Italy. "I wish I were coming with you, Paul. To be with anyone when he first crosses the Alps, but you especially — a young American — *tabula rasa*. . . . Who *is* this man Merryweather ? An editor, yes, I know that — but what sort of person — is he *simpatico* — does he have any idea of his power — to whisk you about the world — London — Dublin — Rome — to offer you, at the impressionable age, such unrivalled chances of experience — some lifetime friendship, maybe, or fate itself, in one guise or another ? Or is it merely that he wants those little articles that you write with such deplorable skill ? "

" Probably only that."

" How unimaginative ! "

" Well, he knows what he wants and he doesn't care what *I* want. I once asked him if I could do the drama criticism, but he said no — I knew too much, he was afraid I'd be highbrow."

" Surely a strain, though, as it becomes harder for you to find subjects you know nothing about. Or perhaps it doesn't ? "

" That's where travel helps. Widens the circle of ignorance. The unsophisticated viewpoint on Rome — I'll get it, you see."

" Rome might even make you *feel* unsophisticated. It has a unique society — or rather two societies, one based on the aristocracy and the other on the Vatican. I must give you some introductions."

" Thanks — I'll be the Iowa farm-boy amongst all that — it'll suit Merryweather fine. Because in spite of Emily Post, America loves the guy who isn't sure what knife and fork to use."

" Aren't you ? "

" I try not to be *too* sure. And where finger-bowls are concerned I guard all my innocence. Haven't you caught me at it ? "

" No, but it fits well with your somewhat complex behaviour. You're an exceedingly complex character — did you ever realize that ? A certain charm, when you care to use it, hides your arrogance, and your arrogance hides your humility, and your humility hides . . . what, I wonder ?

. . . I don't know, and nor do you — you can't know — *yet*. Meanwhile if I can help you. . . . I shall write a few letters you can take to Italy — Briggs will give them to you before you leave in the morning. They'll be to quite influential people — but Mussolini isn't among them, unfortunately. He's something new in the Roman firmament since my day."

"You know Rome well ? "

"As a youth I lived there several years — till soon after my father died. I was being trained for the priesthood."

"And then you found you had no vocation ? "

"To be less dramatic I found I had a brewery. My father had left it to my elder brother, but when *he* died suddenly I got it. . . . Of course you're quite right — I couldn't have had any real vocation."

Paul thought this over and then said : " I suppose what you did proved it. And yet, isn't it a bit too neat — that everything's all for the best, whether you give up something or not ? I'm lucky — I know what I'll never give up, and anyone can put me to any test they like." He checked himself, realizing that there was in all this an implied condemnation of the other, anxious also to avoid an exchange of confessions. He had a curious feeling that he and Rowden could understand each other if they tried, but he did not want to try; on the contrary, he felt embarrassed and evasive, as if he were discovered without a passport at a frontier. He said : " I wouldn't be surprised if I've been talking a lot of nonsense. . . . Of course I'll be glad to meet your friends, it's very kind of you to suggest it, though I don't know how long I'll be in Rome. It all depends on Mussolini——"

"May I give you a word of advice ? " Rowden leaned towards Paul across the table. " Just this. Let the big man talk. Don't tell him what a fool he is if you can possibly avoid it."

Paul was almost ready to resent this as a second return to an issue that had already been terminated, but with relief inside him now rising to enthusiasm, he found it possible to laugh heartily.

Rowden laughed too. "You know, Paul, I've been searching for a word to describe what's the real trouble with you, and I think I've got it . . . you're not *world-broken*."

"*World-broken?* What's that? . . . On the analogy of——"

"That's it. You don't care what you do — or where. And to continue the metaphor, you'll end up shivering in an outdoor kennel instead of basking on the hearthrug in front of a warm fire."

"Okay, Michael. . . . So long as I have even the kennel, to hell with the hearthrug." (It was the first and last time he ever called him Michael.)

"You're probably still young enough to be able to make the choice. How lucky you are, indeed!"

.   .   .   .   .   .

Paul said his goodbyes in the corridor outside their bedrooms, and Rowden left him with a cordial invitation to visit Venton League again. Paul promised he would, though with a premonition that it would never happen. There was so much in the man that he liked and admired, and much too that he felt he could make use of — not in any sense of exploitation, but rather as part of the process of self-enlightenment. He wondered whether Rowden guessed that Venton League was the first house he had ever visited where dressing for dinner was routine and not show-off, where vintage wines were drunk ritually but not snobbishly, and where servants shined shoes and packed for guests. His own packed bag faced him now, and on top, where Briggs must have placed it as a reminder, lay the *Martin Chuzzlewit* from the city library. With that as a goad, the thought of Carey leapt at him unleashed and with extra strength because all day, it seemed, he had been holding it at bay. Now that he was alone the enormity of having cancelled the planned excursion sank in his mind with an effect of sickness. He contemplated the possibility that he would never see her again, that Rowden and Merryweather had between them set an end to the relationship, the one with a touch of forethought and the other unwittingly, while he himself had weakly acquiesced.

He knew he could not sleep with such thoughts in his mind. He paced the room, staring at the furniture, the pictures, anything that might stir some feeble counter-interest. Suddenly he saw the volume of Rowden's verses on his bedside shelf, hard to miss if he had ever before given the books any attention. He sat on the edge of the bed and read a few pages. The title was " Leaves ", it had been privately printed, and there was no publication date. He soon decided that Rowden's low estimate of its worth (however insincere) was the plain truth. It was interesting, though, as a clue to the man's tastes and personality. Somewhat in the style of Swinburne or Baudelaire — perhaps written as long ago as that, when their kind of writing was in vogue. Paul re-read a few of the poems and tried to decide on an adjective for them. ' Unpleasant ' would never have entered his mind had not Rowden laid such stress on the word ; as it was, with an idea thus implanted, Paul diagnosed here and there a sort of strained morbidity, perhaps considered decadent at one time, but nowadays merely outmoded. Of course the items in Latin and Greek were beyond him. Having skimmed the book through (it was very short) he put it aside and forgot it was his own property, Rowden having inscribed it for him ; so that the next day, after he had gone, its presence still at the bedside conveyed a far more crushing verdict than any he had formulated. Though he never knew this, it was the reason why Rowden did not reply to several letters Paul sent him during the next few weeks ; and, indeed, it was the end of their fleeting contact.

Next, and in some sense as an antidote, he picked up *Chuzzlewit* and turned to the American section ; its sheer readableness diverted him for a few moments, but all the time he was imagining what Carey might have thought of America and Americans whilst reading it. Perhaps he should write her a letter to go back with the book ; Briggs could mail them to the theatre the next day. He went to a desk and filled several sheets of notepaper, chiefly about *Chuzzlewit*; it was his first letter to her, indeed, except for the mere note he had sent with the roses. Then he noticed that the inside of the book-cover contained a library card with her address in Terenure, and an idea was born in him that speedily rose to huge dimensions. For he knew now where she lived, where she was at that moment — and she had said it was less than a mile away. Why shouldn't he walk over to her house before going to bed and make his own delivery of the book and the letter? Of course she would be asleep at such an hour, but he could come close to her for a moment, perhaps for the last time, and she would later know that he had been there. It was odd how satisfying that was to him as he contemplated it.

Venton League was locked and bolted, but the garden door had a simple latch, and he knew there was a side gate several hundred yards from the house that led through unused stables and another gate into a road. He also knew the general direction of Terenure, but that was all. Fortunately he soon met a late-homing tram-driver who directed him to the address. As he approached it he heard, in the very far distance, the crackle of rifle shots. It spurred him, matching his own feeling of excitement in what he was doing — walking at this late hour (and he disliked walking at any hour) through the unknown streets of an unknown city. A mysterious schizophrenic city, he reflected, passing the suburban villas one after the other, each one dark and silent, while a few miles away on roof-tops a handful of zealots risked their lives to make history. He could not help thinking of it theatrically — the vast populous inertia of the sleeping suburbs as a background to the silhouette of the lone man wide awake with a gun. The idea fascinated, then grew larger as he tried to imagine the play whose staging he had already pictured with the eye of his mind. He had no political intelligence, but for that reason he sometimes caught a whiff of events that the analysts and short-range tipsters missed.

When he reached the house he was surprised to see lights

in several of the windows, both upstairs and down. He walked up the short path to the porch and dropped both book and note in the letter-box as quietly as he could. But someone must have heard, for before he reached the street again the front door opened and Carey's voice called out : "Who is it?" Her voice sounded curious rather than startled. He turned back a few paces into the zone of light from the doorway ; then she came rushing out to him with an eagerness equally curious. "*Paul!* . . . Won't you come in?" That startled *him*. She almost dragged him into the house, leading the way to a small room opening off the narrow lobby — a den, it could have been called, with an old fashioned roll-top desk, shabby chairs, and of all things, a complicated gymnastic apparatus of ropes and pulleys. He felt again the overmastering physical ease of being in her presence, the relief of finding her eager to see him despite the fiasco of the cancelled trip ; but in addition there was a strangeness he was just faintly aware of, a tension in her face and attitude that he had not seen before.

He began rapidly : " You must think me crazy to be here this time of night, but the fact is, I'm leaving for London early tomorrow and I wanted to return the book. . . . I wrote this note too — never thought I'd see you . . . nothing important in it — mostly about the book."

" The book? "

" *Martin Chuzzlewit* . . . don't you remember? "

She answered, almost dreamily : " I didn't know you knew where I lived."

" That was in the book, too — on a library card."

" A *library* book? Oh yes, I do remember. . . . Would you — would you care for a drink? "

" Thanks, no — I'll have to be going in a minute. Must have some sleep. The boat sails at eight."

" Why are you going away so soon? "

" My editor cabled me. I've got to do a job for him in Italy."

" Italy? And before you've finished all you wanted to do here? "

" Looks like it. I certainly haven't done much, have I ?
And I'm specially sorry about Glendalough."

" That couldn't be helped — you had the party instead.
Was it interesting ? "

" Very — but I was missing Glendalough all the time."
How untrue that was, and yet how revealing, even to himself,
of the truth ; for it was now, with her in that small room,
that he was acutely missing something, of which Glendalough could well stand as a name and symbol. " If I'd
guessed it would be my last chance, I don't know but
what——"

" Oh no, you couldn't possibly. And it was just as well."

" Why do you say that ? "

" Because . . ." She hesitated, then chattered on :
" You'll probably get to hear about it . . . no, you wouldn't,
though, if you're leaving so soon. Anyhow, it's nothing that
affects you, but if we *had* gone to Glendalough it would have
been worse . . . for me."

" For *you* ? "

" I'm sorry — it's my fault for not getting to the point. . . ."
She seemed to steady herself as if for the repetition of a
lesson, then said in a level voice : " My stepfather died this
morning."

" *What?* " He stared at her, disturbed by her look and
manner as much as by what she had said. " Carey ! Oh,
I'm sorry. . . . Had he been ill ? You didn't tell me . . .
was it sudden ? . . . But if you'd rather not talk about
it. . . ."

" I don't mind. . . . He was all right, early this morning — I saw him before he left for eight-o'clock mass at
St. Peter's — that's the long mass. I went to the nine
o'clock at St. Columba's — that's the short one. I was back
here by half-past ten after meeting you, and I could see he
was back, too, and had had his breakfast — then I heard the
water running in the bath upstairs. The water's never hot
enough early in the morning, so on Sundays . . ."

She hesitated as if the details were becoming too trivial,
and he made a murmur of encouragement.

65

" Well, it became a sort of Sunday treat — he always stayed in the bath a long time and had his grammar books with him — he was learning Gaelic. . . . After the water stopped running I heard him saying over the words . . . but he was there so long I began to wonder if anything was the matter, so I called out and knocked at the door, but there was no reply. Mrs. Kennedy — she's the housekeeper we've had since my mother died — she said he'd been all right at breakfast — quite chatty and cheerful with her. But after a time I told her I was nervous, so we broke the lock and found him . . . in the bath . . . he was dead by then."

She paused breathlessly and he made haste to offer the only comfort he could think of. " Carey, I know there's nothing I can say that can really help, but of all the ways to die, it might have been the easiest — a fainting fit — suddenly — the hot bath on top of a meal——"

" No, I don't think it was that."

" Why . . . why not ? "

" It wasn't *like* that." She gave him a strained look.

" What did the doctor say ? "

" He said what you said — more or less. But I still don't think——"

" Did you tell him you didn't ? "

" No, I haven't told anybody that — till now."

" Carey, what's on your mind ? "

She said in a level voice again : " I think he killed himself."

" But — how — why — what on earth makes you . . . : Look here, you'd better tell me what really *is* on your mind."

She went on : " He had asthma sometimes. He took pills for it with opium in them, and the doctor told him never to take more than two at a time, no matter how bad the attack was. They were in a little bottle that he carried in his vest pocket. Today, when I looked, it was empty. He must have taken at least a dozen."

" But how can you possibly know that ? Didn't the doctor ask about the pills ? "

" No. It wasn't the same doctor that gave him the prescription — that one left the district, and this is a new man who hadn't seen him before."

" So what *did* he say ? "

" He thought it was a heart attack. I told him he had been warned by the other doctor about his heart."

" Had he ? "

The strain touched her lips now, making them veer and tremble. " I told the doctor he had."

Paul didn't speak for a moment ; he was pondering. Presently he said : " I'm still puzzled — I can't see that you've any reason to draw the conclusion you do. When and where did you last see the bottle with pills in it ? "

" On his bedside table. It was nearly full. I was taking him a cup of tea before breakfast. A few days ago — perhaps a week."

" Then how can you be certain about what happened this morning ? Any time during the past week he could have——"

" But he wouldn't, unless he had an attack, and he hadn't had one since — oh, months."

" How do you know *that* ? "

" He'd have told me, or else I'd have noticed. He always coughed so much and it left him weak afterwards. It's not something you can hide from people in the same house."

" That may be, but I still say there's no proof that he took all those pills this morning."

" I think he *must* have."

" But *why* ? Surely you don't *want* to think so ? And if the doctor was satisfied — he was, wasn't he ? "

" Yes — after I talked to him. He wrote out a certificate, but I don't think he would have if he'd seen the empty bottle."

He said sharply : " What did you do with the bottle ? "

" That's why I'm glad we didn't go to Glendalough. I broke it into little pieces and buried them in the garden."

" You *did* ? Let's hope you were lucky and nobody saw you. . . . And don't you ever tell anyone else about all this."

" Oh, I won't. But there's something I haven't told even you — yet." She went over to the roll-top desk and opened it. " This was the Irish grammar he worked from, and the pencil and exercise-book he used. They were on the chair by the side of the bath, and there was a note clipped to the book, written on a torn page. Here it is. Nobody else has seen it."

She took it out of the pocket of her skirt and unfolded it. Paul read the carefully pencilled script :

" DEAR CAREY — I know now it was a mistake ever to come to Ireland but I did it to please your mother and I pretended to be happy here, but I'm not, and actually I never have been. It's a terrible thing when all at once you realize you're learning a language that bores you and going to a church you don't really believe in. I turned Catholic too, you know, to please her. They don't like me at the office, they don't like my English accent, they have a nickname for me — they call me Fitzpomp. It's odd how all sorts of things can go on and on for years and you can stand them, and then suddenly you feel you can't stand a single one of them for another minute. Well, why should you ? There's a line in some Latin writer — Seneca, I think — that says : ' We cannot complain of life, for it keeps no one against his will '. So I don't complain, and this letter, though it may tell you more about me than you have ever suspected, is really no more than a . . ."

The letter ended at that, and had no signature ; it was as if the writer had been seized with illness in mid-sentence.

Paul was wondering why she had not shown him the letter at the beginning ; it would have saved so much argument. The detached part of his mind caused him to pick up the exercise-book and compare the writing in it with the note ; they were the same, there was no doubt of that. He saw her watching him make the test, but he could not guess what she was thinking.

He said at length : " How old were you when your mother married again ? "

" Twelve."

" And your real father . . . you remember him ? "

"I was ten when he died. . . . We lived in Kildare near the Curragh. He used to hunt with the cavalrymen — oh, you should have seen him on a horse. We had a farm, but it never paid . . . such wonderful times, though — and every Christmas he took me to the Theatre Royal to see the pantomime. That's when I first decided I wanted to be an actress."

"You didn't have such good times with your stepfather?"

"No . . . but he was all right — we got along quite well."

He handed the letter back. "You were lucky to find this too, before anyone else did. Are you going to keep it?"

"You think . . . you think I'd better not?" She hesitated a moment, then struck a match and held the paper to it. When the flame was down to the last corner she crumpled the charred pieces into an ash-tray.

He said: "Perhaps that's wise."

"You don't blame me, do you?"

"*Blame* you? Blame *you*? What on earth for? Did you ever guess he was so unhappy?"

"I never guessed anything he said in the letter. That's what makes it all such a shock. How could he not love Ireland, the poor little man? . . . though dear knows it's had its troubles. And I never heard that they called him Fitzpomp at the office. *Fitzpomp*. . . ." She spoke the word as if sampling it. "He seemed so keen on learning the Gaelic — he didn't have to do that if he didn't want to — he'd been looking forward to taking an examination — it must have been on his mind at the end because he was saying over the words — I *heard* him . . . and the last thing — almost the last thing he did was so normal — so tidy . . . just as he always was . . . so tidy. . . ."

"What was that?"

"He screwed on the top of the empty bottle and put it back in his vest pocket. That's where I found it."

Her voice had a note that made him exclaim: "Carey, you must pull yourself together — isn't there anyone else here in the house to help you?"

"I'm all right. My aunt and uncle came over from Sandymount — they'll stay till — oh, till afterwards. And there's Mrs. Kennedy too. I'm all right now — really I am. I'm glad I told somebody the truth and I'm glad it was you. I expect I told you because you're a stranger and leaving so soon. And I'm glad you made me destroy the letter."

" I didn't make you, but——"

" I know, I know, and you were right. Ah God, he wasn't a bad man. He was kind to my mother — she bossed him a lot — it's true he did everything to please her. He was lonely after she died, but he seemed to manage. He took up all sorts of things — hobbies — studies — memory-training — those things in correspondence lessons to help with the Gaelic. Every evening he'd put in a couple of hours. And the machine over there — he bought that — it's supposed to develop muscles. . . . I got so used to him, I don't know yet how much I shall miss him. I'm watching myself, in a sort of way, to find out. It's like when you're on the stage — you don't exactly *feel*, you *feel* yourself *feel*. I suppose that's the trouble with me now — I'm really *acting* — I can't stop it — I've been doing it all day, more or less — I had to with the doctor — and then with all the others since. . . . Are you shocked? Is there something wrong with me to be like that?"

He wasn't shocked, of course; he had already diagnosed that she was acting; the problem, to him, was in the fact that he himself was not directing. If their conversation since he entered the house had really been stage dialogue, he would have known exactly what the 'playing attitude' should be, but because it was all happening in life he was uncertain how to behave. He knew that his compassion was one of the warmest excitements he had ever felt, but he could find no words for it. Fortunately she had now given him the kind of cue he could pick up. He said, taking her arm a little roughly: " There's nothing wrong with you at all. Don't you know how natural it is for any artist to come to terms with an emotion through the medium of his own art? It's the great thing that compensates him — whatever he suffers, he has that outlet that nobody else has — he can use up what he feels, he can *do* something with it, create something out of it, so that even pain, in a sort of way, seems worth while. If, for instance, he's a writer, he can make personal sorrow work for him in a book — a musician can put it into his music — a painter can see it on canvas. And all that never surprises anyone. But with the actor, the art is *acting* — so that whenever something happens to you that matters enough, that's just what you do. Most people wouldn't understand it, because they think of acting as a kind of pretence or sham — anyhow, they don't often notice it in a good actor, because it's his art not to seem to be acting at all. But he is, and he knows he is, and — as you say — he can't stop it. It's really the highest form of sincerity — and since you liked your stepfather, it's a tribute to him that you should be doing it . . . as you are now . . . *so well*."

"*Am* I ?" She was moved almost to tears, and he did not tell her that his long speech had been a repetition, personalized and slightly adapted, of a paragraph in an article on acting which he had submitted to various magazines so far without success.

She added: "Paul, since you say that, is there — do you think — any chance for me ?"

"As an actress ?" Trying to assemble his judgment, he was excited by her emotion ; it was intoxicating to think that she must assume his eloquence to have been improvised.

"I know it's the most awful time to ask," she went on, noticing his hesitation. "But I *have* asked, so won't you answer ? Is there the merest outside chance ? You're leaving so soon and you can help me either way. If you say no, I'll give up the whole idea, because I don't want to waste my time. But if you say yes, then . . ."

His judgment still balked, and he could only remember what he had realized from the first — that she possessed the genuine histrionic personality plus a quality of her own that the stage might either destroy or magnify, depending of course on how she was trained and directed. What was it ? Talent ? Some half-physical attribute ? He answered: "Yes, I think you might have a chance." His words had the kind of delayed sincerity that made him feel, a few

71

seconds after speaking them, that he hadn't been insincere at all. (For presumably she did have a chance, at the Abbey, of being properly directed.) He went on, gathering confidence : "Why, sure — of course you have."

"You *really* think so ? "

"I do . . . I do. . . ."

The answer made the thing seem like some sort of ceremony involving them in vows and pledges ; I do, I do, his mind kept echoing, incredulously.

"Oh, bless you, Paul — even if you don't mean it . . . no, don't argue — not another word — I know you have to go—"

Actually he didn't want to go now at all ; he wanted to explore a relationship that had begun to fascinate.

"But Carey——"

"Dear, no, I've talked too long already — I'll bet my aunt and uncle are wondering who that man is. Thank you, Paul — you've helped me so much — in so many ways——"

"Will you do something for me, then ? As soon as I've gone, go to bed and try to sleep."

"Yes, yes, I promise that. I promise."

In her changed mood she was almost shooing him out of the house.

"And I'll write to you from Rome——"

"Yes, if you have time — but you'll be so busy——"

"I'll find time, Carey . . . because I . . ."

"Goodbye, Paul — goodbye." They shook hands in the lobby as she opened the door. All the way back to Venton League he wondered why he had not kissed her. It did not seem important till he himself was in bed and trying to sleep. Then, with the mail-boat to catch in a few hours, he felt hemmed in by timings and mistimings.

.   .   .   .

Paul wrote to her from the Holyhead boat the next day — a constrained letter, oddly aloof, because there was a battle going on in his own mind. He was fated, it seemed, to fight too late, when the issue could not be affected and the victory of second thoughts could only bring regrets and remorse. This time it was the fact that he had left Carey in such trouble, deserting her when she might most need him. Actually he doubted whether he could have helped her more than he already had by his advice and encouragement; but this prompt physical departure from the scene had an air of callousness which shocked him when now he contemplated it. Surely it would seem to her that he could cancel anything except business, and for anyone except her. If she mattered to him, he ought to have stayed in Dublin for at least a few days, even if he had left Venton League and taken a room at a hotel. But perhaps, he reflected, the fact that he was now on his way elsewhere proved that she *didn't* matter to him. It was an argument that made him uneasy, as if, in his bones, he *wished* her to matter to him and would suffer if it were proved otherwise.

He wrote to her again from London, but there was no time for her to reply before he was off to Rome; he gave her an address there. If she didn't reply, it might mean that she too had sized up the situation as one calling for caution, or at least for a meditative pause. During his first week in Rome he glanced many times across the hotel desk to the pigeon-hole where his mail was put when he had any; he was curious, but not too anxious yet. No letter came from her; and then, as if to make that a bad start in retrospect, other things began to go wrong too. Mussolini was neither in Rome nor willing to see him, and from a succession of urgent cables it was clear how confidently and absurdly Merryweather had been counting on a repetition of the Lloyd George fluke. Paul almost wished he could share the editor's concern; as it was, he felt only increasing distaste for the kind of fraud he was beginning to think he was. Perhaps the sooner he failed as a journalist the better, but it must be quick and catastrophic, before he could rescue himself by another fluke. Because he so nearly *had* pulled off that interview with Mussolini, and the reason for missing at the last moment had been nothing but his own caprice, if one could let it go at that; he had neglected to exploit one of Rowden's letters of introduction to an Italian of wealth and influence. The man had evidently liked Paul on sight and been ready to pull some final string, but Paul, after one short meeting, had fought shy of him from a personal squeamishness as hard to admit as to ignore.

So having fluffed, he left Italy and travelled to Paris to await further word from Merryweather; if none came he could take it that there were no more assignments for the time being. He certainly did not feel he could return to Dublin to face Rowden's curiosity, whetted by some likely communication from the Italian friend. The one thing that tempted was the chance to see Carey again, but even this did not preponderate till after a certain evening in Paris. He had gone alone to a performance of the *Magic Flute*; he did not as a rule care for operas, because he found their dramatic foolishness hard to take, but this was a superlative blend of music and spectacle that made everything else forgettable and therefore tolerable ; he sat entranced, and later, strolling along a boulevard, suddenly realized that not to see Carey again, not to follow up their relationship, would be like avoiding Mozart because one had once been bored by Bizet. At a sidewalk café he stopped for a drink, the goggle-eyed American in Paris to all misleading appearance; for in truth he was lost in abstractions that soon became self-incredulous — how *unlikely* that a seventeen-year-old Irish girl whom he had talked to for no more than a few hours could not only have occupied his mind since then, but could now reach out to touch the troubled parts of it ! It occurred to him also, and as an afterthought, that no one before had so attracted him by sheerly feminine qualities — the lilt of her voice from the first word of that first encounter, her lips twisting when she smiled, even the piquantly all-wrong quality she had given to a small stage part (the director's fault, not hers). But most of all, and never an afterthought, was the mystery she shared with all (and how few they were) who had it in them to make a finger-point of contact with life through art — a feminine, creative mystery, the secret nerve that could break down every withholding in himself, whether from man or woman.

He wrote again that night, telling her whimsically that Mussolini had refused to have anything to do with him, so he would soon have to return to America, his travel fellowship year being almost over ; but he would like to see her again before that. He didn't think he would revisit Dublin, but if by any chance she could travel part of the way — to Holyhead, perhaps, or Liverpool . . . of course he could well imagine there might be circumstances to prevent that, and he would fully understand, but still, if it were at all possible to arrange a rendezvous . . .

Even while he was writing he knew that part of him was counting on a negative answer or none at all, a rock-ribbed alibi for the rest of his life, so that he could always tell himself he had done his best, he had asked her anyway, it was fate and not he that had foreclosed. But at this the battle was joined again, the feeling in his bones against the arguments of his brain. Eventually he tore up the letter and wrote another, shorter and much more urgent ; he told her he *must* see her again ; he would come to Dublin if necessary and if she were still there, but if not, then somehow, somewhere, *anywhere*. . . .

By return came a note as short as his own. Legal matters, she said, had cropped up in connection with her stepfather's small estate ; there was a lawyer in London she had to visit almost immediately — wouldn't London be as convenient for a meeting as Dublin ?

More so, of course. He left Paris the next morning, having wired her to reach him at the Ellesmere Hotel, Euston Road. It was a cheap but respectable place, all he could afford, and he remembered it because during the war he had worked in an office of the U.S. Army just across from Euston Station. That part of London he knew as well as New York, or Reedsville, Iowa, and for the same reason : he had been lonely there.

. . . .

The battle continued during his cross-Channel journey ; first he was buoyant at the thought of seeing her so soon, then he half regretted having planned the meeting at all. As he entered the gloomy lobby of the Ellesmere Hotel he even hoped for some unavoidable hitch (but it would *have* to be unavoidable) — perhaps his wire had never been delivered, perhaps her own London trip had been cancelled. Yet when, at the desk, he asked if there had been any enquiries for him and was told no, he felt acutely dismayed. The dismay increased during the next few hours; he couldn't think what he would do with himself in London if she did not come; perhaps he ought to wire her in Dublin again. He unpacked in the comfortless third-floor bedroom; once the telephone rang, but it was the manager asking if he were a British subject — " I shouldn't have bothered you, sir, but I noticed you gave an address in New York — we have to keep a record, you know, sir." Paul had sprung to the instrument with such eagerness that he hardly knew how to reply through the deflation he felt; he stammered: " What's that ? Yes — I mean no — not British . . . American. . . . By the way, I'm expecting a call — you're sure there hasn't been one so far ? "

It came much later, about nine o'clock, and he had waited in the bedroom all the time, not caring to go out for dinner — having no appetite, he discovered, and as time passed, not even the inclination to read. He lay on the bed and wondered what was still happening to him — a new experience, and he had always thought he would welcome one, whatever it was ; yes, he *did* welcome it ; all over the world there must be millions of young men concerned, as he was, about a girl ; reassuring to find himself like so many others . . . or *was* he ? Suppose someone were to offer him there and then a play to direct, a great play, wouldn't that have power to preoccupy, to excite, to thrust everything else out of his mind ? Wouldn't it ? Or would it ? After her first words — " Paul, is that you ? " — he knew the answer ; by God yes, it's I, it's me, bring on the play, bring on a thousand plays, here I am, Paul Saffron, you haven't heard of me yet, but you will, you *will*. . . .

" Carey. . . . Where are you ? "

" I didn't know when you'd arrive — I've only just got here myself — the train was late. . . . Oh, darling, it's so good to hear your voice again."

" It *is*? *You* feel like that too? . . . Carey, I . . . I've so many things to ask. . . . Where're you staying? How long will you be in London? I want to see a lot of you. . . . I do hope you won't be busy all the time. . . ."

" As much as you want — it'll be several days at least. I'm staying with an aunt at Putney."

" *Putney?* "

" That's not far out. About an hour. . . . Oh no, I'm not there yet — I'm at the station — Euston — I told you — I've only just arrived——"

" *Euston?* . . . Then what are we wasting time like this for? Just across the street! Listen, Carey — under the clock in the station hall . . . got that? . . . A couple of minutes . . ."

He hung up, raced down the stairs rather than ring for the crawling lift, and on his way across the lobby called out to the clerk in sheer exuberance : " Yes, I'm American — what do I have to do — register with the police or something? "

" No, sir — just for our records. Was that the call you were expecting? "

He snapped out a " You bet " that was lost in the segments of the revolving door.

Crossing the Euston Road (and it was drizzling with rain as it had been so many times before), he thought of Dante's saying that the bitterest of all pangs was to remember happier days ; put that in reverse and it was equally true, for there was actual relish now in thinking of the war year that he had spent so safely and drearily in London. Not that it had been London's fault ; he had liked the people and the city too, so far as it belonged to them in his mind and not to the associations of army life. That he had hated, utterly and absolutely, more probably than he would or could hate anything else in life. The little square where the hut had been was now just a square again, rain-drenched lawns covering so much drab and unrecorded experience; he could still call back the smell of that interior, its mixture of stale smoke, gas heaters, chewing gum, human sweat. Men had swarmed in continuously from the great near-by terminals — Euston, St. Pancras, King's Cross; and it had been his job (the snob job, given him because of his better education, forsooth!) to handle the officers, telling them where they had been allotted rooms, what to see in London during a few days' leave, the best shows, where to find the best women. (Much joking about that, especially from an angle neither flattering to him nor true about him — but what could he do, or say? So he had joined in the laughs, Pagliacci-style.) It was all so 'cushy', to use the over-worked British adjective then current — 'cushy' to sit out the war in London with a telephone in one hand and filing cabinets within reach of the other — practically a hotel clerk in uniform, humorously servile, falsely jocular. He and a dozen other clerks took turns at the job, day and night; they fed at a canteen and slept on army cots in a commandeered boarding-house in Southampton Row. They had varicose veins, weak hearts, hernias; he had his pituitary trouble. They were decent fellows, and he tried to conceal from them his passionate hope that when the war was over he would never see any of them again. Once or twice there were air raids, spicing the routine with excitement rather than danger — Zeppelins like silver cigars in the blue-black sky. On his time off he wandered all over London, visiting museums and art galleries, but his secret contempt for the who, what, and when of military life made him fumble into all kinds of trouble about dress and saluting. He got to know a few girls, one of whom, chance-met in the next seat at a concert, became a friend until she had waited for him once outside the army office and been shocked by overheard badinage. Neither of them had had enough importance to the other to be able to think it merely funny. He had made one man friend also, an English policeman who sometimes idled into the office at nights for a chat over the stove. The policeman had a sister in Alberta and a romantic feeling about America as a whole. He took Paul several times to supper at his little house near the Angel, Islington. Paul liked him from the moment he had said : " If I 'ad your job, mate, I'd shoot meself. 'Avin' to put up with all them jokes from them officers and no chawnce to answer back — it's worse'n bein' a bloody bar-tender. Specially when they all think you've got it so cushy." It was true ; he knew how he was envied by some of the men on their way to the Front, and how little they guessed there could be any way in which he envied them. Yet he did, and then he didn't, so many times ; there had been conflict, even in those days, between physical distaste (fear, too, but no more than anyone else had) and a mental longing to put himself to the test, to find out if he could face what other men faced.

And now, four years later, he entered Euston Station, happily remembering how miserable he had been.

.   .   .   .   .   .

As soon as he saw her he knew that their relationship was on a different level, established at the house in Terenure that night, but since fortified by time, absence, and — who could say ? — perhaps by a telepathy of awareness between them. She rushed up to him in the station hall and laughed her first words above the din of porters and luggage trucks. " Oh, Paul — Paul — I never dreamed I'd see you so soon — I didn't know how to answer your letters at first — they sounded so cold, as if you didn't want to see me again, but then when you said you did——"

" Carey, I did — I do — I've missed you — in such an extraordinary way. Carey, you look unbelievable. . . . Had dinner ? No ? Nor have I. This aunt of yours in Putney can wait. . . . Where's your luggage ? Just the one bag ? We'll take it along, then."

They drove to a small French restaurant in Lisle Street that he knew of — quiet, informal, expensive. He had economized by staying at the Ellesmere, but now he would be extravagant — he would ask Merryweather for more work, would write a hundred articles, would interview Lenin,

79

Gandhi, Bernard Shaw, Suzanne Lenglen — the whole who's who of the world. That was his mood as he consulted the menu. Normally he was no gourmet, and his appetite was voracious rather than fastidious. But now he suddenly hankered after delicacies — terrapin, caviare, frogs' legs — careless of how they mixed or what they cost; and it was she, in tune with his emotion yet thinking of his pocket-book, who talked him out of the wilder whims. Eventually he compromised on smoked salmon, *poulet en casserole*, and a bottle of Heidsieck — forgetting that Rowden had called champagne a wine for cocottes. And meanwhile they talked almost antiphonally, as if their respective concerns matched each other — his failure in Rome, her own bereavement in Dublin; the *Magic Flute* in Paris, a new play at the Abbey in which (sure enough) she had been offered the fourteen-year-old part. But she had had to turn it down in order to come to London. She didn't care — any more than he cared about Merryweather's disappointment. It was one of the few times in his life he had found anyone who could talk as much as he did without seeming to interrupt or to wait anxiously for chances to butt in; a musical simile again occurred to him — that they were somehow improvising on a keyboard of speech while their underlying thoughts made deeper harmony in what was left unsaid.

Over the coffee he remembered that aunt of hers. "Carey, hadn't you better telephone you'll be late?"

" She doesn't know I'm coming at all till I do telephone."

" She doesn't? Oh, fine. Then we don't have to worry, except that if the old lady goes to bed early——"

" She's not old. She's not much older than I am."

" No ? "

" My mother was the eldest of fifteen and Sylvia's the youngest. She's married to a landscape gardener. They have three children and I don't know how many dogs — they breed them — wire-haired terriers all over the place. It's good for children to live in an atmosphere like that. They've won any amount of prizes. The dogs, I mean." She made a grimace. " All this must be so enthralling to

you. Now tell me things like that about your own life — I
wish you would — I hardly know anything about you."

" You know all that matters."

" Ah, yes, but tell me something that doesn't matter for a
change."

" You mean I'm too serious ? I talk too much about
my ambitions ? "

" Darling, no — how could you — to me ? Our ambitions are so alike——"

" That's where you're wrong. Acting's a completely
different function from——"

" I dare say it is." She began to giggle. " I wouldn't
argue about it for the world. Oh, Paul, you've got to humour
me — I want some personal thing — about your childhood,
schooldays, family — any little detail—"

He looked at her, stern at first because of the note of
raillery in her voice, as if she were daring to be amused by
him. Then he softened, as one who can indulge a whim out
of some deeper geniality of the spirit ; he didn't really mind
her laughing at him ; his tolerance of that had been set at
their first meeting.

He said : " Not much to tell, Carey. I was born in
Reedsville, Iowa. Small town. I went to grade school there.
Then to high school and Iowa State University. My father
was a farmer. He came from Pennsylvania — Pennsyl-
vania-Dutch stock — Germany before that. My mother's
still living — she's in Milwaukee with my brother and his wife.
That's about all there is. I have no other brothers and sisters."

" And no girl ? You don't have a girl in America ? I
don't know why I never asked that before."

" I don't have a girl anywhere."

" You say that either forlornly or proudly. Which is it ? "

" Neither. Just a fact. To tell you the truth, I — I
don't seem to score very heavily with the other sex — as
a rule — except as friends. At least I haven't so far."

" So far," she echoed. " That's not very far."

He went on hurriedly : " How about you ? I expect
you're popular enough with all kinds of men."

" Some kinds. But I don't know many — even as friends. You can't, when you're only free one evening a week. They won't put up with that."

" Nonsense ! If a man were to fall in love with you — hasn't that ever happened ? "

" Yes."

" Well, did he object ? "

" *Object ?* "

" To your work — to seeing you only one night a week ? "

" He saw me every night. He was acting with me."

" Oh, then it was simple for you——"

" No — it didn't work."

" Why not ? Didn't you love him ? "

" I thought I did at the time. Perhaps I did. But it wasn't a success."

He asked sharply : " Why not ? What happened ? Which of you broke it off ? "

" Oh, Paul . . ." She began to laugh. " You suddenly get so — so pouncy — like a prosecuting counsel — as if I were on trial——"

" Well, I'm curious. You were curious about me — you asked for something personal. What went wrong in this affair you had with this man ? "

" It wasn't an affair — at least not *that* kind of affair. Perhaps that's why it went wrong. He wanted it to be."

" And you didn't ? "

" No."

" Why ? Moral reasons ? "

" Partly. Maybe."

" Because you're a Catholic ? "

" Maybe."

" But you're not sure ? "

" The way you're cross-examining me I don't feel too sure of anything. You'd make a terrifying lawyer."

" I'm sorry. And I think you were quite right to refuse — at seventeen. . . . Though it's none of my business."

" It isn't really, is it ? And I was sixteen then. . . . But it's my fault, I admit — I began all this questioning. . . ."

82

" No, *my* fault — I'm much too inquisitive. *Sixteen!* Good God ! "

" Now tell me if *you've* ever been in love."

" *Me?* Why . . . Why, yes . . . hundreds of times."

" That's like saying never."

" Carey, I assure you, I fall for every clever or beautiful woman I meet — you mustn't think because I'm not a Casanova that there's anything about me that's — that's *against* women. It's just that — well, I suppose I'm not quite the type for these headlong passions, though no doubt one of them will come along some day and bowl me over completely——"

" How convenient to have it come along like that ! Nothing for you to do but just wait."

" No, that's not my attitude, because — really — I should like — very much — to — to . . ." He began to colour, then looked at his watch and laughed. " *Now* who's cross-examining ? "

" It's my turn again — isn't that fair ? Besides, it's good for both of us. Wouldn't you like us to get to know each other really well ? "

" Of course I would." He signalled the waiter and asked for more coffee. She said relaxingly : " Oh, I'm so glad you did that. When you looked at your watch I thought you were going to say it was time we were leaving."

" It is, but I don't mind."

" Nor do I, though I haven't an idea how to get to Putney if I miss the last train."

" We'll take a taxi."

" *We?* But you needn't bother to——"

" I certainly wouldn't dream of letting you go alone at this time of night — I don't know how far the place is or what it's like — it's absurd for you to think of——"

" All right — all right — I give in."

The waiter refilled their cups. She said after a little silence : " I'm finding you unbelievable too. When do you have to go back to America ? "

" When the cash runs out. Not that I have any there

83

except what I earn, so perhaps I could starve in London just as well. . . . I'm kidding — I know I won't starve. I can always write something. I'm not a bad writer. Not *really* good, but not bad either."

" I wish you were going to direct a play here."

" I wish I were going to direct a play *anywhere*."

" But here especially, then you could give *me* a chance."

She had said that jauntily, so he answered in the same vein : " And you're quite positive I'd do that ? "

" Yes, because you said just now you were curious about me, and I think you'd be curious to find out what you could make of me."

" I *know* what I could make of you." The boast startled him by its promptness, then appalled him a little when he gave it a second thought.

" I half believe you, Paul."

He said, continuing the joke : " And the other half I resent. Still it's good to know you'd even be willing to stay in London if you were offered enough inducement — say Candida or Desdemona, with your name in lights and a thumping salary."

" You don't really think I'm as arrogant as you, do you ? "

" So you think *I* am ? "

" You have to be. You couldn't make anything of me — or even of yourself — unless you were. . . . See, I do understand you a bit. Will the cash last a week — or ten days perhaps ? "

" Could *you* stay too ? How soon will your business with the lawyer be finished ? "

" Darling, there isn't any lawyer. I didn't really have to come to London at all. Now you know."

He felt an unclassifiable emotion for a second, sharp and intense ; then he diagnosed it as sheer pleasure and took extra pleasure in so doing. " So you wanted to see me as much as I wanted to see you ? That makes us quits. But why invent an excuse ? "

" In case you felt burdened with responsibility for bringing me here. In case you'd changed your mind about me

84

again. You do change your mind. First you like me — then you think because I'm a girl you can't like me. Or else you don't want to dare to like me, or don't dare to want to like me, or something. So I thought if that were to happen you might feel better if I had another reason for coming."

He said seriously : " That was very considerate of you."

Because in a way he knew it was, and he was impressed ; he was also aware that their whole conversation since meeting had been a succession of moods on both sides, never clashing but never identical, as if they were both breathlessly sparring for position in some game that had as yet scarcely begun and might turn out to be not entirely a game.

He added : " But you've told me now. You've burned your boats. Or burned mine. Which is it ? "

" I don't know. But I promise you this — if you do change your mind again I'll go back to Dublin without any fuss."

" That's a threat, not a promise. And all this about changing my mind — I'm not so fickle — it's only that I'm a bit scared when I remember other times I've tried. . . ." What he really meant but would not exactly say, was that his few previous affairs had disappointed him as aesthetic experiences while at the same time they had satisfied him as biological demonstrations. " And that's why . . . with you . . . the closer I get to knowing you the more I like you, and therefore the more . . . the more I want to take care not to have anything spoil the relationship. Like betting on the same number — the oftener you win, the more amazing it is, and the more nervous you get about doubling the stakes." He stirred restlessly, then forced a laugh. " Far too subtle, all this. The really worst fate for any human relationship is to be analysed to death."

" Paul, perhaps the mistake you made was to try too hard — those other times."

" I didn't mean *try* in the sense of *make an effort*. I meant *try* like — like *sampling* something."

" Oh, I see. To *discover* how you felt ? "

" Yes. An experiment that wasn't too successful. But with you I almost know how I feel."

85

" In advance ?   Without the — the sampling ? "

" That's how it seems.   Remember the Oscar Wilde remark — about the spire of a cathedral ?   It's *that* kind of moment for me now — meeting you like this . . . here. It's — it's superb.   In fact the real danger is if I were to develop one of those headstrong passions — I never have before, but——"

" Oh, darling — for *me* ?   If only you would."

" You — *wish* — that ? "

" It would be fun.   Maybe that's what you never had before — fun.   And I'm quite enough in love with you — I dare say you guessed——"

" You — *what* ?   Carey, you're joking——"

" I'm serious too.   Did you never guess how *I* felt ? "

" I — I wondered — sometimes — if — if such a thing were possible."

She touched his arm across the table.   " Oh, Paul . . . don't . . . don't be so humble."   Her eyes brimmed over. " I expect it's the first time anyone ever said that to you — and a few minutes ago I was calling you arrogant.   But where's the danger ?   I don't see any.   Because I'm too young ? "

" No, not exactly — though that's a reason why it would be specially unfair to you if it didn't work out."

" But it might.   At least it *might*."

" It didn't between you and that actor."

" I told you why that was."

" I know, and an excellent reason, as I said."

" But I don't think it could apply to us — to you."

" Oh, and why not ?   Why are you so sure I wouldn't want what he wanted ? "

" Paul, don't pounce on me like that — of course I'm not sure at all——"

" Then why couldn't it apply to me ? "

" Only because of my answer if you did ask.   I'm different now — not only a year older . . . but — well, I told you — I'm in love with you enough."

He was so touched he felt shocked, as by the revelation of

86

some hitherto unsuspected compound of guilt and innocence inside himself. He muttered : " Carey, what the hell are we talking about ? Let's get the bill."

  •   •   •   •

  They didn't go to Putney, but to a hotel in South Kensington. On a very few previous occasions when Paul had embarked on an adventure like this, the moment when he first knew there would be no refusal had been one of dismay, even dejection, as if his sufficient pleasure had been in the mere pursuit of an uncertainty. But now there was no dismay, and its absence would alone have made the experience unique. There was, however, between Carey and himself a more positive novelty, and this he discovered gradually and with delight ; it was a tenderness that flowed over the raw edges of rapture and gave to all functioning an aspect of inevitability. Till then he had sometimes thought that if all forms of sexual behaviour could only be energized artistically in terms of theatre or ballet, then his problem would be solved, since directorially he could be the spectator or participant in any proportion he chose, and nobody would question or deny his credit. But now, with Carey, the problem was non-existent ; and with this perfect outcome the quality that had attracted him first of all in her voice was able to entrance over the whole range of sensibility. It was as if, he told himself at the time and later told her, it was as if her body had *brains*. Naturally from him this was the supreme tribute, causing him to add another to his short list of ambitions : it was to marry her.

  So they were married, after the necessary period of waiting, at a register office in the Strand. A Catholic priest had previously declined to solemnize a mixed marriage except on conditions, but later, on learning that a civil ceremony had already taken place, he complied. The service, at a church in Putney, was attended by Aunt Sylvia and her husband ; after which the couple enjoyed a gay wedding breakfast among the wire-haired terriers. Paul was, for the first time in his life, superlatively happy ; a cloud that had seemed to overshadow him was lifted, and in the unimagined radiance he realized how dark it had sometimes been. He wrote exultant letters to his mother, to Rowden, to Merryweather, and to half a dozen others. All sent their congratulations except Rowden, and Merryweather was generous besides; he suggested some articles about England and enclosed a cheque on account.

They spent a week at a seaside hotel by way of honeymoon; then one afternoon Paul took Carey to Hampstead, a part of London he especially liked. Careful search yielded nothing they could afford except a small second-floor flat (first floor, as the English called it), but it was conveniently close to the Tube station as well as to an old-fashioned public-house where, of an evening, writers and artists mingled with artisans and clerks in mutual unawareness of any trick successfully performed. Paul fitted easily into this society, and it was soon known who he was; he made friends and enemies as promptly as always, but fewer enemies than usual, since much was forgiven a stranger and a good talker, and it was also possible that his private happiness surrounded him with a visible aura of fellowship. Anyhow, it was in this pub that he met a man named Henry Foy who owned and subsidized a theatre in the neighbourhood — an old barn of a place, full of dry rot, moth-eaten scenery, and other drawbacks, but not too far from the Tube, and therefore accessible to a London West End theatre audience. Comfortably off, unmarried, and in his fifties, Foy was something of a dilettante; he had produced and directed plays himself, but so poorly that critics had generally ignored him except by attending his parties, which were frequent and colourful. He was a likeably gregarious personality, and there was no doubt that if he ever did anything remotely worth while everyone would jump to praise him. Besides a passion for the theatre which did not quite amount to devotion, he had a certain flair for new ideas and a willingness to try them which a more balanced mind or a more restricted pocket-book might well have checked. He had put on such plays as Brieux's *Les Hannetons*, Hauptmann's

Hannele and Ibsen's *Little Eyolf*, but none of these had done well, or attracted much comment. Not till he tried Ford's *'Tis Pity She's a Whore* did fortune smile; certain local groups objected to the title in lights over the theatre entrance, a newspaper controversy was stirred up, and many Londoners thereby discovered the existence (and even more important) the whereabouts of the Nonesuch Theatre. It was just after this *succès de scandale* that Foy met Paul and was instantly captured by the idea of an all-Negro *Othello* except for a white Othello (that random product of good wine and good talk at the Venton League dinner-table). Foy wanted to stage it immediately, for it was the sort of thing he had always been happy to lose money over, like *The Duchess of Malfi* in modern dress, or *Hauton Timorumenos* as a musical comedy. They left the pub arm in arm, Carey between the two men; at Foy's big house in Well Walk they talked till long past midnight, electrically conscious that something important had happened in their lives. Unfortunately, as they found no later than the next morning, there were not enough Negro actors then in London to make the project feasible; but by that time Foy was keen on the play even if it were to be produced normally; or rather, he was hypnotized into a belief that anything with Paul in control would be better than anything else. It was luck indeed for Paul to have met such a man. Within a few hours Foy had engaged him to direct and choose a cast, and what had once been a joke became suddenly and fatefully true — Carey Arundel as Desdemona. A great chance for her, undoubtedly, and in grabbing it she was to learn much about acting and Shakespeare and herself, but even more about the man she had married.

.　　　.　　　.　　　.　　　.　　　.

The first thing she discovered was that his work made him a changed person. He was possessed, and by something that could excusably be called a devil, since angelic possession exacts no price in sweat and fury. It had one curious and immediate effect; he was only in his late twenties, yet as soon as he took the stage he seemed old enough for no one to think of him disparagingly as young — at least ten years were added in appearance, plus an indefinable quality that made Foy once remark to Carey : " Is he aiming to be a *maestro*, or does it come naturally ? It's a continental trick — English and Americans as a rule don't pick it up." Carey was more surprised than Foy, because her own limited theatre experience had prepared her so little for the effort that Paul demanded from everyone around him, including herself. It was a demand outrageous enough to stifle the protest that anything more reasonable might have drawn. For he had made it clear from the outset that he must be taken as he was or not at all ; that being established, the situation left no opening for lukewarmness or compromise. Very soon she came to know what he had meant by defining a director's role as the communication of excitement. Hour after hour were spent, not in speaking or memorizing lines (which, in the beginning, he made light of) but in discussing the play from every angle until a law of diminishing returns seemed to operate and arguments became sharper without being more helpful. Up to that point, however, he had incited controversy ; one dispute over the precise motivation of Iago's behaviour grew so heated that the actor taking that part walked off the stage in a huff. Paul dragged him back, exclaiming loudly enough to be heard by all the rest : " D'you realize what you've been doing ? Here's a complex academic point in the interpretation of a character in a play written three hundred years ago — yet today on this stage you were almost coming to blows about it ! "

Iago began to stammer apologies.

" No, no," Paul interrupted. " It's wonderful ! Because it shows we've taken the first step — we're beginning to think the characters matter to us — we're shouting about them as if they were people we know. That's what I hoped for. But now comes the next step. Understanding is a *basis* for emotion, but no substitute. From now on we must begin to *feel*. The mind has had its feast — now comes the turn of the heart."

Paul had a store of such gaudy sayings about acting and theatrecraft — " Just as the stage is larger than life, so words about it can afford to be bigger and more extravagant," was another of them. They did not always probe deeply, but they decorated his instruction and were apt to seem talismanic towards the end of a gruelling rehearsal. He got along well with the cast ; he was thoughtful of them as artists, and the excitement he generated helped them to endure his occasional tantrums. As usual, there was no one at the Nonesuch Theatre shrewd enough to find out exactly how little Paul had done in New York, so he could magnify that achievement, not only for personal vainglory but because he knew that the greater they thought he was the luckier they would think themselves. In all this he was sustained by his own passionate belief in himself as a child of destiny in the theatre ; he was like a poor man writing post-dated cheques for large sums but with complete assurance that he was honest.

During this time his private happiness with Carey was equally sustaining, though he spent few daytime hours alone with her, and there was no moment of their lives, however intimate, which he was incapable of turning into a lecture or a lesson or some fragment of a rehearsal. In a half-amused way she relished this, for her own ambition had been rejuvenated and she was beginning to realize, not yet how much she was learning, but how little she had ever known before. She found she could help him too by her own greater tact in handling countless small situations — a stage-carpenter he had unwisely yelled at, the landlady of their flat who objected to Mozart on the gramophone at 2 A.M. He was usually inconsiderate about such matters. One thing, however, seemed large enough for her real concern — his attitude towards Henry Foy. Paul had become cool to the man, treating him offhandedly at rehearsals, sometimes omitting to consult him on points that were clearly in a theatre-owner's and play-backer's province. Carey rather liked Foy, who was always genial, conciliatory, and generous alike with hospitality and advice. But Paul declined to weigh all this. " Look, Carey, let's face it — at bottom he's an amateur, a dabbler — he's actually a nuisance at rehearsals — if I can make him stop attending them so much the better."

" But surely the man has a right to potter about his own theatre."

" No, not if he gets in the way. When he signed me to direct he delegated his rights — it's like a ship that carries the president of the line — the captain still gives the orders even though the other man owns the outfit."

" But I'm sure a tactful captain tries to say a few polite words to the president now and again."

" I've never been impolite. I'm just too busy to go to his parties and sit up half the night listening to pseudo-artistic claptrap."

" I thought you enjoyed his parties. That first night we went to his house and stayed for hours — you were so enthusiastic."

" Only because I knew I'd talked him into engaging me. I thought most of his ideas were half-baked, but it was worth while to let him believe I was impressed."

" You know, Paul, you scare me sometimes — you're so utterly shameless. Don't you ever feel that Harry's giving you a big chance ? "

" I'm giving him a chance too. So far he's done nothing but lose money and fool around, but now he's due for a huge success and his precious little flea-bitten theatre will become famous all over London."

" You really are quite sure of that, aren't you ? "

" Yes. Aren't you ? "

" Darling, of course."

He went on, scrutinizing her : " I think I can read your mind. You're wondering if I was equally sure in New York. You *were* wondering that, weren't you ? " (It was true, she had been.) " Well, the answer's yes. And the plays flopped. I don't admit that to others, but you probably guessed anyhow. . . . And what does it prove ? That I can be wrong ? Does that *need* proving ? . . . All I can say is, count on me this time. Carey, it's terribly important that you should feel about it as I do. You *have* to."

She smiled and told him she did. She knew by now the rich support he took from her, and her satisfaction in that was almost enough to create the faith he asked for.

With her own performance in the play he was both patient and severe. After the first week she said unhappily : " You don't seem to like anything I do. I'd hate to spoil the play, and from the way you criticize——"

" I criticize the others just as much, only you don't hear me. I never criticize anyone in the presence of anyone else."

She was a little relieved by that, but still troubled. " I can't help wondering, though, if I'm equal to a part like this. Perhaps some actress with more experience in Shakespeare——"

" Carey, you're not losing your ambition ! You wouldn't give up *now* ? "

" Not if I can satisfy you, but if I can't — I couldn't bear not to — and there'll be some other play later on — something easier maybe——"

" Oh ? " He assumed the attitude which she called his ' pounce '. " And what makes you think you'd be any better in anything easier ? I suppose you're hankering after some frothy little comedy where you have to light cigarettes and mix cocktails all the time ! Don't kid yourself — you'd be just as bad in that if you're bad at all. But you *aren't* bad, and you're going to be good — you're going to be *very* good ! Don't you believe in yourself yet ? "

There was no answering this sort of thing. Logical or not, it had rallying power. But she could not help marking the contrast between his first cautious opinion of her in Dublin and his unbounded optimism now ; surely the change which that represented was in *him* far more than could possibly have happened in the quality of her acting. Yet she felt also that there was no conscious insincerity in his enthusiasm — that his own mind, under the hypnosis of the task, swung continually between the same poles — never satisfied,

D   93

always confident. But what really tickled her was the way this attitude extended itself even to the play and the author; in Dublin he had often criticized Shakespeare, but now, as the rehearsals progressed, Shakespeare became faultless and *Othello* the greatest play ever written in the history of the world.

One afternoon she met Foy in the street near his house. He asked her to come inside and see some designs for scenery that had just arrived. " Oppeler should have sent them to Paul, not to me — try to convince your husband this is no plot against his authority." His eyes twinkled as he said this, and she liked him for sharing with her an understanding of Paul that the latter would have vehemently denied.

The designs she thought excellent, though she knew she was no judge. They had been suggested in a general way by Paul himself after long sessions with the artist; Foy's willingness to spend freely and his almost naïve pleasure in giving Paul anything he wanted, touched her as it always did. She stayed for a while, enjoying conversation that was comfortable and, for a change, unexciting. Then, with the designs under her arm, she returned to the flat.

Paul was sitting hunched over the living-room fire. He had taken a chill and had been dosing himself unsatisfactorily since early morning. He was inclined to baby himsel. over such things, and she thought there were signs in his posture, as if he had assumed it too quickly on hearing her footsteps on the stairs. She was beginning to find out these things about him now, and to love him all the more generously for most of them. He was a bad actor, as he often said; indeed, he said it so often that she wondered if he hoped that some day he would be contradicted. But she was willing enough to humour him, to fit herself into whatever drama could compensate for him for a bad cold. She put her arm affectionately round his shoulder and felt him pretend (she was sure it was that) to be startled. " Hello darling — still feeling rotten ? . . . Look at these — Harry sent them over." She gave him the folio of drawings, watching his face for a verdict. To her surprise he glanced at only a few of them, casually, then let them slip to the floor

" Don't you think they're good ? Or would you rather not bother about them now ? They can wait. . . . How about some coffee, or a stiff drink, maybe ? "

He said sharply, looking up : " Why did Oppeler send them to Foy ? "

" I don't know, and neither does Harry — he particularly asked me to tell you it wasn't his fault they didn't come direct to you. They should have, he knows it."

" That relieves my mind enormously."

" Oh, now, Paul, don't talk like that. How could he help it if the artist made a mistake ? "

" These drawings seem to be another of his mistakes."

" You really haven't looked at them yet."

" Enough to know that I'd rather do without scenery altogether. He'll have to try again."

" They're as bad as that ? "

" How bad do they have to be ? If they aren't good enough, they're bad."

" Are you sure Oppeler's the right man ? Perhaps some-one else——"

" Of course he's the right man. He's the best set designer in London if he ever gets a chance to prove it."

" Tell him that, then he'll *want* to try again." She won-dered how far his obduracy was loyalty to the artist or to his own judgment in choosing him, but whatever it was, the switch from attack to defence was characteristic. While she was thinking of this he turned on her suddenly. " How did it happen you got these from Foy ? "

" I met him in the street and he told me they'd just come."

" He had them with him ? "

" No. They were at his house."

" So you went to his house ? "

" Yes."

" What time did you meet him ? "

" I — I don't know — about two o'clock. Or soon after."

" It's four now. How long did you stay at his house ? "

" Perhaps an hour. Does it matter ? "

" How *could* you spend a whole hour there ? He's such a bore——"

" He doesn't bore me. We just talked."

" What about ? "

" The theatre, of course — the play — you — me — him — he likes you so much." She said that because he always liked to hear that people liked him, even if he didn't like them, but this time there was no response except the sort of sarcasm that might have come from a bookish schoolboy ; he said : " Again my mind is infinitely relieved."

She faced him with dawning astonishment. " Paul . . . what's happened ? Why are you talking about Harry like this ? "

" *Harry* ? . . . So you call him *Harry* ? "

" So do you. So does everybody — we did from our first meeting, didn't we ? Paul . . . *please* . . . it can't be that you — oh no, that would be too ridiculous."

He stood up with his back to the fire, his face flushed, eyes glinting. " Carey, I'm not a fool — do you suppose I haven't noticed the way you look at that man every time he comes to the theatre ? And his manner to you — he knows he attracts you — no wonder he won't miss a rehearsal. And the other day when he made all that fuss about something in his eye — a childish manœuvre——"

" But there was something, a little fly, and I got it out."

" He didn't have to ask *you* ! Any excuse, though — these drawings are another——"

" Paul ! This is really funny . . . almost . . . you think a man puts a fly in his eye just for the pleasure of——"

" Carey, tell me this, why *should* he ask you to his house ? Why not send over the drawings by messenger — he has servants and it's only a few blocks away ! And an hour — with *him* — just for talk. How much do you expect me to swallow ? "

She was speechless for a moment ; it was now beyond a joke, and as full awareness of what was happening took possession of her, she found she had no voice for anything but a few scattered sentences. "Paul, you know I love you. Are we actually quarrelling — and about something so utterly beyond reason? . . . I don't know what to say, except that . . . your suspicion . . . any suspicion you can possibly have . . . about anything . . . is just plain silly. You believe me, Paul, don't you?"

He stared at her with hard eyes. "I believe you're becoming a very good actress."

That changed her mood abruptly; she stepped away from him in a cold rage that made her feel physically sick. "All right. What more can I say? . . . It would be wasted time. I'm going out for a walk. . . . Take your temperature and see if you still have a fever. Maybe that's what's driving you crazy."

She dashed out of the room, snatching hat and coat on the way to the door. In the street a car just missed her as she ran across. She knew people were staring; she heard the man who had nearly run her down calling after her in anger. She checked her pace and turned into the first side-street. A few yards along this she heard footsteps overtaking her; Paul, dishevelled and panting, seized her arm and pulled her roughly to a standstill. "Come back — come back—" he gasped.

Even at such a moment there was faint comedy in the thought that he who hated to run had actually been forced into a chase. She might have begun to smile had not she seen that his own gasps and chokings were partly of laughter. That made her more furious than ever. "No — leave me alone — I don't want to talk to you."

"Carey — come back — I'll explain everything——"

"Please let me take my walk."

"But I want to explain — I can't talk to you while you're walking — Carey, darling — come back. . . . I've got a temperature — I oughtn't to be out here in the cold air—"

Two things leapt to her mind — first, that he had called her 'darling'. He never had before — it was a word that did not come easily to him, except ironically or extravagantly when he addressed others. The second thing was his temperature. A gust of anxiety shook her about that. She let him lead her back to the flat without further protest and went straight to the bathroom for the thermometer.

"Only just over ninety-nine," he said, following her and waving the instrument aside. "I took it just now — nothing to worry about. Let's have that drink."

By this time her own emotions were too confused to seek expression. She felt weak and empty of concern, one way or another. "I must rest for a minute, Paul. This kind of thing upsets me."

He came beside her, kneeling on the floor by the chair and pressing her hand to his face.

"Listen to me, Carey — no need to be upset . . . just let me explain . . . don't interrupt. . . ."

"I'm too tired to interrupt."

"Carey, I want to talk to you — about jealousy. Sexual jealousy. It's a terrible thing. It destroys the mind, it warps the judgment — it can make clever people stupid and stupid people murderous — it infects — it poisons — and when the victim's innocent the others become innocent too, but in a horrible kind of way. . . . Do you remember how you first reacted — the feeling you had when I told you my suspicion? You were *stupefied*. Not indignant, at first — not angry — not even protesting . . . but *bewildered*. The look on your face — blank — expressionless — uncomprehending. Then later you told me very simply how much you loved me, how wrong I was. . . . Only after that, when I said I still didn't believe you — only *then* you got mad and lost your temper . . . for which I don't blame you a bit. . . . Did you ever notice the eyes of a dog that hasn't done what he's accused of, but because master is master his only reaction is innocence itself — the sheer acceptance of limitless injustice from the limitlessly beloved? You have to think of animals nowadays to visualize that — a modern heroine isn't capable of it. But Desdemona *was*, the poor sucker, and it's the key to the whole interpretation — you have to play the first two attitudes — bewilderment and pure

98

heartbreaking innocence — without ever touching the third one — anger! See? . . . And by the way, there was one true thing I said — that you were becoming a good actress. That's what struck me as funny — to pay you my first real compliment and have you stalk out of the room as if you'd been insulted! . . . But those two things — hang on to them, won't you? — first the bewilderment, then the simple statement of innocence. . . . Why, what's wrong? What's the matter?"

"I think I'm beginning to find out — what's the matter — with you."

He laughed again, but comfortably now — a chuckle, as at a practical joke so comic that the victim should at least be sporting enough to smile. "Carey, don't you see? — I wanted you to learn from the heart, not from the mind! And you did — even my bad acting took you in completely. Good God, it must have done, for you to think *that* . . . and Harry of all people! . . . But I believe it'll help you to feel the character — she's a difficult dame, probably the hardest of all Shakespeare's heroines, because the way she takes a beating isn't really meekness, it's a sort of strength in disguise — fascinating the way it builds up during the course of the play — if you'd like us both to go over it again — the handkerchief scene, begin with——"

"Oh no, no. It isn't so much the part that's troubling me now."

"Good. I'm glad you feel more confident."

She couldn't control her tears, of pity for him as well as of fading anger and growing relief, but there was a glimpse of horror in his ready assumption that all was well, that his explanation, once made, could instantly undo all the mischief.

He continued jauntily: "Remember in Dublin I said that when an actor feels an emotion intensely it's natural for him to act? Here's the corollary — that to make him act you must sometimes make him feel intensely . . . shock treatment . . . to get the final rightness — to pin it down once and for all. We'll know tomorrow if that's happened to you."

99

" Something else may have happened too. Isn't it a bit dreadful, Paul, to be willing to risk so much ? Supposing you hadn't caught up with me in the street — suppose I'd had hours to walk and think and worry . . . wouldn't it have mattered to you at all ? Perhaps you'd have laughed all the more. . . . And I nearly got run over." She began to laugh herself at last, though with a touch of hysteria. " Quite a joke, on every score. And all those things you said about Harry — the nonsense you invented — how *can* you use your friends like that ? "

" Now look, Carey, I only called him a bore — and I think he is, but if you don't, that's fine — he's not a bad fellow, we both know that. . . ." Then he caught a note behind her laughter that made him add, in simple wonderment : " You aren't *really* upset, are you ? . . . Oh, if you are, I'm sorry. I'm a son of a bitch at times like this — I have the damned play on my mind — I don't think of anything else. But if you ever leave me I don't know what I'll do . . . that's what I was thinking all the time I was talking the nonsense — I was thinking, suppose it *was* true, suppose you *were* carrying on with Harry or some other man . . . what *would* I do ? "

She was laughing now in the sheer pleasure of hearing him confess so much. " Stifle me, perhaps, as in the play ? "

" No, I'd think you were lucky and I deserved what I got, because I know I'm not good enough for you. I mean that, Carey."

They made love, then had drinks, then looked over the drawings to decide what had to be changed. By that time it was dusk and he declared his cold so much better that he would enjoy a good dinner in town, so they went to the restaurant in Lisle Street in a mood of celebration. After the bizarre events of the day she was very happy.

The extraordinary thing was that when she rehearsed in the morning there was such a marked improvement in her performance that she startled herself as well as the others. For the first time in her life she enjoyed an experience that was later to become the thing aimed for — a sudden swimming bliss in which her own self split effortlessly into two identities, the one Desdemona, the other a calm observer of herself acting. When she finished there was no need for Paul to tell her she had been excellent. She knew it in her bones, with a warm satisfaction that made it pleasant to reply quietly : " You said I would be, didn't you ? "

Paul, of course, enjoyed no such serenities. Nor, she was sure, did there ever come to him a sense of incredibility in the contrast between this terrific emotional and creative effort on the part of a dedicated few and the apathy of the multitude which, if the play were to succeed, it must conquer and divert. She had an idea that Paul regarded audiences too arrogantly even to think of this, much less to be appalled by it ; he would give people not what *they* wanted, but what *he* wanted, thus involving him in the further task of making them *want* what he wanted. No one could essay this without an eagerness to be consumed, and it was true that, as opening night approached, Paul reached flashpoint ; his whole being clenched into a total effect of alertness, so that it could be said that he neither saw nor heard, but constantly watched and listened. She wondered how he could keep it up, but she guessed that some of the physical energy he forbore to expend was somehow transmuted into these more combustible channels. Yet there was nothing of the conventional ascetic about him ; he ate prodigiously (he could do this without gaining weight during such stressful days), drank quite enough, smoked cigars all the time, sat up half the night and fell into dreamless sleep from about 4 A.M. till 10. While he was asleep his breathing was often imperceptible, he rarely turned or stirred, and his face, usually pale because he spent so little time out of doors, became paler still ; there was only one word that occurred to her, though she tried never to think of it — he looked *dead*, as if he had switched off the waking turbine by some act of deliberation. Physically he grew lazier as the ultimate ordeal approached ; he would call a taxi for the short distance to the theatre, and during later rehearsals he would sit in one of the back-row seats for hours on end, summoning actors next to him for private talk. Or else Foy would arrive with news about programmes, posters, advertisements, box-office arrangements, and be regally motioned to another adjacent seat to wait his turn. Paul had a lively finger in every pie, and was quite capable of making the size of the ticket-stubs an issue for first-class bickering. It was against his nature to delegate authority, he much preferred to enlist willing slaves; and perhaps Carey's appeal to him to treat Foy more generously did have some effect, for during the final weeks of preparation Paul received him back to favour in the role of an overburdened but unfailingly cheerful office-boy.

To Carey the kind of man she had married became a source of increasing wonderment. She was aware of his separateness in a world she could not invade with him, and when he returned to her, as from this world, it was often to talk of its glories in a way that might have bored her had she not loved him. She knew him too well now to expect him to share so many simple things that she enjoyed — a few hours taking pot-luck at a local cinema, fun with the landlady's cat, a walk on Hampstead Heath in the morning, with the yellow autumn sun peering through mists above London's roof-tops. Yet she remembered that their first real acquaintance had been during a long walk in Phoenix Park and that on the night before he left Dublin he had actually walked the mile or so from Rowden's house to her own in Terenure. Walking thus became a symbol of what he had once done, for her and with her, but would no longer do. Was it because, as with his first cordiality to Foy, he could always bring himself to do things if he thought them worth while for some personal end? She did not much care. If he had been so keen to know her that he had paid a price of any kind, it only proved how keen he had been. And he still was, she knew that, because he had explored so much more of the ways in which she could help him. She sometimes thought that after the crisis of love-making came a second and perhaps to him a deeper one that had grown up out of her own subconscious desire to play whatever part he cast her for; in this she would cradle him in an embrace that was almost sexless, yet as close to him (she felt instinctively) as she could ever get.

Once he talked about his mother in Milwaukee. " She doesn't get on too well with my brother and his wife. The first thing I'll do when I've made some money is to take her away somewhere else — New York, London, anywhere — she wouldn't mind, so long as it's near me. . . . I suppose you're surprised to find I have an ambition in life that isn't connected with the theatre ? "

" Yes," she answered. " But I'm rather glad. It seems to give me a chance."

．　．　．　．　．　．

It would be an exaggeration to say that Paul Saffron's *Othello* (Shakespeare's being a name too well known to be worth mentioning) at the Nonesuch Theatre, Hampstead, on December Twenty-Seventh, Nineteen-Twenty-Two, made theatrical history ; it was, however, a big event in the lives of both Paul and Carey, because it was their first success together, so they could both feel they were lucky for each other. The London press was favourable, and since praise for a Shakespeare play is primarily for the production, Paul could not have found a better vehicle to advertise himself. Carey was praised too, her performance being hailed by one important reviewer as " the only Desdemona I ever saw who didn't seem more dumb than innocent ".

In other respects Paul's optimistic prophecies proved wrong. Foy did not make any fortune, nor did his theatre achieve the fame that would establish it in the regular West End firmament (indeed, the controversy about *'Tis Pity She's a Whore* had given it far more spectacular publicity). The truth was that only a limited number of people wished to see *Othello*, however well done, and only a limited number of these would make the journey by Tube to Hampstead. The play, moreover, had been staged so expensively, to meet Paul's every whim, that it could yield only a moderate profit if the house were always full, and after the first few weeks there were enough empty seats to whittle down any accumulated surplus. All of which might have been called a disappointment by those who remembered Paul's extravagant forecasts. Paul was not one of them. He seemed unperturbed, even bored by the box-office returns, and once he casually remarked that he had never expected financial success at all, and that the excellent critical notices were a complete satisfaction of his aim. Whether or not this was true, Carey reached a tentative conclusion that in the larger sense he was indifferent to money; what he did want were plaudits, power, prestige, and the satisfaction of a boundless artistic ego — plus, of course, enough of someone else's money to spend and, if necessary, to lose. There remained, however, a question she could not answer either then or whenever afterwards it recurred — was his tremendous all-embracing optimism before the opening night of any of his plays authentic, or part of an enthusiasm deliberately generated as part of the basic strategy of stage-direction? Or, to put it another way, did he always fool himself when he fooled others?

Something else emerged as an insight into his make-up; the play being now launched, he clearly suffered a kind of spiritual anti-climax. He idled and became restless, flinging himself into occasional re-rehearsals as if in desperate intent to recapture something. During the nightly performances he would watch from the wings in a state of excitement mainly self-induced because he felt it his continuing duty to inspire and encourage, but the effort wore thin at times, and on the way home afterwards he was often morose until she had cheered him, as she always could and did.

Othello lasted twelve weeks and then ended not because of Foy's insistence on a profit (as Paul wrote years later in a book of reminiscences, though it would not have been too unreasonable even if true), but because Paul himself had by that time received several offers to direct plays in the real West End and had already chosen one of them — with a part for Carey, of course. Foy sized up the situation shrewdly and was amiable enough to do so without resentment. It had been all right while it lasted, he told Carey, though he added: "You probably think Paul and I have got along pretty well, but actually there've been a few times when I'd have punched his nose if I hadn't remembered that hitting a genius is like hitting a woman — except that they deserve it oftener."

"So you'd call Paul a genius?"

"I wouldn't dare deny it if someone else challenged me. Just watching him taught me more about the theatre in four months than I'd learned before in twenty years. He made me feel an amateur."

She knew him almost well enough to reply: "That's what he said you were", but it would have been too much the sort of *riposte* that Paul himself could never have resisted. Yet there was, between her and Foy, and later between her and many other people, an awareness of Paul as a phenomenon to be discussed in a spirit of detached investigation, with no sense of personal disloyalty and little capacity to be startled or even hurt by what was revealed.

"So you see," Foy added, "it's been an experience for me and a stepping-stone for him — now he can push ahead and discover the facts of life, such as how many seats in the house, how much per seat, how much on the weekly salary sheet — that kind of thing. He's so wonderful at everything else, he really ought to learn arithmetic. . . . Anyway, I wish him well and I hope he scores a real hit with the new play."

Paul didn't. It was a flop — so instant and ignominious that he crossed the Atlantic immediately.

PART TWO

ONE day about six years later she was driving with Paul to the Pocono Mountains. Their play had closed down for the summer and it was a relief to escape from the heat of New York to the scarcely cooler but much more endurable countryside. They had a house near Stroudsburg and would spend July and August there; Carey loved the place, and if Paul treated it as a necessary boredom to be lived through from time to time, she was sure it did him good in many ways he would have strenuously denied. The servants from the apartment had gone on ahead and everything would be in order when they arrived — much more so, doubtless, than ever again during their stay, for Paul had a habit of disrupting household arrangements in town and country alike.

She had made this journey often enough for the Delaware Water Gap to have become a symbol of holiday, the mental border-line of work and relaxation. Now, as she saw it again, she could not restrain her delight. " Paul, it's so good to be here at last — it makes me know how much I needed this." The words and the way she spoke them sounded older than her looks, which were at the full radiance of twenty-four; but early success and early marriage had built in her an illusion of maturity that was at least as real as a part well played. She sometimes thought that the ways in which Paul had never grown up were compensated for by those in which she herself had done so fast and far.

Paul did not answer because he had fallen asleep. He was a little overweight (a long run always did that to him), and the drive had combined with a rather dull play script to make him drowsy. She gave him the warm yet wry scrutiny of a woman who had been married a number of years to a celebrity; that is, she enjoyed the spectacle of the hero unheroic — the large lolling head, papers crumpled under a finicky hand, the face dubiously sombre and far too pale. Enough of the world conceded now that Paul was a great stage director, including those who also thought she herself was a pretty good actress. She treasured that tottering compliment ; it seemed to suit her private thesis that if she were even near good it was because she was near Paul.

As always when he was asleep he had that look of absence that sometimes scared her, making him ageless, so that it was odd, rather than hard, to realize he was only thirty-six. Probably he had only escaped being called a boy-wonder because in public he had never looked like a boy. But in this, as in so many other things, he ran to extremes — babyishness at moments, usually for her alone to witness and indulge ; at other moments the air of being biblically, almost Mosaically old. Yet at all times in his work he wore the authority of one whose years had had no real meaning in his life. She often wondered what their children would have been — either geniuses or idiots, she told people, glossing over with a joke the fact that they could have no children.

She watched the familiar road as it curved alongside the river. Their house was half-way up a hillside a few miles ahead ; fat maples surrounded it, which could have been why it was called Mapledurham, though there was a place in England of the same name that might have some connection. It was a pleasant house, old enough to have been worth an expensive modernizing ; the rooms were large and cool to the eye ; the gardens not too formal. And on their arrival there would be tea waiting, English style (coffee for Paul) ; Walter would have put on a white jacket and transformed himself from a caretaker to a butler of sorts, and his Airedale would break established rules by nibbling from her plate. All this to look forward to as the Packard covered the miles on a summer afternoon.

In sheer exuberance she chatted with Jerry during the last lap of the journey. He was a good-looking southern boy whom they had employed as chauffeur for several years and who had developed an affectionate tolerance for the habits of theatre people. He said now, offhand as usual : " Mr. Paul got another play in mind ? "

She said no ; the one they had been in all the year would be resumed in September.

" I just figgered he might have, though — he's bin acting like he wanted one, these last few weeks."

This alarmed her a little, for she had caught a whiff of the same misgiving herself. But she answered decisively, as if saying so could make it final : " He needs a rest, Jerry, and so do I. That's what we've come here for. I don't care how bored he is, he's got to rest."

It had happened before, and doubtless would do so again — that Paul, having launched a highly successful play, had tired of it after the first few months and was secretly longing for it to end, so that he could give his undivided attention to something else. Whereas Carey was always happy throughout a long run, because it meant comparative ease and assured prosperity — things she was human enough to enjoy as long as they would last. Of course Paul was comfortably off ; they had both had luck during recent years, and a flop now and again could not harass them financially. But there was more than money in her reckoning. A new play was an ordeal, increasingly so as both Paul and the critics expected more of her ; the weeks of rehearsal could become a nightmare of hard work and high tension — thrilling if it all ended in triumph, but no experience to be sought wantonly. And this wantonness was in Paul. It was not that he did not enjoy success himself — he worshipped it ; but he was like a mountaineer who cannot relax on a summit to enjoy a smoke and the view, but must itch immediately to descend and climb another.

At Mapledurham not only the tea and the Airedale were duly waiting, but also, standing up as they entered the drawing-room, there was a tall slim young man who introduced himself as Malcolm Beringer. The name was unknown to her, and the elegant way he pronounced it did not remove her suspicion that he had no business there, or at least that his business was of a kind they didn't want to be bothered with on their first day in the country. " I hope you'll excuse this intrusion . . ." he began smoothly, whereupon Paul looked him up and down and snapped : " You're damned right it's an intrusion. I don't know you, and I don't care who you are or what you've come for, you can't see me or my wife without an appointment."

Carey turned back into the hall where Jerry was dumping bags from the car. She hated scenes, and this was a type she could never get used to. She was usually torn between solicitude for Paul, who needed protection from all kinds of crackpots and time-wasters, and sympathy with the adventurers who wanted him to read their plays or give them acting jobs. But today she had no such sympathy; it seemed intolerable that a stranger should actually stalk them to their retreat. She sought out Walter. " Why on earth did you let that man in ? What does he want ? How long has he been here ? "

" 'Bout an hour. I didn't know whether to let him in or not, but he said he knew Mr. Paul would want to see him. Something about a play, he said."

" Oh, Walter, how *could* you be so easily handled ? . . . Well, we can expect to see him thrown out on his ear any moment now . . . you know what Paul's like." It was natural for her to speak of him as Paul to those within the household ; they called him *Mr*. Paul, with the Mister somehow a mark of deference to her rather than to him.

Ten minutes passed, and Paul's voice from the adjoining room, at first upraised, had become mysteriously inaudible. Carey felt she must investigate ; once a similar silence had been due to a young man fainting. She re-entered the drawing-room with the upset feeling that Paul's behaviour so often caused her. Surprisingly, however, she found a quiet, almost a cosy conversation in progress, and when Paul turned to her there was the beam on his face that was usually reserved for a good performance at a final dress rehearsal. It disconcerted her now, and still more so when he called out briskly : " Oh, Carey, I've asked Mr. Beringer to stay to dinner. Will you tell Walter ? And by the way . . . you remember I once said Wagner might have done *Everyman* as an opera, but he didn't. . . . Well, now, here's this Mr. Beringer with another idea. . . ."

Carey smiled wanly, murmuring something, and was glad of an excuse to get away. Oh God, she thought, *Oh God.* . . . For this sort of thing, too, had happened before.

She did not conceal her ill-humour when she joined them at the table a couple of hours later. It was maddening that this first evening at Mapledurham, which she had hoped to spend alone with Paul, chatting unimportantly, strolling in the garden with the dog and going to bed early, should be taken up by an outsider. During the meal the subject of *Everyman* did not crop up again, and she was heartily glad of that ; she was in no mood for any kind of shop talk. She wondered if Mr. Beringer were canny enough to sense this, for once or twice he seemed to steer conversation away from the theatre when Paul was inching towards it. He was certainly an entertaining young man, if one had wanted to be entertained. As it was, she treated him with a minimum of warmth and excused herself as soon after the coffee as she decently could. Paul and he would doubtless discuss their precious *Everyman* when she had gone. Hours later, while she was still reading in bed, she heard the front door bang but no sound of a car starting. Then Paul came in. He was in the condition she often called ' basking ' ; it occurred whenever contact with some new idea or personality swept the accumulated dust of boredom out of his mind.

" I told you, Carey, this fellow Beringer has an idea for *Everyman.*"

" Has he ? Who is he, anyway ? "

" A neighbour — he's staying at Moat Farm. He walked over. Pity it was tonight when you were tired, but I suppose he was anxious to break the ice of a first meeting. You certainly gave him that . . . the ice, I mean."

" And you bawled him out at the top of your voice."

" Yeah, I did at first, didn't I ? " He laughed as if it were already a reminiscence of long ago, to be savoured with amazement. " Well, we'll be seeing him again and you'll probably like him better."

There was no use opposing the inevitable. She said, summoning cheerfulness : " Darling, I'm sure I will, and if he's going to be a friend of yours I'll be specially nice to him next time."

" Oh, you don't have to put on any act. It's me he wants to impress."

He had the look in his eyes she knew so well and was afraid of, because it was both shrewd and guileless, so that in recognizing that the young man had sought to impress him he did not debar himself from a willingness to be impressed.

" What is it he wants you to do ? " she asked quietly.

" He has an idea, that's all. He thinks *Everyman* would make a motion picture."

" And of course he wants to interest *you* in the project ? "

" There is no project, but I *am* interested in *Everyman* — you know that. Seems he read some piece I wrote about it years ago. That's why he came to me rather than any of the picture people. He wanted my advice."

" Only advice ? "

" That's all. I told him I knew nothing at all about motion pictures."

" Then what kind of advice could you give him ? "

" Oh, now, Carey, you're splitting hairs. There's all kinds of advice I can give a bright young man if he's interested in something I'm interested in. You know I've always had an idea to do *Everyman* on the stage."

She could see his face in the mirror ; he was taking his tie off with a gesture she felt she would remember if she were to go blind and deaf and forget his looks and his voice. He had once told her, apropos of some discussion of ballet, that of all the movements incidental to male undressing, only the removal of a bow tie could be done with flair ; the others, particularly the stepping out of pants, were banal. . . . She said sleepily : " So long as you don't get yourself stuck with anything, Paul. You promised you were going to take a real rest.'

He nodded. " I know, and if that damned play weren't reopening in September . . ."

The implication was that if the play, their almost fabulously successful play, were not reopening in September he could have all the rest he needed ; and this, she knew, was nonsense ; only the play kept him from the far more arduous business of staging its successor. But it had got to the point now when the play was a scapegoat ; he hated its guts, though towards the end of August he would order a few frantic corrective rehearsals in which he would behave as if it were a masterpiece. There was, of course, no compelling reason why he could not put on another play while the successful one was still running, but he shied away from this, partly because he wanted a part for Carey in everything he directed, but mainly because he shrank from proving that anything he had once started could possibly continue to exist without his constant attention. Nor could he tell himself rationally and mundanely that here was a harmless little comedy hit that might run another year, maybe longer — easy on audiences, because it didn't make them think, easy on Carey because it was tailor-made for her, easy on the pay-sheet because there was just one set with a cast of five. True, it was a trifle, but since he had chosen to do it in the first place, why complain because it was making a small fortune for everyone connected with it, including himself ?

She said : " Look, Paul, get to bed and don't lie awake thinking about plays or anything else. I'm going to sleep the clock round, and then tomorrow . . ." She was about to say she would take a long walk, but that was one of the things he would not share with her, so she changed it to : " Tomorrow we'll sit in the garden and pretend we haven't a care in the world. Not much pretence needed, either. We're very lucky people — doesn't that ever occur to you ? "

" Sure, but we mustn't sit back and *hoard* luck. That's just the way to lose it."

It seemed to her about the most disquieting answer he could have given.

.   .   .   .

Carey had received several offers from motion picture companies but had turned them down because she would not think of doing anything without Paul, and though Paul had received feelers himself, they had never in his case reached the point of a firm offer because he had always made it clear that he would want complete control of everything — story, cast, direction, production, cutting, and music; and as he was prompt to add that he knew nothing about motion pictures and hardly ever saw them, the movie moguls were doubtless intrigued, but not enough to buy Carey at such a price. Actually all this was very much of a pose. He knew a great deal about motion pictures and had seen many. It was also a fact that shortly after their marriage he and Carey had lived in Hollywood for about a year. That year had been one of failure, and as if to propitiate obscure deities he would never talk of it, or even admit its existence. Carey had no such feeling herself, but she was aware of his, and made it one of her own secrets also. It was thus without any sense of untruth that Paul could indulge in one of his favourite confessions — that when once he had been stranded in Los Angeles for a few hours he had been curious enough to ask a taximan to drive him around Hollywood, but the expedition had covered such dreary territory that he could only (in fairness to such a world-famous name) conclude that the driver must have lost his way.

But now a few conversations with Malcolm Beringer, a young man of no particular standing or importance, were enough to effect a change — not, it is true, in his attitude towards Hollywood, but certainly in his angle of aloofness towards motion pictures in general. Perhaps Malcolm's deficiencies were even an asset, for Paul was no respecter of big names and rather enjoyed the caprice of paying attention to the unknown, always provided they had qualities to attract him. Malcolm, moreover, was fey, and Carey, being Irish, was on her guard against this from the outset. After his second visit to Mapledurham, she tried to find out how far Paul was in danger of losing his normally keen judgment, but all she got was another discussion of *Everyman*. Then suddenly, to her direct question, Paul answered: " I'll tell you one reason why I like him. It's because he reminds me of myself at his age. No money, no name — just ideas and ambition."

She had to laugh at that. " It can't be so long since you *were* his age, Paul. He must be thirty at least. So don't treat him like a son."

" Of course I wouldn't. To him I'm just an older man who's already made his way in the world. A very pleasant relationship can be had on that basis."

" Like you and Mr. Rowden in Dublin ? "

" Perhaps . . . though I hadn't thought of it."

(She knew she had touched a nerve. Rowden was dead ; they had seen it in the papers some years back. Paul had been sad after reading the obituary and had said then, without subsequent explanation, " I don't think I treated him very well. He wanted to help me and I wouldn't let him.")

She answered : " Perhaps, then, it isn't Malcolm who's anything like you used to be, but you who fancy yourself growing up to be like Mr. Rowden. . . . Only I hope you won't."

" Oh ? I wouldn't be ashamed of myself if I did."

" But I still hope you don't."

Some sort of major issue was being stated by them, but n a minor key and without emphasis. He said after a pause : " All I meant is that Rowden was kind to me and I wasn't as kind to him as I ought to have been, in some ways. You don't know all the facts."

It was on her tongue to reply : " Perhaps you don't, either " — but she checked herself and smiled. She said instead : " Darling, we're getting into deep waters. Just don't let Malcolm tempt you into anything you don't really want. That's all *I* mean."

He laughed and said there was no fear of Malcolm tempting him at all — either into what he wanted or what he didn't want. " I only tempt myself," he added. " And then, invariably, I yield." This being the kind of epigram, half purloined as a rule, with which he liked to end an argument, she was satisfied to say no more for the time being.

But Malcolm still remained, to her at least, a somewhat

mysterious person. *Everyman* to him was charged with modern significance; he read into it some vast cosmic meaning that Carey would not for the world have disputed. Paul, on the other hand, saw it theatrically — as sheer spectacle and drama. They were probably well matched as collaborators, which is what Carey soon discovered them to be; and again it alarmed her, if only because it was unlike Paul to be able to collaborate with anybody about anything. Then it appeared that Paul was actually planning picture shots while Malcolm was writing a script.

She pretended to be casual. " It's all right if it interests you, Paul, but what does Malcolm expect to come of it? I hope you haven't promised him anything. It's so easy nowadays to get yourself in a tangle."

" Oh, he's not that kind. We have no written agreements, anyway. Nothing to sue about."

" He can't be working like this for fun, though."

" Why not? What would you have him do for fun? Play golf? "

" All right, darling — enjoy your joke. Golf wouldn't do your figure any harm."

" I'm thinning it down again now. I lost two pounds last week."

Another bad sign. She said, still trying to disguise her seriousness: " Paul, why don't you tell me what's in that busy mind of yours? "

" Sure. There's no secret about it — never has been. I've always said that one of these days I'll make a picture."

" But when will you find the time? The play's quite likely to run all through next year."

" If it does it won't need me to keep it going."

This was the first time he had ever said anything so sensible, yet in another way so ominous. She replied, still casually: " True, of course. Plenty of people commute between New York and Hollywood."

" Hollywood? Good God, you can't imagine anyone there would be interested in *Everyman*? "

" Who would, then? "

Expansively he answered: " Only the public. Only Thomas, Richard, and Henry, to whose pursuit of happiness the movies ought to be dedicated. Only the kind of people who paid to see Shakespeare and hear Wagner and read Dickens — only the world audience that never has missed a good thing whenever one comes along."

This was the surest danger signal of all, because she knew he did not mean it. Artistically he was an authoritarian; he did what pleased him and had small regard for popular taste as an arbiter of quality. But when it suited him he could take the opposite and currently fashionable view, and chance acquaintances who caught him in such moods were apt to retain a wrong impression for life. Carey, however, was not taken in. She knew that when he said something he did not mean he must be meaning something he would not say.

She said quietly (ignoring Thomas, Richard, and Henry, as well as Shakespeare, Wagner, and Dickens): " But what about Malcolm? Has he done film work before? Come to that, Paul, has he had any theatrical or dramatic experience at all?"

Paul gave her an affectionately derisive pat. " You're so practical, Carey. I'm glad I can answer yes. Malcolm once worked with Reinhardt in Germany."

" I shouldn't have thought that would have recommended him to you."

He began to chuckle in lazy anticipation of a point about to be scored. " Ah, but Reinhardt *fired* him. I checked up on it. They disagreed. You know, Carey, he practically told Reinhardt to go jump in a lake!" He added, still chuckling: " And in German, I hope."

He had had this grudge against Reinhardt ever since their first and only meeting, though the real reason why the two had apparently disliked each other on sight was doubtless that they were both dictators and perfectionists. At any rate, they had had a fantastic tantrum about something— fantastic because in its final stages Reinhardt had volleyed in German and Paul in English, both shouting together, with a Reinhardt minion translating like mad between them, and Carey standing by in much embarrassment but with an awareness that she would find the incident exquisitely funny in retrospect. Which she always did — as now.

.   .   .   .   .   .

For the one thing she had held on to, throughout all the routines of effort and failure, effort and success, was a sense of humour. It was an odd humour, rooted in a profound acceptance of the incongruities of life and perhaps also in that background of Ireland and Catholicism which, though she might seem to have lost both, was — at a deeper level — beyond her power to surrender. Paul, she knew, did not laugh in the same way or at the same things ; especially he could not laugh at himself. But gradually, over a period of years, he had grown used to the way she laughed at him, and at themselves ; he believed he had conceded her the privilege, and she never let him realize it was something neither of them could have prevented. Nor did he know how many times her own special humour had eased him out of trouble. When he was most unreasonable there was a way her mouth could twist which was hardly a smile, yet could bring the temperature down like a breeze through an opened window.

So in admitting that she would have been nothing without him, she had private knowledge that he without her would have made extra enemies and kept fewer friends. The one field in which he was almost impeccable and infallible was the theatre itself — that abstraction which to him was far more than the building or even the play. The theatre freed him from all that made muddle in his life, so that on the stage decision came to him purely and instantly from something deeper than his mind and sharper than his brain. When he directed her in comedy he seemed even to understand her sense of humour, doubtless because he was then in control of it. To understand anything he had to be in control. " I'm right when I do what I want," he had once told her. " I'm wrong when I try to compromise or please others." He meant, of course, in his work, but it was perhaps natural that an arrogance so unarguably justified should tend to become a habit elsewhere.

Those weeks at Mapledurham during that summer of 1929 were somehow crucial to Carey; it was as if the *Everyman*-Beringer affair acted like a catalyst, intensifying a vision of things already seen obscurely. Her life with Paul, she realized, had acquired a texture. She must guard him constantly from the kind of mundane error he was prone to; on the other hand, in anything touched by his infallibility she must not try to influence him at all, and for her own ultimate sake as much as his. The problem lay in the delimiting of worlds. Perhaps it was a good thing, she reflected with a twisted smile for herself alone, that popes should not marry.

Thus, when she saw that the *Everyman* collaboration was more than a whim, she ceased to be openly critical of it, though she kept a watchful eye on Malcolm. That young man spent most of his time at Mapledurham, walking over from Moat Farm early in the morning and returning late at night; he and Paul were closeted together (the old-fashioned phrase seemed to suit the situation) for five or six hours each day. Usually Paul had discussed all his work with her, seeking not advice, but a sounding-board for his ideas; about this *Everyman* project, however, he became gradually less confiding. Once when she taxed him with this he answered that he knew she didn't approve what he was doing, so he had chosen not to worry her.

" But Paul, I'd worry still more if I thought you had secrets from me."

" Well, it's no secret any more. I'm going to make a film with Malcolm in Germany."

" *Germany?* "

" They have the best techniques there — and in France — they're the only places where the art of the film isn't dying of infantile paralysis."

" And it's all . . . arranged . . . already ? "

" Practically all."

" Including the financing angle ? "

" Sure.   No trouble about that."

She was at the breakfast-table with him (the only meal of the day guaranteed to be without Malcolm) when this conversation had sprung up, and she had an idea that unless she had broached the subject he would not have told her, even yet.   She said at length, calmly : " I suppose you're sure what you're doing is the right thing, Paul."

" No, I'm not sure, this time.   It's a new venture — an experiment.   That's why I've kept you out of it. . . . But if it's a success you can count on me — one of these days I'll make you into a movie star."   He laughed and added : " Besides, you'd hate to walk out of a play that still has a few hundred nights to run."

" I would, I'll admit that.   But it isn't going to be easy for me, away from you."

" Oh, you'll manage.   A play like that can jog along."

" I wasn't thinking about the play. . . . When do you go ? "

" Sail on August twenty-fifth."

" You've even fixed that ? "

" Have to book far ahead, the boats are crowded."

" Yes, I know, but . . . well, when do you expect to come back ? "

" Before Christmas. . . . Carey, you're not really upset, are you ? "

" Darling, if you're doing what you feel you have to do, then everything's fine so far as I'm concerned.   That's the way I discipline myself — if I didn't, you'd never put up with me.   It's a bit of a miracle, really, the way we manage to put up with each other.   But I'll miss you, Paul.   That's something I *can't* help."

.   .   .   .

She didn't miss him nearly as much as she had expected ; indeed, she was rather startled to find how much smoother in many ways life was without him.   Provided he was doing what he wanted in that infallible world of his, she could face the few months of his absence with something more than equanimity. She missed him most at the rehearsals before the beginning of the new theatre season, for she knew there were things he would not have tolerated, that the play could have benefited from the kind of sprucing-up he would have given it ; on the other hand, it was booked solid till January and the audience at the reopening laughed as loudly and as often as ever, not noticing (she was sure) the lack of that little extra quality that Paul could always squeeze out of a performance. Perhaps the squeeze did not matter so much, in a comedy. She was torn between a schooled integrity that insisted it did matter, and a feeling of relaxation in being able to do a competent job night after night without having to worry about what Paul had said to offend one of the carpenters, or the house-manager, or somebody from a newspaper.

He wrote to her, fairly frequently but irregularly, from Berlin, giving her little information about the *Everyman* project, but conveying an impression that all was going well with it. He hardly ever mentioned Malcolm, and her own gossip about New York and the play never drew his answering comment. She was not surprised at any of this. Again, so long as he was all right, doing the work that satisfied him, she was content. She went to a few parties and enjoyed herself, discovering reluctantly how pleasant it was not to watch for danger across a crowded room, for Paul's feuds with so many people had always made acceptance of a party invitation something of a risk. More often, though, she spent pleasant hours by herself — reading, shopping, attending matinées of other plays on her own free afternoons. Life went easily — at the theatre, at her apartment, and in a curious way within her inmost self.

Towards the end of that October came the big break on Wall Street. Like most people she and Paul were ' in the market ' ; not to do what everyone else was doing would have seemed perilously close to that act of selling America short, which was, of course, a sin as well as an error. So, as they had accumulated more cash than they could spend, they had acquired the services of Andrew Reeves to manage the surplus — an elderly, highly respectable, and even conservative stockbroker who recommended only the blue chips and was cautious about too much buying on margin. All had gone well, and there had come a time when Carey could reckon, without undue excitement, that they were probably worth a quarter of a million dollars between them. Carey, in fact, was the one who dealt with all financial matters; she and Paul had separate accounts, but Paul had told Reeves that Carey was the one to say yes or no to any specific proposition. For Paul was fundamentally bored with money except when he needed it, so that the less he needed it the more bored he became. He would sign cheques and documents without looking at them if Carey had approved them first, and she doubted that he knew the names of the stocks that had given him quite large paper profits.

Carey did not follow the affairs of Wall Street with any day-to-day preoccupation, but she could not miss the headlines on October 23rd, when market leaders plunged as many as fifty points. Alarm was in the air by then; it was already affecting theatre audiences. At her apartment after the performance she found a wire from Reeves asking for additional margin on certain stocks she held. The amount was not more than she could afford, but the drop in prices was so different from anything she or Reeves had considered possible that she wondered if she should sell out the stuff on which she and Paul still had a profit. It was a nuisance his having left without giving her legal power to act for him, but perhaps she could contact him by cable. The next morning she visited Reeves in his office on a day long to be remembered. Alarm had now mounted to panic, and she was aware of something in the atmosphere that touched her far beyond any question of personal loss — something she had not felt since those homeward journeys from the Abbey Theatre when there was shooting in the Dublin streets. She fought her way through yelling crowds into the broker's sanctum and at last managed to get a word with him. She was dismayed by his appearance and by his wan smile as he struggled to close the door of an inner office so that their voices could be heard, but what shocked her most was the way his telephone kept ringing and

he made no move to answer it. This, from a man so punc-
tilious, seemed to her an utmost symbol of disintegration.
She liked him, they had had many lunches together at downtown restaurants where he was obviously pleased to be seen
with her, and he had attended all her first nights and had
been half-affectionately proprietary when he paid his respects
in her dressing-room afterwards. There had always been in
his attitude a sense of kindly guardianship; his eyes upon
her told others that here was a beautiful young actress who
naturally knew nothing about business, so she had put her
financial affairs in the hands of safe old Uncle Andy and
could henceforth sleep at nights without worrying her pretty
head about them. It was a fairy-tale relationship, harmless
enough, and Carey had not discouraged it. And now Uncle
Andy was running his fingers through his whitening hair and
refusing to answer telephone calls — perhaps from other
pretty heads. " I can't figure what's happened, Carey. Of
course it's absurd — U.S. Steel under 200 — that shows you
how absurd it is. . . . Too bad you didn't take Paul's
advice."

" Paul's ? . . . He never . . . why, what about Paul ? "
He was too bewildered to notice her bewilderment. He
went on, still with the same wan smile : " One of the few I
know who got out right at the top. Good for him."

Amidst the bedlam of that morning she finally elicited that
Paul had actually visited the broker's office in late August,
had shown a lively interest in his holdings and what they were
worth, and had shocked Reeves immeasurably by giving an
explicit order to sell everything. It was obeyed, of course,
and a few days later he had collected a cashier's cheque,
again in person. What he did with it, if and how he rein-
vested the whole or any part, Reeves couldn't say. He had
naturally assumed that Carey had known all about it. " I
was surprised," he said, " that you'd let him act like that,
though God knows he was smarter than either of us."

Carey made the obvious guess as to what had happened to
the money, but she did not mention it to Reeves. What
troubled her most was not what Paul had done, but the way

he had done it; it was the first time he had failed to consult her on the business angle of any enterprise. She wrote to him, as soon as she got back to the apartment — a short, straightforward letter, saying she had learned he had sold out, which in view of what had happened since was fortunate, but why had he kept it so secret? And had he put money into the *Everyman* project? If so, she hoped he had a reliable lawyer or business manager in Germany to look after his interests. After she had mailed the letter, Reeves telephoned. He told her things had steadied a little during the afternoon, Morgan's were supporting the market. Late that evening he telephoned again. He would be working all night, he said, to help his clerks bring some kind of order out of chaos. She hardly recognized his voice; it sounded not only strange, but the voice of a stranger. He added that after studying her account he was afraid the extra coverage she had agreed to send would not now be nearly enough. He was terribly sorry — it was for her to decide whether to put up more cash and hang on, or sell out and take the rather heavy loss. He was sorry it had come to that, of course she wasn't the only one, there were thousands in the same position or worse — some had been wiped out completely. And he was sorry he couldn't advise her what to do — after all, his advice hadn't been so good lately, she would admit. True, if one believed in America at all, the market was bristling with bargains — U.S. Steel at 200, for instance — on the other hand some people, probably bear operators, believed prices could go lower. So that was how it was, he simply couldn't advise her at all. He kept repeating that he was sorry till at last she realized whom he was reminding her of — an English butler they had had once who hid brandy in vinegar bottles and always apologized profusely when found out. She smiled then, knowing how utterly unlike a drunken butler Reeves could ever be, unless he and the whole world were to go as crazy as the market. It was cheering, anyhow, to find something to smile at. She said lightly: " Sell the stuff, Andy, and let's get it off our minds. I was all for taking medicine at one gulp when I was a kid.

And I never worried about money when I had none — why should I now ? Besides, there'll be some left, won't there ? "

"Oh yes," he answered eagerly. "You aren't nearly as badly off as others."

Less was left than she had expected, though there would have been nothing at all had she delayed action ; she had that much consolation. She did not definitely worry, but it was discouraging to find that taking one's medicine in one gulp could not close the issue, for all around her as the days passed and the market fell further, reverberations affected her life in countless ways — through the changed fortunes of her friends, the atmosphere in shops and restaurants, and by a sharp down-turn in theatre prosperity. There was talk of cutting admission prices and salaries, and though nobody had yet suggested the play should be taken off, already it looked as if it would not last far into the new year. People said how fortunate that it was a comedy, since in bad times everybody wants to laugh. Carey heard this truism so often that she began to feel like medicine herself, and she wondered if it made her act better or worse ; Paul could doubtless have informed her.

One of his most irritating habits was that, in letter-writing as in personal argument, he was capable of blandly ignoring what had been said or asked by the other party. He did this in a way that would have been almost more forgivable had it been deliberate, but Carey knew that it represented the absence from his mind of any real concern for anything outside the circle of his own dominating interest at the time. Thus, in reply to her letter, he made no comment about the sale of his stocks, and neither confirmed nor denied that he had put money into the *Everyman* project. And when, in a second letter, she told him frankly she had lost heavily herself, and that all phases of New York life were hard hit, including Broadway — to all this he replied by a casual suggestion that maybe she could sell Mapledurham — he had always thought it was too expensive for what they got out of it. The rest of his letter was about the beauty of some lakes near Berlin where he was apparently working on the picture. And in a postscript he added : " Sounds like a bad theatre season over there. I hope mother isn't worried. Try to cheer her up."

This reference to his mother further exasperated Carey, because, of all the people she knew, Paul's mother had least to worry about. The first thing he had done when success came was to fulfil an ambition to bring the old lady from Milwaukee to New York and set her up in an apartment of her own ; then, with the profits of his first long run, he had bought her a comfortable annuity. All of which had been very dutiful and sensible, but it did, Carey felt, put Mrs. Saffron in a position where she needed less cheering up than a great many younger people. She was a woman of strong character and personality, rather terrifying in some ways (' fabulous ' was the adjective she tried to live up to), and Paul's devotion to her was probably the most consistent emotion in his life. As such, Carey had been careful to respect it, but she was constantly amused by the aspect of angelic boyhood he assumed whenever he was with his mother. Play-acting himself down to the level of a teen-ager, he was often quite ridiculous ; yet there must have been something in it, for no matter how dark or tempestuous his mood, he could always appear frolicsome with her.

Carey made a special visit in response to the postscript. Paul had been in the long-established habit of paying his mother a short call every day, except on Sundays, when she came over to dinner ; since he had been away Carey had kept up the Sunday dinners and made one or two return calls during the week. This could have looked like kindness to a lonely soul, except that Mrs. Saffron was neither lonely nor the kind of person who is called a soul. She enjoyed her independence, she could afford a daily maid, and she had a visiting clientele of elderly admirers who accepted her domination and constantly lost small sums to her at pinochle ; moreover her health was good, and most mornings she pottered briskly about the Fifth Avenue shops with an eagle eye for a bargain. Carey always felt during her visits that she was being treated to a special demonstration of how close were mother and son, for invariably Mrs. Saffron could produce a letter from Paul which she did not show or read in its entirety, but quoted a few sentences from here and there. Apart from the fact that these letters were longer and more regular than the ones he sent to her, Carey thought them unremarkable; Paul was not a good letter-writer. This time, however, Mrs. Saffron's voice was charged with extra emphasis as she made the usual opening announcement: " I've just heard from Paul, my dear. . . ." She went on, as if she couldn't wait for even the most perfunctory response: " He says you've been losing money in the stock market."

" Oh yes, a little." So Paul, despite his anxiety that she should not worry, had given her the news.

" I'm sorry you weren't as smart as he was."

Of course that explained it. Her own loss made a neat dramatic contrast to the good news he had been able to give his mother about himself.

She said : " Yes, I am too."

" Of course, he talked to me about it beforehand, and I said to him, ' Son,' I said, ' it's your money, you made it, you do what you want with it.' So I guess that's what made him sell at the right time."

Carey had no comment.

" It's rather funny what he said about it in his letter." Mrs. Saffron put on her spectacles, searched for the page, and ran her finger down with a great show of omitting other things. " He says . . . this is what Paul says, my dear . . . he says, ' I've just seen some American papers and oh boy, Wall Street certainly did take a beating. I can just imagine how old Reeves must feel. I didn't dare tell him I was going to bring the cash to Germany to make a picture — he'd have raised such a shindig — but golly, even if the picture's a flop I won't be worse off than if I'd left things as they were. . . .' "

How true that was, Carey reflected, and how character-istic in a letter to his mother were such expressions as ' Oh boy ', ' shindig ', and ' golly ' — a kind of slang he would never have dreamed of using elsewhere.

Towards the end of November he wrote that the picture

was going well but more slowly than he had expected, so that he couldn't return till some time in the New Year, perhaps March or April if he could manage it. For the first time, in that letter, he showed interest in her affairs — he hoped the play was still making money and that she hadn't lost ' too much ' in the market crash. If she had, and had any use for a thousand dollars or so, there was that much cash in a safe-deposit box of his (he gave the number and location) which he had forgotten to empty when he left — she was welcome to it. As for the picture, it was going to be wonderful. It was also the first time he had sounded such an optimistic note about the work he was doing.

News of the delay in his return did not prevent this letter from cheering Carey considerably. She was touched by the evidence of his concern for her, even though the form it took had a typical streak of impracticality. She replied: " Darling, it was sweet of you to tell me about the safe-deposit box, but I really don't need the money and in any case the bank wouldn't let me touch it if it's in your name — didn't you know that ? . . . The play's still running and audiences seem to be picking up a little, and I've been approached in a vague way about several other plays next year, so I don't think I shall be out of work. Even if I were, I could enjoy a holiday, and I'm not *penniless*, you know. So please don't worry about me, and take all the time you need for what you want to do. . . . I see your mother regularly and she tells me you've lost ten pounds and are very proud of it — I know what this is a sign of — the creative yeast beginning to ferment, didn't you once call it that ? Don't work too hard, though, and give me more news of the picture — I'm so happy about it. . . ."

She spent a busy but enjoyable Christmas, and on New Year's Eve she wondered sentimentally but not anxiously what Paul was doing, and figured out that it was already New Year's Day in Europe. She sent him a cable.

The play finally petered out in the third week of January, and though she was not definitely signed for a successor, there was another comedy by the same author shaping up and

127

with an obvious part for her. She took a trip to Florida with theatre friends and was back in New York by the beginning of March, the earliest month that Paul had said he might possibly return. Recent letters, however, had not confirmed this, or indeed mentioned the matter again. His last letter had been from Riesbach, near Interlaken, Switzerland, where he had taken part of the company on location, so he said. He did not explain further, and Carey wondered how Swiss scenery could become necessary in a film of *Everyman*; but she was not especially surprised.

Then one Sunday as she was walking through the lobby of the Plaza for lunch she ran into Malcolm Beringer. She almost literally ran into him, and was sure from his instant look that he would have avoided her if he could. Even his suavity deserted him a little as she made him stop. "Malcolm! I didn't know you were back from Europe even — Paul never tells me things. Can't you sit down for a moment and give me all the news?"

She practically forced him to a chair and hoped he did not see her hand trembling as she offered him a cigarette. She had a sudden premonition of things not quite right. "So you left Paul there? How is he? Tell me about the picture. . . . He writes that it's going ahead well."

"I believe it is," Malcolm agreed, but without enthusiasm.

"You *believe* it is? Don't you know?"

He said: "I left Berlin in November. I can't say what's been happening since."

"But I thought you and Paul were working together?"

"We were . . . till then." He continued, with a faint smile: "It's a long story — much too complicated to explain."

"I'll bet it's complicated. Anything to do with Paul usually is. What did you do — quarrel?"

Then his faint smile vanished altogether. "We didn't see eye to eye about certain things."

"Of course you didn't. I was always surprised how well you got on at Mapledurham. Paul's not what you might call one of nature's collaborators."

" It wasn't exactly that."

" Oh, wasn't it ? "

He fidgeted to the edge of the chair, scrutinizing the passing crowd as if hoping for rescue by someone. " You'll excuse me, Carey, I ought to be looking for a man who's coming to lunch with me."

" So ought I, but both of them can wait. You've just time to tell me very quickly what happened."

" Why, nothing happened — particularly." He stubbed out his cigarette and let his long slender fingers tap some message of uncertainty on the table-top.

" Then what is it that's too complicated to explain ? "

" Why don't you ask Paul ? "

" How can I ask him about nothing particular — and that's what you say happened ? "

" It's all too personal, Carey, and if Paul doesn't mention it perhaps he thinks it's of no importance. And perhaps it isn't."

" You must know how that kind of answer scares me."

" I'm sorry. I don't think there's anything to get scared about."

" Mysteries always scare me. You've made me feel I want to leave for Germany tomorrow."

" Switzerland now, I understand."

" Yes, that's right. Some place near Interlaken."

" You know that ? He told you where he was ? "

" Of course. Why shouldn't he ? "

A very elegant young man approached the table, bowed slightly, and had to be introduced. Malcolm did not ask him to join them. Carey said lightly : " Pity there isn't time for a longer chat. Maybe we could have dinner together soon—"

He murmured something about having to leave for Washington. She didn't believe a word of it and she knew he knew she didn't. She added, shaking hands : " Well, I might take a trip to Interlaken one of these days — would you recommend that ? "

" They say it's a very beautiful place."

Oh God, she thought — couldn't you have thought of a

better exit line, and you supposed to be a writer ? . . . And then she remembered something that Paul had once said, that all the time-worn clichés that sound too absurd nowadays for any modern play are still used in life by people who are either too unsophisticated or too disconcerted to think of anything more original. And of these Malcolm could clearly belong only to the second class.

She acted a part throughout lunch, appearing very carefree ; it was easier to overdo it than merely to quell a mounting nervousness. Later that day she wrote to Paul, saying that she had met Malcolm accidentally and that he had given her the news. She did not say what news, and hoped that the equivocal phrase might evoke some revealing answer. But it failed to do so ; the letters Paul continued to write, both to her and his mother, were no different and contained no mention of Malcolm at all. It was maddening, the way he could ignore things. After a month of it, and with the new play still not definitely lined up, she came to an abrupt decision. She *would* go to Interlaken. To Mrs. Saffron she made the excuse of another trip to Florida ; what the old lady would think when no letters from Florida arrived she neither knew, nor in the mood she had reached, particularly cared. She caught the *Olympic* and reached Paris on an April day whose flavour gave her a pang. She and Paul had spent much time in that city, and had loved it, but now she merely hastened across from one station to another. Travelling all night, she arrived in Interlaken the next day about noon. She had never visited Switzerland before, and the loveliness as she stepped out of the train was overpowering. A cab-driver said that Riesbach was several miles away, a tourists' resort with a hotel, approachable only by steamer across the Lake of Brienz. It sounded so remote she didn't think she would want to stay there if Paul had gone back to Germany, which was a possibility ; so she booked a room at an hotel near the station and left her luggage. Then she took a cab through the town to the lakeside and boarded the tiny paddle-steamers. She was already more, or perhaps less, than entranced ; she felt that the beauty surrounding her hit below the emotional belt. And how industriously the Swiss had exploited everything, never vulgarizing though sometimes prettifying, building their parks and esplanades into perfect line with the white cone of the Jungfrau, running funiculars here and there to catch a special view, electrifying their trains into docile cleanliness; it was unbelievable that people should have come to such cosy terms with grandeur. The whole place, with its keen bright air and gay decorum, had an air of holiday that made Florida, steeped in stock-market and real-estate gloom, seem like a melancholy shambles by comparison.

The boat chugged across the lake, putting in at various resorts before arriving at Riesbach. Only a few passengers alighted there. The hotel was perched high above the water; a funicular climbed to it from the dockside. Every step in this long verifying journey from New York seemed to have increased her excitement in geometric progression; the ocean crossing, lasting a week, had been tense but endurable; the overnight train from Paris had left her restless; the boat trip across the lake had been an excruciating dream; and now these few minutes in the funicular seemed the culminating race of her heart to some kind of extinction. But at the very end, at the hotel desk as she asked if a Mr. Paul Saffron were staying there, she was becalmed. Yes, they said, but he was out at the moment — he was probably taking a walk in the woods. Doubtless he would be back soon. Would she care to wait? She agreed, and sat down in the lobby for a while. Then she went to the terrace and saw the trail leading into the woods with romantic deliberateness, the little sign-post giving time in hours as well as distance in kilometres — all so neat and satisfactory, so safe in an unsafe world. She began to walk along the trail, not intending to go far, in case Paul might return by some other route. The woods were cool and fresh-scented, sloping to the lake at an angle that gave sudden glimpses of blue amidst the green. Wild flowers, buttercups, and crocuses speckled the undergrowth, and at pleasing intervals a waterfall tumbled over rocks that seemed too casual not to have been arranged.

After ten minutes or so she turned a corner and saw two people some hundred yards ahead, and one of them, she thought from the slow walk, could possibly be Paul. The other was a girl. But what surprised her was that he was carrying a huge clump of wild flowers and that every few yards both he and the girl stopped to gather more. This was so totally unlike Paul, who cared for flowers only enough to buy them at high prices, that she almost doubted her own recognition till she came closer and could see the familiar head balanced heavily on the familiar shoulders. The rest was less familiar, for he was wearing shorts, woollen stockings, and boots spectacularly different from anything in his American wardrobe. Then she noticed that the girl had straw-coloured hair of the kind usually provided by wig-makers for use in Wagnerian opera.

Carey caught herself insisting that this encounter was a joke which they must both share with the girl, whoever she was. She was afraid they would hear her footsteps and turn, and for some reason she wanted to choose her own time ; she stopped therefore, partly to gain breath and partly in the sheer fascinatedness of being able to count now in seconds, after the minutes, hours, days, and weeks of waiting. She felt curiously elated. And the flowers and the girl's hair and the blue seen through the green and the snow-capped mountains dazzling in the distance — it *was* all rather like an opera, or like that recurrent crisis in an opera when something silly but quite tuneful is about to happen. " *Paul!* " she cried out abruptly. She had not known till then how silent everything was, except for the murmur of the waterfalls. Strange, she thought, that she had not heard them talking together. It was so odd of Paul to be walking, and even odder for him not to be talking.

He turned, stared, muttered something either to the girl or to himself, then began back along the trail, towards her, the girl following him. He was somewhat short-sighted and could not, she knew, recognize her at such a distance, but surely he must have known her voice. But then she realized that her voice had not sounded like her own voice at all.

"Hello," she said conversationally, but projecting a little, as she would have done on the stage.

Then came, in a rush, the inevitable exclamations and counter-exclamations. "*Carey!* For heaven's sake! *You?* You didn't tell me you were coming! Why on earth didn't you write? Carey, I can't *believe* it's you. . . ."

"Oh, Paul, I ought to have let you know, but I made up my mind so suddenly and I thought if you'd gone back to Germany I didn't want to interfere with your plans — I mean, if you hadn't been here it would have been all right — it's such a glorious place and I needed a vacation — it was either here or Florida, and there's no comparison, is there? And besides, *you* don't tell *me* everything, why should I tell you? — that's fair, isn't it? . . . My goodness, you're looking well!"

It was true. His usually pale face was bronzed, and he had lost nearer twenty than ten pounds, she would have judged. She had never seen him in such condition and it was doubtless absurd of her to reflect that, in a certain sense, it didn't suit him.

Then the girl came up, and Carey gasped, for she was a blond beauty, Wagnerian perhaps, but slim and exquisite, the flaxen hair framing the face like an ivory miniature.

Paul said: "This is Miss Wanda Hessely — she plays the lead in the picture." He turned to the girl and said, in very bad German: "This is Carey Arundel."

Carey smiled and the girl smiled back.

Paul said: "She doesn't speak English and I still can't manage much German, but I can tell you she's a fine actress."

"That's wonderful. I hope I'm not interrupting your morning."

Carey hadn't intended that to be sarcastic, it was simply what she sincerely felt, but as soon as she said it she wished it had sounded differently. Already she was half-regretting the whole trip; to meet Paul was one thing, but to sneak up on two people gathering wild flowers in a wood was somehow too naïve. Besides, she knew Paul had his own ways of rehearsing privately with actors — perhaps there was a flower scene in the picture and they had been taking themselves off to some quiet spot where Paul would have her go through a part. But to think that was perhaps also naïve. Already she knew that any twinge of jealousy she felt had not come from seeing the girl, but from hearing Paul call her a fine actress.

Paul said : " Oh no, we were just out for a stroll. Nowhere special. Wanda loves flowers. Let's go back to the hotel and have a drink. . . . She talks French, if you can remember enough."

They walked back together, Paul between them. The girl was not only lovely, she was charming and spoke enchantingly, with a quality of voice that Carey knew must set her high in Paul's regard ; and though Carey had not used her French for years, it began to ripple fast between them by the time they reached the hotel. Paul, indeed, was left rather out of things ; he kept glancing first to one side and then to the other, as if uncertain whether what was happening was altogether what he wanted. He was a bad linguist, and could not follow the conversation. " So you *do* remember your French," he commented ruefully, as they chose a table on the terrace.

" Of course. And since she doesn't know English I'll tell you this much in front of her — she's just about the loveliest thing I've ever seen. Is she well known ? "

" She will be. She's my discovery — she used to work in a department store. A natural actress. You should see some of the rushes."

" I'd like to. May I ? "

" They're in Berlin."

" But aren't you making part of the picture here ? "

" We were shooting a few mountain scenes, but that's all done now. We're just killing time for a while."

" A nice place to do it. Everybody must be very happy."

" No, the others have gone back to Germany till there's more money. Mine turned out to be not nearly enough. You've no idea how costs run up. I sold out half my interest. I had to — we couldn't have gone on without."

"So you spent all your money and now you only own half the picture?"

"Maybe not even that, by the time we're through. But if I'd kept it in stocks, what then?"

"Exactly. You were so right."

"I didn't know I was right. I just knew I wanted the money. . . . And it's a good picture, Carey, really it is."

"Oh, Paul, I'm very happy about that."

"Are you? You *look* happy."

"Why shouldn't I be? I've owed myself a real vacation for years. Last summer at Mapledurham wasn't much of one."

"I know. Because you didn't like Malcolm. Maybe you were right about him just as I was about the stocks."

"You mean accidentally right?"

"Well, you couldn't have *known*."

"Couldn't have known what?"

"Oh, well, let's not hold a post-mortem."

"He told me he hadn't seen eye to eye with you — that was the phrase. I suppose you had a big row."

"An *impossible* row, Carey."

"You're pretty hard to collaborate with."

"Oh, it hadn't anything to do with that."

"So he said, too."

The waiter came and Paul, without consultation, ordered three double Amer Picons, which Carey thought rather massive for that time of the day, but she was too preoccupied to ask for anything else.

"What was the row about, then?"

"Wanda, mainly. He didn't like her."

"You mean, in the part?"

"That as well."

"As well as what?"

"Oh, it was all rather personal."

"Perhaps he was jealous."

"Not in the way you'd expect."

She laughed. "Darling, how do you know what I'd expect?"

" That's enough in English. Say something to her in French."

She spoke across him to the girl; she said : " My husband tells me you're very wonderful in the picture."

She watched the girl's response, and saw shock (if there were any) mingle with pleasure at the compliment into a cool shyness, half disconcerted, half serene. The more Carey studied her the more she found her utterly delightful. They talked on till the drinks came, less and less importantly ; by that time Paul looked forlorn again and was itching for a chance to interrupt.

" You two seem to be hitting it off together," he said, at the first opportunity. " Hitting it off " was his favourite phrase for success in any and all human contacts.

" Paul, I think she's adorable."

" How do you like the Amer Picon ? "

" I'm not used to drinks at all, so early, but it's no more unusual than my being here, is it ? I left my luggage in Interlaken, by the way."

" The hotel people can send over for it."

" As a matter of fact I booked a room there at the Splendide — I wasn't certain you'd be here, and Interlaken looked very nice."

" Sure, but you can cancel it now. Let me go to the desk and fix things."

She talked with Wanda till he came back a few moments later. " They've put you in the room across from me for tonight," he said, " but tomorrow we can switch to the royal suite — it's probably that — two bedrooms with a real bathroom in between — quite sensational for these parts. And I asked them to telephone the Splendide to cancel your room and send over the stuff. It won't arrive till tomorrow, but I don't suppose that matters."

She could not help thinking how strange it was for him to have made all these businesslike arrangements. Usually when they travelled it was she who did everything at hotel desks, booking and inspecting rooms, checking luggage, and so on. It was certainly strange of him to be rushing to handle such details himself, and courtesy seemed laughable as a possible explanation. Perhaps, though, it was no stranger than the walking in the woods, and the flowers, and the shorts. As for the arrangements themselves, they were quite normal. For years he had been apt to sit up half the night reading and smoking cigars, and for this reason separate rooms had become a habit, and in hotels whenever possible they had always tried to fix up a two-bedroomed suite.

Then, in the swiftly gathering dusk, she noticed a small group of people at the end of the terrace staring in a certain direction, some with binoculars. Paul explained that it was the Alpine glow transfiguring the snow peaks, evidently a much-esteemed local spectacle. They moved over to join the group. It appeared often in clear weather, Paul went on, with something of a chamber-of-commerce pridefulness, but this evening's show was the most colourful he had yet seen. " That *incredible* saffron . . ." he remarked, adding quickly : " And no joke intended."

" That makes it a better one," she laughed, feeling the drink in her head and legs simultaneously. " Because you *are* that incredible Saffron, and I only wish I could translate it into French for Wanda. . . . Anyhow, it's pretty — the colour, I mean. Just like slabs of pink blancmange. . . . I think I'll find where my room is now and get myself freshened up."

" Sure, I'll take you."

They entered the hotel, leaving Wanda on the terrace, and climbed the staircase to the second floor. Everywhere looked rather empty, and Paul explained that it was in between seasons, the snow being now too soft for skiing and the yearly influx of vacationers having not yet begun. He talked with a satisfied air of proprietorship, as if the hotel as well as the girl had been his own discovery. " It's just the spot to rest and relax," he said, amazingly when she recollected all the other country places which with her he had found just the spots to get bored in. He unlocked the doors of both their rooms, then strode across hers to fling open the windows. " No screens, of course, they never have them out here, but there aren't insects either." Screens were his fetish; it was the one feature she had to look for first when she was booking at an American hotel, and how often they had passed up a good one for lack of them. "I think you'll like it here," he went on. Both rooms were bare-boarded, cheerful, spotless, but austere by American standards; Paul's was smaller than hers, with a single bed and not much of a view. He said he had taken it because it was cheap, which she could well believe. She was wondering how much tact she need employ to offer him a loan (probably none at all if he needed the money) when he said with a grin : " Carey, what really made you come here ? "

" An idea I got suddenly. I just wanted to see you. I wanted to make sure you were all right. Malcolm scared me."

" What did he say ? "

" Nothing. That's what scared me. I got so that I had to find out for myself."

" I don't blame you."

" That's nice. I knew you wouldn't."

" Well, I mean it, Carey. I *don't* blame you."

" And I don't blame you either."

He did not reply, but went on grinning, and after a pause she continued : " Anyhow, you look so well and happy . . . and why shouldn't you be, with a good picture nearly finished ? "

" Yes, it *is* good. I wasn't certain at first, but I know now I can do a great job for the screen just as for the stage."

" I'm glad you haven't changed, Paul."

" Don't you think I have ? I've lost a lot of weight."

" I meant that if I ever found you modest I really *would* think something had happened."

He laughed. " You know me pretty well, don't you ? "

She laughed with him. " Does Wanda think you're going to make her a great actress ? "

He became suddenly serious. " She nearly is already. You'd agree if you saw the rushes."

" But I can't, can I ? She's a better actress than me, I suppose ? "

" Yes."

" When you say so, as solemnly as that, I know how true it must be."

" It's also true that I've missed you, Carey."

" You *have*? Really? I wouldn't put it past you, as they say in Dublin."

" There's one thing Wanda hasn't got."

" That makes her human, anyhow."

" But it's something I miss — though perhaps it's only due to the language barrier. . . . A sense of humour, Carey — the kind you have."

" And the kind I need, too, darling. When do we get dinner? "

" Six. We'll drink champagne."

" Provided you let me buy it."

" Thanks, and since we're on that subject, do you think you could lend me a little cash? I'm a bit short till we get some more out of Germany."

She began to open her purse. " Anything you want, Paul — within limits. We're neither of us as well-heeled as we used to be. Matter of fact, this room suits me perfectly — why bother making any change tomorrow? We don't need a suite when the hotel's so empty — it's no hardship to walk down the corridor to a bathroom."

. . . . . .

The dinner was good, and in a somewhat under-populated dining-room the explosion of champagne corks seemed a ceremony to announce the season yet unborn. The hotel manager smiled his approval and sent them cognac on the house. Carey talked a good deal to Wanda, and Paul offered his constant interruptions, irrelevantly but not without a sort of bizarre harmony. In the rays of the table lamp Wanda was an Alpine glow herself, something to be stared at like a natural phenomenon. Her beauty was of a kind, Carey thought, that would make anything she did forgivable, while the beauty itself remained unforgivable — because in an imperfect world nobody had a right to such flawlessness.

Even the flaw Paul had mentioned was more likely to be his own than hers, for Carey guessed that Wanda did have a sense of humour; it was Paul who had failed to discover it because he hadn't nearly so much himself, as his stress on the language barrier showed; for it was wit, of which he had plenty, that required speech; humour could pass wordlessly from eye to eye, as Wanda's did to hers, even when their chatter in French was quite ordinary and serious. And they need not tell each other much about Paul, Carey thought, because they could *look* at each other about him; and this they had been doing all the time so far, with Paul presiding between them with an air of performing a conjuring trick that nobody was interested in.

It was during the later stages of dinner that Carey realized how impossible it would be to find out anything that could be called the absolute truth. She knew Paul well enough to know how rarely he could be attracted sexually; she knew, too, that there was nothing in the outward appearance of his attitude to make it certain that Wanda was, or had been, his mistress. He adored beautiful women, extravagantly and romantically, and a beautiful woman combined with a fine actress would surely drive him to every kind of distraction — with only one possible but not quite guaranteeable exception. It might well, for instance, expend itself in an ecstasy of gathering wild flowers, wearing shorts, and losing twenty pounds of superfluous weight. During the seven years Carey had lived with Paul she had witnessed the strangest manifestations of his enthusiasms for other women, yet she had never really believed him to be unfaithful, and had only very occasionally wondered about it. For she had the best of reasons for knowing how hazardous he found the relationship of man and woman, a problem worth solving once in a lifetime, if at all, and then to be given up not so much in despair as in thankful disregard.

And yet, looking at Wanda, Carey could not be sure. From the girl's angle a liaison with Paul might easily seem desirable as a means of keeping him interested in her till he had given what he had to give — and if she were a good actress, let alone a great one, she would know how much that was. There was a composure about her that Carey could not interpret, but admired because she knew from stage experience how hard it was to simulate if it were not felt; so that in Wanda it must either be sincere or else a piece of acting equally to be envied. She wished she could see the rushes of the picture, not because she doubted Paul's word about their merit, but to reach in her own heart that point at which envy must spill over into hate or love; for she had never hated anyone yet, and wondered if she could.

She decided then that she was not jealous, but mainly curious, with a curiosity disciplined by her own surmise as to what would happen if she were to ask Paul a plain question. Because, whatever his answer, she wouldn't know whether to believe it. She could imagine him, in pride that was a sort of self-defence, assuring her that of course he and Wanda had had an affair — what did she think he was made of? (Once or twice in the past he had hinted at conquests which later she had found to be mere boasting.) Or she could imagine him answering no, with much indignation, merely to spare what he would assume to be her feelings — such an assumption being often no more than a reflection of his own high opinion of himself. " I didn't want you to be hurt," he would say when he would be hurt himself if she ever told him she hadn't been.

And if she were to put the same plain question to Wanda there would be an equal impasse; something transfiguring would happen again, a glow on top of a glow, the look that could come to the same bashful terms with guilt or innocence, as Carey had seen already in the girl's response to that deliberately testing phrase " my husband ". And there was nothing more to be learned.

Except one matter, which Carey held herself justified in probing at the first chance. It came when Paul left them at the table to buy a cigar. Carey said then, changing the subject abruptly: " I saw Malcolm Beringer in New York before I sailed. He gave me an impression that he and Paul had quarrelled while they were working on the picture."

" Is Mr. Beringer a friend of yours, Mrs. Saffron ? "

" No, I wouldn't call him that. Why do you ask ? "

And then a long cool silence, until the girl continued :
" You see, it has been hard for me to exchange ideas with
Paul, because of the language, but Mr. Beringer spoke
German well — so he acted as interpreter amongst all of us."

" Yes, I can understand that, but how did it affect the
quarrel ? "

Wanda smiled. " He was able to say things about Paul
that were not true."

" I see. And when you found out they weren't true . . . ? "

" Yes, then there was the trouble."

Paul was already returning with the cigar. There was no
time to explore further, nor perhaps any need either. Carey
said, deliberately gay for Paul's benefit : " Paul's quick
enough at most other things, I wonder why he's so slow at
picking up languages ? "

" I will tell you why," Wanda answered, in the same key.
" First, it is because he does not really listen when others
are talking. And second, it is because he feels the whole
world has no right not to know English."

Paul sat down and lit his cigar, pleasantly aware that they
were having some joke at his expense ; he did not know
enough French to enjoy it with them, but he was sure it must
be harmless.

. . . .

Carey stayed at Riesbach for a week, and in many ways
it was a very pleasant time. All the things she had long
wished that Paul would care for, he now apparently did care
for — hours of sheer laziness in deck chairs, rowing placidly
on the lake, picnics in the woods, even walking, if it were not
too athletic. Wanda was wise enough not to persuade him
to do other things that she herself enjoyed ; she used her
power, if it existed, with a sparing scrupulousness. So when
she felt in a mood to climb a mountain or play tennis or take
part in the impromptu dances that often sprang up at the
hotel after dinner, she made no attempt to drag Paul along ;

and of course there were always young men anxious to fill the gap. Paul seemed to have no jealousy when he saw her in the arms of some handsome ski-instructor; he and Carey would sit watching, Paul relishing the spectacle theatrically and passing frequent remarks on Wanda's beauty and accomplishments.

Carey did not need to be told that Paul was happy. He gave every sign of it, and the loss of weight and healthier life had added a new kind of vigour — more physical, less nervous. In a sort of way Carey found him less like himself, which could also be called in some ways a change for the better. She noticed that he ate, drank, and smoked less, that he would choose fruit as a dessert instead of chocolate pudding, that he did not smoke his first cigar till after lunch. Little things. Once as the three of them were returning from an afternoon on the lake, wind-blown and sun-brown, they passed a large mirror in the hotel lobby, and Paul, in the middle, drew them both to a standstill with encircling arms. " Don't we look wonderful ? " he exclaimed, and it was true that they did. But at the very moment of joining in a laughing assent, Carey caught Wanda's eye in the mirror and saw in it something so friendly, yet at the same time so inquisitive, that she felt Paul's question was being repeated rather than answered. Carey said : " Well, we ought to, with the kind of life we're leading. Sunshine and fresh air and no work."

Paul said : " One of these days I shall make a picture about children, and when I do I shall remember Riesbach."

He drew them away from the mirror, but the look in Wanda's eyes which Carey intercepted before they left it was less inquisitive now, had more of shared awareness, as if she were saying : We both know that cryptic kind of remark, don't we ? . . . And Carey returned the look, as if to answer : Of course we do, it's his way of clinching something in his mind by a dramatic attitude, as he would have an actor do the thing on the stage . . . and just to prove it isn't as silly as it sounds, he probably *will* make a picture about children some day and it'll be so good that people will think what a lovely childhood he must have had himself to understand it so well, but the truth is, Wanda, his own real childhood wasn't lovely at all — he hated his father, he was miserable and lonely and insufferably precocious . . . this Riesbach interlude is a dream of his and we are the playmates he never had before — he's seeing us now, with his arms round both of us, symbolically as well as actually, in a mirror. . . .

One morning the Riesbach interlude came to a sudden end. She had cabled her address to Bill Michaelson, her New York agent, merely as routine, but on the breakfast-table there was a cabled reply saying that the new play was now finished, should he mail it over, or was she likely to be returning soon? Had this come alone she might have wondered whether to ignore it, at least for the time being; but for Paul also there was a message, summoning him to Berlin to complete the picture, new money having at last been raised. As they sat, the three of them, drinking coffee on the terrace in the mountain sunshine and exchanging these items of news, it seemed quite providential that so much had happened simultaneously, thus cancelling out blame, remorse, and responsibility. They packed that morning and took the lake steamer to Interlaken in the afternoon. The spell was over, and Paul was more normally nervous and excitable, fidgeting over trifles and almost absent-mindedly enquiring about the New York play. Carey told him what she knew, which wasn't much, except that it was another comedy guaranteed to be a winner like the last one. He said moodily: " It's about time you were bored with comedy," which she knew was his oblique way of telling her that he was, or rather that he was so interested in something else that the idea of coming back to New York to direct the play wasn't touching even remotely the fringe of his mind. Towards dusk at Interlaken station they boarded two trains that left, again by coincidence, almost at the same moment and in opposite directions — Wanda and Paul to Germany via Lucerne, Carey by the express to Paris. Two days later she was on the *Berengaria*.

As soon as she embarked at Cherbourg she felt tired and lack-lustre. It was as if the Riesbach interlude, now that it was over, had withdrawn its own illusion of well-being, leaving only the memory of an enchantment too slight to lean on. The goodbye to Paul, so far from upsetting her, had been in some sense a relief, and though he had said he planned to be back in America by September, she was surprised to find that the idea of his return did not fit into her mind as something terrific to look forward to — rather, in her present mood, as merely another and a further horizon of ordeal. For the new play was already the nearer one, and although she knew how difficult Paul was when he was directing, the thought of some other director made her feel very glum. But of course it could not be helped. Thank goodness Paul's all right ; he's happy ; let him get back to his work and I to mine ; in this spirit she could face any future. On the boat she surrendered to something else that was harder to analyse — not quite depression, but a deep lassitude of the body that matched an inner indifference the like of which she could not remember in her life before ; it centred on the new play, which of course she would study as soon as she reached New York, but she was actually glad she hadn't it with her during the trip — she lacked even a desire to read it.

She spent the first four days at sea in her room, the weather being rough. On the fifth day, approaching the Grand Banks, the skies cleared and the rolling lessened, so that many of the passengers, like herself, appeared on deck for the first time. She did the regulation walk, then found a vacant chair, a rug, and a novel. Next to her in the long line was a grey-haired man, rather good-looking and apparently asleep. There was something about him that made her think she might have seen him before — not that she could know him personally, for she had a good memory for acquaintances, but perhaps his was one of the faces that sometimes emerge from the blur beyond the footlights, randomly and as a challenge when an audience is cold — see that man at the end of row three, centre aisle — he's not laughing, *make* him laugh, make *him* laugh . . . occasionally in comedy one got as desperate as that, and it was significant that now, with the new play distantly on her mind, such desperations were easy to remember. She was staring at the man, still wondering and remembering, when she realized he had opened his eyes and was staring back at her.

He smiled and said slowly : " Miss Arundel, isn't it ? "

She was used to this kind of thing, and though it was sometimes a nuisance, she knew that if it ever ceased happening she would have much more to worry about ; apart from which, in this instance, she had been staring first. So she returned his smile. " Yes, that's right."

" I thought I recognized you." She was glad he didn't try to get up or perform any polite manœuvre, tucked in as he was under a very luxurious fur rug. " I'm one of your countless admirers, Miss Arundel. My name is Bond — Austen Bond."

" My real name is Saffron. Mrs. Paul Saffron."

" Ah, yes." She couldn't be sure whether the name Saffron meant anything to him or whether he was merely being cool towards the revelation. " Are you coming back to New York to give us a new play ? "

It was the one thing she didn't want to talk about. " I expect so," she prevaricated, " sooner or later."

" I hope sooner."

" Thank you."

" No, no, it's I who should thank you for giving me so much pleasure."

To which by all usage she should have murmured vague appreciation and changed the subject, thus ending the see-saw before it began to be ridiculous ; but instead she let what was uppermost in her mind dictate a reply — she said : " Don't forget the director also — and the author — they have a lot to do with a good play."

" Of course. And I notice you put the director before the author."

" That was accidental — or perhaps it's because my husband *is* the director — *was*, that is, of my last play."

The steward came with bowls of hot soup. The effort of dealing with them seemed to make the conversation more intimate, if also more scattered. They discussed foreign travel for a time (she told him she had been visiting Switzerland, and he said he had been on a business trip to Sweden); then the novel on her lap led to gossip about books and writers. He talked intelligently but not learnedly. Now that he was sitting up she could see he was less elderly than she had thought at first; the grey hair was misleading, he did not look more than fifty. He had a proud, strong type of face, the kind that looks sculptured, and there was a sense in which his voice and accent conveyed rather than betrayed the fact that he was American. If he were an actor, she reflected, Paul would probably not cast him for the part of an ambassador because he looked too much like one.

Presently he asked if she were travelling alone, and when she said yes, he asked if she usually dined alone, or had made friends on board. She answered ruefully that so far on the trip she hadn't dined at all.

" I think there'll be better weather from now on," he said.

" I hope so. I'm not a good sailor, though I'm probably not the worst one either."

" Then perhaps you'd care to join me for dinner this evening ? "

When she hesitated, not knowing whether she wanted to or not, he added with quick tact : " That is, if it keeps smooth." He got up with rather surprising agility and stooped to lift her hand. " Shall we say seven o'clock in the bar near the small restaurant ? I'll look for you there, but if you don't feel equal to it, please don't bother. I'll understand."

She noticed as he walked away that he was tall and had a good figure — perhaps he was still in his forties and the grey hair could be regarded as premature.

By six o'clock she had almost made up her mind not to keep the appointment. He had given her an easy out, and it was true that the wind was freshening and the sea not quite so calm. But most of all she felt in herself a renewal of the inertia of indifference, plus a somewhat professional feeling that if she were not in a mood to be attractive she had no business to inflict herself on an audience, even a chance-met male audience of one. Then suddenly and for no reason she could think of except again a professional awareness of challenge, she decided to meet Mr. Bond at least for a drink and, if that much bored her, to excuse herself from dinner afterwards. The challenge thus accepted, even in part, she felt immediately encouraged; she dressed carefully and gave herself cautious approval in the mirror. She looked a little off colour, but the reason for it was obvious, and a drink was doubtless one of the things she needed.

He was waiting when she got to the bar, and in a dinner-jacket he had the kind of anonymous distinction that the English have succeeded so well in making fashionable. Only perhaps by someone Irish could the thing be seen through and at the same time admired as an accomplishment. She smiled a greeting and began : " Well, I managed it. I won't prophesy, but I think I can last out a martini."

He took her to a table. " Good. It must be very trying to be travelling alone when you don't feel well."

" Oh, I haven't been really ill. Just resting and reading."

" Lonely, though."

" No — or rather, if it has been, I've enjoyed it. Such a change from one's normal life — whole days of nothing to do, nobody to argue with, no problems, no appointments, no worries. . . ."

" Do you usually have worries ? "

" Doesn't everybody ? " The play that she hadn't wanted to talk about came in useful now. " I think an actress always worries about her next play even before she knows what it will be."

" Don't you know yet ? "

She told him about the new comedy by the author of her recent big success; she would read it as soon as she got to New York, it was partly for this she was returning. " I suppose it won't come on till the fall, so there'll be plenty of time for rehearsing and polishing up — rewriting this scene and that and the usual mood of wondering whether it's a masterpiece or a piece of junk."

" Somehow you don't sound as if you were looking forward to all that."

" Oh, I'm used to it."

" But not looking forward to it this time ? "

He had a very quiet, persistent, but kindly way of refusing an answer that evaded.

" To tell you the truth," she said, and wondered why she was doing it, " I'm too tired right now to be looking forward to anything."

" You'll feel better on dry land." The drinks arrived, which made him add : " Too bad it *is* a dry land."

So they had the usual exchange of views about Prohibition, and that led to general chatter about American affairs, including inevitably the stock market. She told him she had lost money and gave a light-hearted account of her husband's action in selling at the top in order to finance a film-making enterprise in Germany. " He'll probably lose it that way too, but how much more worth while."

" Why should you think he'll lose it ? "

And she had to ask herself the same question. She answered, honestly, after a pause : " I expect it's my own conceit. You see, this is the first time he made a deal on his own without asking my advice."

" Would your advice have been against it ? "

" I don't know. I don't know what the deal is. And what right have I to pose as business adviser anyway — I haven't proved myself so smart lately."

" Nor have a great many business people. . . . Would you like another drink here or at the table ? "

She smiled and he asked her why. She said : " It reminded me of what they teach waitresses. Years ago, when we were hard up, I was one for a while, and whenever anyone ordered pie we were told to ask whether they wanted whipped cream or ice-cream with it. The customer who didn't want either had to make a stand."

" I hope you won't make a stand now."

" No, I haven't the strength. Four customers out of five hadn't. It was good psychology."

"That's very interesting." He gave the order to the waiter, then said : "So you've had your hard times?"

"Oh, nothing very dreadful. Before we made our first hit we went through a few bad patches, that's all."

"In New York?"

"Yes — and other places. It was in California that I was a waitress. Only for a short time — till Paul found a play."

"You've worked together as a sort of team?"

"Not deliberately—but I suppose it has been, more or less."

"Until this German enterprise?"

"Oh, well, I couldn't expect to be in that. I've had no picture experience."

From his silence she knew he realized how stupid the remark was, except as a revelation of things it did not say. Presently she went on : "Don't let me bore you with all this talk of my own affairs."

"How could I be bored when I've been asking all the questions?"

That was so. She replied : "Yes, but theatre shop can be pretty dull to those outside the business, and I rather imagine you are."

He nodded. "Yes, my own profession is far less romantic — and popular. . . . I'm in a broker's office." The second drinks arrived and he raised his glass. "Well, here's to the new play. Whatever it turns out to be I shall make a point of seeing you in it."

"I'll send you tickets for the first night."

"That would be very kind of you."

It would indeed, she reflected, considering they were so much sought after and he was someone she had met for the first time that day. She added : "If you promise to laugh at all the jokes, no matter how hard it is."

"I promise. But why should it be hard?"

"Well, for one thing, they may not be such good jokes. And then, too, it must be pretty hard for a broker to see a joke in anything nowadays. My own broker's having a nervous breakdown. . . . Andy Reeves. . . . I wonder if you happen to know him?"

" I'm afraid not."

" He's much older than you, I should imagine."

" Now how old would you imagine I am·? "

" I guessed fifty-five when I first saw you but you've been growing younger ever since."

He seemed amused by that and she felt the beginnings of a mood she sometimes got into when she was emerging out of fatigue — a sort of impishness, making her say things that were quite helplessly silly and only funny to others if she found them funny enough herself.

Then suddenly she keeled over and would have slipped to the floor had he not held her. It could hardly have been the drink, for she had had only one ; the bar was rather stuffy, perhaps that was the reason. People made way for an emergency that had happened many times before on ocean liners, except that in this case it wasn't that particular emergency at all. As soon as he had helped her to the fresh air on deck she fully recovered, but he led her to her cabin and summoned the stewardess. He was very gracious and attentive and took his leave when the stewardess arrived. She didn't feel ill, or quite well either, so she swallowed some aspirin, undressed, and went to sleep. The next morning the seas were rough again, so she stayed in bed all day. He sent flowers.

.   .   .   .   .   .

The morning after that the *Berengaria* arrived at New York. Amidst the last-minute scurry of packing and formalities she half wondered if she would see him again, but she did not look for him, and when the ship docked she followed her usual habit of waiting till nearly all the passengers were off before making her own way down the gangway to the customs. She soon found her luggage, among the last of the " S " group, but as she approached it an elderly stranger touched his hat, evidently recognizing her. " Mrs. Saffron ? Mr. Bond asked me to help you through."

" Well, that's very kind of him, but I haven't anything dutiable, so——"

" It'll be easy then. Your car's meeting you ? "

" No, I'll take a taxi ; but please don't bother—"

The man had already stepped to the customs officer and was saying something in his ear, with a result quite astonishing — the immediate passage of all her bags without inspection. Normally she disliked being singled out for special favour, but this time the act was performed so simply and quickly as to give her no time for embarrassment, and she was grateful besides, for she had had experience of customs men who seemed to have a special distrust of actresses.

While the man was giving further instructions to a porter she said half jokingly : " That's one of the most impressive things I've ever seen. Thank you, and please thank Mr. Bond. He really must know the right people."

" Well, Mrs. Saffron, I dare say he does. . . . He also asked me to give you this letter."

She couldn't figure quite what the man was — a servant, an employee ? He hadn't introduced himself by name and he was dressed as nondescriptly as an hotel detective. She thanked him again and read the letter on the way to her apartment. It said merely : " I'm sure you consider we owe each other at least one dinner. Will you let me know an evening that suits you after you get settled ? Yours sincerely, Austen Bond (aged forty-six)."

Not till several days later did she happen to mention Mr. Bond to a friend as " the only man I spoke to during the entire trip — tall and rather handsome — something in a broker's office, he said."

" My goodness, not *Austen* Bond, by any chance ? "

" Why, yes."

At which the friend laughed raucously. She was a lively old snob who fancied herself as a connoisseur of that overworld which is, in its way, quite as secret as the underworld ; everything in her private who's who depended on what *kind* of duke, what *kind* of millionaire, even what *kind* of actress. Carey happened to be her kind, which was the kind that could be invited to the Colony Club. She said : " Well, darling, I guess you could call him something in a broker's office if you wanted. D'you really mean you've never heard of him ? . . . I suppose that's possible — he's not the type that goes popping toy balloons at night clubs. Neither are you, for that matter — you two ought to get on well together."

" Oh, I don't suppose we shall meet again."

" You mean you won't call him up ? "

" I'll be so busy with the play from now on. I think I'll take it to the country and let it simmer in my mind for a few weeks."

Michaelson gave her a typescript the next day, after which she went to Vermont to stay with the Whitmores, old friends whom she had known since the year of the struggle as she called it to herself — that first year in America when Paul couldn't find any kind of job. The Whitmores had been the means by which he had finally got the chance he needed. They were comfortably off, but not rich, and the small paper-mill which they owned and in which Harry Whitmore worked was a mile from their house at the other end of the small town. An open invitation to visit them any time she could spare was her only effective consolation for having sold Mapledurham, and now, she was quick to avail herself of it. She read the new play in the Whitmores' garden, and thought it pretty good, but even while she thought so she was distrusting her own judgment — *was* it good, was it *really* good ? Of course there were comedies that made one laugh aloud at a first skim-through and later proved complete flops on the stage ; perhaps the reverse could also operate. She certainly did not laugh or even smile during the several hours she gave to a careful reading, and afterwards she picked up a published copy that the Whitmores had of her last play and tried to imagine that that too was new — would it have seemed amusing either ? But of course the test was invalid — the lines came to the ear as well as to the eye, and with the remembered laughter of an audience as punctuation. When Michaelson telephoned later in the day, eager to know her reaction, she had to tell him that she liked the new play well enough, because it would have seemed absurd to confess that her lukewarmness was probably due to some private mood of her own.

A few days later Michaelson arrived with contracts. He had made a special trip to get her signature. Somehow she had not expected there would be that degree of urgency, but such evidence of being sought after gave her a touch of cheerful panic. She signed, measuring the weeks till August, when rehearsals would begin. Plenty of time to work up the right mood of enthusiasm.

Towards the middle of July she returned to New York and met the author, who took her to lunch and proved, almost by algebra, that he had written a sure-fire successor to a success. But later the same day at a party she met another author who said he had heard a rumour that the new play was a bit of a let-down — what did *she* think ? She used up all her new-found confidence in denying it vehemently.

That evening at her apartment she read the play again, speaking many of the lines aloud, and in the midst of so doing she remembered Paul's remark : " It's about time you were bored with comedy." Was it that ? Or was she still just tired ?

Suddenly she doubted if she would be any less bored or tired had it been a tragedy and the greatest play ever written. And in that mood, a rather frantic one, she ransacked her desk for Austen Bond's note and dialled his number. She knew, by then, who he was.

PART THREE

AUSTEN BOND was not well known in the modern metropolitan sense — that is, to newspaper columnists, head waiters, and the man in the street. He was rich, and had his own importance, but the firm of investment brokers of which he was head was not one of those on everybody's lips and he had no ambition to make it so. There was something in his mental attitude that always preferred quality to size, and his place in financial circles was of this kind also; he was satisfied to make a personal fortune just less than sensational and to influence, occasionally and obliquely, those who had greater influence. The stock-market collapse had not affected in the slightest degree the routine of his private life, which had long been unpretentious. His attitude towards the future, including his own, was affected by his unspoken opinion that capitalism had begun to die. He did not think this was good, but he believed it was inevitable; and he had found, from a few scraps of early experience, that many people assume that the man who prophesies something, also wishes it to happen. In his case this was not true, and would have been absurd if it had been; but his knowledge of how easily and dangerously he would be misunderstood made him keep his mouth shut. He was less tempted to open it because he also believed that, on the scale of events that he foresaw, nothing he could do or persuade others to do could change the outcome to any worth-while extent. He therefore confined his activities to certain machinations of the market, in which it would have been as naïve to be a Marxian as a Seventh Day Adventist.

Within this somewhat chilly circumference the intimate structure of his life had developed, up to a point, quite genially and not very remarkably. He had been left money and a job by his father, a Wall Street man of the old school, while his mother had contributed good looks and an equipment of innate good taste in the arts. Education at Groton and Harvard had followed, after which there had been years of hard work. In 1920, aged thirty-six, he had married a New Hampshire girl who loved horses and dogs and enjoyed New York only as a visiting country cousin; so he had bought some land in Connecticut and there they had spent much of each year quietly and very happily indeed. In 1925 she had died in an influenza epidemic, leaving a boy of three named Norris. After that he had lived even more retiringly, but mainly in the old family house in the East Sixties that he had inherited from his father. He had an unmarried aunt who often played hostess at his small and not too frequent dinner-parties; he belonged to a few good clubs and liked to go to plays, art exhibitions, and concerts. During school holidays, when Norris was at home, he sometimes took the boy to places like the Metropolitan Museum and the Statue of Liberty. He had, behind a reserve that was hard to penetrate, a quietly inflexible will and a loyalty to those who worked for him, so that those who knew and liked him best were doubtless his employees and servants.

Austen had hardly expected to pick up an acquaintance with an actress on board the *Berengaria*. Not that he felt superior to the acting profession; on the contrary, he had a playgoer's affection for its leading figures, and Carey had often pleased him from the other side of the footlights. But he would not, had anyone forecast it, have agreed that he was at all likely to take the initiative in getting to know her. What had made him do so was that she looked unhappy. Minutes before she saw him he had recognized her; then he had closed his eyes to wonder what could be the matter, for though he was not simple enough to think that comedy stars must always be gay, the contrast between his recollection of her on the stage and the way she looked in the adjacent deck-chair had been too startling to ignore. Perhaps it was just the effects of a rough crossing; he hoped so, but he wished he could find out. Finally a kindly curiosity had made him speak.

And of course she had proved to be a mixture of everything he remembered and much that he could now so pleasantly discover for himself, once the plunge had been taken; she still looked unhappy, yet she was good company, and certainly hard to put out of his mind when the trip was over.

During dinner on that first evening at home he had said to Dunne, his butler: " I suppose you got Miss Arundel through the customs all right ? "

" Yes, sir. And she asked me to thank you. A very charming lady . . . and I *mean* a lady." (Dunne, a Scotsman, was careful to avoid the behaviour of the stereotyped English butler — he was not obsequious, and he never used the phrase ' if I may say so '.)

" Oh, and what makes you so sure of that ? "

" She knew better than to tip me."

Austen laughed — which did not mean that he failed to take the diagnosis seriously. He had a very high regard for Dunne's social assessments; there was something professional about them, as if he himself were to offer an opinion of Portuguese Fours. Indeed, he had a high regard for the man altogether. As his father's butler Dunne had been his boyhood friend, had taught him chess, and to ride a bicycle, and how to identify different birds in Central Park; Dunne had taken him for vagrant walks along Madison Avenue, explaining the difference between real and sham antiques in the shops; Dunne had lent him money when he had overspent his schoolboy allowance, had visited him at Harvard after his father's death to break the news that his mother was seriously ill. And Dunne, after Fran's death, though no one knew about this, had helped him through the worst crisis of bereavement. Austen had sometimes wondered if in an improved world, where there would doubtless be no master and servant, any other framework for such a relationship would be devised. If not, he would consider the improvement overrated.

When Carey telephoned, he felt a stab of pleasure as he heard her voice. After the long interval he had ceased to expect her to call; he assumed she must regard their acquaintance as a mere shipboard freak. He had a genuine modesty that made him consider himself dull by the standards that professional entertainers might set, and that an actress should seek his company must mean either that she liked him or that she was coldly appraising his social and financial eligibility. All his instinct was to believe Carey incapable of the latter.

He invited her to dine with him the following evening at his house, and her prompt acceptance sounded so much like that of an old friend that he let himself forget that they knew each other so slightly. Their telephone conversation was short, and that too pleased him; she could not, he reflected, have known how he disliked telephoning and how rarely he gave anyone his private number. Then he asked himself why he had, since the postal address would have sufficed, and the reason he fastened on was that he had wished to give her a better chance to act on impulse. After all, it was impulse that had made him speak to her on the *Berengaria*, and impulse, having begun so well, might claim a right to be encouraged. For him it was at least a novelty in a life so largely reasoned and reasonable. He sat in his favourite chair in the dark panelled library and meditated long after he had spoken to her. Only once did he have a flash of misgiving — when he wondered again if she would find an evening with him pretty dull — if, for instance, she would expect a lively party, or even for that matter a *tête-à-tête* — for of course his old aunt would be present, he would observe all the proprieties, at any rate until friendship had become established. And he must tell her, he decided, why it was that he hadn't invited her to a restaurant.

He told her while they drank sherry together in that same room the next evening. He noted her dress — black and gold, very becoming, and also tactfully suitable to whatever he or others might have been wearing, for in the brevity of his invitation he had given her no clues. He noticed also her grey-blue eyes and the little gap between one side tooth and its neighbour, a gap too small for a dentist to fill, yet a pleasing imperfection, especially when she gave the slight twisting smile that matched her prevalent mood.

He was saying : " I hope you wouldn't have preferred going to a restaurant, but the fact is, as long as Prohibition's the law of the land I don't care to break it publicly." He smiled. " You can judge how moral that attitude is from the way I'm willing to transgress in private."

" I think it could still be a moral attitude," she answered. " They're apt to be stronger than morals — or rather, they can hang on long after morals give up."

Wondering what was in her mind, he went on lightly : " It also happens that I hate noise and commotion and sitting amongst strangers — except, of course, when it's all made worth while by a good play. Tell me, how's the new one coming along ? "

He saw a shadow cross her face till she made the effort of dismissal. " Oh, pretty well. I've read it and signed the contracts, but we don't begin rehearsing till August, so there's nothing much to do just yet."

" No learning of lines ? "

" Not till after the first readings — the stage-readings, I mean, with the cast and the director. So many changes are made then, as a rule — it wouldn't help much to be word perfect in the play as it is. . . . But learning lines isn't hard once you get the real feel of the play. If you're absorbed you seem to memorize even when you read it privately."

" Is that happening to you with this play ? "

" Well, no — not so much."

" Then the play hasn't absorbed you — yet ? "

" Not altogether . . . which means that Paul might be right — Paul, my husband."

" Yes, I know. What did he say ? "

" He hasn't read the play, of course — he's in Germany — but when we met recently he said it was time I was bored with comedy."

" And are you ? "

" Oh dear, I'd better not be. He just put the idea into my head. I suppose I ought to be used to that by now — he's so full of ideas — they shoot out like sparks when he's directing."

"And the director of the new play doesn't have any sparks?"

"I haven't experienced them yet. Maybe he will. Or maybe it'll be my fault for not being electrified. I hope all this doesn't sound too occult."

"No more than my own work would sound to you if I talked about it."

"But you don't — and you set me a good example."

"No, no — that wasn't what I meant. I'm really interested in the theatre — not only as a playgoer but — well, for one reason — because of you. So please go on. I wish I knew more about it — what rehearsals are like, how the director functions, and so on."

"Come along and see, some day, if you think you'd enjoy the experience."

"To a rehearsal?"

"Yes. I dare say I could sneak you in." She laughed a little and his questioning look made her add: "I'm laughing to think how impossible that would have been if Paul had been here. One of his inflexible rules — no strangers at rehearsals."

"I can't say I blame him."

"You would, if you'd ever seen him turn somebody out."

"From the look on your face I can see you don't blame him either."

"Not with my heart, because I think I understand him but with my mind I've called him all kinds of names."

The way she said that made him catch his breath, for the words had a beauty that seemed to belong out of their context, as if she were speaking some kind of benediction on a vastly larger matter. Then his aunt came into the room and introductions broke the spell. Aunt Mildred was in her late sixties, obviously though not slavishly devoted to her nephew, a serene good-humoured woman. She had developed the technique of being an unobtrusive hostess without ever accepting the role of mere chaperon, and she and Carey liked each other in an instant way that neither of them took any trouble to conceal.

The dinner, Austen thought, was a definite success. Of course the food and drink were excellent, they always were (another of the advantages of home, or rather of being able to afford a French chef), and the conversation did not flag amongst the three of them. He knew Carey must be enjoying herself, because he could imagine that a stranger meeting her for the first time would not think her unhappy at all, though he himself still caught a darker mood behind her gaiety — not that the gaiety was ever false. It was strange to feel such confidence that he understood her, so that after coffee, when Aunt Mildred excused herself to go to bed early, he hinted at a movie with the near-certainty as well as the hope that she would decline. She said : " Frankly, I'd rather see pictures in the afternoon when I've nothing else to do."

" Good. Then let's take it easy."

They went by elevator to the roof above the sixth floor, where a small secluded garden had been laid out in tubs and boxes. The air wafted the flavour and sounds of the streets, yet it was a pleasant place to relax on a summer evening. When she finally left, not long before midnight, she said warmly : " I *have* enjoyed myself — I like going somewhere without being involved in terrific plans to go somewhere else — I like sitting and talking to someone who doesn't feel it's boring to do just that."

He said : " I hope we're going to meet again — often."

" Oh yes. And don't forget to come to a rehearsal. Not just yet — one of the last would probably be most fun for you. That would be late in August."

" And in the meantime . . . during the hot weather . . . I have a farm in Connecticut — sometimes I invite a few friends there for the week-end — if you'd care to . . . if you like the country . . ."

" I love it. I was born on a farm. So was Paul — but he hated it. That's a strange difference between us — or perhaps between Iowa and Ireland, though I've never seen Iowa."

" Then I'll arrange something quite soon. Not a big party. Do anything — or nothing — swim, dance, play bridge——"

" Which of them do *you* do ? "

" Bridge I rather like, but that won't matter — there'll be others who don't play, and the effort to entertain you will be very slight indeed. For myself, during the daytime I mostly potter about with the man who runs the place for me — sometimes I ride over a few fields and try to think I'm a genuine farmer."

" But you really enjoy it — pottering about like that ? "

" Oh yes, I wouldn't do it otherwise — why should I ? It's like you with a new play — if you didn't like it, you wouldn't feel you had to act in it. . . . May I fix a date, then, and let you know ? We might drive out together."

There were many things that surprised him after she had gone. To begin with, that he had invited her to the farm at all, and also that, in doing so, he hadn't told her the complete truth. He was a little appalled by what faced him now — a reopening of old memories, an ultimatum to grief, arrangements and complications and decisions, the welcome of local people who hadn't seen him for years and would regard his return as evidence that a new stage in his life had been reached. And perhaps it had. In the morning he told Dunne of his intention and actually asked the old man whom he should invite — he was as uninterested as that in all his guests except one. Dunne pondered and spoke a few names. They were not of close friends, for Austen hadn't any, except Dunne himself ; but there were many people he knew fairly well, and liked, and who liked him. After a list had been compiled he said : " I think I'll ask Mrs. Saffron too — she's charming, isn't she ? I could see you were thinking that yourself last night."

" I was indeed, sir."

Austen looked up gratefully. He wondered, at that early stage, how he would have acted had his butler disapproved

.   .   .   .

The farm was about two hours' drive from the city and a dozen miles inland. A house dating from Revolutionary times formed a nucleus that had been cleverly added to there was a large barn where dances and parties could be held, as well as a group of modern guest cottages. The land sloped from the main building to a stream, widened in one place to make a swimming-pool that seemed a part of the natural landscape. Trees fringed a formal garden, and there were woods beyond, rising to a ridge. The whole property covered six or seven hundred acres, most of it tilled; there was a second farmhouse, not so old and much more practical, in which Grainger lived. Grainger, like Dunne, had worked for Austen's father.

When Austen arrived with Carey towards evening on the last Friday in July he braced himself for the shock of seeing again the place where he had been so happy, but the shock was not what he had expected; it struck, but without the leaden bruise; it was more a sharpness that made him specially sensitive to Carey at his side. " Well, here we are," he said, as they drove up. He hoped she would catch, as he did, the beauty of the old brick in the sunset glow, and when she remarked on it, as surely as if he had pointed it out, an unbelievable pleasure filled him. They left the car, Dunne (who had been there since morning) helping them and taking the bags; the familiar entrance and hall beyond faced him without challenge. He had thought he would remember Fran; but instead he could think only of Carey.

Several other guests had already arrived; more were expected later. They were not celebrities, though not nonentities either — the Peter Rushmores, he an architect, had probably the best-known name. There were no brokers or financiers. Austen did not like to talk his own shop, but other people's interested him — he had a wistful curiosity about such things as how to run a woman's page, or excavate for a sub-basement, or cook clam chowder. All the people he liked enough to have at the farm were working people, in an extended sense; it was not that he did not care for drones, but that drones were usually the kind of people he did not care for. And perhaps because the people he did care for were attractive and hard-working, they were often successful in their own fields — successful enough for them not to think of him primarily as a person 'worth knowing'. He was, indeed, immensely wealthier than they were, and quick to help them in any financial emergency (there had been some lately, since the stock-market collapse), but he liked their own success to guarantee him against the fear that their friendship could have any ulterior motive. To this extent, wealth had been a restrictive influence in his life; it had made him cautious in affection, not because he was afraid of being sponged on, but because he shrank from an emotional investment that might turn out humiliatingly. In a profound sense he knew the corrupting power of wealth, and on a scale impossible to convey to anyone outside his own business; he knew that not only individuals but whole classes and generations and empires could catch the Midas infection, and it was his belief (private, like most of his beliefs) that America in the 'twenties had been so infected. Apart from the personal havoc which was tragic and obvious around him, he could not regret what had been happening in Wall Street since the previous October; but he would never say so, because his own position as either Cassandra or moralist would be clearly impossible. Once again his impulse to be secretive was geared to the likelihood that few people would understand him. On perhaps the worst day in Wall Street's history a frenzied speculator had somehow pierced his line of clerks and secretaries and demanded face-to-face how he could reconcile it with his conscience to profit out of national disaster. Austen must have been disturbed or he would not have replied, as he did: " The national disaster is not that prices should now fall, but that they should ever have been forced so high. To that disaster I did not contribute — on the other hand, my own operations tended to prevent them from going higher. And today, my friend while you have been adding to what you call the disaster by selling, I have been supporting prices by buying back. The fact that I personally profited is immaterial." It was the only time (and an ill-chosen one) that he attempted a logical indeed a classic defence of his own function, and the reason (illogically) was that the troubles of other people did affec him, and all the more because even to say so would have seemed hypocritical.

That week-end at the farm made proof, if he had ever needed it, that Carey could come close to his heart and mind if she wished. Whether this was likely he could not yet decide. But he guessed that her husband's return (in September, she had said) would set limits to whatever had not been accomplished before.

"You must be looking forward to it," he said, as they inspected the stables and milking-sheds that Sunday morning.

"Oh yes," she answered eagerly, and then added, as if she were having to think it out : " Yes, I think so."

"Only that ? "

She laughed. " It's really quite a lot. I couldn't ever really explain just how I *do* feel about Paul."

He took that as a closure of the subject till she went on : " It's strange — I'm quite happy without him so long as I know he's happy. I don't miss him, exactly, and I know when he does come home what a to-do there'll be — everything upside down, the whole of my life in an uproar. He *consumes* people. It's probably good for me, though — I'm naturally rather lazy."

"How's his film progressing ? "

"All right, I suppose. He doesn't write much about it."

"Don't you ask him ? "

"Yes, and he doesn't answer."

"So he doesn't answer, and you don't miss him, and you don't really want your life to be in an uproar, and yet . . . there must be an ' and yet '."

"There is . . . but I don't know what it is."

"It might be love."

"Yes, it might, mightn't it ? I expect we all love differently."

They walked some way while he told her about the farm, the way he had acquired it, and his plans for development. Apparently it had been only half arable land at first, and he had made a point of reclaiming more and more each year, clearing, liming, and fertilizing ; he had taken a scientific interest in soil conservation and had experimented with different kinds of crop rotation. Everything that modern farm management could do was still in progress, for he had good men working for him; but the way he talked of it somehow conveyed a revival of his own interest after a long interval, and he could guess that she sensed this. So he said abruptly: " I misled you when I asked you here. I gave you an impression that these week-ends were a normal thing for me. Actually this is the first time I've been here since my wife died."

" Yes, the Rushmores told me."

" You must have thought I hadn't been very frank."

" I don't think it matters, now that I know."

" I'm glad you know. Fran and I were so very happy."

" I was told that too."

" I didn't think I'd ever have the nerve to face all the memories — places we did this and that, the walks we took — Sunday morning walks just like this. . . . My boy Norris comes home from school soon. Will you spend another week-end here and get to know him? "

" I'd like to very much."

He took her arm. " Good — because we must make the most of our time, mustn't we, before your play opens? "

" Yes, I'll be pretty busy then, one way and another."

He was fairly sure that the same interpretation of that was in both their minds.

.   .   .   .   .   .

She visited the farm again in August, but this time he had no one else there except Norris and Aunt Mildred. He had expected Norris to like Carey, and the boy did, but it somewhat amazed him that she seemed to enjoy the meeting for its own sake. He himself was devoted to his son, but he found it hard to establish contact with a somewhat difficult eight-year-old, and he had set the age of fifteen in his mind as a date from which he and Norris could really begin to understand each other. And of course it would be easier still, later on. He looked forward most of all to a young man, home from Harvard, discovering his father as an equal.

" He's so friendly and intelligent," Carey said. " It's fun to talk to him."

" Because you know how."

" Well, most children are actors, so we have that in common. . . . Paul used to say he could make an actor of any child under ten — and *until* he was ten."

" Did . . . does Paul like children ? "

" I think he would have, if we'd had any. Whenever he directed children in a play he was like a rather sinister Santa Claus, if you can imagine such a thing. They were fascinated."

" As you were too."

" Me ? Oh no, I wasn't taken in for a moment."

" I meant that you must have been fascinated in some kind of way — when you first met him. . . . A man so . . . so remarkable. . . ."

" Oh, *then* ! Yes, I was seventeen and he came to Dublin on business. He was the first brilliant man I ever knew. And the *most* brilliant. He always has been. I only wish he'd be brilliant now about the new play."

" It's worrying you ? "

" Not exactly. It's just that I'm not excited enough. One ought to be excited about a new play."

" Or else not be in it at all ? "

" But the part's made for me — written for me, in fact. I don't know what there is wrong — maybe nothing. I expect I'll be all right on the night. That comes under the heading of famous last words."

" You don't get nervous ? "

" Heavens, yes. Paul does too — he can lose ten pounds during rehearsals. And that doesn't do him any harm either."

" He's a big man ? "

" *Big ?* " The word seemed to amuse her. " Well, he's . . . I think I've got a photograph."

She opened her handbag and found a snapshot. " I

took this several years ago — it's good because it doesn't flatter like the professional ones."

Paul was unlike anything Austen had in the least expected, and from then on, in a curious way, he thought of Carey a little differently.

He said : " A personality — one can tell that. . . . And what a pretty garden ! "

" It is, isn't it ? Only a small place, near Stroudsburg, not really as beautiful as here, but I used to love it."

" You don't go there any more ? "

" We had to sell — or rather, I had to — last year. I lost a lot in the market and I didn't think I could keep up two homes."

" Didn't you once tell me Paul sold out at the top ? "

" Oh yes, *he* did. He was smart — or else lucky."

He gripped her arm. " I'll tell you one way he's lucky, and that's to have you. . . . I hope he realizes it."

" But I'm lucky too. I'd never have been successful on the stage without him."

" You're very modest to say that. Does he agree with you ? "

" You bet he does. *He's* not modest."

She laughed, and he had again a feeling which only now he was able to put into words for his own private consideration later : that Paul did not make her happy, but that in some incurable way she was able to take delight in him.

. . . .

She had scored such a definite hit with Norris that it was obvious to assume another meeting soon. Austen was pleased on the boy's behalf, but he was also glad for himself because it meant a further stage in their own advancing friendship. He knew by now that he was very much in love with Carey.

They met often during the weeks that followed. She visited the farm at week-ends, when there were sometimes, but not always, outside guests ; she dined frequently at the house in the East Sixties, where there was usually only Aunt

168

Mildred with them. He realized that she found, both at the farm and at the house, some kind of comfort that appealed to her. As the rehearsals for the new play got under way, he guessed that what he could offer, if nothing else, was actually a refuge from the theatre — a place where she could not be reached on business, where she need not talk or even think about it if she wished not to. He had once called for her at her own small apartment, and during the short time he was there had heard her end of several long telephone conversations; they had sounded to him as if the play were in trouble of some kind, though when he hinted this she said lightly that it was no more than usual. But she had seemed harassed and glad to escape.

One evening she arrived at his house with a look that did not wear off after the first drink. He gave her time to tell him anything amiss that might have happened, and when she kept up the effort to talk gaily he asked what was the matter.

" The matter ? . . . Why ? . . . So I really *am* a bad actress ? "

" It's because you know you don't have to act with me, and that makes you half-act."

" Oh, well, if that's the case, I'll tell you, though it's not startling. I mean, it's the sort of thing that's happened before — and doubtless will again."

" Trouble with the show ? "

" *My* show. . . . No, not particularly. I had a letter from Paul this morning."

He did not reply, and was surprised to find how fast his heart was beating.

She went on : " He's in some kind of a mess with that film."

" Serious ? "

" I don't know. It's hard to tell from his letter what exactly has been happening, but he seems to have had trouble with the people who're putting up the money. They're trying to dispossess him — or something like that. . . . *Can* you be dispossessed of a film you've made yourself ? "

" I should think so. It's like any other property."

" Well, of course to Paul it isn't. He didn't mind when I sold the house in the country — in fact, it was he who suggested it — but his *work* . . . that's different. It's like an artist having his own canvases seized for debt."

" That could probably happen too, in certain circumstances. Is the film finished ? "

" He says it is, but they want a different ending and he refuses to make one. I suppose it depends on the kind of contract. . . . Well, let's not have it spoil our evening. I didn't intend to tell you — after all, why should you be burdened with someone else's worries ? "

He said : " If I had to answer that, I'd ask why you should be burdened by a rather difficult little problem child who doesn't happen to be your own."

" I see. Your son and my husband . . . you'd class them both as problems ? "

" Aren't they ? "

" But I like Norris, and I don't think you'd like Paul. Unless he happened to be in one of his charming moods."

" You think I'd find him irresistible then ? "

" I've known it to happen."

" Does his letter ask your advice ? "

" I'm afraid he's had that — I told him at the outset to make sure of a good lawyer. I wish I could help him, but what can I do — from here ? And if I went over to try to straighten things out — I can't, of course — I'd probably find that the people he's up against have a case."

" You've known that happen too ? "

" Yes."

" Tell me . . . well, no, it's little use even discussing things at this range. . . . Would you like another drink ? "

" Yes, I would. And I *can* talk of something else, I assure you. I'm not going to worry."

For the rest of the evening it seemed that she didn't, or perhaps she was only keeping a promise not to ; they talked of other subjects and in some ways their conversation had never been livelier. Aunt Mildred, before she went up to bed, even commented on Carey's high spirits — how well she was looking, evidently the week-ends at the farm agreed with her and so on. Later, when they were alone in the library, Austen said : " I don't want to intrude, but I have certain contacts in Germany . . . people who could probably find out the facts about Paul's situation . . . strictly for ourselves — Paul wouldn't even need to know it was being done. Would you like me to write to them ? "

She seemed touched by his offer, then amused by it. " You're so tactful — you say Paul wouldn't even need to know about it. As if he'd care."

" Well, so much the better. Just an outside and impartial report. Until we have that there's nothing else can be done."

" I never thought there was. It's kind of you, though, to suggest writing to your . . . contacts. They're not private detectives, by any chance ? "

He wondered what was in her mind to have said that. " No, just financial people, quite respectable, but they have a good nose for other people's affairs."

He cabled that night, after she had gone, and for ten days there was no reply except an acknowledgment ; nor did she hear again from Paul. She told him that such a gap in her husband's letter-writing need not be of any significance ; he was alive and well, she knew that much from his regular letters to his mother. More and more Austen was getting acquainted with the structure of her life, and Paul's mother was clearly a part of it. He was reluctant to put personal questions, but he did ask her once if these letters to the old lady contained any fresh news about his business troubles.

She answered : " Oh no, and they wouldn't be likely to. She only gets *good* news. He adores her — she's the last person he'd worry if things were going wrong."

A few days later Austen received a long communication whose contents made him postpone rather than expedite his next meeting with Carey. He had much to think about and decide. When he had done so he invited her to the farm for a week-end. On their usual Sunday morning walk

Grainger was with them at first, discussing crops and animals ; then when they were alone, Austen began with no preamble : " I have some information about Paul. He's in the midst of a legal mix-up, and he does have a lawyer, of course, but I'm afraid — as you guessed — he hasn't got too good a case."

" They can't put him in prison if he loses it, can they ? "

" Oh no, it's a purely civil action. . . . Why, what makes you . . . ? "

He paused, reconsidering the question as too personal, but she answered without reluctance : " He once got into trouble in England over some money he'd borrowed to stage a play."

" What happened ? "

" The judge said he didn't think he'd actually intended to defraud anyone . . . and anyhow, by that time a play I was in was making money so we could repay the amount."

" I can see you've had your difficulties."

" Yes . . . but after that Paul left all money affairs in my hands — that is, until recently. What sort of people is he fighting ? "

" A few Berlin business men who're much like other business men — they don't like to lose money."

" First of all, though, Paul spent his own money."

" Yes, and to be fair, he seems to have been just as extravagant with that."

" How about the film itself ? Is it good ? "

" My informant didn't say. It's probably the last thing anybody's wondering about till the lawsuit is over — except you and Paul."

" He's not wondering. He *knows*. He told me it was good."

" Then why did you ask, Carey — unless you think he could be wrong ? "

She suddenly put her hand to her eyes. " Yes, why *did* I ask ? He told me, and if I ever lose that kind of faith in him, I lose it in myself . . . perhaps that's what's been happening to me lately."

" *Carey!* "

She had a puzzled look. " It's true, though. I don't seem to be able to act any more."

" Are you serious ? "

" Yes, that's the trouble. After all, it's a comedy, and if I'm serious I'm no help." She began to laugh, then. " Perhaps it's only temporary, till I get used to a new situation. It's odd — when I was a girl I had ambition to be a *great* actress, which was absurd, because I haven't it in me. When Paul came along he soon convinced me of that, but on the other hand he did make me a pretty big success — he saw *something* in me and developed it more than I could ever have imagined or hoped for. But in a way I surrendered everything in the process — even ambition. I didn't *need* ambition, with him around — his was enough for both of us, and of course everything he did included me — until lately. So now I have to get hold of myself, I suppose."

From that moment something that Austen had already dreamed of became in his mind a possibility to be handled with care and calm and infinite patience. And to do this, to envisage the remote chance and guide it, partly following it, to the safe haven of happening — this was a task for which few minds were better equipped.

What he already dreamed was that Carey should some day divorce Paul and marry him. But that, in itself, was not enough, or even desirable, unless it came about in a positive way — not only by her own realization that he, Austen, could make her happier than Paul had, but by her own desire for that extra happiness. Mere disillusionment with Paul would not perform the miracle ; Austen had no desire to capture her on any kind of rebound. And yet, at the right moment, disillusionment might help. He had given the matter much thought, and he believed he would know the right moment if and when it came — or at least he would know when it had not yet come. For this reason he did not tell her more than a fraction of what he had learned about Paul. His German informants had done a thorough job, but the weapon as handed him was too clumsy ; he shrank from the practice of emotional blackmail, even if it would work. But beyond his fastidiousness was a sense of timing as subtle, in its way, as an actor's. It was not the first time he had had to judge when the day was rainy enough to make necessary the disclosure of a hidden reserve. There was no such urgency — yet, and on Paul's return the whole thing might even have to be postponed indefinitely. In that case he, Austen, would be thankful for not having precipitated the kind of crisis that would make his own future relationship with Carey impossible. She would have time ; indeed, it was hard to realize she was still so young. Perhaps it was self-flattery that he always thought of her as older than she was ; or perhaps it was the one thing Paul had done — unwittingly, unforgivably, yet fortunately — for his successor. He had *aged* her.

After dinner that evening Austen said : " I expect you've been wondering how we can help Paul. How would you like me to buy an interest in the picture ? "

" *You* ? "

" It wouldn't be so far out of my line."

" But how would it help ? "

He smiled. " You were upset this afternoon — that's why I didn't go into details then. As I size up the situation, there are a group of business men who originally had faith in Paul. All they want now is to cut a loss and be rid of him. Specifically, they want to bring in another director to change the ending of the picture — to make it more commercial, I suppose. That's what the legal sparring is all about. But I've an idea that if someone were to come along and offer to buy their investment at so many cents on the dollar — and perhaps not so very many at that — they'd jump at it."

" It mightn't be a profitable investment for you."

" Listen. . . . You said the picture must be good because Paul told you so. I'll take your word for it, just as you take his."

" But I meant good artistically."

" Let me keep my cynical belief that there can be money even in art."

" But how — if you did buy — how would it help *him* ? "

"By ending all the legal tangle, with him left in full artistic control, because naturally I shouldn't interfere. It's not, by the way, a very costly picture, by American standards. When I said he'd been extravagant, I meant relatively."

"Austen . . . it's terribly generous of you, but I can't see why you should do it."

"I won't, unless I can get a bargain, so don't call it generous. Anyhow, there's no harm in having my people over there feel things out. And in the meantime, not a word in your letters to Paul. This kind of negotiation has to be done rather secretly. I hope he won't mind."

"Oh, I'm not worrying about that. He'll be happy enough as long as you leave him alone."

"I'll leave him alone, all right."

A couple of weeks later they had news for each other. They met at his New York house and he told her as casually as he could that he had bought the film. "It was pretty much as I thought — which means that the price was low. So low, indeed, that I really don't see how I can lose."

"Then why did they sell?"

"I don't know, but if you want me to guess I'd say that Paul's been such a headache they're glad to get out at any price."

"That's possible."

She seemed so disinterested that he waited for her to reveal why. After a silence he went on: "You don't seem very excited."

"I'm sorry. I'd already heard about it from Paul. I had a letter this morning."

"Oh, I see. And what's his attitude?"

She shook her head as if in despair at being able to convey it. "He's unpredictable — I'd have thought he'd be glad, or at least that he wouldn't care . . . but the kind of letter he sent me . . . about some Wall Street millionaire buying the picture over his head — you'd think he'd been insulted."

"Perhaps he doesn't realize yet that I don't intend to interfere. When he does he may feel differently."

"I doubt it. Now that the picture's finished and the

trouble's all over, I'll bet the whole thing's already half out of his mind. He's like that. . . . He's not coming back just yet, by the way."

" No ? "

" He'd planned it for next month, but now he says he can't get away till later in the year."

" That's too bad . . . for you."

" Yes, it's disappointing, isn't it ? But the reason he gives is funny — he says he's working on an idea for another picture, only this time it'll be all his own and he's not going to have interference from anybody."

She began to laugh, rather wildly, at that. He came over to her chair and touched her shoulder. He had never felt more tempted to put the issue to some kind of test, but caution prevailed. He said : " I'm glad you're not upset." (Although he wondered if she were.) " Personally I'm looking forward to seeing his picture. I've asked them to ship me a print and I'll find some place we can have it run for us. Now tell me about your own affairs. How's the play going ? "

" It's shaping up. We open for a trial week in New Haven after Labour Day."

" Then I'd better fix a time for coming to one of your rehearsals."

" Yes, if you still want to. I thought you'd forgotten. You might find it interesting."

He did indeed, for it was a completely novel experience to sit in an almost empty theatre and watch a play without benefit of scenery, adequate lighting, or audience response. As an outsider he was struck at first by the improvisations — the stage manager's ' ting-a-ling ' to indicate a telephone call, the way in which non-existent properties were assumed to be touchable and movable by the actors. It was as fascinating as the inside of a piano to a little boy who sees it tuned for the first time, and there was enough of the little boy in Austen to keep him preoccupied for at least ten minutes. After that he began to listen with an effort to judge the play as a whole. Never before had he taken a deliberately critical mind to a theatre ; usually, like most patrons, he went to be entertained, and either was or wasn't, with no particular need to decide why. He realized he had no specialized critical equipment, still less any experience that would enable him to discount the conditions of a rehearsal. Yet the intelligence to know what he lacked was itself a sort of equipment, and on this basis he found himself doubtful, half-way through the first act, that the play was good enough, and sure, half-way through the second act, that it wasn't. By ' good enough ' he meant, modestly, the kind of play he would have put money into had he been the kind of speculator who backs plays at all. That was the only way he felt qualified to make a decision, and fortunately he hadn't to make it. Later he privately decided that the play's only chance of success was in the stratosphere of some miraculous carnival mood, if the latter should take hold of Carey ; there was no sign of it yet, or even that it was possible. At least, however, he would give it no discouragement. So he told her, when she met him afterwards, that he had enjoyed himself and thought she might have another winner.

" You're very sweet, Austen. Paul was like that too — a play before it opened was always going to be the biggest hit that ever was. Salvation by faith, I suppose. But it didn't prevent him from taking the actors aside and telling them separately how bad they were."

The reception at New Haven was more favourable than Austen had expected ; the house was sold out and applause, especially for Carey, considerable. Yet he returned to New York the next day with a strong feeling that the theatre was another of the things he must rescue her from. His inside glimpse into the lives of actors had fascinated him, but without enchantment ; he had been chiefly impressed by the strain and uncertainties of their work, the last-minute anxieties and confusion, the wear and tear on the nervous fabric.

The New York opening also went better than he had expected, but by then he had come to expect so little that this was faint praise, and the applause seemed almost an effort by an audience that liked Carey to make amends for not having laughed enough at the play. He went to her dressing-room afterwards and joined in the general chorus of congratulation; he felt that nobody was sincere, yet that the play had not failed so conspicuously as to make insincerity mercifully impossible. He was sensitive to atmosphere, even in an unfamiliar world, and excused himself from an after-the-show party chiefly for the reason that he doubted how long he could match the professional make-believers in their make-believe. Carey understood, or he thought she did; she seemed relieved to let him go. The next day, calling at his house, she confirmed that the party had been a progressively dismal affair, culminating in the reading of the notices in the morning papers. He had read them himself at the breakfast-table, and they had scarcely surprised him, except by the extent to which some confirmed his own personal yet hesitant opinions.

She said, sinking into a chair: "Well, Austen, there's one consolation — now the bad news is out, we can all relax."

"How long do you think it will run?"

"After those notices? A week . . . maybe."

"It's a pity . . . all that effort . . . time . . . hopes . . ."

"To say nothing of money. Fortunately it wasn't mine. . . . Oh, dear, why did we all kid each other? If only someone had had the guts to say — 'Look, this is junk — what are we going ahead with it for?' Nobody really believed in the thing from the start — *I* didn't — I don't think you did, either, after that rehearsal. But you were too polite — or else you didn't want to be the wet blanket. It's incredible — the way we all sleep-walked into it — why didn't somebody wake up?"

"Why didn't *you* wake up, Carey?"

"That's a fair question. I suppose the truth is that once rehearsals begin it's always a question of jobs — you don't like to do anything that throws people out of work, especially these days. And the author had written hits before — he

kept saying this would be another. Maybe he believed it
. . . you never can go by what an author thinks of his
own work, Paul always says."

" Do you think with Paul as director it could have been a
success ? "

" He'd have got far more out of me and everyone else,
that's certain. And the play isn't so much worse than
others that have been hits. . . . And yet I'm doubtful.
Somehow I've an idea Paul's neatest trick would have come
when he'd first read the script — he'd have said *No*. And
then he'd have telephoned the author. Believe me, that was
something to listen to — Paul saying no to an author."

" You mean he was brutal ? "

" Usually he was charming, and especially on the telephone. He would talk one way and look at me another. He
didn't really *like* authors, but he knew they were a bit
necessary in the theatre business."

" It would have saved him trouble if he'd written plays
himself."

" Oh yes, he tried, but he used to say it cramped him to
think theatrically in terms of mere words. Isn't that a
beautiful way to admit there was something he couldn't
do ? "

She laughed, and her cheeks were flushed ; she did not
look as if the fate of the play were distressing her much.
But perhaps it was something else, for he had often noticed
that when she talked about Paul and especially when she
reminisced about him, she could launch herself into an
almost hilarious mood, as if he were still a core of pleasantry,
if not of pleasure, in her heart.

She said, sighing : " Oh, what a cool calm house this is,
Austen. . . . It's such a relief to be here."

" I always hoped you'd find it that. What are you going
to do when the play closes ? "

" Look for another, I suppose."

" It wouldn't do you any harm to take a rest."

" Sure, it would be fun to be unemployed if I didn't have
to earn a living."

" You don't have to worry about earning one immediately."

" Oh no, I'm not quite on the rocks. And perhaps Paul's film will make a fortune." Then she evidently recollected the facts and added, with some embarrassment : " A fortune for you and success for him — that'll be all fair and square." She seemed still more embarrassed at that, as if the joke had made it worse instead of better. " By the way, when are we going to see it ? You said you were having a print shipped over."

Expecting her to be unhappy about the play, he had planned to postpone giving her the latest news about Paul, but now he thought he might as well. He said : " I'm afraid there may be some delay."

" Oh ? Why ? "

" Paul . . . it seems . . . isn't pleased with me for having intervened — as I thought — on his behalf."

" So I gathered from that last letter he wrote me, which was weeks ago. The Hidden Hand of Wall Street, Art versus Dollars — it had some ringing phrases. . . . Anything happened since ? "

" He evidently likes litigation."

" What makes you say that ? "

" He's already changed his lawyer and started suit against me."

" Against *you* ? What on earth for ? "

" He disputes my title to the property."

" You mean the film ? But *can* he ? "

" Naturally he can dispute anything he likes, but an honest lawyer would tell him when it's no use. Apparently his original lawyer *was* honest, so he had to find another."

" Oh dear, I'm so very sorry."

" Carey, it isn't *your* fault."

" I wasn't apologizing. Sorry can mean — sorrow . . . can't it ? That's what I feel."

And suddenly she looked it. He sat on the arm of her chair and tried to comfort her. She soon controlled herself and pressed his hand. " Oh, Austen, don't worry about me. There's nothing you can do."

"Carey, I know your trouble. I think I've known it ever since I met you on the boat. Or part of it. Carey . . . may I be very frank — even at the risk of putting my nose in where I shouldn't? You're a success, that goes without saying — one flop does nothing to disprove it — and I've admired you on the stage just as thousands of others have . . . but since I've got to know you personally I've admired you . . . so much more . . . in other ways . . . that . . . that . . . please remember this is none of my business unless you wish it to be . . . I've wondered . . . lately . . . is it *enough* for you? Do you have a sense of vocation that makes everything worth while? You're so happy at the farm — doing simple things — talking to Norris, having a quiet time . . . you somehow don't fit in with all the scurry and bustle of stage life."

"I wonder."

"Of course you're the first actress I've ever known, I admit that."

"Yes — and this is the first play you've ever been on the inside of, isn't it? That's a pity, because it really was exceptional. Most plays have a chance — or at least you genuinely think they have — you wait for the opening night like judgment day, but not like the electric chair. From the first reading to last night's fiasco the prisoner marched confidently from the condemned cell to the death house. . . . I've never known anything quite like that before. So please don't generalize from your one play — or from your one actress."

"I wish my one actress would take a long vacation — a year at least to rid herself of all kinds of trouble."

"*All* kinds?"

"It ought to be possible, if you let yourself face the future realistically."

"I'm glad we've stopped talking of me as *herself*." She began to laugh. "Like an Abbey play. . . . And what kind of future do you think — realistically — I have to face?"

He said tensely: "That's a straight question, but I can't answer it without talking about Paul."

" Oh, talk about him, I don't mind. *I* talk about him to you."

" Carey . . . do you really love him ? "

" I've told you I don't *miss* him — except his better judgment in saying no."

" So you're not really upset by the delay in his return ? "

" I'm upset by the mess he seems to be getting himself into over there."

" Yes, I know, but if a cable came now that he was arriving in New York tonight — how would you feel ? "

" Oh, my goodness — *horrible* — because I'd hate him to see the play."

" But apart from that ? "

" It's very hard for me to think of Paul apart from plays."

" That's been your life together — principally ? "

" Yes — you could say so. Principally. Except for a short time — at first."

" Then we're back to what I said before. It isn't enough. You've gone without a great deal."

" Oh, I'm sure I have."

" You ought to have had children of your own."

" I don't know whose fault that was — Paul's or mine."

It seemed to him an answer to a question he wouldn't have presumed to ask. He went on, after a silence : " Carey, it all boils down to this . . . how long are you willing to endure a situation that can't make you really happy — your nature being what it is ? "

" Is there an alternative ? "

" Of course."

She said, almost flippantly : " Oh, you mean divorce him ? Sure, I could do that — he's probably been unfaithful with somebody or other . . . but what exactly would be the point ? "

In a single sentence she had blunted the weapon he had furbished for some possible use at a clinching moment. He knew now it would be anti-climax to give her certain facts about Paul; worse than anti-climax, it would recoil ignominiously on himself. He was devoutly thankful he had made good taste the better part of wisdom.

He said simply : " The point, Carey, is that I'd want to marry you if you were free."

She looked up with interest rather than surprise or enthusiasm, then exclaimed, still flippantly : " You *would*, Austen ? Why, you've never even made love to me ! "

" That isn't because I . . ."

" I know, I know, you've been so careful not to spoil things — I'm sure that's how you've thought of it, and that's why it's so funny when you talk about my nature being what it is. You just don't know my nature."

" You think I don't ? "

" I'm sure you don't. Or else you do, and you've been a bit afraid of it."

" Carey . . ." He took her into his arms, yet amidst his joy, the overwhelming joy of finding himself not rebuffed, he was aware of her laughter limiting as well as inviting him.

" Oh, Austen . . . you're very sweet not to have understood me for so long. That's why I'm laughing, not because I'm not just as serious as you are."

.   .   .   .   .   .

The play came off after four nights, and Austen was sheerly delighted. Now that he had entered on this new relationship with Carey, everything else was in order ; he was happy again, after an interval of years which, in retrospect, seemed like a tunnel from which he had just emerged. He had had affairs during that period, not very many, but they had all been rigidly circumscribed, if not furtive, and never had any of them led him to the most abstract contemplation of marriage. But now, with Carey, the fulfilment of a desire reinforced the ambition he had had (he could now realize) from the beginning.

They went to the farm and found all the familiar things doubly enjoyable in a new emotional context — the walks and rides, the pottering about, the first fires of autumn, a long day's drive to the Catskills to catch the trees in deepest crimson. One brief conversation, at a moment when both were in a mood for practicality, had settled the future as far ahead as could be ; it was understood that she would ask Paul for a divorce. Austen did not verify if and when she had done so, and not till a month had passed did he bring up the matter at all. She said then that she had written, but that Paul had not replied. It was like him, of course, not to write for long periods — or perhaps, if he were on a trip somewhere, he might not yet have received her letter. She said she would write again, and Austen wondered, pre-occupyingly but not urgently, why she had not thought to do that already.

Nor did they ever discuss whether she would retire permanently from the stage or merely take a long vacation. Austen sensed how unwise it would be to mix this question with the so much more important one of their lives together ; if he could make her happy with him, he felt fairly sure she would have a strong impulse, not so much to surrender a career, as to cling to the kind of life which a career would prohibit. He was always ready to barter the shadow of intention for the substance of likelihood. Out of her very happiness he aimed to build a defence against whatever lure the stage could exert ; he would make her life comfortable but not placid, exciting enough yet without strain. He not only loved her, but was a connoisseur of qualities he had found in her, and this gave his love an aspect of guardianship.

As for his feeling for Paul, it was hard for him to make up a cool mind, since he so much resented the harm he believed Paul to have done. Yet because Carey usually seemed amused when she talked about Paul, he knew he must never invite her to share his serious condemnation ; he must pretend that he too thought Paul a forgivable genius, whom one could no more enchain by marriage than escape from by divorce. For she had said to him reflectively when they had first discussed the future : " I don't quite know what Paul and I had in common — it certainly didn't make a marriage." He had heard that with joy, especially the past tense of it. But then she had continued, less happily for him :

184

" So what it did make, if anything, perhaps a divorce can't take away." He had quelled his mind's retort that he hoped Paul and all Paul meant to her would be taken away, eventually and finally, not only by legal instrument but by the passage of time and the growth of compensating joys.

She kept up her visits to Paul's mother, and he did not suggest that she make any change in this. He asked her once if Paul and his mother still corresponded regularly and she said yes, just as usual, once a week, like clockwork and about as interestingly, if one judged from the excerpts that Mrs. Saffron read aloud when she visited her.

" It seems to prove, though, that he must have received both your recent letters, so that if he doesn't reply to them it's only because he doesn't choose to."

" Yes, probably."

A few weeks later came Thanksgiving, the second since Paul had left America. The previous year she had visited Mrs. Saffron, but had found her in such large company, all eager to finish dinner and play pinochle, that she almost wondered if the old lady had invited her just to demonstrate how little need she had of filial duty. This year Carey saw no reason to repeat the experience, apart from her own desire to spend the day with Austen, but she thought it polite to announce the change in advance and as tactfully as possible. She came to Austen's house direct from this encounter, and her face, flushed and a little agitated, told him at once that something had happened. He took her into the library and knew better than to start a cross-examination.

She sat by the fire and drank a glass of sherry before ceasing to chatter about unimportant things. His house seemed to give her calmness whenever she needed it. Then she exclaimed : " Oh, what a terrifying person, Austen ! No wonder Paul always capered with her. *Capered*, yes. I can see now he had to do *something* in self-defence."

Austen poured a drink for himself and threw a log on the fire. " Does she mind if you don't eat with her on Thursday ? " he asked with deliberate matter-of-factness.

" Oh no, that's all right. She's the centre of a sort of

salon — she won't be alone. But we got on to much more dangerous topics than Thanksgiving. . . . She's *incredible*, Austen. She's been writing to Paul about us for weeks."

" *What?* "

" Writing to him . . . all the time. . . ."

" You'd better tell me how all this cropped up."

" Yes . . . quite a scene it was, believe me. I've never pretended I didn't know you, but since she didn't mention you to me till today, I never did to her . . . yet all the time, it seems, she's been gathering information — gossip, I suppose — and sending it on to Paul. In fact they've been having a long correspondence together — about you — and me. She knew, for instance, that I'd asked Paul to give me a divorce."

He said, in a clipped voice that was a further attempt to suppress his own tensions : " Does she know whether he will ? "

" She hates me, so she's in favour of it . . . but she wants Paul to bring the suit himself and she'd like him to make all kinds of accusations. Involving you, I'm afraid."

" Except for your sake, Carey, I wouldn't give a damn. But never mind what *she* wants — what's he going to *do* ? — that's the issue."

" Nothing."

" Nothing ? . . . *Nothing ?* . . . How can anyone do nothing?" He added, taking her hand : " I'm sorry, I really must keep my temper."

She nodded in sympathy. " I know. Paul always had the most subtle ways of being a nuisance."

" It's not subtle and I'd call it worse than a nuisance."

She did not reply to that, and after a silence he continued : " So he just won't give an answer at all . . . is that what it amounts to ? "

" No, he's been quite frank in a letter to his mother. He says I can go through any legal procedure I want, but *he* won't do anything. He won't contest it, or agree to it, or acknowledge it, or discuss it with me or anyone else — he won't accept or sign any papers or answer letters — he simply won't make a move of any kind." She began to smile and there came from her a sound that was amazingly like a giggle, but her face had lost its flush and was now very pale. She was clearly under a strain perhaps as great as his own.

He said, in a level voice: " Well, I think we can handle all that if we put it in the right hands. The main point is that he won't contest — unless he changes his mind."

" Oh, I don't think he'll do that, from the mood he's in. . . . He's different from his mother, although in so many ways she's made him what he is. He turned down flat her idea of accusing me . . . of us . . . of anything. I saw the letter. I was surprised at the tone of it — I don't believe he ever squashed her quite so utterly before. He doesn't really want to harm people."

" Carey, he couldn't harm *us* if he tried. Take my word that he couldn't — he's in no position to — he's . . . oh well, so long as you realize that, let's not argue. It's something, of course, that he isn't as vindictive as his mother, but I don't think I'll express any gratitude. I'm not one of those disappointed authors whom he makes a specialty of charming."

He would have regretted and apologized for the sarcasm had he not seen her smiling again, in the way that hurt him immeasurably, yet which he did not dare comment on, much less rebuke her for. She said: " I'd like to see him *trying* to charm you, though," — and then continued, as if eased by the thought: " She showed me the letter. She was so angry I don't think she realized that some of it was what she wouldn't have liked me to know. I mean, the part where Paul told her off. . . . I didn't think he was capable of it. . . . Imagine, though, she'd been storing all this up for weeks — never a word about it all the times I've been meeting her . . . till today."

He could well imagine it, being schooled in such reticences himself, but he answered: " Put the whole thing out of your mind, Carey, if you can. It's just a lawyer's problem from now on. So long as we both get what we want in the end, and we know what that is, the details aren't of any consequence."

"But some of them are so funny, Austen — such as when he said in the letter that every true Catholic would applaud his attitude. Actually, yes — these were his words! He isn't a Catholic, and nor is she, and it's due to him, probably, that I'm not much of one myself, any more — yet he can talk about every true Catholic applauding him! You'd think he was leading the Counter-Reformation or something! Just how important does he think he and his attitudes are?"

Even though the mockery was against Paul, and quite scathing, he could not share the spirit of it, because there was nothing in what he knew of Paul to impel him to any kind of laughter. He said, bringing her back to seriousness: "Well, after what happened this afternoon, you certainly won't want to see his mother again."

"Probably not. I'm not good at having rows — they upset me. That's why I'm a bit upset now."

"I understand that, Carey. I hate rows too. I never want to see again a person I've quarrelled with."

"And I hate to quarrel with anyone I hope to see again. Is that the same thing?"

He took some satisfaction from thinking it might be. At any rate, the old routines of her life were breaking up, and, as he planned it, the new ones under his guidance would presently take possession.

The next day he had a long interview with his lawyers, as a result of which Carey visited another lawyer recommended by them. Austen was anxious that she should have as little as possible to do with the actual machinery of the suit, that she should not even know the state of its progress, beyond what was necessary; and for this reason he rarely referred to it during the weeks that followed, though he himself was kept informed of every detail. His lawyers had served him for years and he trusted them enough to be perfectly frank about his own interest in the case; he told them also of the somewhat peculiar attitude to be expected from the husband. Doubtless they passed this on to Carey's lawyer, whom

Austen was careful not to meet or have any direct dealings with. He was all for employing that discretion which was the better part, not only of valour, but of getting his own way. Nor had he been completely candid with Carey in saying he would be indifferent to any accusations made against him, nor was it true that Paul had no power to harm by smearing. The power to do this, as he well knew, is conferred by the person whose position is high enough to be smearable, and though ordinary scandal could not affect him professionally he was personally sensitive to it and had an almost pathological distaste for publicity. All these things were much on his mind, while he never spoke of them.

Christmas and New Year passed with nothing accomplished. Letters to Paul from Carey's lawyer were not only unanswered but presently came back as undeliverable, which seemed to indicate that Paul had changed his address and might well succeed in hiding himself if he were so determined. In the meantime he had apparently dropped the suit about the film — perhaps to facilitate his evasion of the larger issue. As week after week went by with no sign of escape from the impasse, Austen caught himself yielding to the beginnings of obsession ; he resented Paul not only on account of Carey, but because he felt they were at hostile poles in their entire techniques of thought and action. Although he was relieved that Paul had refused to bring counter-charges, he would have disliked him for them no more than for this nonsensical and exasperating obstructionism — so baffling because it was in essence so childish. Perhaps he disliked him most of all because he could not understand him — he could not understand why, if Paul wanted Carey, he did not return and seek to reclaim her ; or why, if he did not want her, he would not gladly unload his responsibility on a successor. There seemed no logic in the man, not even the logic of unregeneracy.

And all this while, during the interval of wasted time, Austen's relations with Carey were in some danger of languishing. Knowing more of the complications than she did, his were doubtless the greater restraints, yet she too

189

had her own, and it was an extra anxiety that he could not always discern them. That she was happy with him he was confident, but he wished he could see into her mind and heart about Paul, yet he knew better than to ask, or even to mention Paul's name. He had the feeling once or twice that the pending case had disappeared from her thoughts, which was almost too much what he had wished for ; and when papers had to be signed she did so with such little apparent interest that he remembered a remark of hers about the play fiasco — that she had sleep-walked into it. He hoped she was not sleep-walking into marriage with him, though even if she were, he would still want her.

The only thing she asked about fairly often was the *Everyman* picture, and there was nothing more to tell for the reason that though Paul was no longer claiming ownership, the actual physical film had so far been impossible to locate. Here, too, was bafflement that made Austen feel not so much defeated by an adversary as scorned by a child who thumbs his nose from a safe distance. He wanted a print of that film as part of the establishment of adult discipline, though if it should arrive he had decided to conceal the fact from Carey. Whether it was good or bad (or perhaps especially if it were good), he did not wish her to see it yet ; as a product of Paul's mind he was afraid of it.

Towards spring the print still had not come, but he was no longer baffled, merely determined. For he had sized up Paul's outlandish weapons, and had devised counter-weapons of his own ; one of them was guile. In this new mood (not really so new, for guile was part of his professional equipment), he made a fresh approach to the major problem. Hitherto Nevada had been thought of as the place to bring suit, but now, in face of Paul's continued inaccessibility, Mexico came under consideration. A divorce there would be more dubious legally, but there were procedures in certain of the Mexican states by which Paul's tactics could be circumvented if it could be shown, evidentially, that he had expressed an intention not to contest the case. And he had — though only in that letter to his mother which Carey had seen.

Thus, at the extreme of the dilemma, Austen found himself acting in a way so contrary to what he would have said were all his normal principles that he could only conclude that his affection for Carey amounted to sheer self-abandonment. He was startled to discover this, for he had not suspected himself capable of it; and perhaps he was secretly gratified, for to a man of his age a grand passion is a renewal of youth. He had loved Fran very deeply, but never to such a point, unless it was merely that he had won her against fewer obstacles and had thus escaped the test. Like all men who govern themselves austerely he was shocked to think he was in the throes of any desire that he could not control, and ashamed to employ the ruthlessness which a weaker man would have enjoyed. Yet here again he was secretly excited; it was a new thing in his life at a time when most things were already getting to be old. Actually his self-knowledge did not go far enough to see the whole thing in perspective — to realize that the average routine of his daily business was just as ruthless as his behaviour now in a different field, and that most of his desires were uncontrollable in the sense that if he wanted something enough there were few plans he would not put into operation to get it. His shock and shame, therefore, were in the nature of sentimental luxuries — or at most, the fastidiousness of a man who normally does unpleasant things at such long range that he escapes all personal contact with the event.

There came a day when he called at his lawyers' office and was told that certain information he had asked for could now be furnished.

"But you understand, Mr. Bond, that's as far as we can go. We've no idea what kind of organization these people have — we certainly do *not* guarantee or recommend them in any way. The whole thing is really far outside our province."

"I know all that. And if they do what I want it won't be a testimonial to their respectability — I know that too. I hate this sort of thing, but I can't see an alternative."

"Then be sure you take precautions. There's always a

chance of blackmail, especially if they find out who's paying them."

" They won't. Dunne will arrange everything, and for for cash. He's discreet."

" So long as you realize there's a risk."

" I don't think there's much, but what there is I'll have to take."

A week or so afterwards, Dunne returned to the house late in the evening after a day filled with Oppenheimerish detail, for he had used a variety of subways uptown and downtown, and had taken several taxis in confusing directions. Entering the library with a tray, he approached Austen in a manner so carefully customary that he was obviously relishing the drama of the occasion. Austen had been dozing in a chair and woke to stare sharply, then exclaimed : " You're back, then ? . . . What happened ? "

" It's here, sir. In this envelope."

" What ? . . . You've got it ? Already ? "

" Sure. And I paid them. They didn't try to welsh on a bargain either."

Austen stared at the envelope, controlling his excitement.
" Did they tell you how they managed it ? "

" I didn't ask for details. After all, you couldn't expect them to reveal their methods."

" I suppose not. I was just curious."

" I got the impression, though, that they used the daily maid, and they did say it was stuffed away in a drawer with a lot of other letters. So it may not be missed, and if it is the old lady may think she lost it."

" Fine. . . . So there was no hitch of any kind ? "

" Apparently not. They're reliable people, I should guess, in their way."

" But what a way ! "

Now that he knew the thing was in his possession he had no eagerness to inspect it. He did not open the envelope till some time after Dunne had gone ; then he read the letter once before mailing it special delivery to his lawyers. Photostatted, it might do the trick, but he could not forgive Paul for having made all this necessary. Again, it was his blind spot; he did not realize that the daily tricks of his trade were so similar in degree that their difference in kind was not fundamental.

Two months later Carey obtained a decree of divorce, and the next day, in the same Mexican state, she married Austen. She did not know the devious means by which Paul had been held to be a consenting party or the high cost of deviousness in fees to all the deviators, and as the documents were in Spanish, there was not much likelihood of her finding out. Publicity, too, was at a minimum, for the story did not leak till it was already stale, and the news item as reported lacked sensation. The pair stayed in Mexico for several weeks, then took an extended motor trip in New Mexico and Arizona. They were in Santa Fe when Austen received news from his German lawyers that Paul was showing *Everyman* in Berlin, and what should they do about it? He cabled them to take no action, but to send him news of what the film was like, how it had been received, and so on. And in the meantime he still said nothing about it to Carey.

Not till they were back at the farm in July did he decide to mention it, partly because for some time she had not asked, and he thought her silence might have been deliberately aimed to please him at a cost to herself. He said one morning when the mail arrived: " Oh, by the way, here are some clippings from Berlin papers about the *Everyman* film. You know German? Quite good notices on the whole."

She must have translated them somehow or other, because at lunch the same day she said: " The critics call it wonderful, Austen — I'm so happy for Paul's sake. When can we see it over here? "

" I don't know exactly. I must find out what the situation is."

The situation was clear enough, had he made it so, but he was content to let it acquire and remain in obscurity, with the result that *Everyman* never reached America and was hardly seen at all outside Germany. It was not a commercial success even there. For some reason, also, fewer prints than usual had been made, and several were destroyed in a fire. Soon the film entered the category of those that are far more talked about by connoisseurs than seen by the public, and in due course it became somewhat legendary, like the reputation of its maker.

PART FOUR

In 1936 Norris was fourteen, a shy sensitive boy, hard to make friends with. He was so far advanced in some of his studies (English and history, for instance) and so backward in others (mathematics and French) that teachers held widely different opinions of him, especially as he did not care for organized games and would not even pretend to. He was physically delicate, yet fond of long walks and uncompetitive outdoor exercise ; in a quiet way his personality was effective, and at school he was never bullied though quite often bored. He adored Carey, whom he treated as he might have an elder sister, certainly not as he would have his mother, had she lived. Carey had been promising for years to take him on a vacation trip to Ireland, and at last, during this summer, the chance came, made easier because it could be fitted in with business visits that Austen had to make to various European capitals. Dublin was not one of them, so it was arranged that Carey and Norris should join him in London before returning to America.

Carey was thirty-one and something seemed to have happened to make her beautiful. She had never quite deserved this adjective during childhood or girlhood, but now there was a special ripeness about her that was conspicuous even in the company of other beautiful women ; it was this that attracted artists, and several had done portraits of her that had been widely exhibited. Her marriage with Austen had been a happy one ; they got along well, enjoying the domestic tranquillity that both valued so much and that made each of them precious to the other because they knew how shared and contributory it was. Austen was in his fifties, not much older in looks than when Carey had seen him first, but increasingly busy in a field which, amidst depression and the collapse of currencies, had become increasingly mysterious if not sinister. He remained unknown to the man in the street, though his marriage to Carey had made him slightly more newsworthy to gossip columnists had there been anything in his life to gossip about. There never was.

Carey and Norris left the ship at Cobh, while Austen went on to Southampton. She was looking forward to her first revisiting of Ireland since she had left it fourteen years before, but most of all she wanted to show Norris the country as if it were a gift to him from herself. They stayed in Cork for a night, rented a car the next day, and set out on the westward road through Bandon. Norris drove. Probably he was not supposed to at his age, but he was an excellent driver and tall enough not to be questioned. She relaxed in the small two-seater and watched the boy's eager profile against the green background of Irish hills. Though he was not her real son, the experience came near to a fulfilment so profound that her eyes were proud, yet she did not know whether it was her pride in the country as seen by the boy, or in the boy as seen by the country. Because people did stare at Norris, or so it seemed to her, for she was never fully aware of how often they were staring at herself, or at the remarkably handsome pair of them. Norris, as he drove along the winding lanes, looked radiant. It was the first time they had ever faced a long spell together without Austen, and she knew he was happier now than if Austen had been with them.

They reached Glengarriff by evening and stayed at a hotel perched somewhat inland on a hill, with a view of the harbour over waterside woods. It was an old-fashioned place where the food was excellent, and where, in the absence of gas or electricity, oil lamps swung yellow beams into the shadows and guests carried lighted candles upstairs to their high-ceilinged bedrooms. All of this was the exact opposite, Norris said, of those places on the Boston Post Road where things are done by candlelight because the proprietor considers it part of the atmosphere he charges extra for. Norris had the wit to express a thought of this kind, and Carey was delighted because it seemed to her a sign that he would accept Ireland without too much regard for plumbing on the one hand or shamrock on the other. She knew how hard it was for Americans abroad to be neither condemnatory nor sentimental.

The next day they drove through Kenmare to Killarney, where the hotel was less primitive — indeed, in a forlorn and stupefying way, rather grand. Norris diagnosed Killarney as the kind of show place that every country needs, since it concentrates in one spot all the naïve elements in tourism, thus preserving other places equally and sometimes more beautiful. This verdict, Carey thought, was too cynical; but after all, he was at an age when cleverness runs to that and when the deliberately unromantic view-point almost achieves a romanticism of its own. In an earlier generation (hers, by a slight stretch of arithmetic) he would have been influenced by Shaw and Mencken; as it was, he gyrated amidst a vague flotsam of assorted disillusionments about war, peace, government, capitalism, religion, and sex — all of which created in him a personal attitude not more than skin deep. One of the troubles that Austen gave himself needlessly (and which made it harder for him to get to know the boy) was that he took at its face value so much that Norris said when he was merely flexing his mental muscles to satisfy an exhibitionist whim of the moment. Carey, as an actress, understood this intuitively.

" It isn't what he says," Austen had complained once, " it's his whole outlook. He seems to have no faith in anything. Even if certain beliefs are questionable, one shouldn't lose them till later on in life."

" Austen, I think that's far more cynical than anything Norris has ever said."

Austen had tried to understand what she meant by that. But he remained (to his distress) incapable of coming to intimate terms with Norris, and the greater his effort the more intractable yet polite grew the barrier between them.

Norris had once asked her glibly : " What does father do all day to make him so serious in the evenings ? "

Carey had answered : " What do *you* do all day to make

you bait him so much when he comes home tired after his work ? You seem to store up sharp things to say, and if he takes them all seriously maybe that's because he doesn't think they're funny."

But now, in Ireland, clouds such as this had lifted and it was clear that, without Austen, Norris was a less combative though still disputatious personality. They drove on through Limerick and Nenagh to Dublin, detouring on the way through the place in Kildare where she had lived until she was ten years old. The house was unchanged, but the farmland looked better cultivated, and in the neighbouring town there were modern stores and neon signs. Approaching Dublin she noted much development — streets of new houses that might have been on Long Island or outside London — " the sprawling anonymity of the suburbs ", Norris called it, pleased with his phrase, and Carey thought it good too, though not quite valid, for the brownstone houses that made up so much of metropolitan New York, or the Regency streets of Limerick, were in their own ways just as anonymous. And come to think of it, anonymity was honest, and if there could be anything more depressing than a row of identical suburban villas, surely it was one of those streets in which the builder makes each unit deliberately different from its neighbour. She chattered on these lines to Norris, and they were still arguing about it when they arrived at the Shelbourne. Then followed a week of sightseeing — art galleries, churches, the Zoo in Phoenix Park, and a long excursion to Glendalough and the Wicklow Mountains. But here again Glendalough, a show place, did not appeal so strongly to Norris as Glenmalure, the lonely dead-end from which the mountains rise steeply to the peak of Lugnaquilla. By a coincidence they went that same evening to the Abbey Theatre where Synge's *The Shadow of the Glen* was in the bill. Norris was much taken with it. He had been to the theatre often in New York and had even seen the Abbey Players there during one of their tours, but the Dublin performance made him conscious of something in a different dimension. He tried to explain this to Carey, who was herself warmed by memories that came to her not only of the play but of the physical stage, the red seats, the black-and-gold striped curtain, and the tricky Dublin audience. She had told him, of course, that this was where she had made her first professional appearance, and he naturally put questions, all of which she answered as truthfully as she could till he asked : " What made you leave Ireland and come to America ? "

" It's a long story, Norris — too long to tell during a theatre interval."

" You were married in Dublin, weren't you, to your first husband ? "

" No, not in Dublin — in London."

" You don't mind talking about him, do you ? "

" Of course not." After all, it was Austen who would not talk about him any more, who had doubtless never told Norris of his existence, though it was clearly impossible to keep the boy always in ignorance of such a plain fact.

" Is he alive ? "

" Oh yes. We were divorced."

" I knew that. Dunne told me. But that's about all I do know. What sort of a person was he ? "

She smiled, sampling the enormity of the question. Then she said, with far greater ease than she could have anticipated : " He was . . . *is*, I mean . . . a very clever man . . . quite brilliant. He directed plays — I believe that's what he's still doing. That and motion pictures."

Norris pricked up his ears, for he was a patron of the screen far more consistently than of the stage. " What's his name ? "

" Paul Saffron." She saw no reason not to tell him, but more pressingly she could not think of any sensible way to evade the question. Yet she knew it would have displeased Austen.

" *Paul Saffron?* . . . Oh, you mean those German pictures — *Ohne die Wahrheit* and *Donnergepolter*. . . . Wonderful ! . . . I saw them at a little theatre on Ninety-Fifth Street — there weren't even any English titles dubbed in, but you could understand without knowing the language."

" I didn't know you'd ever seen them, Norris. You never mentioned it."

" It was last Easter, just before you and father came back from Florida. I'm glad now I didn't happen to mention it."

" Oh ? "

" Well, father wouldn't have liked it, I'm certain."

Had he gained *that* impression from Dunne ? Or by intuition ? She was relieved when the curtain rose on the second item of the one-acter programme — Lady Gregory's *Workhouse Ward*, an old favourite and so ineluctably Irish that it could hardly survive a journey across the Channel, much less the Atlantic. Norris seemed to enjoy it to the full, but at the next interval he plunged immediately into a renewal of the earlier conversation. " Carey . . . where does Paul Saffron live ? "

" I don't know exactly. On the Continent somewhere."

" Is he foreign ? Is it Saff*ron* ? " He gave the word a French pronunciation.

" No — American. He was born in America."

" I'd certainly like to meet him some day."

To hear him say that gave her a shock which only in retrospect she found tantalizingly pleasant. She said : " You might, possibly, if you travel abroad later on, though I'd have to warn you against him." And then, realizing how he might misunderstand unless she said more, she continued hastily : " I mean — he'd probably be rude to you if you didn't have any particular reason to see him."

" But if I said you were married to my father, wouldn't that be a reason ? "

" Oh, my goodness, I don't know."

" You think he'd be mad at *me* ? After all, I couldn't help it even if you *were* my mother — and you're not." He went on, thoughtfully : " I'll bet he'd be interested in me on account of you. . . . What broke up your marriage with him ? "

Carey felt herself flushing deeply ; this was going too far, no matter how preordained it was that he must eventually explore an   chart the situation.   She contrived a laugh as she said : " I can't discuss it, Norris.   I'm sorry."

" You think I oughtn't to know things like that till I'm older ? "

" Maybe — and if you *were* older you wouldn't ask.   Now please let's talk of something else."

" Sure.   I didn't mean to upset you."

" I'm not upset at all, darling, but you mustn't ask any more personal questions of that kind."

As if to signify acceptance of her taboo he changed the subject abruptly by saying : " It's odd, isn't it, that I've never seen you act.   Were you very good at it ? "

" What ? "   She hadn't been listening.

He repeated the question, adding : " Is *that* too personal, too ? "

" Not a bit.   It's just hard to answer except by a plain no.   I wasn't *very* good . . . that is, I wasn't a Bernhardt or a Duse.   But I must have been *fairly* good, or I wouldn't have been able to take leading parts on Broadway."

" With your name in electric lights ? "

" Oh yes."

Clearly he was impressed by that.   He mused after a pause : " I've often wondered if people like them — Bernhardt and Duse — would disappoint us if we could see them today.   There's no way of knowing, exactly, is there ?   It's different with an old film — you can make allowances if the print's worn or the style's out of date — the acting still comes through.   But great stage actors — after they're dead, how *can* you tell what they were like ? "

" It's true we can't judge them ourselves, Norris, but we can read what people thought at the time — critics and others who wrote about them.   We know from all that how good they must have been."

" Just as *you* must have been."

" Except that I was never in their class at all.   And I'm not dead yet either."

" It's the same kind of argument, though.   Circumstantial evidence. . . . I still wish I'd seen you, Carey."

She laughed. " Maybe you will, one of these days. We'll get up a play some week-end at the farm. The Rush-mores would love it, I know."

" Oh, amateurs," he said, not contemptuously, but with the most crushing disinterest. She did not wish to approve such an attitude, yet she could not bring herself to dispute it. She was relieved again when the curtain rose on the third and final item. It did not hold her, perhaps because it was a recently written playlet that evoked no memories — or perhaps because of the cross-examination she seemed barely to have survived. It *was* odd, though, that Norris had never seen her on the stage, so that he could not know that part of her which was professional and accomplished. Her life since marrying Austen had been too peaceful to provide acting moments off-stage, and even if it hadn't been, she was probably too proficient to be suspected of them. So she was ruefully sure he had no idea how good she was ; and she had a sudden vision of him, amazed and starry-eyed, bursting into her dressing-room after a triumphant opening night . . . ' Oh, Carey, you were *wonderful* !' . . . the word he had used about Paul's films.

And yet, when she came to think about it, she did act occasionally — even with Austen. Sometimes, when she was the gracious hostess at a dinner-party, the thought had come that she was playing the role of his wife — not *instead* of being it, but in addition ; so that he was getting double service. But Norris, she knew, got only single service — she never played any role with him, if only because she did not know what it would be. Stepmother ? The word seemed as unfitting as any she could think of. That there was deep friendship between them she was certain, a warmth that had helped her reclaim him from the category of problem child. Or rather, she had tried to make Austen see the problem as the larger one of himself, herself, and the world.

And so in Dublin with Norris, and without Austen, she was thoroughly enjoying herself. One day they took the Terenure tram and walked past the semi-detached villa where James Fitzroy had learned his Gaelic to the last.

Another day they visited Kingstown and climbed the hill to her great-uncle's old house ; he had died only a few years before, and a new house built close by obscured the view of the harbour on which he had so often trained binoculars. She remembered the spot (to within a dozen yards) where she had first mistaken Paul for an advancing gunman . . . only fourteen years ago, yet it seemed, and was, in another age, for by now the gunmen were in office and grown respectable — a typical Irish progression. Even the Abbey Theatre had followed it, becoming by now a rather conservative institution whose leading personnel had mostly left for the fleshpots of America, and in which the early plays of O'Casey were exhibited from time to time like upheld relics of an uproarious past. She felt not only a stranger in Dublin but a stranger to the kind of city it had become, and this made her feel a stranger to the kind of girl she had once been herself — not merely innocent, then, of what the world was about, but ignorant of the fact that the truth was not to be discovered. As the wife of a rich American she was doubtless now envied, and as a beautiful woman she could be admired, but as an Irishwoman she had been suspect from the moment the porters at the Shelbourne saw her Hartmann luggage and knew she would throw half-crowns about like sixpences. She was aware of all this, but it was Norris who gave it meaning. He, with his American birth, background, and accent, was *real*; and she noticed also that he was far less shy than in his own country. It was as if being a foreigner gave him greater confidence to be himself.

He kept his word by asking no more personal questions (that is, about her previous marriage), but he often skirted the subject, and sometimes her unsatisfactory answers must have told him he had touched it. As when, for instance, he probed her acting career in Dublin — what parts she had played, how she had become successful, had it been easy or hard, sudden or gradual. She was deliberately vague, until he sensed she was concealing something ; he then said : " Don't you like to look back ? "

" I don't mind, Norris. Why should I ? "

" I just thought you might have some regrets."

" Darling, if you only knew how little I did here to have any regrets about. They only gave me the smallest parts." She hoped the evasion would satisfy him, but of course it failed to.

" That wasn't what I thought you might regret. It was the idea of giving it all up — later — after you'd been a success. I wondered if coming back here and thinking about it might make you wish you hadn't."

" Oh no. I was *glad* to give it up — you've no idea how exhausting the theatre can be, even if you are successful. Perhaps *especially* if you're successful. Anyhow, I've been very happy since, and if I ever wanted to, I dare say I could go back." She added mischievously : " Would it give you a thrill if I did ? "

" *Me ?* You bet. But not father."

" I didn't ever promise I wouldn't go back."

" All the same, he doesn't expect you to."

" That wouldn't matter, if I wanted to do it."

Then she checked herself, a little appalled. She wasn't sure she had spoken the truth, but even if she had, it was hardly a thing to have confided in Norris. She must not let this vacation, with all its chances, generate a conspiracy between the two of them against Austen. She went on hastily : " Of course I don't really mean that. It *would* matter, but I'm sure if I wanted to do it your father would wish me to."

To which Norris retorted derisively : " Why don't you try him one of these days and see ? Tell him Hollywood's offered you a big contract to star in a film."

" *Hollywood ?* Why should I say that ? "

" Well, it *could* happen, couldn't it ? Didn't they ever go after you ? "

" Yes, but——"

" Why did you turn them down ? "

" Oh, there were many reasons — so many I can't even remember them all."

He said judicially : " You know, Carey, I think you'd be

good on the screen. You're so beautiful — you'd be a joy to photograph."

" Well, thanks. I love compliments."

He went on, still judicially : " And also, as you said, you aren't one of the *very* great actresses. In films you don't have to be. . . . No, I mean it — I'm not kidding. I know something about films — at school we have a society to study them and I'm president of it. I'd like to direct films some day. That's why I'm such an admirer óf — of Paul Saffron. . . ." He looked embarrassed to have mentioned the name, as if he felt it might constitute a breach of the agreement. " Anyway, what I said is true — I do think you'd be a success in films. You have the face and the voice and the personality."

" Plus a slight knowledge of acting which I could forget if I found it a nuisance. . . . Yes, I dare say you'd make a good director."

" Oh ? Why ? "

" You've already learned how to flatter a woman one minute and squash her the next, so that she doesn't know whether she's in heaven or the doghouse."

" Is that what they do ? "

" Some do."

We're still talking about Paul, she reflected, and Norris guesses it. . . . She took the boy's arm (they were walking along O'Connell Street near the Pillar) and said : " Let's go to a movie, if you're so keen on them." It wasn't a specially good one, but he responded excitedly as to ice-cream, animals in a zoo, a catchy song, or any of a dozen other simple enjoyments. He was old for his age, perhaps, but there was also a sense in which he was young for his brains. Nor did she take too seriously his announcement that he would like to be a movie director. There was already a long list of trades and professions, from lion-taming to private detection, that he had declared himself in favour of.

A few days later they drove north to Belfast and the Giant's Causeway, then crossed to Scotland and toured the Highlands. By this time Austen had finished his European business trips and was waiting for them to join him in London. They had an enjoyable week there, sightseeing and going to theatres, but perhaps the most interesting event was again one in which Austen had no part. It was during a day he had reserved for business appointments in the City ; Carey and Norris were strolling along Oxford Street when a poster faced them outside a small cinema — it was of a youth and a girl, hand in hand, against an idyllic background of forest. Over it was the title in large type *Passion Flower*, and in brackets under it in small type : *Erste Freundschaft*. Clearly the English exhibitors had felt themselves able to improve on a literal translation. To Norris, however, the two titles offered more than a joke ; he exclaimed, tugging at Carey's arm : " It's one of Paul's pictures . . . *your* Paul. . . . Oh, we *must* see it. . . . Carey, don't you want to ? "

She didn't know whether she wanted to or not. Several times, in New York, she had seen films that Paul had made, and had enjoyed them under difficulties, aware that Austen would have been unhappy had he known about it, and half-conscious of guilt because of that. She wondered how she had happened to miss *Erste Freundschaft* : maybe that was the year they had spent so little time in New York. Norris was chattering on : " It's probably our only chance, with father not with us — an old picture too — we mightn't ever catch it anywhere else. . . . Carey, even if you don't want to see it, may I ? Do you mind ? I'll be back at the hotel by five. . . ."

She was staring at a name in even smaller type on the poster — " Wanda Hessely ".

" I'll come with you," she said.

The girl at the box-office told them, with complete lack of enthusiasm, that the ' big picture ' had been on about ten minutes. They went inside. It was an old-fashioned building dating from the early days of films — very oblong, with a steep slope and bare walls. Not more than forty or fifty people were scattered about the middle. Carey and Norris found seats in an empty row. The print was old and flickered badly. The occasional English dialogue, flashed on the screen on top of the picture, was often absurd and always distracting. The sound track was worn, so that both voices and music sounded metallic. Twice during the performance the film broke and there were moments of dark silence that fidgeted everybody. And yet, against all these disadvantages, a vivid beauty was alive on the screen and somehow communicated itself, not only to Carey and Norris but to the small English audience who might well, after seeing the posters, have expected something very different.

For *Erste Freundschaft* was, in essence, nothing but a story of first love, but portrayed with such warmth and tenderness that its simplicity was almost disguised. There was no need for the overprinted English dialogue ; one almost felt there was no pressing need for the German voices even if one had understood German. It was really (as Norris acutely remarked afterwards) a silent picture with the kind of accessory use for sound that silent pictures had had — no more.

Carey was glad the theatre was darker than most, for the film moved her in places, not so much to tears as to a helpless acquiescence that would have made her speechless had Norris offered any comment, but he did not ; he seemed as enthralled as she was, though of course less personally. For he did not know she had met Wanda Hessely ; and, come to think of it, the picture must have been made only a short time after that meeting at Interlaken. Carey's acquiescence was partly with Paul's opinion of Wanda — that she *was* a great actress, great enough to weave her personal beauty into the total spell of the picture ; or perhaps this was Paul's achievement. But it was when she came to thinking about Paul himself that acquiescence became most helpless yet also puzzled ; for how had he ever managed to tell such a story ? The man who made this picture is a man who understands love, she would have thought, had she not once been Paul's wife. Yet the impact of what she had seen on the screen was so great that eventually she was thinking : he *does* understand, or did, in his own world, however far that has come to be from mine.

When they left the cinema dusk was falling, and neither she nor Norris had much to say during the short taxi ride to the hotel. She wondered whether he was old enough not to have found the theme sentimental. He had been so enthusiastic over the other Saffron pictures; it would be ironic if this one had pleased him less.

" I thought it was very beautiful," she said simply.

He replied, as they climbed the steps to the hotel : " I wonder why he called it *Erste Freundschaft*? That means ' First Friendship '. But it was love, not friendship."

That evening Austen took them to the theatre to see a popular play that none of them liked, and the next morning they left for Southampton and boarded the *Normandie*.

.   .   .   .

One morning in the spring of 1939 Carey was walking along Fifth Avenue when she saw a man coming out of a shop who looked so much like Paul that she caught her breath. She stared fascinatedly while he sauntered across the pavement to signal a taxi, lighting a cigar as he did so. Then, because he suddenly saw her and spoke her name, she caught her breath again, with astonishment not only that it was Paul indeed, but also, and illogically, that he had changed so greatly.

" Carey, this is really incredible. How *are* you ? "

They shook hands, and for a moment she could not call herself to any kind of order. It was not so much that he looked older (after all, it was almost a decade since she had seen him, and presumably she looked older too), but he had become weightier in a way that somehow suggested mental rather than physical substance ; his head seemed bigger and his eyes brighter and smaller, and there was a sombre twinkle in the greeting he gave, stooping slightly over her hand with a gesture that offered the verdict she had been fumbling for in her mind — that he looked every inch, and in all dimensions, a *maestro*. Which was (as Foy had once said at the old Hampstead theatre) a Continental trick ; and in a flash of whimsy she saw this changed Paul, dressed more Gallic-ally, but with the same brooding effervescence, on some Paris poster advertising an apéritif.

" Carey . . . have lunch with me. . . . Of course you will. . . . Taxi ! . . ."

A cab came up, and before she could think of an objection (if there were any) he had bundled her inside and ordered the man to drive to Twenty-One. A bit of a character, this driver, independent-spirited but not surly, and honest enough to remark that since Twenty-One was only round the corner it was hardly worth getting in for. Whereupon Paul replied, mock-suavely (exactly as to some callow actor's suggestion that a line in a play be changed) : " May we have a ride, please, instead of a geography lesson ? " To which the man retorted, with a shrug : " Okay, buddy, any way you want it." This little incident, so convincing in its message that Paul had not changed altogether, would have amused Carey had she not been gathering her wits to realize what would happen if they did lunch at Twenty-One — a minor sensation on the spot and later in gossip columns. She was not going to let herself in for this at any price, but she had barely time to countermand Paul's instructions and tell the driver to turn on Sixth Avenue and enter the Park.

" Okay," Paul then said, grinning at her. " Any way *you* want it."

" I'm sorry, Paul. I hope you don't mind. But some other place——"

" Of course — wherever you like. Now tell me about yourself — all the news of what's been happening to you."

But it was not so easy to begin, besides which she knew how incapable he was of letting anyone else talk. Nor did he help by exclaiming, loudly enough for the driver to hear : " So you married Moneybags in that Mexican place that dogs are named after." He spoke indulgently, as of a childish escapade for which she had already been forgiven, and she recognized his familiar technique of making a remark in such thoroughly bad taste that there was nothing to do but put up with it or start a row. As she did not want to start a row she said merely : " Please don't shout, Paul."

" Are you happy, that's the main thing ? "

" Yes."

" You've retired from the stage ? "

" I suppose so, though I've never definitely——"

" You like being idle ? "

" I'm not idle."

" Any children ? "

" No."

" Just the two of you, alone and rich ? "

" My husband has a son by his previous marriage — a boy now at college. Rather clever. He's interested in films. He's studied your work and admires it."

" Well, bully for him."

She said, after a short pause : " You've been away from this country too long."

" I have ? "

" People don't say ' bully ' any more."

" I know. I was a boy when they did. But *I* didn't, not then. I never cared to be in a fashion."

" I suppose you speak other languages now ? "

" French and German like a native. . . . So he's interested in films, is he ? You're not by any chance asking me to find him a job ? "

" I think he'll find one quite well himself when he leaves Harvard. What he seems to want to do is to write."

" For films ? "

" Not particularly. Not at all, so far as I know."

" Written anything already ? "

" A few short stories. You might like them."

" Are you hinting I should buy them for pictures ? "

" I don't believe they'd do for pictures, and apart from that I wouldn't recommend anyone to have business dealings with you."

" Listen — I've made money lately. I can pay top prices for all the movie rights I want."

" I dare say. I've followed your career. You've done very well."

" So have you, by God."

And then they both laughed. Antagonism between them, though genuine, had always had to take its turn with countless other emotions. She knew he had been trying to be as rude as he could, and she hadn't been too polite herself; it was all some kind of preliminary bout, not to be held of much importance even if the traded blows were hard. She said seriously: "I saw *Erste Freundschaft*. A great picture, Paul."

His face lit up with a delight in being praised that had enough wonderment in it to make his boasting almost tolerable. "You really think so? You *mean* that?"

"And I liked *Als ob nichts vorgefallen sei* nearly as well."

"You liked *what*?"

"*Als ob nichts vorgefallen sei*." She did not know much German and to repeat the words, possibly mispronounced, with his smile widening on her, made her blush with embarrassment. "Isn't that right?"

"Sure. . . . But your native sounds even worse than mine."

She began to giggle. "Paul . . ."

"And you laugh just the same — and as if that were not enough, you're lovelier than ever when you do it. I hope our friend in front realizes how privileged he is."

"You bet," the driver called out over his shoulder. "I've driven 'em all in my time — Groucho Marx, Dorothy Parker, Katie Hepburn, Maurice Chevalier, Sophie Tucker . . . Who are you two?"

"Did you ever hear of Carey Arundel?"

"Who?"

"Carey Arundel."

"Can't say I . . . sounds kind of familiar, though. Are you him?"

"No, my friend. But you are so right about the name. It sounds familiar, yet nobody remembers it. . . . Well, Carey, what did you expect after ten years?"

She laughed again through her fresh embarrassment, and thought how exempt she had been from this kind of thing during the years of what Paul called 'idleness'. Just to imagine Austen exchanging three-way badinage with herself and a taxi-driver was as fantastic as the concept of some natural law in reverse; yet she knew it did not prove that Austen was a snob, or even that Paul was democratic. It proved nothing, in fact, except that Paul was still Paul.

She said: " I didn't expect to be remembered, so it doesn't bother me at all to find I'm not. You, of course, can't understand that. . . . Why don't we lunch somewhere on Upper Broadway ? "

" Suits me. Take us to the best place you know, driver."

" On Upper Broadway ? All among the hoi polloi ? Okay, buddy."

He drove them to a restaurant that was supposed to look like an English chop-house. Paul tipped him extravagantly and was very regal with a head waiter who was not used to regality; the table waiter, however, turned out to be a Frenchman on whom he could lavish exuberant conversation in that language. Carey noted that though his command of it was fluent, his accent was execrable. Eventually, having manœuvred themselves into the centre of a whirlpool of fuss, they were served with exactly the kind of average food they would have got with no fuss at all. Paul ate voraciously, seeming not to be aware (thank heaven) of any deficiencies. She remembered he had always had that sort of innocence; a steak that sizzled was good, and *crêpes suzette* pleased him so much as a spectacle that he could enjoy them even when they were leathery. Until the coffee stage they had the waiter almost constantly at hand for Paul to demonstrate his French on and his personal importance to; finally, however, having brought Paul a double brandy, he edged behind the scenes with obvious readiness to escape.

And then for several moments Paul had nothing to say. She wondered if he were actually uncomfortable to be alone with her, and if his behaviour had been designed to postpone that as long as possible; he looked deflated, as so often when the stimulus of an audience had been removed. How well she knew that look, the look that said: " I have spent all my brilliance on others; now you, my wife, are privileged either to share my silence or talk me out of my fatigue. . . ." But she was not his wife now, nor was she disposed to assume an old function. She watched him quizzically, till at length he broke the silence himself by saying, with a sudden sweetness that touched her more than she had been prepared for: " It's good to see you again, Carey. I'm glad you're happy."

She controlled herself to ask how long he intended to be in New York.

" I'm sailing in a few hours."

" Back to Europe ? *Today?* "

" Midnight. It's been just a short visit. Less than a week. I was in time for what I came for."

" Some of those top-price movie rights ? "

" No. My mother died."

" Oh, Paul. . . ." She reached out her hand to touch his across the table. " I'm sorry. I didn't know, or I'd have——"

" Nothing anybody could do. A chill and then pneumonia. She kept herself alive till I got here."

" I can believe that, Paul. She was always devoted to you."

" Yes, she really was, and so was I to her. I had her over with me in Europe for a few years, but she hated foreigners and after the Munich crisis she insisted on coming back. She wanted me to come back also, and I promised I would, as soon as I'd cleared up existing commitments, but I wonder if I should have. I wonder. The promise made her happy, anyway. And now, of course . . ."

She said : " Now you don't have to do anything unless *you* want to."

" That's about it. When something happens like this you feel lost and free at the same time. . . . *You* didn't like her, did you ? "

" I liked her more, I think, than she did me."

" That may have been partly my fault — I mean, how she felt about you. I let her think I didn't care for you much. It pleased her. But then, of course, it made her think I'd be better off without you."

It was on her tongue to ask : " Have you been ? " — but

she quelled the impulse, feeling nevertheless that he read the question in her eyes. After a pause he went on, perhaps evading it in his own way : " And once she got an idea, no matter how absurd it was, she wouldn't let it go. For instance, she insisted there was going to be war last September. I told her it would all blow over, as of course it did, but that didn't stop her fidgeting."

" It hasn't stopped a good many other people, Paul."

" I know. And there'll probably be more scares. But actual war — my bet's still against it, and I do have hunches about things, don't I ? Remember when I sold out at the top before the crash ? "

She remembered. She remembered also that it had not been any hunch of his at all, but the simple fact that he had wanted money at a particular time for a particular purpose. Presumably since then he had built the whole situation into drama, with himself as the clairvoyant speculator ; and if that could give him pleasure at such a time as now, she had no wish to spoil it.

She said : " I only hope you're right about things in Europe. I'm not nearly so optimistic."

" You read too many newspapers. If you were working you wouldn't have time. What kind of job could an artist do if he worried over headlines every morning ? The artist never did believe in security, so he isn't upset to find it doesn't exist. And he'd always rather take chances than play for so-called safety. Why, I'm taking a chance now merely being here."

" How do you make that out ? "

" Your husband could cause me a lot of trouble if he knew I was on this side of the Atlantic. He could sue me over that *Everyman* affair — maybe he could even have me arrested or jailed or something."

" Oh, don't be silly, Paul. First, he wouldn't, and second, I'm pretty sure he couldn't. Anyhow, if you're really going about in fear of arrest, why did you want to lunch at Twenty One where just about all New York would recognize you ? "

" Taking a chance, as I said."

But she knew it wasn't that at all. It was just a secondary drama he had improvised to embellish the occasion. More and more, as she talked to him, she wondered how she could ever have accepted his tricks and tantrums, all that mercurial pretence and deviousness, as part of the norm of life ; she wondered how her nerves had survived the wear and tear of those feverish years. And yet she knew she was excited to see him again, an old excitement without any of the old heart-strain. For she had no qualms about him now, or anxieties on his behalf ; he was a success, as he had always wished to be, and she could enjoy the spectacle warmly, but with detachment. Her enjoyment, moreover, eased everything between them, so that he began to bask in it happily — too happily even to show off his French again when the waiter reappeared. He ordered another brandy, in English, and launched suddenly into a declaration of his future plans — a picture, he said, based on the Book of Job. For over an hour he talked about this, not grandiloquently or boastfully, but with the subdued eloquence of a mature mind operating at a peak of capability ; and she was entranced. She knew then that the years had increased his stature in his own infallible world, and listening to him, she felt a certain dreamy contentment, a pride in having been once his wife, in being still whatever she was to him even if they should never meet again. She wondered if they would, not hoping it especially, but with an awareness that she was storing up a reserve of memories impossible yet to assess or classify. To have met Paul, for these few hours before he returned to Europe, to have heard him talk about something which in due course the world would perhaps find worth talking about — how remarkable it might all seem in retrospect. Presently she realized he had stopped talking and was staring at her.

" You're not listening, Carey."

" I *was* . . . I think it's a great idea . . . *great*."

But this time he seemed to derive no pleasure. He said, in a troubled voice : " You say you're happy. Tell me, what sort of a man is he ? "

" Who ? "

" This Austen Bond."

" Oh, *him*. . . . He's . . . why, he's older than — than you, and rather quiet in manner, and . . . and he's kind."

" Sounds like an epitaph."

She smiled, glad of his change of mood to break the spell she had recently been under. " If it does, Paul, it isn't such a bad one." She looked at her watch. Four o'clock already — she must be getting back home. It was all over.

He knew that too, and signalled the waiter.

They shared a taxi as far as Saks', where she said she had to make a call. During the journey they talked incessantly and quite trivially. As the cab drew up outside the shop she said : " Paul, I'm glad we met. And I do hope you keep on having success. . . . Goodbye, Paul."

He took her gloved hand and put his lips to it, whether impulsively or from Continental habit she could not tell. " God rest your soul, Carey. We'll see each other again." (Drama in that too, doubtless, both in the Catholic invocation and in the emphatic prophecy of something so uncertain.)

She smiled and kept smiling from the kerb till the cab drove away. As if to complete an ordered cycle of events, she entered Saks', walked round, then left by a different door and took another taxi home. Norris was at college, Austen had not yet returned from downtown, and Richards (the butler whom they still called ' new ', though it was four years since Dunne's death) said there had been no calls. She sat by the fire in the library and glanced through the afternoon papers. News from Europe looked bad again. She thought of Paul packing in his hotel room, having dinner somewhere (he could find company if he wanted it), perhaps going to a theatre, then driving down to the pier to catch the boat. He had not named it, and she consulted the list to find what sailed at midnight. The *Bremen*.

Austen came in, and they had the usual drink before going up to change, then another drink before dinner. She gazed at him admiringly, challenging herself to think how handsome he was for fifty-five. And so *kind*. . . .

" Carey, you look exhausted."

" Do I ? Goodness knows I haven't done much — just a few odds and ends of shopping." (*Idle?* Could the word be used about her life ? She managed Austen's domestic affairs efficiently, she was on committees of various organizations, she gave teas and lunches to raise funds for good causes. . . .)

" Must be the weather, Carey. When it began that sleeting drizzle this afternoon I kept wishing we'd stayed a few weeks longer in Florida."

She hadn't really noticed the sleeting drizzle. She said : " We can look forward to the summer. It's nearly April already. . . . Do you think there'll be a war in Europe ? "

" I imagine so."

" When ? This year ? "

" Oh, I can't say that. I thought you meant within the foreseeable future."

" How far into the future can you foresee ? "

He smiled. " Why do you ask ? The news in the paper ?"

" It's serious, isn't it ? "

" I think it is."

" Isn't there *any* kind of security anywhere ? "

" You mean some country to run to or put money in ? "

" More than that. Isn't there some way of feeling that whatever happens certain things in one's own life are safe ? Maybe that's a selfish feeling, but it's what I mean by security."

" I'd call it only an *illusion* of security at best, but of course for those whom it satisfies it's all right."

" Well, how can one get it ? "

" I don't really know. I suppose some people *buy* it — hence the uses of good investment stocks. And others imagine it — perhaps religion helps in that."

" Oh dear, what an icy way of looking at things."

" It's an icy world, Carey, except for the small corner of warmth at one's own fireside."

She knew he was telling her, obliquely in his fashion, how much he loved her, and it was comforting, but at the moment she found it easier to be disturbed by the remarkable similarity of Paul's views and his about security. Nothing, she felt, could symbolize insecurity more than their agreement.

On an impulse to treat him as frankly as he deserved, she said : " Guess whom I saw today on Fifth Avenue ? . . . *Paul* . . . of all people."

Just as Paul would make drama, so Austen would destroy it if he could. He answered, in a tone that could have been a parody of an Englishman receiving news that his house was on fire : " Really ? What was he doing in New York — or didn't you stop to talk to him ? "

" He's sailing back to Europe tonight. He dragged me off to lunch, and it was all I could do to keep him from taking me to Twenty-One. We went to a place on Upper Broadway. I don't suppose anyone saw us."

" Doesn't much matter if they did. How is he ? Quite prosperous nowadays, I believe."

" He seems to be. His mother died. That's what he came over for. Just a short visit. He has big plans for a new picture."

" Still in Germany ? "

" No, France now."

" Well, that makes a change. He's really a true internationalist — he doesn't care where he lives provided he can do the work he wants. . . . He didn't talk of coming back here to direct any more plays ? "

" No, and I don't think he will. The stage doesn't give him the chance to be such a dictator. Or so I gathered, though of course he didn't put it that way. In films he can control more people more of the time."

" Provided he makes it pay. One flop and that kind of dictatorship can end up pretty badly. The same, by the way, applies to Hitler. He can't afford to have a flop either As long as he goes on winning he's safe, but sooner or later something else will happen and . . . By the way, has Paul married again ? "

" He didn't say. I should imagine not."

" You mean you didn't ask ? "

" To tell the truth I never thought about it. Paul married

or unmarried makes so little difference to the kind of person he'd be——"

" And which he still is, I presume ? "

" Oh yes. I thought at first he'd changed a lot, but it was only the shock of seeing him. He doesn't look much older."

" Fatter ? You always told me he put on weight easily."

" Perhaps. Or perhaps not. He looked more . . . to me . . . it's hard to think of the right word. . . ."

" Well, now, what *did* he look ? "

Austen was smiling and she answered honestly, yet knowing it would take the smile from his face : " He looked *greater*, Austen."

.   .   .   .   .   .

It had always been Austen's dream that as Norris grew older their misunderstandings would disappear and a friendly father-and-son relationship develop ; but this did not happen by the end of the boy's schooldays, and Harvard, which was to have performed the miracle if nothing else could, proved a special disappointment. For it was there that Norris became *avant-garde* both artistically and in politics, and this worried Austen all the more because he found it difficult to tell either Carey or Norris exactly why. Clearly it was not because he was shocked by the boy's opinions as such, and it annoyed him to guess that Norris thought so. But it was one thing for himself, in private and with regret, to doubt the future of the capitalist system, and quite another thing for Norris to do so openly and disputatiously. Thus even the feeling they shared was a barrier rather than a union, especially with the approaching need for Norris to consider what he was going to do in the world.

Years before, when a brash newspaper reporter had asked Austen to what he attributed his business success, Austen had been stung to the epigram : " I always sell too soon." Actually this was true ; he had sold out, and what was more, sold short, as early as 1928, and during the first half of 1929 it had required iron nerve not to admit himself wrong and get back into the market. The years that followed had trebled his fortune, and during this period there had doubtless developed the tight-lipped ambivalence of his attitude towards life. For he was a genuinely kind man, devoted to the few whom he considered his friends ; and the spectacle of ruin all around him, the ruin that was of such profit to himself, gave him a complete absence of personal pleasure as well as grim satisfaction in finding how right he had been.

And by the same principle of ' always sell too soon ' he had decided, about midway during the 'thirties, that the planning of Norris's future demanded a sacrifice from himself on the altar of that long-range expediency which was so often his almost unknown god ; he would *not* urge the boy to follow exactly in his own footsteps, entering the brokerage firm, learning the ropes, and eventually taking over. Since Norris had never shown any wish to do this, the decision presented no problem at the time ; the real problem would come later, when Austen's more positive plan would require skilled unveiling. Briefly, it was that the boy should graduate into the same world as his own but under slightly different auspices — the slight difference, perhaps, between something that had a past and something else that might have a future. Banking was the profession he had in mind, but not ordinary banking — rather the new semi-governmental kind, of which the Bank for International Settlements at Basle was but the first of probably an illustrious succession. With his influence he might find Norris a job of that sort in which the boy could start a career that might conceivably lead to high and highly secret places. In all this Austen was pushing antennae, as it were, into the years ahead — a vastly more subtle accomplishment than mere indulgence in prophecy.

Father and son had once come close, but not nearly close enough, to a discussion of the issue, during which Austen had been driven to say : " Even assuming that all your extreme ideas are correct, don't you realize that even in Russia financial experts are necessary ? Of course there'd be no place for a firm such as mine, but banking people, fiscal and treasury officials . . . why, I've met some of them, Norris — brilliant fellows — I've sat in conference with them. Naturally they didn't talk politics — they didn't have to — because the field we were all specialists in is by no means tied to Wall Street or the so-called competitive system or any other particular *bête noire* of yours. Every country, no matter what economic road it takes, has currency and exchange problems."

All this time Norris had been listening more and more cryptically. Presently he said : " You know, father, I'm not easily shocked, but you almost do that to me. Are you seriously suggesting I should enter a bank and learn the tricks of the trade so that when the time comes I can be Commissar for Currency and Exchange ? "

This was the kind of remark that grieved Austen immeasurably, bringing him to the edge of a mental abyss. He retorted sharply : " Don't be so naïve. All I'm suggesting, if you want to know . . ." And then he hesitated. Even if Norris did want to know, did he want Norris to know ? He had all the embarrassment that fathers of an earlier generation were supposed to have when faced with the problem of telling their sons the facts of life. But the facts in those happier days had been merely sexual ; now they were economic and cosmic, and in Norris's case complicated by the chattering likelihood that he knew them already and was wondering how innocent his father was.

" Yes, I would like to know, father."

The tone was ironic, forcing Austen to make some sort of a reply. This he did, coming to grips with the situation as squarely as he ever could or did. " All I'm suggesting, Norris, is that the world of the future will be increasingly in charge of experts, and that politics, of the street-corner or even the Congressional variety, is becoming very much of a smoke-screen behind which the real rulers quietly get to work with the real issues. If you'd rather be a part of the smoke-screen, fine — though you'll find it tough going, in the direction you favour, and I shan't be able to help you. Whereas for the expert, life will continue to offer fascinating

H

employment, a secret choice of sides according to the dictates of one's mind and heart, and a very fair chance of surviving catastrophe. . . . Technical brains, remember, are the booty that the modern conqueror cannot afford to destroy — while mere soldiers and shouters are a dime a dozen in all countries."

Norris was silent for so long that Austen added, more uncomfortably than ever : " Well, it's your future, after all — you *have* the brains — no one else can finally decide how you use them. Perhaps at least I've given you something to think about."

Norris answered, in a bemused way : " You sure have. You've really opened my eyes. I'd no idea you had such a . . . a mind. *What* a mind ! "

The matter was never again broached with such near frankness. He was less certain now that he wanted to be a writer, despite his ability to sell an occasional magazine article or short story. With rare self-criticism he admitted his lack of everything but talent, and a spiritual arrogance made him feel that talent was not enough. Presently it came to be understood that after finishing at Harvard he would take a year for travel during which he would make up his mind what he wanted to do, not merely what he wanted not to do — an apparent surrender on the part of Austen. But of course Austen never really surrendered, either on that or any other matter ; it was his campaign plan of life to avoid direct challenge, to stave off the final no, to make opposition to himself a bore even if it were not to be a hazard.

Meanwhile the war had started in Europe, and once again Austen was faced with his familiar cross : something which he foresaw as inevitable yet also deeply regretted. This was America's intervention. Liking the cause of the European Allies as little as did the *Chicago Tribune*, yet as anxious for them to win as was the William Allen White Committee, he found himself gagged as usual by his own awareness of how readily he would be misunderstood ; and among those who would misunderstand was certainly Norris. So he would hardly discuss the war with him, though he noted with some satisfaction the boy's utter confusion about it ; at one moment he was violently anti-Hitler, at other times pacifistic, the two often blending into a ' plague-on-both-your-houses ' cynicism. All of this seemed to Austen relatively unimportant compared with the extremely practical problem of what Norris should do when the war (as Austen was certain it would) engulfed America. Since Norris would be of military age he would have to get into uniform somehow or other, and Austen's idea was to pull strings to have him commissioned as soon as possible in one of the services ; then other strings could be pulled. Unfortunately all this was the kind of thing Austen knew he could not discuss with the boy without risking a direct rebuff, and during the summer of 1941 the relations between them grew strained to the point of an infinite politeness. Sometimes Norris talked to strangers in the Park far more freely than he ever could or did at home, and once he got into an argument that led to a fist fight. He had happened to remark that it was strange that people who professed to follow a religion founded by a carpenter should be so derisive because a certain ruler had once been a house-painter. Part of the small crowd took this to be anti-Christian, another part took it to be pro-Nazi ; and as Norris was neither, the whole episode became a lesson to keep his mouth shut such as (though he never guessed it) his father had well learned in his own youth.

A few weeks after returning to Harvard Norris suddenly settled the whole issue in his own fashion by an act which to Austen seemed quite appalling ; he volunteered for the American Field Service which was then sending ambulance units to work with the British in Africa. When Norris announced what he had done, Austen could not hide his grief nor the boy a certain sardonic comfort. " I don't know why you're worrying so much, father," he said. " America's bound to get into the war soon, and then I probably wouldn't have any choice."

" *Choice?* . . . But my dear boy . . ." It was impossible, of course, to say what was in his mind.

" Besides," Norris went on, enjoying the effect of his

own casualness, " if I waited to be drafted I think I'd have to be a conscientious objector. So you ought to be glad I've spared you that to worry about."

Actually Norris was only just in time, for he was on a troopship in mid-Atlantic on the day of Pearl Harbour.

. . . . .

For Austen the war, on the emotional level, was his anxiety over Norris. The boy was at Tobruk, then at El Alamein; he was risking his life, and it was not part of Austen's plan that this should have happened. In a sort of way he was proud, and he was also aware that countless other parents were suffering like himself; but neither pride nor anxiety increased his sense of fellowship with his countrymen as individuals, any more than the fortune he had made after the market crash had diminished his sympathy with the victims. So far as his own personal affairs were concerned, it was not too difficult to bring even the war into the master plan. Indeed, one of the changes it made in his life suited him very well, for within a few weeks of Pearl Harbour he had accepted a dollar-a-year job in Washington, and it could truthfully be said that he had never worked so happily as when he found himself serving his country. Was this patriotism? He was honest enough not to assume so, and sensible enough not to deny it if others called it that. The truth was that the war, by enabling him to take a Government post without giving up his firm, had made it comfortingly possible to serve God and Mammon, had put the future and the past in some sort of temporary truce.

As for Carey, the war led indirectly to the fulfilment of her own teasing dream about Norris — that he should, some-time, see her in a play. But it happened far differently from anything she had envisioned. To begin with, it was not a first night, but nearer a hundred and first, and Norris, who should have been starry-eyed, was almost condescendingly cynical. Perhaps this was just another disguise for his real emotions, whatever they were, but she had not reckoned on it any more than she had pictured him clumping into her dressing-room in a uniform that made him both shy and truculent.

She herself had returned to the stage in the autumn of 1942, and for a number of reasons, none of them separately decisive, but all contributing to the event. First, there were Austen's frequent absences on business, that took him mysteriously by air across oceans and continents, so that she was left increasingly alone and for the first time in her life lonely. Austen had never had a wide circle of acquaintances, and this had suited her well enough when he was with her all the time, but as soon as he was gone (and with Norris also away) she realized how many friends she had practically given up since her marriage. Most of them were in the theatrical world, and once she re-established contact with them it was inevitable that the idea of a play should crop up. She was still remembered by producers, and since her biggest success had been in a rather trifling comedy, the fact that wartime audiences favoured light entertainment brought her many approaches. The lure of the stage, so harped upon and romanticized, did not specially operate; on the contrary, the *fear* of the stage, the memory of strain and tension, nearly made her say no to every proposition. Then a play came along that exactly suited her style; she was good, the critics were warm, it made a hit, and at the back of her mind was always the escape clause that if she got bored, or felt herself too spent, she could give up. Perhaps because of this she enjoyed success for the first time in her life without qualification.

Nor had Austen opposed the idea; if he had, she would probably not have indulged what had originally been hardly more than a whim. But he merely cautioned her against overwork and stressed the escape clause. He seemed to regard the whole thing as covered by some aura of wartime expediency, like his own missions abroad and the loss of his butler to become a butler in uniform.

Norris had enlisted in the A.F.S. for a year, but it was the spring of 1943 before he came home for transfer to a regular medical unit. He had sailed from Egypt on a slow boat round the Cape; it had dumped him in a southern port where red tape had held him for days before he could get a furlough. It was like him not to wire the news of his return until he could give the time of his arrival in New York; he did not want his father to start doing things on his behalf. As it happened, Austen was away at the time, and it was Carey who met him at Penn Station. The train was late and, after an almost frantically embarrassed greeting, she had to leave immediately for the theatre. She had thought he would want to go home for a good meal and a rest, but instead he said he would rather have a bath at the station, see the show, and take her to supper. She was too excited to argue about it, so she arranged for him to have one of the house seats and asked him to come round to her dressing-room afterwards. This he did, joining the group of admirers whose shrill and fashionable chatter made him stay in the background till she caught sight of him. By this time her excitement over his return had become part of her usual exuberance after a performance, and she could view him with a certain detachment. He was handsome enough, she perceived, to transcend the ill-fitting uniform; that is, it looked even more eccentric on him than he did inside it. She gave him a lavish welcome, her pride masquerading as motherliness, for she felt, as always after a show, extravagant in all her emotions, both genuine and acted.

" *Well!* " she exclaimed, embracing him as she wouldn't have done except at such a moment. " What's the verdict ? How did you like it ? "

" I laughed," he answered, and then, with careful timing, added, " quite often."

He had probably thought this out as a thing to say, and it served a purpose by giving him status among the elegant civilians.

She exclaimed gaily as she introduced him around : " Can you imagine — Norris has never seen me in a play before ! That's a fact ! Darling, don't you dare tell what you think of me ! "

" Oh yes, I will. You were much better than I expected."

More amusement, amidst which he thankfully reverted

to the background till the others had left and he could remind her she had promised to have supper with him.

" Why, of course. I've been looking forward to it all evening. Oh, Norris, did you *really* enjoy yourself ? I warned you it wasn't the kind of play you'd choose."

" It wasn't," he answered. " But to see you on the stage was fun. You're *good*, aren't you ? So sure of yourself, up there — the audience eating out of your hand — your eyes bright and your voice and movements so perfectly controlled . . . but I guess all that just proves I'm as naïve as father says I am."

" I didn't know he did . . . but please go on. I'd rather have your opinion than most people's."

" Well . . . the sheer competence of it all impressed me — just as I'm impressed by championship tennis or Capehart record-changers or H. V. Kaltenborn adlibbing . . . The way you got the laughs — even the fact that you remembered all the lines. And then, on a different level, I was impressed by the play."

" You *were* ? "

" Because of the remarkable team-work between actors and audience. Both had to forget how stupid the thing really was."

She giggled. " I shall quote that as my own. . . . You did laugh, though, or were you just saying so out of politeness ? "

" Sure I laughed. Couldn't help it. You had me eating out of your hand, too. But I'd have enjoyed you better in something more important — something worthier of your abilities."

" How do you know anything more important *would* be ? I'm not really an important actress, Norris. I just happen to have something that pleases an audience if it's properly exploited — that is, in a certain kind of play. It doesn't have to be a great part."

" I still think you'd be good in films."

" So does Hollywood, apparently. I've had one or two interesting offers lately."

" But you're still not tempted ? "

She shook her head. "I have a feeling I wouldn't like it there. . . . Let's have something to eat. I'm starving."

She took him across the street to a restaurant much favoured by theatre people where the food was good and she knew she could get a table. "Now tell me about yourself," she said, over their first drink. "You haven't said much in your letters."

"There's not been much to say that's sayable."

She sensed a cloud of meaning and felt aching sympathy. "Have you . . . have you had a bad time?" she asked.

"Not particularly. Did you think I would?"

"Well. . . . I worried about it, and so did your father. Not the dangers only, but . . . the whole army set-up. It didn't seem the sort of thing you'd easily come to terms with."

"It wasn't. That's why I avoided rank. Stay as low as you can when you know you're on the wrong ladder. Be anonymous. I've found I can get along pretty well with most people — fellows in the same tent and Italian prisoners and Arab kids and girls we sometimes met in Cairo, and so on."

"Girls?"

"Sure. Anonymous girls for anonymous men."

"I don't believe it."

"You don't believe what?"

"That even you could be anonymous so — so personally. That is, if it meant anything to you."

"Who said it did?"

"Then it will, one of these days. . . . Coming back to your opinion of the play, didn't you think——?"

"No, let's explore the other subject, it's the most cheerful we've struck so far. Since you raised the point, I'd like you to know that all women are anonymous to me — with one exception."

He looked excited, as if the first taste of liquor had released stored-up emotions that the entire evening had generated.

She answered: "I didn't raise any point, Norris——"

" Then I will, because it's about time. I fell in love with *you* when I was a boy. Didn't you ever guess that ? "

Of course she laughed, then felt herself blushing deeply.
" Norris, that's absurd. . . ."

" True, though. All that vacation we had together —
Glengarriff, Killarney, Dublin — everything we did and
said — I haven't forgotten a thing. *Erste Freundschaft*. . . .
Couldn't have been more appropriate, though at the time I
missed the meaning of it."

" I remember a lot, too — we certainly had a grand time.
So if you did fancy yourself in love with me then, it must be
rather delightful — as well as amusing — to look back to. . . .
Shall we catch the waiter's eye and order some food ? "

" After another drink."

" For you, Norris, not for me."

" Oh, now, don't get angry."

" *Angry?* My goodness, how could I possibly —— ? "

" You're just refusing to take me seriously, is that it ? "

" I'm not in a very serious mood, I will admit."

" That's too bad."

" But I earn my living by not being, remember. Oh,
darling, don't *you* be serious either. This is such fun — I
always dreamed about it — you seeing me on the stage and
then meeting me in my dressing-room and taking me out
to supper. . . . How long are you home for ? A good long
leave, I hope."

" Furlough, not leave. That's for officers. I've got to be
back in New Orleans by Wednesday, which means I have to
start on Monday."

" Oh dear, is that all you have — and after all this time ? "

" They're in a hurry to put me in a real uniform, I suppose. They probably have a feeling that the A.F.S. was a
bit amateurish. And it was, in the beginning."

" So tomorrow's your one whole day—" She was just
realizing it and thinking of nothing else.

" I'm afraid it is, so if you can spare any more of your
time——"

" Of course I can. Lucky it's Sunday."

H*

" And you aren't by any chance giving a lunch party for the Jugo-Slav War Relief or Bundles for Timbuctoo or something ? "

" If I were I'd have you along to help out. But I always try to keep Sunday as lazy as possible."

" I'll bet you need it, and from now on I promise to conform to all the proper habits — I'll not be serious — I'll be just as lazy as you want — get up late — breakfast in bed——"

" Oh, not *too* late — say ten. Then we can take a walk in the Park——"

" Fine — once round the reservoir and home for lunch——"

" No, lunch out somewhere. While your father's away the servants go, on Sundays, after breakfast——"

" The Plaza, then. And home after that with the Sunday papers and the radio. A noble routine. . . . Are you sure you won't have one more drink before we order ? "

" Yes, I'll change my mind — and the drink. Let's have a bottle of champagne."

She did not know why she had given such a late signal for celebration, or why the two of them so easily slipped into an air of having something special and personal to celebrate. They stayed at the restaurant till almost two, his dark mood lifting till they were chatting and laughing as if the world were indeed unserious all around them ; then they took a taxi to the house. The watchman, who sat up all night, let them in, greeting Norris and telling them that Austen had arrived after a long air journey and had gone to bed.

" You told him Norris was home on leave ? " Carey asked.

" Yes, ma'am, and he said he was too sleepy to wait up, so he'd get a good night's rest and see him in the morning for breakfast about nine."

Carey and Norris stood close together in the small slow-moving self-service elevator that took them up to their separate floors. Norris muttered : " Ten, *we* said. But *he* says nine. Matter of fact, I still say ten." He yawned and swayed. " And by the way, Carey — it's furlough, not leave. Remember that, even if you forget everything else I've said."

"I'll remember." She pulled the sliding-door for him as the elevator stopped. "Sleep well. Ring for Collins if you want anything. . . . Good night, darling."

. . . . . .

In the morning Austen was still suffering from the strain of travel. He had been down at nine, and had waited in the breakfast-room, drinking coffee and reading the papers. He greeted Norris warmly when the latter appeared about eleven. By coincidence Austen also had just come from Africa, having flown back by way of Bathurst and Brazil; he did not mean to be either pompous or mysterious about it, but Norris made him seem both, and as had so often happened, father and son soon touched the frayed edges of each other's nerves. To Norris his own humble uniform conferred unlimited freedom to deride; to Austen it was a symbol of the boy's obstinate folly. Neither knew of recent physical discomforts that were fairly even between them — that Norris had stood up in a packed chair car across half a continent, that Austen had been bumped about hour after hour over unmapped desert and jungle. But the latter, as a civilian, had travelled with importance, and Norris could not help matching it against his own self-chosen lack. He seemed at once proud and scornful of the difference. But bigger differences occurred to Carey as she looked at the two of them — that Austen was old and Norris young, yet that Austen, however exhausted, had got up early to meet his son, whereas Norris, fresh and eager after a late night and too much to drink, was in a mood to bait his father. She was unhappy about it and relieved when the day was over. The next afternoon Norris left, and, as she had a matinée, it was Austen who saw him off at the station. Later Austen did not say much, except that the train had been crowded and an M.P. had checked Norris's pass and found something wrong with it, though afterwards it had turned out to be the man's own mistake. "But no apologies. Just a surly admission. That's the sort of thing he's up against — the way he had to take insolence without protest, whereas an officer would have——"

"Oh, I don't know, Austen. It isn't all a matter of uniform. Suppose you were insolent to one of your employees at the office, do you think he'd answer back just because he's a civilian?"

She could see he was puzzled by her having asked such a question. "But I'd never dream of talking to anyone like that fellow at the station——"

"I know you wouldn't, but *if* you did . . . my point is that . . . oh well, never mind, it isn't important. And I expect the insolence didn't bother Norris half as much as it did you."

"Actually he seemed glad I'd been a witness of it. As if he enjoyed proving to me how humble and insignificant he was. Does that make sense?"

"Probably — to him. You're a big shot, so he'll show you he's a little shot."

"Sheer perversity."

"Well, it's his method of scoring off people."

"But why should he want to score off his own father? That's what I can't understand. Does he ever try to score off you?"

"Oh yes, often. He enjoys telling me I'm not a great actress. Of course I know I'm not, but he never loses a chance to remind me. And he was scathing about the play."

"Collins also told me he got a little drunk last night."

She was suddenly furious. "Collins had no right to say such a thing——"

"Oh, he wasn't saying it against him. It *isn't* against him anyway — home on leave for the first time——"

"Furlough, not leave. And he *was* drunk slightly — so was I — we went to supper and had champagne."

"Fine. Why not? I wish I'd got home in time myself — I'd have joined you. What I meant was . . . the only reason I had for bringing up the matter, I assure you . . . was that *that* might have been the reason why he criticized your play."

232

She answered gaily : " Oh, Austen, don't try to soften the blow. He was cold sober when he criticized it. He thought it deplorably insignificant compared with today's events on land, sea, and in the air. And it is. . . . But it made him *laugh*. I'm so glad about that. We had a very pleasant evening together."

.   .   .   .

In the late spring of 1945, when the war in Europe was over and everybody's story was beginning to leak out, Carey learned for the first time what had happened to Paul. She met at a party a British naval officer who had been in liaison with the French at Bordeaux during the confused days following the German collapse ; it was near Bordeaux that a camp for internees had been located, and Paul, having been one of them, had passed through the city after his release. The Englishman had spoken to him. " He looked sad. It's not unusual, though. When the first excitement wears off, those who've spent years behind barbed wire are apt to be like that. The reality never turns out to be as wonderful as the dream beforehand. Maybe that was so in his case. But there were others from the camp who read him differently — they said he was upset because the Germans lost the war. That doesn't make sense and I simply don't believe it. Talking to me, he hadn't a good word for the Germans or for his fellow-prisoners either — in fact, he seemed pretty fed up with everybody, one way and another."

A few weeks later she heard from a different source (a journalist) that Paul was back in America — in Washington, trying to stir up official interest in the fate of his unfinished film based on the Book of Job. Nobody in Washington cared, but his technique of being charming and a nuisance in well-adjusted doses was having some result — invitations to cocktail parties, meetings with a few minor government personages, and so on. " He might pull something," the journalist admitted. " You never can tell. A lot of people don't realize he's American — that's in his favour. Being able to jabber French to an attaché counts for more in some

Washington circles than having been born in — where was it ? — Iowa."

" Yes.   How did you know ? "

" I caught the accent and then looked him up in *Who's Who*. But the accent's a bit encrusted by now. You *could* take him for a foreigner — especially when he wears his opera cloak."

" What ? A real opera cloak ? With top hat and gloves and cane——"

" No, you've got the wrong layout. A crushed black Homburg, a walking-stick that he carries into a room and leans on, and a very tattered brief-case. How old is he, by the way ? "

" He must be — let me see — fifty — fifty-two."

" Well, he looks sixty-two. Cultural Ambassador, Liberated War Victim, Man of Genius. It's a good line with the hostesses of our nation's capital. He has a good line with publicity too, if he doesn't overdo it. When he said he'd never heard of Lana Turner he hit the news-wires. . . . Am I being too flippant ? I've often noticed that ex-wives enjoy a good laugh about their ex-husbands."

Carey had been honestly glad to learn that Paul had come through the war years safely ; she had also been amused at the picture of him at one of those Washington parties ; but now she caught a conspiratorial air in the journalist's attitude, as if he were inviting her to snicker a little in private. She said : " Well, I certainly hope he has luck," and managed to catch the eye of someone she knew. She did not talk to the man again.

Nor did she pass on the news to Austen. Since her accidental meeting with Paul in 1939 she had sensed that Austen did not care to discuss him ; she had sensed, too, that though Austen did not blame her for the meeting and had said not a word in criticism, he still wished it had not happened.

One Saturday morning in late August she grabbed up her mail in a hurry and did not glance at it till she was in the car on the way to the farm. Austen was driving, and when they reached the dull high-speed stretches along the park-way she began opening envelopes randomly and without much interest. One of them was a Western Union wire; it said, with a Washington return address: " Can you lunch with me same restaurant on Upper Broadway next Wednesday one p.m. Important. Paul." She felt her cheeks warming as she re-read the message and hastily slipped it with other mail into her purse; the warmth, she soon decided, was largely indignant. The wire might easily have been read over the telephone to Richards. And the phrase ' same restaurant ', as if they had made a habit of secret meetings. Her first impulse was to tell Austen immediately, but then she saw his unclouded face; he was enjoying the drive and looking forward to his first post-war arrival at the farm — better wait till later in the day, perhaps till after dinner when they were both relaxed. But she told him before that. They took an afternoon walk to see what new land could be cleared, and returning across the fields she showed him the wire.

" I'd rather you didn't go," he said, handing it back.

" I hadn't even thought of going."

He walked some way without comment. Then he said: " If it's important, as he says it is, he can write and give you details."

" Yes, of course. This is really too absurd, whatever it is he wants."

" Probably only money."

She felt her indignation suddenly deflate. Austen's mood was so reasonable, but his voice was cold; his guess was as plausible as any other, yet from him it came unsympathetically. It was like the wrong kind of line for a certain type of actor; in his case it was the wrong line for a rich man. She knew he had spoken it simply and uncynically, but somehow it made her switch to an indulgent feeling for Paul, even to a whimsical tolerance of the wire. She said: " I expect he thought it tactful to suggest meeting at that restaurant instead of outside the Players' Club."

They walked again in silence. Near the house he said

ruminatively : " I'm afraid he isn't getting what he hoped for in Washington."

" What was that ? I didn't know you knew he was back here."

" I've heard a few things about him. He's been lobbying, you could almost call it, for support in some squabble he's having with the French Government. Apparently when we entered the war he was caught over there, though he'd had ample warning to get out, and anyone but a fool or a pro-German would have. But he was working on a picture and when the Germans interned him as an enemy alien I'm sure he became anti-German enough for anybody. His chief peeve, though, seems to have been against the Vichy Government for not taking his side. Now he wants the State Department to back him up against the new French Government because they won't let him stay there. Complicated, eh ? It's also rather preposterous. He hasn't a grain of political wisdom and he doesn't seem to grasp the fact that on the scale of current events he and his affairs count for nothing. Still, you can go a long way in Washington drawing-rooms with a well-kept grievance. I heard he'd been taken up by one of the weaker-minded senators, but even this couldn't hold when the latest rumour got around."

" What was that ? " she asked again. It chilled her a little that Austen should have known so much about Paul without mentioning it till now, and that, in substance, it fitted so neatly with what she had learned from others.

" It may not be true, but the story is that he came to be on pretty good terms with the German camp commandant and actually sold him on the idea that he should be let out on some kind of parole to finish the film, but the plan hadn't time to go through before the war ended. Of course it was just the way to be tagged a collaborationist, and it certainly was incredibly stupid when the German defeat was already in sight. Anyhow he made enemies by it, and some of them are over here now, so I guess a Senator can be forgiven for dropping him like a hot potato." He added judicially : " I suspect the real truth is, and has been all along, that he simply wanted to finish that damned film, and to do so he didn't care whom he trafficked with — the Vichy French or the Germans or the Americans or the Free French or the Devil himself. That would be in character, wouldn't it ? "

" So what do you think will happen ? "

" Goodness knows. Trouble for him of one kind or another, but that won't be anything new in his experience. And he usually falls on his feet, doesn't he ? "

There were visitors waiting for them at the house, and the subject of Paul was not resumed when they were alone again. Carey had expected it would be, if only to clear up one point — should she answer Paul's wire in the negative or merely ignore it ? She was certain the matter must have occurred to Austen, and the fact that he did not mention it seemed to indicate that he was deliberately leaving her to do whichever she wished or thought best. She did what she thought he would have preferred — she sent no answer at all, and she somehow knew that he knew and was grateful for her decision. They had reached that point in understanding of each other. Meanwhile Austen was having his first real vacation for years, and as Carey was not in a play and had no plans for one, she could share his enjoyment of it. Norris was in Germany, having come through the invasion campaigns without a scratch and with a certain amount of credit. At a world-moment heavy with destiny Carey and Austen could both feel that their own personal case had been dealt with leniently, so that they could now become spectators for a breathing spell. Every morning Austen watched the tractors and drag-chains at work on his waste-land and at lunch reported progress as if it were symbolically important in their lives, and almost every evening they listened to the radio like a good bourgeois couple and went to bed early. And on his sixty-first birthday they had the liveliest week-end party they could assemble.

. . . .

One afternoon in October the first really cold spell hit New York City and Carey decided not to go out. She sat by the fire in the library, reading a novel, half dozing, and catching the muted sounds of wind and traffic that made more satisfying the sanctuary of the room. Richards, back after demobilization, was taking his day off. Towards four o'clock she heard the front door bell; after a pause it rang again, and then again, so she got up to find out what was happening. By the time she reached the hall Flossie was at the door, closing it on someone from whom she had taken a card. Had she put it on the tray as usual Carey would have made no comment, but she saw her slip it into her pocket, and this stirred a mild curiosity. " Who was that, Flossie ? "

" Oh, nobody, ma'am."

" Let me see the card."

Flossie delivered it with a hesitation that just fell short of intransigence. She was an elderly Scotswoman, unsuitably named, but of intimidating character and loyalty — a breed of domestic rapidly becoming extinct, Austen had sometimes said, with more regret than Carey could muster. Carey stared now at the card, then hurried across the hall. There was a built-out porch with side windows that gave views along the street in both directions ; she could see a man walking slowly, aided by a stick, towards Lexington. She turned back to Flossie.

" Will you please go after Mr. Saffron and bring him back here ? "

" I told him you weren't in, ma'am."

" But I *am* in."

" I told him what Mr. Bond said to tell him."

" Mr. Bond ?   I don't understand. . . ."

" He told Richards if ever a Mr. Saffron called he was to say you weren't in."

(*A* Mr. Saffron — as if the woman didn't know who he was.)

" Flossie, whatever Mr. Bond said, I'm sure he'd wish you to do what I ask. So will you please bring Mr. Saffron into the library. . . . He seems to be lame, so you won't have to run to catch him up."

A moment later Paul was ushered in, leaning on his stick.

He looked old, but his face was ruddy red, and he had a beaming smile for her as he crossed the room. " Paul ! " she exclaimed, waiting for Flossie to leave as if nothing else could be said till they were alone. But after the door closed she could not think of anything to say at all. Her chief emotion was one that had been mounting ever since the incident in the hall — anger, resentment, and a kind of helpless opposition to the all-seeing and all-knowing surveillance that Austen had put around her. Doubtless his motives were of the best, but she knew that if she tried to defend him to herself she would find the whole situation sheerly intolerable, the more so as it affected Flossie and Richards. It was a peculiar thing (and she had often reflected on it) that Austen could win the utmost allegiance of servants and employees — or was it because of his frightening skill in choosing the kind from whom such allegiance was obtainable ? But even that did not fully explain why it was not offered to her. Maybe because she valued it less, and freedom more. All this was in her mind as she took Paul's hand.

" Well, Carey, my dear. . . ." He bowed over her finger-tips, a little shakily, then stood with his back to the fire. " Excuse me for toasting my behind — if I don't get warm before I sit down, you'll never get me up again. . . . Arthritis."

" Oh, I'm sorry."

" You know what happened ? They put me in an internment camp. No proper heating — we shivered every winter for months on end. But I'm getting treatment now. . . . I'm glad I took another chance on catching you in."

" You've been here before ? "

" Twice. What's the matter with that old family retainer of yours ? "

" She makes mistakes."

" I'd cast her for Grace Poole in *Jane Eyre* — well, no, she's too much the type. And your butler, who told me you were out, the last time — a pinchbeck Malvolio. Remember the drunken one we had at Mapledurham ? There's something quite fascinating about English butlers. One of the end products of our civilization. Some time I'd like to make a picture in which God is a butler."

" Hardly box-office, Paul."

" Ah, how necessary that is ! That's why I came to see you. I'm getting a bit desperate."

" Desperate ? "

He nodded, then moved from the fire and sat carefully in an armchair. She studied him with an effort of concentration, ticking off in her mind the many changes which were not, in the aggregate, so very much — hair wilder and completely grey, the bones of the face more high-lighted, the eyes brighter than ever, the chin jutting below the lower lip, the hands red-veined and nervous. He could have been, as the journalist had said, at least in his sixties ; one might also have guessed that he had lost much weight and was beginning to put a little of it back, but into a seemingly shrunken frame. Yet all in all he looked rather well, with something of an old man's polished-apple health.

" I'm broke, Carey, and I want a job."

She smiled. " I don't know about the job, but I can give you some money."

" No, I want a lot of money — enough to work with. I have an idea for a picture — box-office and also great. . . . You know those sons of bitches in France won't have me back to finish the last one ? Won't even let me into the country ! The lies they spread — that I was pro-German, that I offered to make Nazi films for Goebbels — not a word of truth in any of it — not a word ! "

" I'm very glad to hear that."

" But they won't believe me. They *choose* not to believe me." He launched into a long account of his martyrdom, from which he emerged as his own hero and the victim of malicious conspiracy and calculated persecution. He had always had a tendency to consider himself either ill-fated or ill-treated — accepting good fortune as no less than his deserts, and misfortune as some species of deliberate evil planned against him. Carey was surprised to find herself regarding him dispassionately, noting the progress of his obsession; yet at the same time she felt a very simple sympathy. She tried to imagine what it could have been like for him to spend over three years behind barbed wire — the merely physical hardships — confinement, cold, bad food, poor medical care. Oddly, perhaps, it was not of these that he made most complaint — on the contrary, he referred to them almost derisively, and his recurrent phrase 'that damned camp' was in the mood he might have inveighed against 'that damned waiter' in a restaurant, or a neighbour's 'damned radio'. He even joked about his loss of forty pounds in weight (at one time), and the outdoor work in rain and cold that had given him arthritis. From what she could gather the conditions at the camp had been rough, but not vicious; there had been misery rather than cruelty, and the camp commandant seemed to have been merely a stupid martinet. Paul was contemptuous of him — "a man who broke his word to me on every possible occasion". (This, in view of their relative positions, seemed to Carey revealing enough.) But his bitterest grudges were against fellow-inmates who, he said, had spread poison about him after the general release, so that he was now *persona non grata* with the French; and on a special pinnacle of detestation there was a certain Frenchman, formerly his own assistant director, who was now in charge of the company that had been making the Job film. "You can guess why *he* doesn't want me back. A second-rater. If *he* finishes the film, it'll turn into a glorified floor show — that's his type of mind — drilling a few dancing girls and he calls it direction. . . ."

He went on till at length Carey interrupted: " There doesn't seem much you can do about it, Paul, now you're here. And you ought to be glad you're here — I'll bet there are thousands in Europe today who'd change places with you."

" Okay then, so I'm here. What do I care where I am, after all? I can work any place. But it costs more here. I want a million dollars."

She smiled again. " That's a nice round figure."

" I'm serious."

" But you don't seriously think I can write you a cheque for it ? "

" I haven't asked you for money at all. I've merely said I'm broke and I want a job."

" Then let's be practical. I'd like to help you, but what's really in your mind ? That I should ask my husband ? "

" Not if you're going to talk to him about *helping* me. Why *should* he help me ? I'm offering something — something that ought to appeal to him as a business man."

" I doubt if it would."

" You mean he isn't tempted by eighty or a hundred per cent on an investment ? Several of my pictures have made it — he can have the figures if he wants——"

" Paul . . . quite apart from all that, doesn't it occur to you he might not want to do business with you at all ? "

" I never met a rich man who wasn't ambitious to make himself richer. Maybe he's the exception."

" Maybe he is. He certainly doesn't put money before *every* other consideration. You don't know him."

" I don't want to. There's nothing personal in any of this. I ask nothing for myself except employment for my brain, the pride and pleasure of artistic creation, and a pittance to live on."

She laughed, partly because she knew what Paul's idea of a pittance was, but chiefly because she was already transferring some of her indignation from Austen to Paul, and the load being thus more equally distributed made it feel less of a load altogether. She said : " Look, Paul, your affairs are no longer anything to do with me, so this is a free gift of advice. Get off that high horse and don't be so arrogant. Because, if you can bear the truth, you're not quite great enough to get away with it — you aren't a Bernard Shaw or a Toscanini——"

" In my own field I am."

He said that with the kind of simplicity that baffled argument even if it did not carry conviction.

" Well, anyhow, till the world admits you are——"

" Till then I must be on my best behaviour — or perhaps

on my knees . . . is that it ? And if I don't — or won't — what's the alternative ? Starvation ? Even in that damned camp I didn't have to *beg* for a crust of bread."

" Oh, stop talking nonsense — why must you dramatize everything ? You're not going to starve. But you're probably not going to get a million dollars either. . . . In the meantime, have some tea."

" Thank you."

She rang the bell. " And put your health first. It's more important than any other plans you have. Is the treatment you're taking for arthritis doing you good ? "

" Yes, thank heaven."

" I wish you'd let me pay for it . . . please, Paul, let me do that."

" I would, but it doesn't cost anything."

" What ? "

" It's free — at the hospital. If I had some wretched little job bringing in a few dollars a week they'd put me in chains to make me pay, but as I haven't a cent I get it for nothing. Isn't that wonderful ? Only the rich and the broke have a chance these days — the in-betweens are just out of luck."

" But how do you *live* ? *Where* do you live ? Are you in New York ? "

He gave her an address.

" How do you manage without money ? "

He grinned. " You've forgotten, haven't you ? I borrow where I can and run up bills. Didn't you and I do that once ? Don't you remember ? "

" But eventually, Paul . . ."

" Yes, I know. It's a problem. After all, I'm a citizen, they can't intern me here. I'm perfectly free to rob a bank, or hitch-hike to Florida, or panhandle on Forty-Second Street."

She went to a desk and quickly wrote out a cheque for a thousand dollars while he went on talking. He talked wildly, extravagantly, and she only half listened. Then she came back and placed the folded cheque in the side-pocket of his coat.

" Thank you very much," he said casually, without looking at it, but not ungraciously.

243

" I'm afraid it's only a small fraction of what you asked."

And he began to chuckle. " Who gets all he wants in this world, Carey ? Perhaps *you* do. . . . You've had most things. Fame, fortune, health. . . . How's that boy you once talked about — Norris, wasn't that the name ? Of course, you can guess what reminded me of him. I was counting the things you'd had, and I suddenly thought of the one thing you haven't had . . . children of your own. D'you find Norris a good substitute ? "

" I don't find him a substitute at all. He's in Germany now. It's over a year since I saw him, but he came through it all, that's the main thing. . . . Here's tea."

She had seen the door opening, but it wasn't Flossie carrying the tray. It was Austen. She felt a sudden constriction of the heart that made her quite breathless for a moment. Paul in the chair was invisible to Austen as he crossed the room, and by the time the two men confronted each other she was standing between them, vaguely smiling and gasping out an introduction. Austen seemed so little surprised that she guessed he had been told that Paul was there, and Paul, trying to rise with the aid of his stick, eased the situation by his infirmity. Austen gestured him not to get up, shook hands with him, and made some comment to Carey about the weather. She responded, and from then on, so far as she was concerned, it was all acting. Amidst the first exchanges of civilities Flossie entered with the tea-things, and this provided a whole ritual of movement while the two men conversed. Austen was reserved, but formally polite. Paul, to her relief, and presently to her slight amusement, turned on the charm. Never, she felt sure, had he been more genial. The things he did not mention at all were perfectly chosen — films, money, and his own personal affairs ; while the topics that did inevitably crop up — post-war Europe and the general state of the world — were touched upon by him in a mood of urbane wistfulness that (Carey could see) made its own peculiar appeal to Austen. She thought : But for me these two men could be friends — for about five minutes, or until Paul

244

decided it was too much of an effort. But as a spectacle it was fascinating — to see him feeling his way into Austen's personality as if it were a part in a play that had to be interpreted. The climax came when Paul, having been gently pessimistic about the future of western civilization, quoted from a speech made by Serge Diaghileff in 1905 : "'. . . We are witnesses of the greatest moment of summing-up in history, in the name of a new and unknown culture, which will be created by us, and which will also sweep us away. That is why, without fear or misgiving, I raise my glass to the ruined walls of the enchanted palaces, as well as to the new commandments of a new aesthetic. The only wish that I, an incorrigible sensualist, can express, is that the forthcoming struggle should not damage the amenities of life, and that the death should be as beautiful and as illuminating as the resurrection.'"

"All that from Diaghileff?" Austen said, when Paul made a pause.

"Yes. At a dinner in St. Petersburg."

"Far-seeing."

"Diaghileff was a far-seeing man."

"You knew him?"

"Not then, of course. But during the early 'twenties, when I was still young and impressionable and taking my first trip abroad, I had the nerve to write to him and he was gracious enough to meet me at a Montmartre café. How naïve he must have thought my ideas! Yet he listened, and discussed them, and gave me just the few words of encouragement I then needed."

It made a winsome picture — the modest youth from Iowa at the feet of the world-weary Gamaliel in Paris, and the only thing amiss with it, Carey suspected, was that it had probably happened very differently, if at all.

There followed more anecdotes, delightfully told, yet as they continued Carey began to feel some strain in her enjoyment of the performance, as if she were watching the try-out of a new kind of trapeze act. After more cups of tea and another half-hour of chatter she was really quite glad when

Paul rose to go. He shook hands with her, and Austen took him out to the hall. A moment later Austen returned. He went to the sideboard and mixed himself a whisky and soda. By that time Flossie was clearing away the tea-things and drawing the curtains.

" Good talker," Austen commented when they were alone. " Do you think he made all that up about Diaghileff ? "

She knew then that the assessments had not been all on one side. " The speech ? He might have, though he seemed to know it by heart."

" I must see if I can check on it. Really quite worth remembering."

" Paul or the quotation ? "

He smiled. " I must admit I hadn't imagined him quite so affable."

She said : " Yes, nobody can be more charming than Paul when he chooses."

" So he chose to be just now ? "

" Evidently. . . . He's broke, he says, and wants work. In films."

" He won't find it easy to get."

" No ? Because he's made enemies ? "

" Partly. I don't think Hollywood will bid very high for his services."

" Oh, Hollywood. . . ."

" Well, where else can he try ? There's no other place over here."

" What he'd really like is to make a film of his own — maybe in Hollywood, but independently. He did that in Europe, and apparently he had some big successes. Commercial successes."

" I know he did, but the system's different over there — or was, before the war. Anyhow, his European reputation doesn't count at the American box-office, and for four years he's been out of touch with everything."

" You seem to know a good deal about the film business."

" Only financially. My little venture with Everyman taught me a few things."

" I can understand it taught you not to trust Paul."

" Well, no, not exactly. The circumstances were unusual.
. . . I wouldn't generalize from that one experience. He's
a slippery customer, but not, I'd say, from any financial
dishonesty — it's his temperament."

" That's very reasonable of you, Austen. If only *he* were
as reasonable . . . but he isn't. If he had been he wouldn't
have had to lose those four years."

" Yes, that was a pity. Four years is long enough for
most people to forget and be forgotten."

" So you think if he wanted to make a picture now he
wouldn't find anyone to back him ? "

" You mean a personal corporation with a bank putting
up the money ? "

" I — I don't know. Is that the way it would be done ? "

" If it *could* be done. But I don't think there's a chance.
Of course, he might interest one of the big studios in whatever
picture idea he has. But he'd have to sell it for what they'd
offer, and if they employed him on the job he couldn't
expect a big salary."

" I think he wants authority — control — more than
money."

" Unfortunately what he wants isn't likely to matter much."

" That seems hard, when he has such abilities. Do you
have influence with any of the studios ? "

" Not to a point where I could help a man who asks for
the moon. There are only a handful of people in Hollywood
who have real authority and control — it's a rare thing there."

" But you *could* find him a job — a subordinate job — if
he were satisfied with that ? "

" It's possible. One of the smaller studios has connections with some banking people I know. That might work
if I cared to try it."

" If you cared to, naturally. And I wouldn't blame you
if you didn't. There's no reason why you should raise a
finger for him."

" It isn't that, Carey. I'd help him if he were helpable.
But if his sights are too high — ridiculously high, what can

anyone do ? And incidentally, I'd rather you weren't mixed up in this at all. He and I have now met, and I'm not sorry that happened, because he can contact me again, directly, if ever he wants."

" And you *would* help him then ? "

" If he were in a mood to take what he could get I'd certainly put in a word."

" That's reasonable, Austen," she said again. " Very reasonable."

But the word ' reasonable ' was so dubious to her that she could hardly speak it without catching an ironic sound in her own voice. Suddenly she noticed that his face was pale and that he was taking, unusually for him at that time of day, an extra drink.

They did not discuss Paul again at dinner, nor during the days that followed, and the longer he was not mentioned the harder it became for her to broach the subject, though she often wanted to. For there were many things she was anxious to know — whether, for instance, Paul had followed up his meeting with Austen by making any direct request for help. And there was the disquieting possibility that he might have written to her, or telephoned, or even called at the house again, and that on Austen's instructions some message had been intercepted. More than once she decided to take up with Austen this matter of the orders he had given to the servants, but each time when the chance came she said nothing, unwilling to start an argument that might make them both unhappy.

She was conscious, since the meeting with Paul, that some strain was on her life with Austen — probably nothing serious or lasting, just a faint shadow on the happiness she had so long enjoyed.

Then they had news of Norris that took all other things out of their minds.

.   .   .   .

Norris, having driven an ambulance for four years and in two continents without serious mishap, drove a jeep into the Rhine on a dark night six months after the war in Europe was over. He was nearly drowned and had injuries besides. At first these were thought to be severe, but just when Austen was arranging to fly to a hospital at Coblenz, wires he had already pulled began to operate and Norris was flown across the Atlantic. He arrived at LaGuardia on a December morning, Carey and his father meeting him. To their relief he could walk, the damage being mainly to one arm, and within a week (again thanks to Austen's intervention which he never discovered) he was mustered out and convalescing at the farm.

But he failed to recover quickly to normal, whatever normal was, and it was also clear that either the accident or the cumulative experience of war had (to use another of the clichés) ' done something ' to him. *What* was the problem. There was certainly a development from the boy to the man, yet also from the boy who had been precocious for his age to a man who, in a way that was rarely but acutely discernible, seemed to have held on to some delicate boyishness as healing aid to a troubled spirit. The doctors talked of long-deferred fatigue which the car smash and the half-drowning had unloosed ; as a short-range diagnosis it doubtless fitted the symptoms, which were an excitability alternating with long periods of lethargy during which he did not seem interested in either events or people. But perhaps he was, in some way of his own. He read a good deal, and Carey was surprised to notice that many of the books were solid stuff — history, anthropology, religion, mysticism. Fortunately he had the desire for rest, which was what he most needed, and his old hostility to his father was less evident, as if it were part of an energy he no longer possessed. To Austen this dubious change brought great joy. He spent hours with Norris, talking, reading, listening to the radio, often merely sitting silently in an opposite armchair while Norris dozed ; and when business took him to New York he urged Carey not to leave the boy alone too much, though she herself did not think Norris minded being alone. It was certainly quiet at the farm while Austen was away, sometimes for several days during mid-week. Mrs. Grainger, whom Carey liked, did the cooking, and there was no fuss or commotion — none of the well-oiled superfluousness of the routine when Austen brought the other servants along. Carey helped Mrs. Grainger with the house-work, and Norris, using his uninjured arm, seemed to like doing small chores on his own. If he did not speak for hours on end, Carey did not bother him, but if he felt inclined for chatter, or nonsense, or even serious conversation, she was always ready. Once she found him reading Thoreau, about whom he commented: " I don't think I'd have liked this fellow personally, but I admire his pose. Nobody ever did it better."

" You mean the simple life — Walden Pond? Don't you think he was sincere? "

" Up to a point. But to enjoy the simple life you really ought to be simple, whereas to write so well about it you have to be complicated. I've a feeling Thoreau enjoyed it chiefly because he liked to write about it."

" Why don't you work up that idea into a critical article? "

" Trying to find me some occupational therapy? That's what they call it in the hospitals."

" Of course not. I just thought it sounded an interesting idea. For the *Atlantic* or *Harper's*, if it turned out well enough."

" I doubt if it would. . . . If I had any talent, I think I'd rather paint than write."

" How do you know you haven't any? "

" That's the come-on for all the racket schools."

" I know, but if you could get any fun out of it, why not try? "

She bought him paints, easel, canvases, and a book of technical instruction, and to her pleasure he found an interest that at times almost amounted to enthusiasm. If there were sun she would carry his equipment to some sheltered spot outdoors, and on bad-weather days he did still-lifes in one room or another. He had talent, but not much, as he soon became ruefully aware. Sometimes, and also for nothing but fun, Carey painted with him, the same scene or model, and her effort was usually better than his, but still not in any way remarkable.

"A couple of amateurs," he commented. "How you'd despise anyone on our level in the theatre!"

"Probably. One's always intolerant of the non-professional in one's own profession."

"You still feel acting is that — to you?"

"I expect I always shall."

"Any new play in prospect?"

"Not at present."

"Looking for one?"

"Not particularly. I think I need a rest almost as much as you do."

"Father never really liked you being in plays, did he?"

"I wouldn't say he was keen on it, but during the war he didn't seem to mind."

"Maybe he counted it a sort of war work."

"Maybe. Or perhaps he thought the war was an excuse for anything."

"Well, it just about was."

They went on putting finishing touches to their canvases. They had chosen a grouping of fruit and bottles on a tray beside a window, but the lighting and reflections were beyond their skill and the result was only middling. They knew that, yet they kept on, as if impelled by a desire more tolerable because the whole thing so clearly did not matter.

"We're pretty hopeless," she said seriously, studying her own attempt and assuming his was as bad.

"But it's quite as sensible," he answered, between brush-strokes, "as playing bridge."

"I hope so, because I do that badly too, and your father's so good. I always envy him at parties."

"But he doesn't dance and you dance beautifully."

"So do you."

"I'll dance with you when my arm's better."

"Good."

And after a pause: "By the way . . . did they ever give any details about the accident?"

"*Your* accident ?   *They* ? "

" Anybody."

" No — at least I never heard."

" Well, it's not much of a story. I was driving a girl home after a dance. She was killed."

" Oh, Norris. . . . I didn't have any idea of that." She put down her brushes and he did also, neither of them giving another look to model or canvas. She began to tidy up, then. " That's dreadful. . . . Were you . . . were you very fond of her ? "

" Not a bit. I'd never met her till that evening. I was taking her home because my friend, who'd been with her, had passed out. I hadn't had any drinks myself and the whole evening was simply a bore. We were driving slowly when a truck came at us round a corner. I had to swerve and we skidded. The road ran along the river-bank. That's all. But I thought I'd tell you in case you'd heard about the girl and might think there was some romance in it." He paused, as if waiting for comment ; when she made none, he continued : " Yet it affected me a good deal — I think more so in some ways than if I'd known and liked her. And the thing itself was worse than war, if you can imagine what I mean, because killing is what wars are for and you half expect it all the time. Just as you somehow expect girls to be pretty . . . She wasn't, poor thing. But her family owned vine-yards, and, if you dated her, they'd give you bottles of wine. Their whole dream, and the girl's too, was that some G.I. would marry her and take her to America. My pal was after the wine. But for that she'd have been alive today and I'd have been — I suppose — still over there."

She saw his face twitching with some kind of agitation and thought he had probably done well to tell her, as the first step towards forgetfulness. She said, as she began cleaning the brushes : " I'm glad you told me, Norris. . . . I hope it's fine tomorrow — we might try the barn, or if it's too cold to paint, we could do a quick sketch."

But it rained the next day and the skies were so dark that it was hardly worth while to sketch or paint anywhere ; and the day after that they returned to New York for the Christmas season. Austen was waiting for them, happy over the boy's progress to health and ready to give Carey full credit for the painting experiment. Norris seemed fairly happy also, or at least indifferent to where he was taken. Of the three, the only sufferer was Carey, for whom the return was to the secret surveillance which she had not yet complained of to Austen, and could not discuss with anyone else. She was certain now that Richards had Austen's private instructions, yet nothing was provable, since it was fully a butler's job to sort mail, take telephone calls, and so on. And even if, when she dialled a number from her room, she heard the click of an extension elsewhere, she knew there could be a hundred innocent reasons for it. She was always on guard against an obsession, having observed so many in other people ; but to measure every suspicion against the possibility was almost an obsession in itself. Only while she was with Norris could she feel utter freedom, for Austen approved so much the time she spent with him, noting each day the boy's rising spirits. So that in a room where she and Norris were together she did not start at a sudden tap on the door ; it was sanctuary of a special kind, the glass-house where nobody would throw stones.

Because of his injured arm they tried to avoid crowds, though they saw a few plays and movies, but more often they walked the two quiet blocks to the Park and then roamed for an hour or two till dusk approached and it was time to return to the house. Sometimes Norris went out on his own and came back hours later ; she never asked him where he had been, though he would tell her as a rule ; he liked wandering about the city, taking the subway to some distant suburb and finding pleasure in the randomness. To her this was perfectly natural, or at least not astonishing, but to Austen it would have seemed queer, so they kept such expeditions a secret. They had a few other secrets, such as the books he read (she knew because she saw him reading them, but she never discussed them unless he started it), a few records they both liked and that Austen would have played far too often if he had known what they were, and of course the biggest secret of all — that there were no important secrets. In the house they spent most time in a little sitting-room on the third floor — Norris's since boyhood, but not boyish in character, for he had always had an aesthetic dislike of pennants and group photographs, and his entire lack of games prowess had left him without trophies. His mind, Carey thought, was abstractly intellectual rather than artistic, and he had not yet found an outlet for its proper use — maybe writing, eventually, if he developed ideas that could survive his own criticism of them. He would be formidable and fascinating in debate, and in this field it was the power of their sheathed weapons that kept father and son apart. If they ever argued, they soon reached the foothills of disagreement beyond which the mountain loomed unarguably. And the mountain was that Norris, despite facile cynicism and years at war, had certain hopes of the world ahead ; whereas Austen, though he would have thought it naïve to discuss the matter, had almost none. Immortal longings against urbane misgivings was a conflict in which Carey was more on Norris's side than she knew ; in fact she did not know at all till one day, in the sanctuary of the sitting-room, Norris remarked that he didn't think he would stay home long after he was fully recovered.

" Why not ? "

" It's hard to say, Carey, in a way that doesn't make me seem either priggish or ungrateful. I like father much more than I did, and I can see now what a brat I used to be with him — he's so patient and affectionate ; I've treated him pretty badly. And yet my first instincts were probably right, if I'd only kept them under civil discipline — I mean, we don't really have the same ideas about things. I change mine all the time, of course, but I never seem to change them to any of his, and I can't help feeling that's a remarkable coincidence. So it wouldn't be much fun for either of us if I handed my future over to him and said ' Make what you want of it.' "

" But do you think that's what he'd like you to do ? "

" He'd like me to go in a bank. He's often said so."

" That doesn't sound too exciting."

" Oh, it wouldn't be an ordinary job — or even an ordinary bank, for that matter. It might mean going abroad — to Switzerland, and I wouldn't mind that a bit, except that . . . well . . ."

He hesitated and she said : " You feel that if you did you'd be giving up something else even if you're not sure what the something else is ? "

" Exactly. And of course that's where he has a case. He says ' Try the bank and see if you like it '. If I answer ' I don't think I'd like it ', then he says ' Well, what *would* you like ? ' — and I don't know."

" Have you had this argument with him ? "

" Oh, not an argument. Just friendly talk from time to time. All very detached and reasonable. I like the idea of going abroad, though. Too bad I'm not religious, I could be a missionary. Matter of fact, I wish I were a doctor, then I could be a missionary without being religious."

" Why do you want to be a missionary at all ? "

" I'm damned if I know. Does that sound a silly answer ? "

" It's better than trying to invent a reason."

He laughed. " I think I'll travel, when I've got myself a bit stronger. Father's offered to take me on one of his business trips abroad, but I'm not really sure that's what I want. Unless, of course, you went too — then it might be fun. But he never does take you on business trips, does he ? "

" It's my own fault, Norris. He flies everywhere and I hate flying."

" So do I. Loathe it. The Wright Brothers were the Wrong Brothers so far as I'm concerned."

" Perhaps so far as the world's concerned too. There's not much time, is there, to save anything ? "

" That's an odd remark. Fifty years ago the only answer would have been ' Yes, if you begin early, putting by a few pennies each day '. But now the question means something else, doesn't it ? And that, I suppose, is the real grudge I have against any kind of job father would find for me. I'd feel like an old clock slowly running down if I really devoted myself to it. And father does devote himself. Not that I mean he's an old clock slowly running down. . . ." He laughed with some embarrassment. " A very elegant clock, at least. I hope I'll look as handsome when I'm his age."

" I hope I'll look as young when I'm his age."

" Young ? *You* ? " He said shyly, and with a different kind of embarrassment : " I can't imagine you anything but young at any age."

He looked at her across the low table on which all the equipment of afternoon tea was laid out — silver and china sparkling in the firelight ; outside, beyond the curtains not yet drawn, snow was beginning to fall in dark slanting flakes against the window. The book he had been reading lay open on another table near his chair, and an interrupted page was in his typewriter. The deep green walls, with their few pictures, framed the red carpet in a way that was striking yet warm ; bookshelves made their own pattern of colours carelessly mixed. She had a curious impulse she had had before when wakened in the night by something that might be a distant explosion or a minor earthquake shock — an impulse to note the hour and the minute, so that the next day, if she saw it in the papers, she could tell herself : That was *it*. . . . She looked at the clock now ; seventeen minutes past four. It was the word ' young ' that had exploded — but not shatteringly at all, just enough to waken her into a new awareness.

She said with a half smile : " I'm forty, Norris, and how have I devoted *my*self ? I wonder if acting's any better than banking, from your point of view ? "

" Oh, but of course it is. And I haven't got a point of view — I wish I had. I'm just fumbling around trying to find one."

.   .   .   .   .   .

When she saw him across the dinner-table that evening it seemed somehow like the day after and she was reading in the papers about that special moment of the earthquake.

He and Austen conversed politely, and after the meal they both listened to music on the radio.

She did not sleep well, and in the morning, not knowing quite why, she told Norris she had some shopping to do. " Last-minute things for Christmas — perhaps you'd better not come with me — there'll be crowds."

She drove the car herself, as she often did, but not to the shops. It was a hard, bright, icy day, and before she realized it she was on the ramp leading up to the Washington Bridge. There was nothing for it then but to cross, and afterwards she turned north along the familiar road to Newburgh. She came to a small town some thirty miles out and had a sand-wich at a lunch counter. Then she drove back, without much awareness of time. She was in New York again by mid-afternoon, and along Riverside Drive she passed the street that Paul had given as his address. Impulse was too late for her to make the turn, but by a couple of streets further it had become a definite whim to see where he lived. She turned and drove there, already unhopeful about it. Yet in New York you could never be sure, that was one reason why the city was so endlessly fascinating — each street, if you knew it well enough, so subtly different from its neighbours that even number itself acquired unmathematical attributes. Presently she identified a red-brick, sham-Gothic apartment building, several decades newer than the decaying brown-stone houses that enclosed it, and possibly at one time a spearhead of social change now merged and indistinguish-able amidst the general slatternliness of the district. Children swarmed along the sidewalks and gutters, and when she pulled up they stopped their games, not because the car was anything special (an old Buick in days when every bookie had a new Cadillac), but from some instinctive curiosity that met her own as she stepped out. Even then she had no plan to visit Paul — merely to ask for his new address, for she could not imagine he would have stayed long in such a place. But she found there was no one to ask — neither doorman nor desk nor elevator ; merely a cluster of mail-boxes, some of them broken and open. She studied the name-cards, hardly expecting to find Paul's; yet it was there — " Paul Saffron 4K " — and immediately the thought of him, crippled with arthritis and living on a fourth floor without an elevator, became a challenge to pity and then to action. Surely, if he were in, she could at least pay him a Christmas call, and with such an excuse the idea of seeing him grew warmly, easing her mind from the strain that had held it clenched all day after the almost sleepless night.

Paul opened the door to her ring, and his first exclamation was not so much surprise to see her as at her looks. " Carey! What have you done to yourself? Climbing stairs must suit you. . . . Come in. I was wondering if you'd ever accept my invitation."

" Your invitation? "

" To see some foreign films. They run them at a theatre round the corner from here. Nothing worth seeing this week, though."

" You invited *me*? "

" Sure, I've written several times, but no answer. Too bad I didn't know you were coming today, I'd have bought some tea. Will you drink coffee? "

" Why, yes, but don't go to any trouble. This is just a Christmas visit."

" Good. What would we poor people do, I wonder, without you rich people to give us a helping hand? "

Then she noticed the room, inventory-making as she always did: the scuffed Edwardian furniture, ugly types of an ugly period; an oblong of threadbare carpet in the centre of the floor, wallpaper peeling off at the corners, an ancient gas chandelier wired for electricity, the imitation marble mantelpiece surmounting a radiator, a contraption on one of the walls that was presumably a pull-down bed. A further door led to a dark bathroom, and the view from the window was of ancient balks of timber buttressing a half-demolished property.

Meanwhile she was asking Paul about his arthritis, which he said was much better, and his prospects of a job, which he said were non-existent.

" I just thought you might have had some luck. I — I don't know how you'd feel about — about talking to Austen. Directly, I mean — now that you've met him. He knows people, and if he could help you to get something—"

" It would give him a kick, would it, to turn me into a Hollywood office-boy ? . . . No, Carey — thanks to your own generosity I've so far managed not only to keep the wolf from the door but also the termites out of my brain."

" But I know how it used to get on your nerves to be idle."

" Who says I've been idle ? " He pointed to a pile of manuscript on a table under the window. " See that ? I've been hard at work. . . . My life story. I tell the whole truth, that's what makes it unique. Probably a best seller. Full of big names when I get to the successful years. Already I'm as far as *Othello* at Hampstead — remember that ? Here, take it with you when you go — I'd like your honest opinion."

" But if this is your only copy——"

" I have an earlier one in rough, and my typing's not so bad. I *want* you to read it. After all, it's your bounty that's enabling me to write it."

" I wish you wouldn't keep on talking like that, Paul."

But she knew that in his own way he was enjoying the situation. From his earlier word ' generosity ', to this last one, ' bounty ', she could read the progress of a drama in which he was already richly casting himself.

" But you *will* read it if I ask you ? "

" Certainly, though I'm no judge of writing, as I tell Norris."

" Norris ? Ah, the boy who liked my pictures. I remember. How is he ? "

" He's grown up now — back home from the Army. He was injured in Germany after the war ended — a car smash. Not badly."

" And Austen ? "

" The same as when you saw him three weeks ago."

" How could he ever be different ? "

" You were being so charming to him that afternoon I guessed you didn't really like him."

" Why should I like him any more than he likes me ? "

" All right, let's leave it at that."

" Personally I think he's a cold fish."

" He isn't."

" Well, *you* should know."

She could ignore the innuendo all the more easily because his description of Austen as a cold fish hadn't reminded her of her own relationship at all, but of the two weeks that had followed Dunne's last operation, when Austen had visited the old butler daily in the hospital, and of Austen's tight-lipped grief when all was over. The remembrance of this armoured her against the resentment she might have felt had Paul said anything less unfair. She even began to feel a sudden ease in being with someone whose outrageousness, whatever he said or did, could neither surprise her nor change her opinion of him. Let him say what he liked about Austen, Norris, herself, anyone he chose. She didn't care, and it was good not to care. Even the room began to look less depressing. It was warm at least, the ceiling was high, and the derelict house that obstructed the view had a Gothic picturesqueness. Doubtless there were many far worse places where people had to live and find happiness.

She did not stay long after that, for she would already be later home than usual. Before leaving she wrote Paul a further cheque and said she would return the manuscript as soon as she had had time to read it. " Of course I may be too busy during the holidays. . . ." What was in her mind was that she would rather not be seen reading it in front of Austen, so that her chances to do so would require contrivance.

" I don't mind how long you take, Carey, but bring it back yourself."

" I won't promise, Paul — it depends how busy I am."

" But I'll want to discuss it with you."

" I will if I can. How shall I know when you're in ? Give me your number."

" I have no telephone, but I'm always in after three. When I see a picture I go when the theatre opens for the cheap prices."

" Yes, yes, I know," she said tolerantly, as of a play she did not think very good, but could learn without difficulty. With the money she had given him she knew he could not be really hard up at all. She wished him a happy Christmas with a comfortable feeling that, even alone, he might actually have a happier one than hers. He had such reserves of self-comfort, far more than she had herself.

.　　.　　.　　.　　.　　.

When she got to the house Austen was already home, scanning the evening papers by the fire. Norris was not with him. " He's resting," he said. " He said he'd stay in his room till dinner." She was fairly certain that Austen had not been wondering where she was, and that part of his indifference was due to anxiety about Norris.

Norris came down to dinner, looking no longer tired, but rather excited ; the evening passed without special incident and they all went to bed earlier than usual. She did not see him alone till the next morning, when he sought her out in her room while she was writing gift labels. He said hello, and took one of her cigarettes, then he apologized for having behaved oddly the previous evening.

" Oddly ? There was nothing odd, Norris . . . you just looked a bit tense, that's all."

" I was, too. It's stupid, but I'd been waiting for you all day."

" Waiting for *me* ? "

" You weren't back for lunch and you didn't telephone Richards or anyone."

" Norris, darling, I don't always telephone. They know if I don't turn up that's all there is to it."

" Of course, and that's why it was stupid of me — I had all day to wonder where you were — and to worry — I thought perhaps you'd had a car accident — I have car accidents on my mind, I suppose. . . . So I just waited and waited . . . couldn't write anything — couldn't even read by the time you came home."

" Oh, Norris, I'm *sorry*." She gripped his uninjured arm

and faced him; he was smiling now, so she smiled back. "And you know where I went? I changed my mind about the shopping, it was such a lovely day. I drove to the country. Just like one of your own expeditions, only with a car. I wished you were with me, only I knew you wouldn't enjoy being driven. I had my lunch at a place called Mack's Streamliner, just this side of Newburgh. Made up with stainless steel to look like a streamliner. On the left as you go north."

"Did you have a good time?"

"Wonderful. But I'm terribly sorry—"

"Oh no, it was my own fault. One thing, though . . . nearly to Newburgh and back would be — oh, I suppose seventy or eighty miles. Did you buy gas on the road?"

"No. . . . Why?"

"Maybe Foster won't notice it."

"Foster? I don't know what you mean. . . ."

He said uncomfortably: "Perhaps I shouldn't have mentioned it, but . . . well, I mention everything to you sooner or later . . . there's quite a lot of checking up goes on here. Richards with the telephones, and Foster, I think, when you take the car out. I don't *know*, mind you — maybe I'm too suspicious of people who act suspiciously."

"But, Norris, even if he did measure the gas, why shouldn't I drive seventy or eighty miles if I feel like it?"

"Sure, sure. Of course."

She heard the elevator whine as it reached her floor and then the slide of the opening door.

"These labels, Norris. Will you help me? Please read them over against this list of names."

They were so occupied when Richards brought in the morning mail.

.   .   .   .   .   .

On Christmas Day they had a small party of friends, a dozen or so, and it was a pleasant time. Norris could not dance, because of his arm, but he talked with the guests and seemed at ease; she herself danced often, while Austen played bridge. Soon after midnight all the guests left except three players who were as keen on the game as Austen and about as good; it was an almost pathological keenness that Austen had, and since he had been losing up to then, there was an edge to his appetite for more.

They were playing in what was called the billiard-room, where there was a billiard table which Carey could not remember anyone ever using — a large basement room, afflicted with supposedly masculine trappings — moose-heads, ‘ Spy ’ cartoons, and a fireplace far too large for a modern fire. There was an alcove modelled on what some architect had imagined to be a typical corner in an old English pub; it had no virtue except seclusion. Carey and Norris sat there while the bridge went on forty feet away, beyond the billiard table. They talked in whispers, not that they had anything to say that was specially private, but because the subdued ferocity of the game induced an atmosphere of tension.

“ Go to bed if you like, Norris.”

“ No, I’d rather sit with you.”

“ I can’t very well leave just yet . . . though if they go on much longer . . .”

“ I rather hope they do. I like talking to you like this.”

“ But you still need plenty of sleep. I’m so glad you’re getting better so fast.”

“ You really think I am ? Don’t you wish we could take a vacation somewhere — Colorado or New Mexico — with no one to check the gas against the mileage ? ”

“ Oh yes, Norris — I’d love it . . . but we can’t.”

“ Then what are we going to do ? ” He flushed and added quickly : “ I mean separately . . . what are *you* going to do and what am *I* going to do ? Will you be in a play again some time ? ”

“ I might. I haven’t plans, but I wouldn’t like to rule it out of my life. On the other hand, I’m not consumed with ambition.”

“ Were you ever ? ”

“ Oh yes. My first was to be a nun — but the nuns at

the convent knew me better and laughed me out of it. Then I wanted to be an actress and play Juliet, but Paul laughed me out of that. He said I wasn't the type."

" To me you would have been."

" What a sweet thing to say . . . but now tell me your plans, if you've made any."

" I know what I'd like to do. You'll probably think it crazy, but to me it doesn't look crazier than most other things these days. I'd like to go to medical school and later take up tropical medicine. My best friend — the one who took the girl who was killed to the dance — he was in the Pacific during the first years of the war — he told me plenty about it. They need resident doctors on all those Pacific islands. The natives have everything from leprosy to measles. Now the war's over the Government's beginning to realize how much medical work will have to be done in so-called peace-time, though I admit it's a bit illogical to improve the health of a few ex-cannibals when we're all going to be atom-bombed. Perhaps that's why it appeals to me — because it's illogical. When the radio-active manna begins to fall on the world I'd rather be discovered in some relatively pointless occupation such as treating a Polynesian scalp for ringworm . . . instead of sitting in a bank office doing fabulous things with a comptometer." He laughed nervously. " Well, what do you think of the idea ? You're very silent."

She said : " I'm just wondering why you haven't already started."

" Started what ? "

" The medical thing, if it's what you want."

" Carey, you're rather wonderful. I have started. I've written to Columbia asking about entrance requirements."

She saw and heard the bridge game ending across the room and the sudden burst of talk as the score was added up. She had time to say : " I'm glad, Norris, I'm very glad," and then to add quietly : " I think your father's won — he looks so pleased with himself."

Austen came towards them smiling. " Eleven dollars

and thirty cents," he remarked, with a satisfaction which, from him, could only be considered charming.

.   .   .   .   .   .

That night, because again she found sleep difficult, she began Paul's manuscript. She had had it in her possession for over a week, during which there had been several chances for private reading, but she had felt no urgency ; Paul's life story was like Paul himself in her life — close or distant beyond computation in miles or days. But she had promised to give her opinion, and, once she began, it was certainly no effort to form one.

The opening chapters were interesting, without a doubt. She could also (though she was no real judge of this) imagine that some publisher might take a chance on the whole book, if only for its general liveliness and gossip value. But what struck her, amusingly at first, and then appallingly as she went on, was the picture it presented of Paul himself — an absurd picture on the surface, yet beneath the absurdity so ruefully revealing. For he was his own complete hero from the first sentence. Nothing had ever happened but added a mosaic to the finished pattern of the man who was always right (and whose enemies and friends alike were always wrong), a man infinitely wise and desperately victimized, a man who had never done a foolish or a selfish or an unjustifiable thing, but whom the world had treated with constant unawareness of the paragon living in its midst. The picture was flawless (Carey realized) because it was constructed with the awful sincerity of self-hypnosis. Errors, even of simple fact, were numerous and monumental. Poor old Foy, for instance, appeared as a philistine who had cut short the run of *Othello* when it was still making money but not enough to satisfy his avarice, and various other theatrical figures whom Paul had quarrelled with in London and New York were hardly recognizable in their completely satanic guise. For the passage of the years was to Paul no softener into greys, but rather a lens through which the blacks were blacker, and his own white whiter than snow. It was demonology, not autobiography. And all this in depicting the comparatively minor rancours of those early years. (There was, of course, no reference at all to that obliterated year in Hollywood.) What would happen, Carey wondered, when he came to his film-making experiences in Germany (the *Everyman* affair), and the war-time ordeal of the internment camp?

She read with greater misgivings as she proceeded, and with the greatest of all when she turned back to re-read passages here and there. She was sure, by then, that for Paul to publish it (even supposing it were free from technical libel) would be disastrous. Not that it was badly written (it had some of the glibness that had made him, in his youth, a promising journalist of sorts), but there was no quality in it to offset its own angle of distortion, and its sole perfection was for this reason non-literary, clinical, and ludicrous. If he had wished to give the world the documented confession of an egomaniac, this was it, and of value, doubtless, in a psychiatrist's library; but among the informed public those who did not sue would probably laugh their heads off. The whole thing was too true by being not true at all.

And then she suddenly realized, as never before, that Paul's infallible world, the world in which his greatness was real, the world of *Erste Freundschaft*, had nothing to do with either his actual behaviour in life or with his own ridiculous self-portrait. It was as if, indeed, words were a medium that, despite his skill with them, set him far off the tracks of truth. He posed in every sentence, and she remembered that his first success in journalism had been the exploitation of a pose that he himself had scorned. Perhaps that early experience had probed and explored a weakness, so that words were never afterwards to be his authentic weapon. And perhaps that was why, of every craft connected with the stage, he had always got along worst with writers; and perhaps that was also why, when he took to the camera, it was a release from chains, for in all his films there was none of this brawling self-love, but an integrity, a vision of life, and the sweetness of a ripe apple. . . . All this came to her mind as she read the manuscript, and when she had finished it she wondered, not what to tell him, but how. The problem took such precedence, even over others she had, that she felt she must act quickly; she could not endure the thought of him sitting there in that dreary little room, happily engaged upon a task so inept. She drove to see him the next morning, climbing the eight half-flights with the resoluteness of one who intends at all costs to be frank. The real trouble, she expected, would not be to break the news gently but to make any impression at all on his own conviction that he could do no wrong.

"So you've read it already?" he exclaimed, when he saw the manuscript under her arm. "That's *great*! You just couldn't stop, I suppose, once you tried a page or two?" He smiled indulgently as he pulled a chair for her. From the look of things he had been working hard at the continuation, and he saw her glance take in the typewriter and the littered table. "I think I have another couple of chapters for you," he added proudly. "Now tell me all about it."

"Paul . . . let me get my breath. . . ."

"Yes, I know. Those stairs. . . . But isn't it good stuff? How did you like the part about our first meeting? That walk in Phoenix Park and my promise to direct you in a play——"

"That wasn't our first meeting, Paul, and you didn't promise to direct me . . . but it's a fair sample of what's wrong with the whole thing."

"*Wrong?*"

"Yes, because it isn't true. You've just made yourself a hero in everything — which wouldn't matter so much except that you're wasting your time doing this sort of thing at all. You're not a writer. You're a picture-maker. Your mind's eye has no words."

And now, she thought, regarding him dispassionately, let the heavens fall. He seemed preoccupied for a moment, as if holding some answer of his own in abeyance; then all he did was to take a cigar from his pocket and slowly light it — not at all the movement of an angry man. Presently he remarked: "Not bad, not bad. My mind's eye has no words. I like that. Carve it on my tombstone. You know,

Carey, I have an idea some time to make a picture without words at all. The old silents were almost an art when this horrible mess of verbiage dragged them down to the level of mere photographed stage plays. You're pretty smart to perceive that."

She hadn't perceived it at all, but she was dazed by her own luck in finding a phrase that had so captivated him.

He went on, smoking tranquilly: " Do you think I'd waste time if there were anything else I could do ? "

" Well, then, Paul, you *must* find some work, the kind you can do and love to do — otherwise you'll soon become a rather silly old man with nothing but a collection of memories and grievances. Paul, why couldn't you take any kind of job — at first — if it gave you a chance to make films ? "

" *Any* kind of job ? "

" Not absolutely any kind — I mean a decent job, of course, but maybe not one that gives you all the freedom you've been used to . . . a job where you could prove how good you are to those who don't already know it . . . a compromise, Paul. You'll have to make one if you ever want to get back. Couldn't you take a job — say — in one of the smaller studios — and on a not so very important picture — if it were offered you ? "

" Directing ? "

" Yes, naturally — though perhaps not with full control of everything. Hollywood doesn't do things that way."

" Ah, Hollywood."

" Well, where else is there ? Apparently you can't go back to Europe."

" So you offer me a director's job in Hollywood at a minor studio and on a B picture. Suppose I say I wouldn't be interested ? "

" Then I'd begin to lose all hope for you."

" Suppose I said I *was* interested ? How soon could I have the job ? "

" I don't know — I don't know even if there is one. But if you say you'd take it, that's the first step. Austen has influence——"

" Oh, Austen, Austen, *Austen*. I wanted his money, and his answer was no. My answer's the same now — to his influence. Damn his influence. No . . . *No*. . . . What sort of person do you think I am ? "

" That's what I've never been able to decide."

She could see the answer amused him as he retorted : " Maybe *you* ought to write a book about it some day."

" Except that I doubt if I could ever make the subject interesting enough."

" Oho, so that's how you feel ? I bore you, eh ? "

He never did and he never had, but she answered : " Yes, sometimes . . . and I'm in a hurry, I think I'd better be going."

" You won't even have coffee with me ? "

" No, thanks. I really mustn't stay as long as last time."

" Next time I want you to have dinner with me."

" No, I couldn't do that."

" Then when shall we meet again ? "

" I can't promise. But let me know how you are, and if you need anything . . ."

" So you find me a bore," he repeated, not believing it at all (she could see), but turning over the idea in his mind as some abstract curiosity.

" I won't argue, Paul."

" You don't even *admire* me any more ? "

This was too much, so she began to smile. " I do admire you, in many ways. I might even admire your attitude towards Austen if I didn't know it's a mere gesture. You don't *really* feel like that about taking help from people — you haven't that kind of pride——"

" False pride. Of course I haven't. And look, Carey, gesture or not, I don't want Austen putting in his little word for me anywhere. It's not a matter of principle — much more important, it's a whim. If you want me to do the kind of job you described — the compromise job — ask Michaelson to find me one. He's been my agent for the past twenty years — time he did something."

269

"All right," she said, ignoring the further absurdity of that last remark. "I'll go straight to Micky from here." She was surprised that the idea hadn't occurred to her earlier. "But I'll have a cup of coffee with you first."

.   .   .   .

Michaelson had been Paul's agent too, in the old days before the European adventures. He was getting on in years now, and had taken on a junior whom he was grooming for partnership and to be his eventual successor. It was this comparative youngster whom Carey talked to when she called at the office on Forty-Second Street. He was very affable, assuming no doubt that she had come to announce herself in the market again for a good play ; and this, being good business, was good news. But when she said she didn't want a play, but would like to talk about Paul Saffron, he assumed the look of someone who, from then on, was prepared to listen merely from politeness.

"Do you know Paul Saffron well ? " he asked, which she took to be convincing proof of how time could obliterate not only the memory of half a dozen successful plays but of gossip also, and even a breath of scandal.

The irony of it made her answer : "Fairly well. He's one of your clients, anyway. Or didn't you realize that ? "

"Yes, Mr. Michaelson used to handle him — years ago — I guess that's why he still considers himself attached to us. Otherwise I doubt whether . . ."

"I see." She went on to explain what kind of job Paul wanted, how well qualified he was, and how high his reputation had been in Europe before the war. "Maybe you've seen his work. I don't think it's an exaggeration to call him one of the world's great picture directors."

She began to dislike the youth for the way he deliberately poker-faced before answering. "You really think that, Miss Arundel ? "

"Yes, I do."

He poker-faced again. "You know, you actresses can sell a lot of things — face cream, lipstick, cigarettes, home permanents, God knows what. But there's one thing you can't sell, and that's Paul Saffron."

" Why not ? "

" Because he's a Fascist."

" *What ?* "

" He was mixed up with the Nazis during the war — did propaganda for them or something——"

" That's not true ! I know there've been all kinds of slanders about him——"

" All right, all right — so they're slanders. Maybe. But people believe them. And he hasn't enough friends who'll *say* they're slanders. You're the first I've come across."

They were still in the argument when Michaelson entered. He and Carey were old friends and greeted each other affectionately. He introduced her formally to the youth, mentioning the latter as " a bright lad . . . I hope he's been telling you how glad we'll be if you're after another play."

" I'm not, Micky. I came to talk about Paul — your bright lad didn't know he was once my husband."

The youth was not in the least discomfited. " I knew, Miss Arundel, but I thought I could be franker with you if I pretended I didn't."

He left the room, at a signal from Michaelson. She said, ruefully : " So I guess he *is* a bright lad."

" Sure. . . . Now what is it about Paul ? "

She went through the whole thing again, but to a kindlier audience. At the end he said : " Well, Carey, what Joe told you wasn't far off the mark. It's going to be pretty hard to sell Paul anywhere."

" Because of the lies that are going around ? "

" Partly that. And also because Hollywood has 'em all listed either hot or cold, and Paul's like ice — at the moment. Now if it were you, I could make a deal by picking up the phone. You don't know how many enquiries I've had — I don't even bother you about them, because I know how you feel. Look, I say to them, Miss Arundel isn't interested in pictures, she's married to a millionaire, you just haven't an

271

angle with her. . . . But you're hot, Carey. I think I could ask a hundred thousand for one picture and no quibbling."

"Micky, let's get back to Paul. He'll go to pieces if he doesn't find a job soon. They must know his pictures made money in Europe."

"Most of them don't know and none of them care."

"I suppose they take more notice of the lies put out by enemies."

"Look, Carey, it isn't only that. Paul has a reputation for being difficult, and there's nothing worse when you want a job. People who ever worked with him don't forget what he was like — he's not a man you *can* forget. If he were on top, they'd all say what a wonderful experience they had, but now he's out, so they all say what a son of a bitch he was. And he was too, let's face it. I used to quarrel with him so many times I lost count, and when he called on me recently after he got back from Europe he was just as impossible as ever. How he managed to make pictures for the Germans I'll never know——"

"He didn't. That's one of the lies, Micky——"

"I meant *before* the war — don't get so excited. The good pictures he made — they were for the Germans, weren't they?"

"They were for the world."

"Oh, come now, he made them in Germany, they were German language films — nothing wrong about that, mind you——"

"Yes, yes, of course. I'm being silly. I'm sorry."

"Sure, I understand. You like the fellow. So do I — in a way. But as I said, I've often wondered how he managed to get on with them over there. Maybe it's what they go for — the Wagner type. Highbrows and headaches."

"No, Micky, that's wrong too. He's not highbrow. His pictures have been *popular*."

"Not in Paducah, Kentucky. That's the hurdle he has to cross."

"So you think there's nothing can be done?"

"I should say at present, not a thing. Unless you want

me to fix up a package deal for both of you ? Then somebody would have to take the pill to get the jam."

He had said this as a joke to lighten the tension on Carey's face ; and she did indeed respond, but he saw the laugh drain away into a look of different tension. She said quietly : " Could you really make a deal like that with someone in Hollywood ? "

" Sure. You can make any kind of deal if you have something to offer that somebody wants. During the liquor shortage I once sold an actor because I could throw in a dozen cases of Scotch."

" Well . . . go ahead and sell Paul along with me."

" You're not serious ? "

" I am."

From habit he pulled a pencil and scratch-pad towards him, then pushed them away again. " No, I won't need to remind myself of this. You're sure it's not a gag ? "

" I'm serious," she assured him again.

They discussed details, and just before she left his office he said : " Your personal affairs are none of my business, Carey, but it's only fair to mention one thing . . . people are going to draw a certain conclusion from all this."

" That I'm doing it to get Paul a job ? I don't see why they'll know that if you don't tell them."

" It'll leak out from the other end, you bet . . . but that wasn't what I meant. The big conclusion they'll draw is that you're leaving your husband and going back to Paul."

That startled her. " Yes, I suppose they will. It's not true, but I can't help it. . . . It's *not* true, Micky — it's almost comic, when I think of it. I could never go back to Paul. You believe me, don't you ? "

" Why not, if you say so ? But who else will ? "

" Then I don't care. It's no worse — and no less absurd — than the other rumour."

Michaelson walked with her along the corridor to the elevator, and as the pointer swung to their floor number he said : " I know you're serious, and I'm itching to get at the phone, but I'll wait for one hour . . . exactly . . . in case you change your mind."

Half an hour later she was with Paul. " Now for heaven's sake don't *you* back out . . ." she exclaimed, watching his face as she gave him the news, but to her relief he seemed delighted and especially because he would now, he said, have a chance to make a movie star out of her. " You remember I always promised I would, Carey ? You have a good face — the right profile slightly better than the left. I'd like to cast you as an old lady — you'd be beautiful with just a few wrinkles here — and here—" He touched her with his finger-tips.

" Well, thanks, but I'm pretty sure you won't have a chance. They'll give you a certain picture to make and you'll have to make it. There'll also be a story, whether you like it or not, and there'll be a producer to decide how much you spend, and a camera-man who'll think he knows more about angles than you do, and a writer or writers to do the script. . . . Micky told me all this, and I'm passing it on to you now, so that you know the worst." (It occurred to her then that it hadn't been at all a bad idea of Michaelson's to wait for that full hour.) " But there's also good news, Paul — and the best of all is that you'll have your chance, and it'll be a big one, because it's bound to be an important picture if anybody's willing to pay so much for me in it."

" What will they pay for you, may I ask ? "

" Micky thinks he can get a hundred thousand."

" Ridiculous," Paul muttered, under his breath, and then added, thoughtfully : " But of course that's for you and me together."

" I expect so," she agreed tactfully.

The full hour passed, after which she returned to the house. Austen was out, and Norris, she learned, had gone to the Museum of Modern Art. She told Richards, with an exhilarating sense of freedom : " Any time, if there's a call for me from a Mr. Michaelson, I'll take it."

There was no call that day, or the next, but the following morning she talked to the agent from her bedroom while Austen was dressing. " I haven't clinched anything yet, but you're hot, Carey, same as I told you. We were batting it out all day yesterday. Better drop by my office later and we'll talk over what's happened."

She said she would, then hung up. She knew that Austen had heard enough to wonder who it was she had agreed to meet, but of course he was too polite to ask and she felt it would have been challenging to tell him.

By the time she reached Michaelson's office there was a tentative deal to be discussed. It was with Majestic Pictures, not the biggest studio, and possibly not the best, if there were a best, but recommendable if only because it had shown the greatest interest and been the first to make a firm offer. On the whole, though, Michaelson seemed a little disappointed. " I could have sold you to any of the studios," he said " except for Paul. Even the jam wouldn't cover that pill, with some of them. And when I named my price to Majestic they didn't even flinch till I said he had to be in the deal. Then they started to hum and ha. They had their own directors, didn't need another — all that sort of thing. . . . By the way, how much do you think he should get ? "

" Oh, I don't know, Micky, that's your province."

" Ten thousand ? "

" For the whole job ? "

He nodded.

" A hundred for me and ten for him . . . he'd be pretty mad, but I suppose he'd have to take it. I thought a director would get more, though."

" Most of them do. But Majestic already have their own directors, that's what they kept telling me. What would you say to Paul being brought in as a technical adviser — wouldn't mean such hard work for him — probably not much at all — and he'd get the cash just the same ? . . . I presume what you really want is to help him financially without getting into any tax situation."

" And he wouldn't direct the picture ? "

" He wouldn't have to."

" But he *must* — I want him to — that's the whole point. It isn't just a question of money."

" I see. I told them I thought that might be your attitude. . . . Still, don't worry. I can make a deal on those lines, but it won't be such a good one."

" Micky, don't you see what I'm after ? I want Paul to get established in the kind of work he can do——"

" Yes, yes, I know. All right. That's how it shall be then. Seventy-five for you and ten for Paul as director——"

" I thought you said a hundred for me ? Not that I care particularly——"

Michaelson scribbled figures on his pad as if they were too difficult to work out mentally. " I could hold out for a hundred, Carey, and I'm certain I could get it — if you'd settle for Paul on a technical adviser basis. Otherwise . . ."

She smiled. " I see. Seventy-five's okay."

He smiled back. " You think he's worth the difference ? "

She kept on smiling. " The difference less a whole lot of income-tax. Yes, I'll sign. The main things are the details. I want you to protect him all you can — in case they want to put him off halfway through or something."

He kept on smiling. " Seems like we're both expecting trouble with that guy."

" An old habit of mine, Micky. Do your best for him. I don't know what you can ask in the way of authority or control — probably not much. But try to get the limit. I'll be out there to smooth things. I haven't met many picture people, but I guess they're human."

" Very. Human enough to be your admirers." He beamed with gallantry, then became businesslike. " So you approve the deal I've outlined ? "

" Yes."

" And you think he'll approve it too ? "

" My God, he'd better."

" Perhaps he could drop by and see me himself. We'll roll out a bit of red carpet."

" Let me talk to him again first. How long before we sign ? "

" It'll take a week or so to set the thing up." Michaelson continued, on the way to the elevator : " As I thought, they all took it as proof you were going back to him. I told them you weren't, but they offered me odds on it. So what would probably have been only in *Variety* — I mean, about the contract — may hit the gossip columns. If it does, remember it's not my fault — I warned you of a leak from the other end. Hollywood's one big leak — you'll find that out."

.   .   .   .

She knew then she must tell Austen without delay, for it would be unthinkable to let him hear or read of it.

She told him that night, after they had left Norris, and while he was mixing his customary nightcap. After considering all kinds of excuses and evasions, she finally decided on the plain truth. She said she had been offered a good contract to make a picture in Hollywood with Paul directing, and she had accepted. She explained the nature of the deal and spared none of the details of Paul's unpopularity and the unlikelihood of his ever getting a job without herself as bait. " It's his last chance," she said, perhaps over-severely, as if he were a bad boy whom she had to discipline. " I'm giving it to him not because he deserves it but because I think he's good in his own line — too good to be allowed to go on being unlucky for the rest of his life. As for myself, I'm not specially anxious to be in a picture, though I dare say it'll be interesting, but however it turns out I certainly don't plan a new career. It's just this once. I want you to know that."

He was silent for a long while after she had first thought she had finished. She kept remembering additional details and adding them, but still he was silent. Then he went to the decanter and poured himself another drink.

He said at length : " I don't want you to do it at all."

" I'm sorry, Austen. I was afraid it wouldn't please you, but I wish you could realize that I feel I have to."

" I don't see why you feel you have to do anything unless it's what you want."

" Then I suppose it's true that I want to do it."

" As I thought." His voice was quietly strained. " So

for this desire, or compulsion, or sense of obligation — whatever it is — you're ready to break up all we have here together. . . ."

" Oh no, no — why ? — why should that happen ? Surely it has nothing to do with——"

" Carey, it's come to the point I hoped it never would — I've got to tell you what I really think of Paul. Discount some of it, but not much, because I hate him. He's the only person I've ever hated. And it's for one reason only — that he not only drove you half out of your mind when he was with you, but he hasn't let you alone since. The mere thought of him — his very existence anywhere — can threaten your happiness and therefore mine. I've known that for a long time."

" You're really exaggerating, Austen. He never drove me half out of my mind."

" You should have seen yourself when I met you. It's what first made me notice you — because I'm not normally the sort of person who picks up strange actresses on shipboard." He smiled a wintry smile. " But that broken look you had, the look of being utterly lost and spiritless——"

" I don't remember it was as bad as that."

" You don't ? Then that's what living a sane life these last fifteen years has done — the life you're now planning to give up. Perhaps you don't remember the nervous wreck you were while you were rehearsing that play ? "

" The one that flopped ? Oh, heavens, yes, but you can't blame that on Paul. He'd never have let me do it if he'd been around."

" But he wasn't around, was he, and that's the point . . . that he'd deserted you and you were like a drowning person all that time. Fortunately — by some miracle — you began to learn to swim on your own."

" With you to help me, Austen, I admit that."

" I don't want your admission as if it were only my due. I want you to stay here, with me, for your own sake and mine, and I don't want you ever to see or communicate with Paul again. I can't put it straighter than that."

Because he was not a man to plead, the note in his voice embarrassed her, as if she were eavesdropping on something unseemly. She knew he was genuinely trying to master his emotion and not, as an actor might, to exhibit it with an appearance of struggle for concealment. She began tidying things on her dressing-table, to ease both of them through a bad moment; and suddenly, as in times of crisis before, the sense of dual personality came on her and she herself was acting, Carey Arundel playing the part of the second Mrs. Bond.

" But it's all fixed up, Austen."

" Then unfix it. Change your mind — break your word if necessary. And if you've signed anything, leave that to me."

" I haven't signed anything yet. But it's all fixed up."

" You're afraid he'll try to hold you to a promise ? Leave that to me too."

" It isn't that at all. As a matter of fact *he* had to be persuaded, not I. It's just that I *want* him to do this job and he can't get it unless I'm in the thing too. They wouldn't take him without me. I explained it all just now."

" So you really intend to go on with this ? "

" Yes, I do. I'm sorry, Austen."

He came over to her and touched her shoulder. She felt his hand cold. She saw how pale he was, the grey look of misery, and when she reached up to touch his hand it was icy. " It doesn't mean any break between you and me," she said with kindness. " At least I don't know why it should."

" Carey, how can you *say* that ? How can you think of *doing* this ? How *could* you ? " He seemed brought up against an impasse of incredibility. " Without even consulting me. . . . I can't understand it. . . ."

" It's my work, Austen, if you argue it out on those lines. I never promised I'd give it up for good. I don't want to do it all the time — you know that — but I can't think of it as something you have a right to veto."

" I've never tried to, when it was the work itself you wanted. But *he's* your reason now. You've been frank enough to say so. And he'll ruin you. He'll wear you out again — and you're older, you won't be able to stand it. He *consumes* — you used that word once yourself. And he has no loyalty, nor integrity, nor even common fairness. As you say, you don't remember those things now. There are things you probably don't even know of . . . all the time he was refusing you a divorce, for instance, he was living with a German girl — a film actress. . . ."

" Oh, was he ? A beautiful girl, I met her. Doesn't surprise me — I suspected it all along. But how did *you* know ? "

He answered grimly : " I had him watched."

It was his mistake to have said that. It threw her into a different mood.

" Really, Austen ? As simple as that ? You just had him watched ? "

" I thought we might need the information legally, but it turned out we didn't and I was glad. I never intended to tell you anything about it, unless I had to, and for all these years——"

" You've kept the secret ! That was rather wonderful, after having him watched. Do you often have people watched ? "

" *Carey !* "

" Have you ever had *me* watched ? " She was relieved to be able to laugh. " But of course you have — Richards watches me, and Foster, and Flossie — you don't suppose I haven't noticed, do you ? It's your way — you think it's safer than trusting people. So do please have me watched in Hollywood — you have contacts there, I'm sure. It won't cause me any trouble, because I won't be having an affair with anybody, not even my ex-husband. I'm really telling you the truth — there's not love of that kind between me and Paul."

" Perhaps I'm just as jealous of any other kind, whatever it is."

" The kind that hired watchers couldn't give you evidence about ? "

" Oh, Carey, why are you so bitter ? Have I ever done you any wrong ? "

She knew it was because he hadn't that she was bitter, if at all. " Let's not talk any more tonight, Austen. I hate arguments and I know you do too."

" There's nothing more to say, now that we've both spoken our minds. You've told me you intend to do what you want. So shall I — as soon as I know what it is. I don't — yet. I'm too shocked — not by the thing itself but by your reason for doing it — the proof it gives of how little I mean to you, and not only I, but your home here . . . and Norris. What's going to happen to that boy after you've gone ? He worships you — you've been part of his cure since he came back — he depends on you . . . but I suppose all that counts for nothing also."

His mention of Norris brought her to the limit of endurance. " Norris will be all right," she answered unevenly. " I'm not as necessary for him as you think."

" But you *are* — you always have been — you're the only one who can talk sense to him ! He has a preposterous idea of taking up medicine and going out to some island as a resident doctor — did you know that ? — the whole thing is fantastic — it would take years to qualify and by that time, anyhow . . . but it shows the state of his mind — it shows how much he needs your advice and influence, since he won't accept mine. And this is the moment you choose to leave him ! "

He walked out of the room without waiting for a reply, even if she could have made one. It was the first time she had seen him beyond control.

. . . . . .

The next morning at breakfast both of them, for Norris's sake, tried to behave as if nothing was amiss. She thought she herself was acting well enough, but Austen, though he clearly did his best, could not match her, and there was a noticeable tension in his manner that made Norris, after his father had gone to the office, remark to Carey : " What's on his mind ? A new billion dollar loan or something ? "

She felt sorry for Austen and therefore hurt by Norris's flippancy ; she said : " He has personal worries, Norris."

" Meaning me ? "

She suddenly decided to tell him the truth then, instead of later, partly because she was no longer sure she could keep up a pretence, partly also from an urge to discover his reaction. So she told him, explaining the thing pretty much as she had done to Austen. When she had finished he was silent for a moment, then said : " So *that's* what was bothering him."

" Yes. That and your own idea."

" *My* idea ? " He started in alarm. " What do you mean ? "

" The tropical medicine. He doesn't like either of our ideas."

" My God, Carey, you didn't tell him *that* ? What on earth made you——"

" Of course I didn't, but he *knew* — he mentioned it to me and I was a bit surprised to think that *you'd* told him——"

" As if I should——"

" Then . . . how on earth could he know ? "

He replied after a pause, with the schoolboy sarcasm that she knew disguised his emotions so often : " I suppose there are several ways. First, he might have heard us during the bridge game. But I rather doubt that — we talked too quietly. Second, Richards might have been eavesdropping after he brought in the drinks. But I rather doubt that too — I had my eye on him. Thirdly, either of them might have seen the letter I wrote to Columbia. Yes, on the whole, I think that's the likeliest. I left the letter on the hall table to be picked up with the other mail. Somehow I didn't think . . . *letters*."

" Oh, Norris, I'm sorry."

" Hardly *your* fault."

" I think perhaps it is, in a way."

" That father sets up a spy system ? I don't get it. You never promised him you'd drop your profession altogether. At least that's what you once told me."

" No, but that's not my real reason. I told you my real reason just now."

He said, after a silence : " Well, I never met the guy, so I can't say whether I think he's worth it."

" Maybe he isn't. It isn't personal, anyhow."

" Then what is it ? "

" I — I don't know. That's why I can't blame your father for not quite sizing it up. I can't blame anybody. Not even myself. It's my fault, but I don't blame myself for it. Does that give any clue ? "

He smiled. " He must mean a lot to you. . . ."

" Which of them are you talking about ? "

" Paul." He went on smiling. " This is a funny conversation. I still say, though, he must mean a lot to you."

" I don't know. . . . I don't know *what* he means."

" But you're looking forward to the excitement of working with him again. I'll bet you are."

She looked up, transfixed with a certain incredulity. " Looking forward to it ? You really think that ? "

" Well, aren't you ? "

" Norris, I'm *dreading* it."

" Then why do it ? "

" I — I don't know."

" There we are again."

" Yes."

" You just *have* to do it ? "

" Yes, in a sort of way."

" Maybe I know how you feel. We're both built a bit like that. You facing your ordeal and I . . . if I can find one worth facing . . ."

" I hope you can, Norris. And I hope it isn't too much of an ordeal. Mine won't be more than I can help. I shall do my best to enjoy a new experience."

" You make it sound like a school teacher visiting the Carlsbad Caverns."

" Now whatever made you think of that ? "

" I'm trying hard not to be serious. You once asked me not to be. Now I ask you not to be. Let's have a good time till you leave — just a hell of a good time, as if we hadn't anything on *our* minds . . . do you think we could ? "

" I'll try."

And indeed a curious tranquillity settled on them both as they went about together during the days that followed. They had the good time, doing nothing specially new, just the things that had by then become routine. To Carey the whole interval had a quality of swanlike timelessness, as if anchored neither to past nor future. She thought of a river above a fall, the water rolling deep and unknowing.

Not till the last day was Paul mentioned again, and then quite casually by her. It was in her room, amidst the confusion of packing, that he exclaimed: " Carey, I said it before and I'll say it again — you'll be a big success in films. You'll photograph like an angel."

" Paul says the left profile isn't quite so good."

" Oh, he does, does he ? Perfectionist. I'll bet he doesn't understand you half as well as I do."

" In some ways he doesn't understand me at all."

" No ? Really ? I'd like to meet that guy some time."

" Maybe you will." She laughed, but nervously, as if the thought gave her a mixture of fear and pleasure. " It's too bad I once told him you were a writer. He hates writers. But perhaps by that time you'll be a doctor."

The maid entered with extra things to be packed, and there was no more chance to talk.

.   .   .   .   .

On the train to Chicago she had a moment of supreme dejection when she wondered if she were doing the most foolish thing of her life. At the peak of misgiving she would have gone back, no matter at what cost in surrender or complication, but of course it was impossible, and the moment passed.

She had waved through the window at Grand Central and seen father and son standing together as the train moved out. There had also been a photographer from the New York office of Majestic Pictures. She had posed for him on the platform and he had wanted to take the three of them in a group, but Austen, with his usual phobia about publicity, had curtly declined. Or had his reason been only that? It would have been a good way to contradict the rumours already in circulation, if he had wanted to. She could not read into Austen's mind, and she realized now that she had never been able to, completely.

Soon it was evening and she felt less troubled — she could enjoy the cosiness of the drawing-room, the lights of the little towns as they flashed by, the glances of fellow-passengers in the diner, some of whom doubtless recognized her. She went to bed early and slept fairly well, and in the morning, after the transfer at Chicago, settled down to a couple of usefully contemplative days alone. It was for this reason she had not travelled by air or with Paul. He was to fly out in time to meet her, possibly at the train when she arrived.

As the miles passed and she stared out of the window for long stretches, it seemed to her that she remembered more than she observed, for it was over twenty years since she had made this same westward journey, but then by road, with Paul, in a model-T Ford. She herself had driven, and in those days it had not been such an easy trip — long spells of dirt road between towns, changing tyres in the dust, the radiator boiling over on mountain grades, nights spent in cheap hotels, sometimes in the car to save a dollar. But to her (as that vacation in Ireland to Norris) the whole experience was deep in the mythology of the heart . . . the tree-shaded towns of Ohio, a whiff of snow in Kansas, sunrise on the redlands of Arizona. And now the air-conditioned luxury of the Super-Chief was the measure of the years of change.

PART FIVE

ONE day about half-way through the shooting of *Morning Journey* the leading man, Greg Wilson, called Carey to come and look at what was going on. She had been resting during a scene in which she did not appear, and the portable dressing-room, tucked away in the corner of the big stage, had a privacy that no one would wantonly disturb. But Greg, whom she had come to like during their work together, evidently thought the reason good enough. At first glance nothing was unusual. There had been one take already and there was to be another. Technicians were checking the lights ; ·the camera was being reloaded ; the customary appearance of noisy chaos was in full show. Paul had slumped in the canvas chair, his head sunk forward as if he were half asleep — a characteristic attitude that often concealed a sharp scrutiny of what was in progress. Greg, ill-clothed and unkempt for his part, looked very different from the hero of his usual type of film, and clearly he was excited at the difference and a little vain of himself. Two other actors, one a girl, were also waiting to begin. The scene was the interior of a country cottage, nothing special or expensive about it.

Paul said something and the bell rang for silence.

" Well, here we go," Greg whispered to Carey. " Watch me — I'm good, but watch Barrington too — he's better."

Carey watched. *Morning Journey* was really nothing but a cops and robbers picture (as Paul had said scornfully at the outset), and any similarity between itself and life would, in the ordinary way, have been purely detrimental. However, once Paul had schooled himself to the actual job of shooting, the usual change in his attitude took place ; *Morning Journey* became then contemptible only to the extent that it owed its origin to a mediocre novel and its later shape to a couple of script writers. There was, of course, the permanent slur (liable to be brought up at any moment in any argument) of its being a Majestic picture and therefore a victim of over-all and predestined contamination. The odd thing was that with all this Paul managed to combine a tremendous intention of his own to make every scene as good as he knew how, and an overmastering pride in every fragment of his work. The result was something in which life-likeness, if not life itself, sneaked in by all kinds of crannies ; or, to quote a later critic who was mainly hostile, the picture was full of " directorial flourishes ". It was one of these that Greg had called on Carey to witness. The opening situation was simple : at night two escaping prisoners-of-war approach a woodcutter's cottage high in the Bavarian Alps. The men are weary and famished, almost ready to give themselves up ; in this mood they enter the cottage seeking food and shelter. To their astonishment they encounter no one, though lamps are lit, there is a fire burning, and a table is set for a meal. The men fall to on what is to hand — hunks of bread and cheese and pitchers of milk ; then, with the edge of hunger dulled, they become aware that there *is* someone else. They hear footsteps and a girl's voice singing. They stand transfixed when the door opens and the girl, beautiful of course, brings in more food for the table. Amazingly she does not seem to notice them, though they have had no time to hide. The men are desperately uncertain what to do. Should they seize her, gag her, and tie her up, so that she cannot give the alarm till they are well away ? Or should they throw themselves on her mercy ? One of the men (Greg), realizing the truth sooner than the other, covers his companion's mouth in a frantic signal for silence. *For the girl is blind*. But already she has *heard*. They try to edge towards the door while she greets them cheerfully : " Hello. Sit down and have some food. Who are you ? How many are there of you ? Did you find them yet ? They're probably across the border by now. Did you meet my father ? — he said he'd climb to the ridge." The men dare not speak and their silence puzzles her. First she thinks it is a joke. " Hans, I know it's you — answer me — stop being silly. Who is it with you ? " All at once, in the continuing silence, panic is born and she suspects the truth — that the intruders are not the pursuers, but the pursued. Her aim is then as much to escape as theirs is, and in rushing out of the room she stumbles over a chair. The second man, with instinctive kindliness, takes a step to help her, but has to be restrained by Greg. Once outside the room the girl screams for help while the two men make their exit from a side window.

A remarkable scene, if only because the star of the picture had nothing to say in it. But two other things made it equally remarkable. One was the almost intolerable suspense, the ballet-like dumb show of the two fugitives counterpointing the fluttering rhythms of the blind girl. The other was the identity of the actor sharing the dumb show with Greg. He was Jerry Barrington, an old-timer from silent-picture days, whose failing (apart from drink) had always been regarded as an invincible inability to speak lines. But now, in a rather unexampled way, he did not have to speak lines. It was really very fortunate for the picture. Yet that impulse of his to help the blind girl when she stumbled had had a rare beauty in it, something that had momentarily transfigured the face and movements of a rather second-rate performer.

Yet another point might have been noted — that the scene bore small resemblance to anything in the script, in whose mimeographed pages the girl had not been blind, and the men, before they could fill their pockets with food and get away, had had to dodge in and out of rooms like erring husbands in a French farce.

After the word " Cut " there was a spell of continued tension as if even hard-boiled technicians were impressed ; then Paul added : " Print the first one," and everybody laughed. Already he had become somewhat notorious for saying that.

Greg joined Carey at the edge of the suddenly unloosed commotion ; Paul was already talking to the camera-man about the next scene.

"How does he do it?" Greg exclaimed. "An old ham like Barrington. . . ."

Carey said: "I've never seen Barrington before."

"That's the point. Nobody's ever seen him before. . . . How does he do it? Paul, I mean."

She said: "It was the same in the theatre. He had a way of getting things out of people."

Greg nodded. "Now go back and finish your nap. We shan't be wanted for another hour at least."

"I'm glad you fetched me, Greg. It's a wonderful scene. Who changed it this way?"

"Can't you guess? The writers haven't been near the place. They'll probably kick when they find out, unless they know a good thing when they see it, and who does, when it's somebody else's?"

"Did Randolph approve?"

"He wouldn't have been given a chance only he happened to come on the set while the whole thing was being cooked up and re-rehearsed. I don't think he really liked it. He finds it hard to like anything that Paul does at the last minute without consulting him. But the big row was because Paul wanted the girl to speak in German — said it was more natural and the words themselves didn't matter — the voice would give the meaning. Of course Randy wouldn't stand for that, and Paul had to give in. The rest he did the way he wanted it." Greg laughed. "What a way to make a picture! And yet *what* a way — if you can do it!"

She had already admitted Greg to full membership in the conspiracy of those who knew the formula derived from measuring Paul's faults against his virtues.

"Personally," she said, "I agree with Randolph about the German. Paul goes overboard sometimes."

"Sure. Ninety per cent of Paul and ten per cent of Randy make a good mixture."

"I think I'll drop by and talk to him before I go home. Perhaps I can smooth matters down a bit."

"Couldn't do any harm. He likes *you*."

So she called at Randolph's office before leaving the studio that evening. She didn't defend the changed scene, but chatted about it in a seemingly impartial way, and somehow conveyed her own satisfaction with the progress of the picture as a whole. Randolph, frosty at first, thawed under her influence till at last he admitted that some of the scenes *looked* all right. The test, of course, would be in the public's reception. He was a tall dome-headed tweedy fellow in his late fifties, as proud of his Bond Street shoes as he was of his hundred-odd pictures that, over a period of twenty years, had earned fabulous profits without ever collecting a single award or distinction. He was not cynical about this, merely matter of fact. Picture-making was an industry; art was all right, but it usually did not pay. If by chance it did, it was either a fluke, or else the artist involved had been kept in careful check by men of proved experience. He himself was a man of proved experience and he was determined to keep Saffron in check, but Saffron, being not only an artist but also a so-and-so, was harder to check than most artists. This was his attitude, which he did not put into words, but which Carey understood perfectly. She had even a certain amount of sympathy — not with it, but with him, for Paul's habit of rewriting scenes at the last minute was really inexcusable. But then Paul had found many other things inexcusable. His first big row with Randolph had occurred after the first day's shooting when the two of them, along with Carey, Greg Wilson, and a fourth man, had sat in the back row of a projection-room to see the rushes. The fourth man, introduced indistinctly, was ignored until Randolph suddenly addressed him across the others. " Cut from where the girl enters the room to the long shot of the cab arriving. Then go to the two-shot inside the cab." Paul rose from his seat immediately. " What's going on ? Are you joking ? Who is this fellow ? " The fourth man, who had been taking notes, was then solemnly reintroduced as a cutter. Paul erupted for about ten minutes. It was then explained to him that Majestic Pictures Incorporated employed producers to produce, directors to direct, and cutters to cut. Paul said he would do his own cutting or quit. He had had to concede control of production, casting, and music, but there was a limit beyond which he would not surrender. The argument continued in the darkened projection-room until Randolph was fuming and Paul had begun to inveigh against the entire output of Majestic Pictures, hardly any of which he had seen. The cutter sat silent, aware that his salary did not entitle him to an opinion. In the end the matter was left somewhat undecided, with Carey and Greg appealing to both sides to wait till the picture was finished before any cutting was done at all. "If it's good," she said, "surely it won't be hard then to agree on the details." This may not have made much sense (since it would always be hard for Paul to agree with anyone else on anything), but it provided a needed excuse for shelving the issue; but of course Randolph hated Paul from then on, and Paul, who already hated Randolph, began a grim accumulation of ammunition for the eventual fight. One of his procedures was to see earlier pictures that Randolph had produced, whenever the chance occurred, and gloat over the details of their badness.

There were other troubles. Randolph's way of shooting a picture (he had been a director himself in his time) was to make a long master-shot of everything in a scene, then break it up into medium and close shots, ' favouring ' the star — for naturally, under the star system, who else could be ' favoured ' ? The final jigsaw was then assembled in the cutting-room, where, if any supporting actors were so good that they drew too much attention, the error could be corrected by blanketing their voices against the star's close-up. This had been done so often in all Majestic pictures that it had become a formula which Randolph took for granted; even to question it seemed slightly impious. Paul not only questioned it, he called it nonsense. First, he did not believe in master-shots, and he hated close-ups of faces while other actors were speaking. And he liked the camera to move, not to chop and change from one fixed position to another. Nor did he believe a scene could be stolen except by what deserved to steal it — which was good acting against bad acting. He thought Greg Wilson, for instance, was a pretty bad actor, and hadn't wanted him in the picture at all. Randolph, however, knew that Carey had no following among movie-goers, and had insisted on casting Majestic's biggest box-office name opposite her. Carey was prepared to agree that in this Randolph might be wise, but Paul resented it until one day Greg told Paul that no director he had ever experienced had done so well with him. This flattered Paul and made him think Greg not nearly as bad, which was the necessary self-hypnosis before Paul could make him, as he presently did, rather surprisingly adequate.

As for Carey herself, her introduction to a new technique of acting, if it were such, seemed less significant than a return to the discipline of working with Paul. After an anguished rehearsal of the first scene, she wondered what had ever possessed her to undertake a renewal of this ordeal voluntarily ; a hundred memories assailed her, mostly of similar anguish when she had been unable to please him during stage rehearsals ; she might have guessed he would have become no more indulgent with the years. But then one day while she was before the camera in a rather difficult scene, another memory touched her — the renewal of that curious trance-like bliss that told her she was *acting*, and with it the renewal of ambition to act, and of the feeling that what she was doing mattered by some standard shared by other arts. She tried to catch Paul's eye when the scene ended, but he was looking elsewhere ; she heard, however, the inflection in his voice as he spoke the one word " Print," and in that she had her answer. She felt suddenly radiant. It was all worth while. God knew how or why, but it was.

She could have endured and even come to enjoy the strain of satisfying Paul as an actress had there been less to do as trouble-shooter. The ancient contrast appeared again in full force — that most people liked her a great deal while few could like Paul except with a degree of partisanship that made them just as difficult to handle themselves. (Among these few were several actors and a negro set-boy for whom he had performed some unexplained kindness.) The trouble was that there were so many more possible antagonisms on a movie stage than in a theatre — so many more rules, written and unwritten, to be despised and challenged; so many more taboos to tilt against, so many more egos to affront. Typical, perhaps, was the row with the musicians. The scene called for Carey to play the piano, which she did on a silent keyboard while a professional pianist dubbed in from the background. Paul's first complaint was that the pianist played too well; after a second try, Paul complained that he played too badly. Paul then went to the piano, played the thing himself, and declared himself thoroughly satisfied. "There's all the difference," he said, "between a non-professional playing as well as he can and a professional deliberately playing less well than he can." Perhaps there was, but there also happened to be Petrillo's union that would not let Paul play at all. It took an hour or more to convince him that he could not fight Petrillo, and several days to appease the musicians who considered themselves slighted by the whole incident.

Then there was his refusal to admit strangers to the set and his rudeness to a New York executive (and principal Majestic stockholder) who assumed that rules did not apply to him. There were also scenes with the camera-man, who regarded his machine as a Copernican sun round which the picture should revolve, whereas to Paul it was an Einsteinian eye that must move relatively to the actors all the time. Furthermore, Paul wanted to select the lens and teach the man his job; as he was a veteran who had worked for Essanay in nickelodeon days he took this very ill indeed, and the fact that Paul knew all the mechanics of camera work did not mollify him. The sultriest arguments they had were over Paul's frequent use of dolly and boom, which caused extra trouble and higher costs. Yet in another way Paul's methods were too economical to be popular; both camera crew and stage-hands liked a director whose many takes gave them plenty of idleness on the set. But Paul was often satisfied with the first take, and took a second only for protection. His procedure was to rehearse and rehearse, with the camera going through all the motions of the shooting and the camera man doing what he was told instead of presiding over a mystery.

But of all disputes the fiercest were with the writers, since to begin with, Paul had disliked both story and script. The former, supposed to be based on a novel, had really retained little but the title, and this, for all that it signified, might just as well (had they not been used before) have been *Gone With the Wind* or *If Winter Comes*. As for the script, Paul claimed it was intolerably wordy; " Nobody talks like that in life ", he kept on saying, though with scornful inconsistency he could agree that many people did, if they attended movies often enough. A rewrite, made after heated conferences, resulted in a second version hardly more to his taste, but by that time the shooting date was near and there was no time for a further rewrite. Nor, to be frank, was Paul at all anxious to have one. He was perfectly satisfied to doctor the script himself as he went along, thinning out dialogue, changing background, inventing incidents, introducing new facets to character, and generally playing God. The writers had every reason to hate him, but since also they were pretty good writers they were even fascinated by him a little, as by a cross unlikely to be inflicted on them again. One of them took him aside after an especially stormy argument and said, almost affectionately : " Look, Mr. Saffron, you haven't been here long — you don't know the way things work. Maybe, as you say, there's too much dialogue in pictures, but what the hell do you expect us to do — turn out a script full of stage directions ? You know nobody ever takes any notice of what a writer wants actors to *do* — only of what he gives them to *say*. Ever seen a top executive looking over a script ? Unless you can make him yell ' Boy, oh boy, what dialogue ! ' you're out of luck. . . . So you see how it is, Mr. Saffron ? "

" All I see," Paul answered, " is that Mendelssohn would have been in trouble here for writing *Lieder ohne Worte*."

The writers laughed and appreciated him more for this and other sallies than he did them for their considerable patience. There was no doubt that he had never really liked writers since the day he had ceased to be one himself. Of course he would show respect to literary eminence, and in the presence of business men he could even feel distant kinship with any writer at all, as with any muralist or trumpet player or landscape gardener; but as a rule he was on constant guard. Stage playwrights especially he had always been wary of, since they had a relatively privileged status and even he could not cut and change their work without a semblance of permission. But his more recent and heightened hostility had actually sprung from a war-time neurosis; in the prison camp he had seen a few writers occasionally writing, and their self-containedness, their ability to work with a pencil and a scrap of paper in relative secrecy and in disregard of events, had rubbed raw his own grandiose frustrations. It was thus in part a pathological grudge, and now the chance to pay it off was unique. Always quick to grasp a situation before he knew the reasons for it, he had soon sensed that Majestic's professional scenarists, even when high-salaried, carried none of the prestige of the older kinds of writer; so that at long last he had the breed where he wanted it — in subservience to the over-all authority of the show-maker — i.e. himself. It was the one point on which, without realizing it, he was in full agreement with the studio heads — though they, of course, set themselves above him with an equal degree of arrogance.

Finally, he was at odds with the publicity department and the columnists who wrote movie stuff for newspapers and fan magazines. He did not trouble to understand their function, but let them know that even if he did he would probably despise it. On first reading gossip items that he and Carey were contemplating a reconciliation, he had snorted contemptuously, and when asked if it were true had denied it with an emphasis that might have sounded ungallant had not Carey been with him to laugh and back him up. But of course the rumour stayed in circulation, only weakened slightly by an alternative theory that Carey was interested in her leading man. She was; she liked Greg Wilson very much. They often dined and were seen together.

Greg was a big, jovial forty-seven, and quite sensationally handsome. By careful make-up and constant attention to physique he had been playing parts of twenty-five-year-olds so long that there was a certain puppy quality in his entire behaviour and personality. Two marriages had failed, possibly because he was less exciting in life than on the screen; he had now for several years been alone, popular, and extremely eligible. He was also Majestic's biggest and therefore most privileged money-maker, playing golf with the studio heads and fringeing on the kind of society that did not normally admit movie people at all. A likeable fellow, whose love scenes were so wooden that women imagined what it must be like to teach him. He found it hard to memorize more than a few lines at a time. When it was conveyed to him (not over-subtly) that Paul had not wanted him in the picture, he said : " For Pete's sake, why should he ? I don't blame him." When he met Carey he made it almost too clear that he was smitten ; actually he wasn't, but he enjoyed thinking he was. He had all the bluff open-air reactions to most things that his screen characters had — except one reaction that nobody could have foreseen and that had certainly not been foreshadowed in any part he had ever played. This was a curious attachment that he developed to Paul. Paul, he went around telling people, was the greatest director he had ever known. " Look ! " he exclaimed, when he saw the daily rushes. " Would you ever believe that's *me* ? " There was something warm and engaging about him, and Carey found him a constant ally in her efforts to smooth out troubles that arose from Paul's behaviour on and off the set.

* * * * *

Those days of the shooting of *Morning Journey* passed for her in a curious enclosed dream.

She heard from Norris — a warm, friendly note, not very long, discussing mostly the books he had been reading, telling little of affairs at the house. He mentioned that Austen would soon leave on a business trip to South America and had suggested he should go along with him, but he didn't know whether he wanted to.

She wrote a long chatty letter in reply, the kind Austen could see if it so happened, describing her work, the progress of the picture, and the life she was living. She added that the South American trip sounded exciting, maybe it was the sort of change he needed.

She did not hear from Austen, but to him also she wrote a long chatty letter, describing her work, the progress of the picture, and the life she was living.

It was certainly a hard one, much more so than she had expected. She was up most mornings by six, to be ready on the set by eight for hair-dressing and make-up. Paul was always there by then, having stayed up all night (she sometimes concluded) to rewrite the scenes. She and Paul lived in apartments several miles from each other; their first meeting of the day was on the sound stage, and in the evenings, even if they dined together at a restaurant, they rarely said good-night later than ten. On Saturdays she allowed herself to accept party invitations; Sunday was a day of rest unless Greg Wilson drove her to the mountains or the sea. He bored her a little when he talked almost continually about Paul. His favourite remark was that he didn't know how two such wonderful people could ever have separated, and once he varied this by saying he couldn't understand how she could ever have let Paul go.

"But I didn't let him go," she answered. "He let me go."

"Oh," Greg exclaimed and was then silent, as if her reply had led him to an entirely new train of thought.

Sometimes during the lunch recess she and Paul would sit in her dressing-room with sandwiches and coffee, and this was really the quietest time they ever had together, certainly the most intimate. There were few places more peaceful than a studio sound stage during this hour-long interval; the big lights were out, technicians and actors had all left the job, sound-proof doors were closed, the huge building with its high roof, dark interior, and mysterious shapes of equipment and scenery had the air of a cathedral dedicated to some new and strange religion. Paul was human enough then to fall asleep, or smoke his big cigars, or talk of anything that came into his head, or even rehearse something privately with her if he wanted. And she in turn would hear his complaints, give him advice, and sometimes coax him into a more amenable attitude for the afternoon. " Paul," she kept saying till it was almost a refrain, " *do* remember what a chance you have. I know you aren't getting all your own way, but you're getting a lot, and if this turns out a good picture you'll be able to ask for much more. *Do* make compromises. You're so good, Paul, you'll have all you want if you'll only play your cards properly now."

He would often talk to her, in staccato and seemingly unrelated snatches, about his experiences in Europe, though there was one period he rarely mentioned, even inferentially — and that was his three years in the internment camp. Like certain other parts of his life it was clearly destined for obliteration in his memory — the final anathema that his ego pronounced on hostile eventfulness. What he did remember, constantly, were incidents in earlier films of his that illustrated some point in *Morning Journey*. As he progressed further with the picture and revamped more of it to suit himself, it naturally rose in his estimation till he began to feel about it almost as he had done about a new play before opening night — *i.e.* that it was a masterpiece. *Almost* — but not quite, for the different conditions of picture-making involved so many other persons over whom he had no control, and whom, therefore, he could not exalt by such comprehensive praise.

A specific scene in *Morning Journey* called for Carey to show by her expression the horror of discovering hate in the eyes of someone she had thought loved her — a difficult emotion, and Paul had rehearsed the scene several times without being completely satisfied. During the lunch hour that day he told her of a scene in one of his German pictures in which the situation was as follows. A wife had been having an affair with a much younger man who was already tiring of it. At the crisis of a bitter quarrel, the woman turned a revolver on herself; the youth managed to wrest it from her and the quarrel then continued more hotly than ever. At a second crisis he became so incensed that, still holding the woman's revolver, he pointed it at her and pulled the trigger. There was no report, and the woman's eyes conveyed what had happened. *She* had known, but *he* had not, that the weapon was unloaded. *She* had been merely putting on an act to impress him, but *he* had been actually ready to kill her.

"I didn't speak much German in those days," Paul added, "and when I rehearsed the scene I told the actors to say anything they wanted to make it sound like a quarrel. Later on we had a writer, but I never even bothered to have his lines translated for me. It was the woman's expression I was aiming for — the awful awareness in it. I got what I wanted too, because she was Wanda Hessely and Wanda could do anything. Remember her? You met her at Interlaken that time."

"Yes, but I'm not as good an actress, you said."

"That's so. But you're good enough."

"And her scene was easier."

"No — just as hard."

"Anything's easier with guns and things to play with."

"Try it then."

"Our scene?"

"No — the one she did. I'll play the man. This is your gun." He picked up the metal tube that had contained one of his big cigars. "Adlib the dialogue — anything . . . let's go. . . . Why not? Can't do any harm."

They went through the scene after a fashion, but Carey was less adept at improvising dialogue than Paul, and it struck her amidst her own difficulty that in adlibbing a quarrel he was very much on his home ground. The whole experiment was not very satisfactory and they ended by laughing. "Maybe it's helped, though," Paul said.

"By the way," she asked, "what happened to Wanda Hessely?"

He shrugged. " There was a rumour she was killed in one of the Berlin air raids."

" Oh dear, I hope not."

He exclaimed sharply : " You what ? You hope not ? You dare to hope that out of all the millions of innocent people·slaughtered during those horrible years *she* should have been spared — just because you happened to meet her once ! What sublime egotism ! "

The remark was so startlingly outrageous that she would have flared up but for the look she caught in time — the look that told her, out of long experience, that he had spoken thus to conceal some deep feeling of his own. He had always been like that, and only for a short time, just after their marriage, had she been able to free him a little. It was the more curious because in his work he was superbly free ; without sentimentality or shrinking he could examine and expose the tenderest emotions. But off duty, so to say, certain rigidities clamped down, engendering even a perverse desire to appear callous, so that it was often at such moments that he said things that were most remembered against him.

She said, as to a child : " Don't be silly, Paul."

. . . . . .

One evening, on impulse, she visited a doctor — not a fashionable one, or a specialist of any kind — just a local man whose office she had noticed near her apartment. She had begun to feel a peculiar tiredness lately, to which broken sleep had doubtless added. The doctor listened to her vague description of symptoms, examined her heart, and asked what was making her so nervous. She said she didn't know. He then fumbled a few questions that would soon have led to an intimate discussion of her personal affairs, but she discouraged him and he ended by telling her she had a slight heart condition, nothing serious provided she avoided overwork and, above all things, did not worry. He advised a vacation if she could take one and she promised she would, very soon. She thanked him then, paid his fee, and felt both relieved and somehow much older as she left his office.

She told Paul of her visit the next morning. Rather to her surprise he took the matter anxiously and was extremely solicitous. " Oh my God, Carey — we'll have to look after you, won't we ? Less work from now on — I'll watch it — to hell with their schedule — we're ahead of time, anyhow. No shooting after five o'clock — I'll make that a rule."

" It isn't so much the work, Paul," she ventured to remonstrate. " It's trying to pacify everybody you quarrel with, and having to talk Randolph into a good humour, and being nice to newspaper people after you've made enemies of them all . . . if only you'd spare me some of that."

" I will," he promised abjectly. " I know I'm to blame in a lot of things. And we just can't have you getting ill. I know what illness is — I'm not a completely well man myself." She smiled at that, remembering that whenever anyone else had ever mentioned the slightest ailment of any kind Paul had always been able to match it with some private and hitherto undisclosed martyrdom of his own. But now he said, so calmly that she felt he might be speaking the truth : " One or two things happened in that camp I was in — shocking things that I wouldn't ever tell anyone about. They made me ill and I started getting headaches. Migraine. They don't come so often now, except when I have fights."

" Oh, I'm sorry. Then that's another reason why you shouldn't have fights."

" Yes, yes." He clapped his hand dramatically to his head. " I must take care. I know I must."

She said, continuing to smile : " Looks as if we're both getting to be a couple of old crocks."

" *What ?* Oh, nonsense ! "

" I was only joking. My trouble isn't serious at all, I'm glad to say. The doctor assured me I'd be all right if I take care. Try to get a little rest in the afternoons, he said. I do, don't I — in between scenes and rehearsals ? And don't let household worries weigh on you. Well, I haven't any, that's one blessing. . . . As he took me to the door, he said — ' You know, Mrs. Bond, your face reminds me of someone.' I thought he was going to say Carey Arundel and I got all prepared to be gracious, but he went on — 'A girl who was a hostess on United Airlines — were you ever one, by any chance?' I told him no, and he looked quite sad."

"He *did*?" Paul exclaimed with abrupt and cheerful interest. "What sort of a man was he? . . . No, don't tell me — I've got a concept of him in my mind already — middle-aged, quiet, hard worker, faithful husband, respectable citizen . . . but all the time he's carried a vision of a girl he once saw in a plane . . . he never spoke to her — just watched as she walked about serving meals and checking seat-belts . . . a short trip, say Dallas to El Paso — two hours out of a whole lifetime. He fell in love with her then, if he'd realized it, but he didn't, he was shy, he didn't know his own mind enough to follow it, he wasn't the type to say 'Hello, sweetheart' and ask for a date, he didn't even remember her name afterwards . . . but as the years go by he can't forget her, she becomes a symbol of the unattainable, the pluperfect subjunctive — sometimes he sees people — strangers, new patients — who remind him of her, or he thinks they do. . . . One of these days he's going to leave his home, his wife, his patients — everything — and search the world for that girl. . . . Ah, that could be a *picture*, Carey. Not junk like *Morning Journey*."

She laughed at the suddenness with which *Morning Journey* had ceased to be a near-masterpiece; she laughed at his improvisation and at his own mounting enthusiasm for it; she laughed at his growing use of slang and epithets, to which he gave a peculiar emphasis, as of a foreigner waiting to be commended for having picked them up. And she laughed, finally, because in the mood she was in she felt hysterically relieved by doing so.

She said: "Magnificent, Paul. But he's not middle-aged, he's quite young, and he's not married — he told me that — and I think he was just making conversation to get me out of his office."

The crew and actors were beginning to drift in for the afternoon session. As at the pulling of a mental switch Paul returned to duty, and *Morning Journey* rose again in his favour.

He often improvised like that — the slightest cue could send him off into the synopsis of an imagined picture. Once Greg said seriously : " Paul, why don't you get that down in writing and send it up to the front office ? It's so damned good you ought to be able to sell it."

" *Sell* it ? " Paul exclaimed, incredulously. " Why should I sell it ? It's *mine*."

.   .   .   .

He made more trouble (it seemed he couldn't help it, despite all his promises), yet Carey had never admired him so much as during those latter days of making *Morning Journey*. There was something exquisite in his care for detail, especially when one thought of the mass audience to whom minutiae would not count, even if they were observed ; he knew everybody's business, much to their dismay at times — he seemed to be an expert on everything for which special experts had already been provided. Randolph barely tolerated him, visiting the set more rarely as the picture neared its end, evidently feeling that bad or good, the die was sufficiently cast. Two things should have made Paul popular with the authorities — the fewness of his takes and the fact that he was bringing in the picture several days under schedule ; but Paul had an unrivalled capacity for sacrificing credit even where it was due, and Randolph, whose own direction had always been of the laborious sort, found it impossible to believe that so many printed first takes could show good judgment. To him Paul was possibly a genius, but certainly the kind of employee one could not handle ; and as the somewhat peculiar packaging of Carey and Paul together in the contract had not been his responsibility, his real hope was that the picture should fail gently enough for the studio to try Carey in another picture and get rid of Paul altogether. Perhaps he, Randolph, might even direct her himself in the next picture — it would be exciting to get on the floor again. He liked Carey. She was a bit old for stardom — no older, though, than Madeleine Carroll and almost as beautiful; she had that indefinable thing called " class ", and with co-stars like Greg Wilson there was no reason why Majestic Pictures should not use her a good deal. But for less money, if *Morning Journey* failed. Her agent, of course, would hold out for the same, would keep on reminding everyone she was married to a millionaire, but maybe that wouldn't be true much longer if the rumours one heard were correct. Randolph turned it all over in his mind many times as he sat at his desk after seeing the daily rushes. He and Paul did not see them at the same time now, and Carey and Greg did not now see them at all. That was Paul's doing too — he had reverted to an old idea of his that watching themselves in the previous day's scenes was bad for actors. What puzzled Randolph was how Paul could have forced such a ruling on Greg. All Greg had to say was, "You go to hell, Saffron, I'm seeing the rushes just as I've always seen 'em " — but for some reason Greg did not say it. That was disturbing, too, when Randolph thought it over.

. . . .

The peculiarity of this film environment was that one could live in a large American city week after week without feeling intimate with it, without even feeling that it was part of America. The apartment Carey had was of standardized luxury, the restaurants she patronized catered to people like herself, the morning and evening travel in the studio limousine was through streets that all looked the same, with the same stores and bill-boards, the same shadow and sunshine. Even the ocean was somehow disappointing as an ocean. But she loved the mountains twenty or thirty miles away, and solely to drive to them whenever she had a few hours to spare she rented a rather smart convertible.

The studio was the real world — or rather, an unreal world which she explored sometimes with Paul when there were outdoor scenes on the back lot and she could make him take a walk during the lunch hour. The maze of streets and alleys there, where one could step from brownstone New York to Elizabethan England in a few seconds, the stranded Pullman on the two-hundred-yard track, the small-town main street with its false-fronted store buildings — all this was fascinating, a symbol (Paul said) of a world in which emotions themselves were false-fronted (" Tell me any picture Majestic ever made that wasn't "), and in which the symbols of life became substitutes for life itself. " Here on this back lot," Paul said one day, improvising himself into a tourist guide, " are all the signposts of our civilization, from the little red schoolhouse where you learn to the prison death-house where you burn. . . ." He went on in this fashion, considerably enjoying himself, but she was hardly listening ; her mind was preoccupied with a letter she had received from Norris that morning, for he had mentioned in it quite casually that he was getting bored in New York and had thought of coming out to see her, and also to meet Paul. Ordinarily there would have been nothing especially disturbing about this, yet it did disturb her, because she knew that Paul and Norris would not get along, and that an extra burden of peace-making would fall upon her. Frankly, with so much else to do, she could not endure the thought of it. As Paul went on talking she could hear in her mind Norris answering him back and the whole argument that would follow. It would be impossible — that on top of everything else.

Within an hour during an interval between scenes, she scribbled a note from her dressing-room :

" . . . Darling, don't think me inhospitable or that I wouldn't love to see you, but I really don't think you ought to come out here just now, it wouldn't be worth your while, I assure you, because I'm busy all day and have to learn lines in the evening for the next day — this job is really work, though you mightn't think so from all the glamorous stuff you read in the magazines. Please don't come, therefore — if you did you'd be at a completely loose end most of the time, and I can tell you this is a dull city to wander about on your own. I doubt if I could even get permission for you to visit the picture set — the rules are very strict against anyone who hasn't a business reason. As for Paul, he hasn't time for anybody, and as always when he's directing he's inclined to be bad-tempered with strangers. I'd hate you to get a wrong impression of him (for he can be very charming at other times), but I'm afraid you would if you met him nowadays. Perhaps later on, some time, when the job's finished and we can all relax. I'm glad to report that the picture itself is going pretty well — as soon as they ship a print to New York I'll try to arrange for you to see it in advance in a projection-room. . . ."

Norris sent no immediate answer to this, and for several weeks she was in constant apprehension that every ring from the lobby would announce his arrival.

Then one morning another of his letters came — from Rio de Janeiro.

". . . the first few legs of a trip that will end up when and where I don't exactly know, maybe the bank that father is so keen on shoving me in. You remember I once said that he *devoted* himself to his job — I can see now it's the right word for something that does have a faintly religious air about it. Everywhere that we've stopped, so far — Havana, Mexico City, Caracas — there've been exalted personages meeting us at airports, sometimes even in morning coats and top hats — it's been a revelation to me what a big shot he is, or must have been during the war, though I still can't quite fathom what his job was — something to do with government loans and currency, of course, but that doesn't give away much, and nor does he. But it's rather fascinating to get an impression of his importance from the way he moves around and meets people — it reminds me a bit of the Acts of the Apostles — you know, *confirming the churches*. And he does also move in a mysterious way — father, I mean. Perhaps he's right, after all, and the bank wouldn't be a bad solution for me — at least for the time being. Oh God, I don't know — what do *you* think I ought to do? He thinks I've given up the medical school idea and perhaps I have — it's hard, out here, to face the kind of opposition I know he'd put up. This must be all for now, there's a business conference going on in the next room, so it's a chance for me to write. Incidentally, Richards is with us, as a sort of valet and general what-not. We stay here a week or two, then go on to Montevideo, Uruguay, the Hotel Bolivar. . . ."

That evening she wrote to both of them, yet there was nothing particular she felt she could say, partly because she suspected Richards might intercept her letters. She therefore assembled another instalment of the chatter she had been sending all along, and to which Austen had not replied by a single line. *His mysterious way*. The phrase stuck in her mind unhappily, not so much for its wry meaning, as because of her distress that Norris should have been in a mood to employ it. It seemed to signify a return to the cynicism of his boyhood, but now without boyhood as an excuse.

During those days she was immensely glad she had work, and that Paul could magnetize her to it so exhaustingly. The picture was making good progress and even he seemed satisfied, though the deferred problem of the cutting loomed larger on his mind as the job approached completion. One lunch-time, after a morning off, she arrived at the studio to find him stretched out full length on the couch of her dressing-room, eyes closed and a cigar in his hand, declaiming in a way which she took at first to be a speech from some newly minted dialogue but which, after a few sentences, she knew could not be that ; it sounded more like an impassioned address to the stockholders of Majestic Pictures Incorporated, imploring them to unseat the existing board and replace them with men who would have greater consideration for art and artists. Actually, as Paul explained readily enough when she broke in on his oration : " I was just getting my thoughts together. We're going to have a fight, you know, about the cutting. I'll try not to drag you into it."

" I'll try not to be dragged in, but I know I will be."

" If it's cut properly it's a good picture. Not great, but good."

" Let's hope it's a success too."

He went on smoking. " Oh, by the way, how's your heart ? "

" Not so bad. It'll be all right if I don't work too hard."

" You had nothing to do all this morning."

" Yes, I had one whole morning — wasn't that wonderful ? What happened while I was away ? "

"Writers on the warpath again. You'd think those fellows had written the Bible."

"What was the trouble this time?"

"The same sort of thing. I couldn't use any of their barber-shop stuff."

She knew the scene — it came earlier in the picture than the one in the woodcutter's cottage, though later in the shooting schedule. . . . Greg, alone, is forced during this stage of his escape to pass through a town by daylight; he knows he is being hunted and that the hunters may already have picked up the scent. As he hurries through the streets he has a sudden impulse to throw off any possible pursuer by disappearing into a shop, and the one that seems most suitable is a barber shop, where he will have an excuse to stay some time. He has a day's growth of beard and knows the language well enough to ask for a shave. While he is being lathered he sees (through a big mirror) that someone is entering the shop and scanning the faces of customers. This man, Greg feels sure, is looking for him. He figures that his only chance is to do something that will eliminate him from suspicion; and this, in the circumstances, is to do something that will immediately focus attention on him. So with a muttered " Excuse me a moment " to the barber, *and with his face still lathered*, he gets up from the chair, walks right past his pursuer to the rack on which he has hung his overcoat, takes a handkerchief from its pocket, gives his nose a startling blast, and returns to the chair. The pursuer observes him, but (as was intended) automatically puts him out of mind, for surely a man on the run would not deliberately and needlessly draw attention to himself? (Such reasoning being unconscious and therefore all the more reliable, according to Paul.) After completing his scrutiny of others in the shop, the pursuer leaves and the lathered man smiles gently as he submits to the razor.

Once again a scene practically without dialogue, and once again different from the pages of the script. In these the pursuer had recognized Greg and there had been a mêlée with shots fired and mirrors broken; Greg had eventually managed to escape through a back door. If, therefore, Paul's scene could have been called over-subtle, the one it replaced had no subtlety at all. But it would have played well enough, and the original dialogue between Greg and the pursuer had been of the tried and true variety — " Put 'em up or I'll shoot " — " You think you've got me, do you ? Stand back, you—" etc. etc.

The writers had urged on Randolph that Paul's scene, both as to incident and motivation, would not be understood by an average audience, and Randolph (miffed because once again a vital change had been made at the last moment without consulting him) had agreed with them.

" And what's going to happen ? " Carey asked.

" Who cares any more about that ? " Paul began to chuckle. " It's happened. I shot the scene my way."

" Oh dear, you're very obstinate."

" *Obstinate ? Me ?* After all my compromises ? "

" Paul, do you know what the word compromise means ? "

" Sure — it's what I'm doing now by working on a picture like this at all. The only thing it can be, at best, is a bag of tricks. Well, that's all right — I don't expect them to let me produce a work of art. But if it's going to be a bag of tricks, for God's sake let the tricks be tricky enough. And that's what really beats me, Carey — here's this business of telling stories by means of tiny photographs — it's just about fifty years old — fifty out of the thousands since people began telling stories at all — yet already there are factory rules laid down — mustn't do this, mustn't do that. . . . And you call me obstinate because I dare to answer : *Try it!* See if an audience is as dumb as you think ! There they are — the groundlings — all crunching popcorn just like Shakespeare's crowd at the Globe if there'd been popcorn in those days — all you have to do is to give them a *Twelfth Night* — it doesn't have to be a *Hamlet* every time ! "

" I'd like to see you shooting *Hamlet*, Paul — you'd cut half the lines."

" So would Shakespeare if he'd had a camera to play with."

" You must admit, though, you do seem to have a special grudge against dialogue."

" No, not a grudge at all — only a realization of what films have done in their first fifty years. They've broken the bottleneck of words that we've all endured for centuries — they've challenged the scholars and grammarians who built their little private fences round enlightenment — they've freed us from the thraldom of Gutenberg ! . . . You've heard some of the old jokes about producers out here who're supposed to be illiterate ? Too bad the breed seems to be dying out — I think I could have got along with one of them better than with Randolph. Because that fellow *reads*. God, how he reads ! He and his wife, when they get hold of what they think is a good book, d'you know what they do ? *They read to each other aloud*. From chair to chair and bed to bed — a chapter apiece every evening ! He *told* me . . . and with a straight face ! "

Paul's guffaws lasted for some time, and Carey laughed more moderately, reflecting that, for all his tirade against books and Gutenberg, there could be few people on earth who had read more. During the periods of his life when he had been out of a job he had borrowed five or six books a day from public libraries, and when he had been earning money he had usually come home with purchased books under his arm. He had probably spent more time in Brentano's than in all other New York shops put together. And she had rarely heard anyone mention a play or a playwright or an episode of theatrical or dramatic history that he did not seem to know plenty about. It was true he was not a scholar in the pedagogic sense, but his range was wider — he had an artist's acquaintance with all the arts, plus a technician's familiarity with all the theatrical arts, plus an immense if disordered store of general knowledge. He would probably have been a great success on Information Please. . . . But of course the way he digested books was photographic ; he could acquire the sense of pages without taking words consecutively, and the notion of his ever reading aloud a whole chapter of anything or wishing her to read him one, was certainly comic. Sometimes, when she had been driving the car in those old days, she had asked him to read her the headlines in the paper, but before he was through a couple of them he had usually launched into comments or fulminations that had made her exclaim : " Darling, will you please read me what it says and leave what you think about it till afterwards."

Pleasant, in a way, to remember these things now, while his guffaws continued.

.   .   .   .   .   .

The barber-shop scene was cut, entirely ; a conclave of studio executives decided after seeing the rushes that it simply did not ' come off '. As it was only an episode in the chase, the cut did not spoil the finished picture. To Paul, however, it might have been his own lifeblood that had been arbitrarily drained away, and since he blamed the writers for it he looked for an early chance to get his own back. It came when one of them, a quiet, studious-looking youth named Mitchell who had said little during story conferences and had always seemed anxious that his more voluble partner should act as spokesman, chanced to visit the set on some personal business that had nothing to do with Paul. But Paul spotted him and drew him into a conversation that began quietly enough ; soon, however, the youth was the centre of a group with Paul baiting him gleefully. When Carey came up, hearing a commotion, she was in time to catch Paul at his familiar game of repeating before a larger audience something he had originally tried out before her. " Of course you writers don't really like motion pictures — how could you ? Pictures have broken the bottleneck of words that's been your mainstay for centuries — they've freed the world from the thraldom of Gutenberg ! In one silent shot I can tell more of a story than you could set down in a whole chapter ! "

" Yes, but to create a character, Mr. Saffron—" Mitchell began in feeble protest.

" All right," Paul snapped. " Create your character —

write your pages of dialogue to make your audience feel the way you want about him. Let's say he's the heavy — the worst villain you can invent — liar, crook, murderer — Simon Legree and Dracula rolled into one — take fifty pages to put your readers in a fine lather of hate. Then call me in with my camera and I'll undo it all in ten seconds. And you know how ? "

Mitchell stammered that he didn't know how, but Paul was going to tell him anyway. " All I need is a little lame dog dodging traffic at a crossroads. Your villain comes along, picks him up, carries him over, sets him down again. Ten seconds. Not a word spoken. And the audience loves the guy for ever. Do you doubt it ? "

" No," Mitchell admitted, amidst the laughter. Then remarkably he seemed to acquire stature, shaking off the nervousness that had made him till then a rather ineffectual figure. He went on, gathering power as from some unsuspected source : " I don't doubt it at all, Mr. Saffron. It's always quicker to raise a prejudice than plant an opinion. That's part of what's wrong with the world today. You talk about the thraldom of Gutenberg, but it was under that thraldom that men learned to *think*. Today thinking's out of style, it's highbrow or longhair or whatever smear you have for it ; you've learned to bypass the brain and shoot for the blood pressure — all your stuff is really for the twelve-year-old ! "

" *All* my stuff ? " Paul managed to interrupt. " How much of it have you seen ? Did you ever see *Erste Freundschaft* ? "

" Yes. Made in Germany in 1931, wasn't it ? A work of genius. Done anything half as good since ? "

Carey thought this was too impertinent, even from one who had had provocation ; she was taking Paul's arm to drag him away when he shook himself free and shouted, turning on Mitchell again : " I'll answer you. The best thing I ever did in my life was in Paris in 1939 — a picture based on the Book of Job — it was unfinished when the Germans invaded and I spent three years in a prison camp because I wouldn't leave it — in the end it was mauled and butchered and ruined by others — my best work — a *supreme* work — and the goddamned French won't even let me over there now to salvage the cuts ! And when I fought and protested — from over here — what help do you suppose I got from writers ? I contacted the big names — put my case to them — appealed to them as fellow-artists — fellow-*artists*, forsooth——"

" Paul," Carey interposed, knowing from experience that ' forsooth ' was always a danger-word in his vocabulary. " Paul, don't you think . . . the scene's ready . . . everybody's waiting. . . . Mr. Mitchell, let Paul tell you about it later. . . ."

Paul never did ; he avoided Mitchell from then on, but when later in the day, still brooding over the incident, he had to talk to Randolph he took occasion to ask abruptly : " By the way, that fellow Mitchell . . . who the devil *is* he ? Is he *anybody* ? *Somebody* ? "

" Mitchell ? You mean the writer ? Why, no, he's — he's just a writer. Reminds me, his option comes up next week. Think we ought to let him go ? "

Paul was about to take a clinching revenge when his mind somersaulted to the nobler battlefield just in time. He answered insolently : " Sure, it might be the making of him. He's one of the few intelligent people I've met out here."

" I think we'll keep him," Randolph replied coldly.

. . . . . .

But there was another incident that really caused most trouble of all. It concerned an extra scene that Paul flatly refused to have, even though it was he who had first suggested it. The sequence called for a German agent in New York to convey news of wartime ship sailings to offshore submarines (just another item in the bag of tricks that had made Paul dislike the whole story when he had read the original script) ; and Paul had been seized with his own special idea late in the afternoon of the day before the scheduled shooting. As the scene was written, a sinister-looking person worked a radio transmitting set on what appeared to be a waterfront roof-top ; but Paul's inspiration was that the German agent should send signals by having secret operatives among the janitors of a skyscraper, so that the apparently random arrangement of lighted windows after office hours could spell out messages in code. The notion intoxicated Paul as he improvised it quite sensationally on the set — " high columns of illuminated print in celestial newspapers " was his description of the New York skyline at dusk ; and as usual he managed to communicate a rare excitement to others, so that Greg was soon in Randolph's office pleading for the somewhat radical and expensive last-minute change. But Randolph, on this occasion, needed no persuading. For the first time he displayed full approval of something that had emanated from Paul's brain, and by morning his approval had soared to enthusiasm. Unfortunately by that time also Paul had begun to discover flaws in his own idea. Surely enemy submarines could not approach near enough to see the high buildings, and wouldn't it be fantastically difficult to plant a special set of janitor spies in one of them ? These and other objections Randolph stoutly discounted, and the argument that ensued was an ironic reversal of the usual.

" But it was your own idea," Randolph was driven to exclaim, in utmost bafflement.

" That gives me a special right to throw it out," Paul retorted. The wrangle wasted an entire morning (and therefore several thousand of Majestic's dollars), and in the end the producer's only comfort was that he could probably use the skyscraper idea in some other picture. Which he did, in due course, and it is fair to add that nobody found much amiss with it.

Since the scenes had not been shot in consecutive order, it seemed that the whole job ended suddenly, almost unexpectedly. One day the scene being done was the last, and there followed a party on the stage during which Paul could think of nothing but the impending battle about cutting. This lasted for a week, and after the dust had settled it looked as if he had got rather more than half of everything he wanted. But from his attitude one would have thought him abjectly defeated. He sulked and gloomed and then acquired one of those migraine headaches. There was no doubt of its reality. In the small office which had been assigned him Carey found him slumped in a swivel chair, grey-pale with bloodshot eyes and icy hands. She called a doctor over his vivid protests; whereupon he diagnosed his own case as if he were dictating a new scene. The doctor, somewhat intimidated, agreed that probably it *was* a migraine headache. He added, however, that a check-up might be a good thing, since Paul looked as if he had high blood pressure too. Paul agreed to call at the doctor's office the next day, and then, as soon as he had gone, assured Carey he had no intention of doing any such thing. " I'm all right," he said, " if only those bastards would let me do my job without interfering."

Carey then broke down. She saw this man, grey and worn and looking older than she had ever known him; she saw in him something worth everything and worth nothing, something singularly great and appallingly little and, in the deepest sense of all, pathetically helpless. She cried: " Oh, Paul, Paul, what can I do with you? Can't you help yourself? Darling, is there no chance for you at all? "

" A couple of old crocks," he muttered whimsically, touching her hand. " Isn't that what you said we were? But we aren't. You're young, and I . . . well, I've still got that picture about children to do. You know my idea for it? The camera itself will be a child. And as the picture develops and the child grows up . . ."

But somebody came in just then with a message from Randolph, and afterwards, when she tried to get him back to the subject, he would only shake his head mysteriously. " Ah, I said enough. Wait till I do the thing. I will — one day."

But the mere reminder of it seemed to have cured his headache; and a little later, apparently rejuvenated, he was ready for a final battle with Randolph.

This was about billing. He wanted Carey's name to be given prominence equal to Greg's, an absurd demand — first, because matters of that kind were none of his business, and second, because the Wilson name at the box-office meant so much more than hers. To her surprise Greg backed him on the issue, and she ascribed this at first to a charming though mistaken chivalry; but later she wondered if it were merely an extreme example of Paul's influence over Greg. Randolph, who clearly considered her the only one with any sense, detained her afterwards for a few compliments. "You've been very co-operative, Carey. I do want to thank you and to say I hope we'll be working together again." He could not commit the studio, of course; it all depended on how *Morning Journey* turned out; but there was no harm in paving the way.

She was non-committal also in her reply.

He went on: "As for Greg, I don't think I fully understand him these days. He used to *fight* for top billing. What's the matter with him . . . is he in love with that guy?"

Carey smiled. "Paul's apt to do that to people."

"To *men*?"

"Sometimes. You're all for him or else you're all against him."

"Well, I'm neither," Randolph said, untruthfully. "And that applies to you too, I should think."

"I *know* him," she answered, with scorn or pride, whichever he decided it was.

.   .   .   .

After the last day's shooting there came the anti-climax to which there was no parallel in the theatre, where rehearsals mount in a crescendo of tension, culminating in opening night and followed by either level activity or quick extinction. But movie-making offers a unique period of waiting while all the sub-assembly lines catch up—printing, distribution, publicity; and the nearest to opening night excitement that can happen at all is the sneak preview. Nearest, but still distant.

One rainy evening Carey drove out with Paul, Randolph, Greg, and several high personages from various studio departments — a convoy of limousines traversing interminable boulevards to converge eventually on a rather ordinary cinema in what seemed a less than ordinary suburb. Unannounced and unheralded, *Morning Journey* was there to be submitted to the verdict of an audience that had come to see something else. The distinguished visitors to whom it all mattered so much sat in a roped-off row at the back of the theatre, just behind the folks to whom it all mattered so little. There was the end of another picture to be endured, then a Mickey Mouse cartoon and a newsreel; finally, without any fanfare, *Morning Journey* began. The audience was small because of the weather, and Carey, unused to half-empty theatres, thought there was only tepid enthusiasm, but she was aware that the picture itself bored her by now, and that the popcorn noises were standard procedure and did not in any way reflect either the patrons' visual enjoyment or lack of it. She was next to Paul, who kept cursing the music, which had been composed and arranged without his approval. Owing to his unfortunate tiff with the musicians this was actually the first time he had heard most of it, and he disliked it intensely.

There was, however, some scattered applause at the end of the picture, which was also the end of the show. Greg had left a minute before the curtain, anxious to reach the manager's office before anyone spotted him for autographs; the others, unlikely to be so bothered, stayed in their seats while the audience filtered out. Then they joined Greg in the tiny office, waiting for the cards on which each patron had been invited to say whether he thought *Morning Journey* was Excellent, Good, or only Fair. There was also a space for ' Remarks '. (The possibility that any Majestic picture might be downright Bad had been ignored.) About two hundred cards, duly filled in and collected by the ushers, were presently handed to Randolph by the theatre manager, a hard-bitten and presumably unprejudiced fellow who said he had liked the picture himself and thought his people had liked it too, but he couldn't be sure — they were a tough bunch. Carey wondered why Randolph had chosen a tough bunch. Anyhow, the visitors were soon back in the cars, swishing through the endless unknown streets and across flooded intersections. Nobody talked much and everyone was glad to be dropped at his front door. " We'll meet again tomorrow," Randolph announced. Carey also wondered why he didn't look at the cards during the drive ; she decided he was enjoying peculiar power in a peculiar way.

It was still raining in the morning when the same group reassembled in Randolph's office, the cards having by this time been sorted and placed in three heaps on his huge glass-topped desk. His pleasure in delaying the outcome had become definitely sadistic ; one heap was much larger than the others, but his encircling arms as he leaned forward prevented closer observation. Paul was the only one who, not having come to pray, was able to scoff. " Our tribute to democracy," he muttered, staring at the cards as at the trappings of some dubious religion. " He must have liked them because He made so many of them. A *non sequitur* if ever there was one. What about fleas, hookworms, boll-weevils ? " Nobody answered.

At last Randolph spoke, smiling rather coldly as he referred to figures on his desk. " This is what you're all waiting for, no doubt. Out of 215 cards we have 133 Excellents and 61 Goods. I think we can regard that as satisfactory — as far as it goes. Of course we can't predict what the critics will say, or the big exhibitors. . . . Would anyone like a whisky and soda so early in the morning ? "

Put this way, the invitation drew no affirmative except from Paul, who said : " Sure. Why not ? " So Randolph was forced to go to the small refrigerator concealed within an imitation bookcase whose false-fronted books were sets of Dickens and Thackeray. Everybody all at once began to smile and chatter — again except Paul, who glowered over his cigar as he watched Randolph's reluctant hospitality.

Nobody looked at the cards, save at a few that had been put aside on account of some obscenity. These Randolph handed round for laughs. There were always two or three out of every batch. But here yet again Paul was the exception. He did not laugh. Indeed, he was rather prim about certain things — much more so than Carey, who could enjoy most jokes that most people found amusing.

.   .   .   .   .   .

After the sneak preview Randolph decided to shorten the picture by ten minutes' playing time to suit the requirements of double-feature exhibitors. Paul protested, but not so energetically as might have been expected ; he was going through his own anti-climactic period — the mood in which, after a job was done, he found it hard to take continued interest in it. Already, from certain hints he let fall, his mind was beginning to revolve on other ideas. It was during this period also that Carey gained an impression that Randolph would not be terribly disappointed if the picture did not do too well. Not, of course, that he would sabotage his own product, but there seemed a lack of zeal in his proddings of the publicity department — a lack which must certainly have communicated itself. The fact was, he disliked Paul so much that he could take real pleasure from the prospect of his downfall, while at the same time he had an alibi for himself whatever happened, since it was on record that he had objected to the contract that had forced Paul into the company's employment. And at the back of his mind there grew intoxicatingly the notion of a future picture with Carey in it which he himself would direct. His real hope was that *Morning Journey* would turn out to be one of those half-and-half failure-successes in which he could fix praise and blame just where he wanted each.

Carey could not enjoy her leisure during those further weeks of waiting. Unlike Paul, she was unable to generate new ideas to take the place of old ones, and the absence of daily work only made more room for her own private worries. She spoke of these to no one, not only because they were so intimate, but because something centrally sane in her make-up told her continually that she deserved no sympathy ; by so many reckonings she was fortunate. Surely there could be no doubt of it when she looked back on her life. Yet she felt, at times, acutely unlucky as well as unhappy. She did not know what she wanted to do next, or where she wanted to go, and the fact that there were choices made the future harder to contemplate. Perhaps she would stay where she was till the fate of the picture was decided, then take the trip she had vaguely promised herself.

Another thing that few would have thought credible and for which she blamed only herself was that she was often lonely. In a place full of interesting people she had so far been too busy to make friends, and the occasional parties she went to were apt to be unrewarding — not dull, but somehow devoid of a quality for which she could think of no single word but merriment. It seemed to her that many of the interesting people were also too busy to make friends, that many of the laughing people were laughing too hard to make merry, and that many of the interesting, laughing, and busy people were also as lonely as herself. Sometimes, after such a party, she had a spiritual hangover that sent her driving random miles in her rented car, as if to kill the memory of an evening that had been full of excitement yet fundamentally distraught. And even if her personal mood were responsible for much that seemed amiss, there were things to which she felt her own reaction was not subjective at all ; the geographical heartlessness of the city, the miles of streets where nobody walked, the rigid charm of the professionally decorated interiors, the air of insecurity that was more sinister, somehow, than the perhaps greater insecurity of stage life.

One day she made the expedition she had often thought of, but had hitherto avoided, partly from an unwillingness to be sentimental. But now she felt that sentiment was not the guiding motive, but rather a dispassionate curiosity to see a once familiar place with a different eye. She drove, therefore, to a certain street between Western and Vermont. The houses looked much as she remembered them — a little shabbier with age, and there were gaps in what had once been a careful line of palm trees. The frame house she was looking for had been renumbered, but was otherwise unchanged — the same wide porch, and the swing door whose sound in banging she could still catch in the ear of her mind. She drove round the block to see the house again, and as she repassed, the swing door opened and a child emerged. His brown face was so happy that she had an impulse to stop and talk to him, but he scampered into a neighbour's yard before she could think of an excuse. She then noticed other coloured children playing near by, and it seemed indeed that the whole district had undergone that kind of racial change that real-estate people deplore ; but to her, because of the child's face, it was part of a deep content that came on her as she drove back to her apartment.

When she got there, decision had been added to this new mood. She wrote immediately to Norris at the Hotel Bolivar, Montevideo, Uruguay :

" DARLING NORRIS — I'm writing this before I change my mind, before I feel scared about it. I'm so glad you're having an interesting trip, but there was something in your last letter — the one from Rio — that I didn't answer ; I felt I couldn't at the time, but now I suddenly feel I can and must. You asked what I thought you should do about going into the bank as your father wants, and my answer is *No* — not yet, anyhow, till you're stronger and back at home and unless you then feel happy and aren't in the cynical mood that your letter showed. Well, there you are, darling — my advice — you asked for it. *Don't give in* — to anything or anybody. I wish I could offer my own life as a shining example, but you know it wouldn't be — and yet, in a sense, I haven't often let myself be pushed around too far, and when I have it's been my own choice as well as my own fault. And in case your father reads this (and why shouldn't you show it him ? — I'd like him to know my attitude — perhaps it might even influence him a little), I'll add the news that the picture is finished and I'm looking forward to seeing both of you again if he'll send me a line so that I can match my plans with his. Actually I haven't any particular plans — I don't want to make any till I know his and yours. I've missed you both very much but I'm not sorry I came out here for the picture — I think it's turned out the way I wanted it and you know what that is. Well, this seems about all, perhaps in some ways it's more than enough, but the fact is, I'm so used to covering pages with nothing but chit-chat that I'd better send it off before I'm appalled at having had the nerve. But you'll forgive me, because you know how much I care for your happiness. My love, darling, as always. — CAREY."

Without a re-reading she air-mailed it from the box on the pavement outside. Then she took her car and drove to the mountains, returning towards dusk. The fact that the mailbox had been cleared by then gave her the feeling of having made a decision which she did not regret, but whose magnitude she might not yet have fully explored.

.   .   .   .   .   .

During this waiting period, before the film was released, she saw little of Paul, but what she heard about him was characteristic. He had money in his pocket and was spending it, not exactly on luxuries, but with an eccentric abandon that was even more consuming — but of course that would not matter if the picture were successful. And if it weren't, perhaps money would even then be the least of his problems.

She did not see much of Greg, either, though she heard that he and Paul had been to San Francisco together and had later stayed at Greg's house at Carmel. Apparently they were close friends and Greg's admiration for Paul had in no wise diminished. There was an interview in one of the film magazines in which Greg talked of him in terms so extravagant that the shrewd outsider's deduction would be that the picture must be bad enough to need it rather than good enough to deserve it; and so indeed were many deductions made, though not so shrewdly.

Of all the strangers she had met and talked to in this strange part of the world the one she liked most was a man who had nothing to do with pictures — a certain Professor Lingard, who did not even look like a professor. He was an astronomer; about thirty, sandy-haired, pink-cheeked, angular, diffident, not really at home at the party to which, for some obscure reason, he had been invited, yet enjoying himself from an angle schoolboyish enough to be charming.

Carey found herself next to him for supper; he talked about his work at an observatory on a mountain top and was interested because she had driven near it and knew where it was. Apparently he lived there during part of the year, in a small cottage within walking distance of his job; he said she ought to drive up there some night and take a look through the big telescope. She told him she would like to. "Give me a ring first and I'll let you know if the sky's clear enough," he then said, and she wondered if this were an 'out' because she had taken his invitation too seriously.

Later in the evening he whispered to her: "I often wonder what it feels like to be famous," and she was just about to answer modestly but first-personally when she realized that his glance was scanning the other guests and that he evidently didn't take her to be one of the famous ones at all. That's what comes of being friendly to nice nobodies at this kind of party, she thought; they assume you must be a nice nobody yourself. "I don't know," she answered, glad to have spared both of them embarrassment. "Almost everybody here is a household word except me."

"Ah, but you will be soon," he said, "if you're in pictures." He spoke comfortingly, as to a junior who had tried several times for an examination and failed. She was amused and also touched. There was not only a winsome naïveté in his attitude, but a pleasure to her in finding someone who did not know her name, or if so, did not know it *was* a name — who had never heard of her recent role in *Morning Journey* (as had everyone else in the room), but who treated her as if she were a young girl full of dreams and ambition.

She said: "I doubt it. I'm a bit old, you know, for a new career."

"But you *are* in pictures, aren't you?"

"I've just finished a part in my first one."

"Well, the main thing, I suppose, is to get a start. And you really are beautiful."

"Oh, thanks." She even felt herself blushing.

"Do drive up some time and look through the telescope."

323

She smiled and repeated her promise, satisfied now that he really meant it.

. . . .

More weeks passed; the rainy season ended, the first hot spell of the year wiped the freshness off the hills. The skies became tawny-grey, the sun shone as through muslin.

Suddenly two rumours got around, both from sources hard to define or investigate. First, that Carey was separating, or had separated, or was about to separate, from Austen Bond. Previous rumours that she was about to be ' reconciled ' with Paul had somehow ignored the existence of a Mr. Bond, and for that reason she had herself ignored them more easily; but now, in gossip columns and on Sunday radio broadcasts, the stories, though untrue, had greater logic. She did not know whether to take trouble to deny them or not; once a woman telephoned her and, after receiving a denial, made the tart rejoinder : " Okay, darling, but I write a column, so I hope you aren't just saying that on general principles."

Carey telephoned Paul and asked if he knew of the woman. " She called me up just now. Any idea who she is ? "

Paul answered promptly : " Never heard of her." He was busy and soon hung up. But half an hour later he called back to say : " Carey, that woman you asked about — I asked Greg and it seems they're all scared of her out here. So you'd better be careful."

" How do I be careful ? "

" Oh, I don't know. Be what you like. What the hell does it matter ? "

" Well, who *is* she ? Why is she important ? "

" Greg did tell me, but I couldn't quite get the hang of it. She writes, I suppose."

" I know she writes, but why should they be scared of her ? "

" They have scarable ulcers. Don't worry about her. The whole thing is a fine pickle of nonsense."

The second rumour, a pleasanter one, was about *Morning*

Journey. In some mysterious way people were already aware that it was good. Possibly it had been run in private projection-rooms before an *élite*; at any rate, the hint was in circulation that it was something to look for. Then came the press preview in New York with the critics practically unanimous. All of them praised Carey, nearly all praised Paul's direction, most prophesied a big hit, and one said that Greg Wilson had never supplied such a plausible though still invalid excuse for calling himself an actor.

On the day these critiques were reprinted in the trade papers Carey could sense an almost barometric change in the local atmosphere. She could even believe that at her usual restaurant the smile of the head waiter had an extra obsequiousness. People came up to her table to gush and congratulate. The next day an executive of another studio asked her to lunch, ostensibly to show her the New York clippings, actually to sound her out about her plans. " I understand you have no future commitment with Majestic," he remarked with overdone casualness.

" That's so, but I don't know yet whether I want to make another picture at all. I must take a vacation first."

" Why, yes, naturally." And reading her indecision as caginess he said : " Of course nobody knows how the public will react. Critics can't make or break a picture as they can a stage play."

" I know. Better wait and see how it goes."

Having blown cool, he must now blow warmer again. " Personally I enjoyed it immensely — and you were *magnificent*."

" I think the direction counted for most."

" Yes, very good, quite good. . . . How did Saffron get along with people during the shooting — not too well, I heard ? "

" Not too well, but well enough. He just did a wonderful job that'll probably make somebody else a fortune."

" High praise, indeed. . . ."

" And from an ex-wife," she said with a laugh, guessing that the fact was already or would be later known to him.

She added : " Paul's so good in *Morning Journey* that one can imagine if he were given a free hand — a freer hand, anyway — he might be great."

" Sometimes when you give them too free a hand, these geniuses, they make a hell of a mess of things. I'd be satisfied if he stayed *good*."

" I think he'd rather wait for a job in which someone would trust him enough to let him be *great*."

" What, are you — his agent too ? "

More laughter. She couldn't be quite sure she was helping Paul by putting out feelers like this, but she had an impulse to do so. Then she steered the conversation to more general matters and let her host do most of the talking. Just before taking her to the car he said : " Where *is* Saffron, anyway — I was trying to get in touch with him this morning but couldn't."

So *that's* it, she thought gleefully ; they're *already* after him.

But she had to answer, in reply to his question : " I don't know."

.   .   .   .

Paul was on an Arizona ranch, with Greg ; he returned after *Morning Journey* had opened at Radio City Music Hall and broken all records for a first week. Randolph, convinced now that his private dream of a half-success was hopeless, jumped on the band-wagon with full force. He was especially pleased when the picture won the triple awards given annually by the local newspaper critics — Carey, Greg, and Paul being the recipients. The awards were to be presented at a big dinner, and on the morning of the day Randolph could not help summoning the honoured three to the studio for compliments and a briefing. " Of course you'll all make speeches after you get the plaques and somebody ought to bring in that Calvin Beckford is seventy tomorrow." (Calvin Beckford was a local politician who would present the awards.) " Perhaps that would come best from you, Carey. And if anybody should see fit to say something nice about the studio it wouldn't do us — or them — one bit of harm." He tittered self-consciously. " I'll be there, of course, but they don't ask producers to speak. Those newspaper boys seem to think we don't do any of the real work. . . . Incidentally, Carey, I phoned your agent in New York — I wanted him to know how pleased we all are."

Paul had arrived at the office with Greg, but afterwards he drove back with Carey. " Greg wanted to stay on and talk to Randolph," he said, as if the star's absence from their company were something that had to be explained.

Carey, who could be away from Greg without feeling completely lost, sat back in the car and looked at Paul. When she thought of Randolph's recent compliments she did not know whether to feel happy or cynical, but for Paul's sake at least she was happy. She knew he enjoyed compliments, even when he knew they were insincere, and from a man who he knew hated him there was probably a special piquancy.

She said : " Well, Paul, isn't it nice to be on top of the world ? "

Paul seemed to have Greg still on his mind. " Greg's had too much of it. They put him in one picture after another — anything to exploit him. He's getting pretty sick of it all."

" I don't know what he has to be sick about. He gets five thousand a week and he can't act."

" He's a good fellow, Carey — really he is."

" I know it, and I also think he's lucky."

" Because I directed him, you mean ? "

" He was lucky before that."

" He wasn't *bad* in the picture."

" He wasn't as bad as usual."

" He told me he never believed he had it in him."

" I don't think he had. I think you performed an optical illusion."

" He certainly gives me all the credit."

" Why shouldn't he as long as he keeps the salary ? "

" You're very waspish today, Carey."

" I'm just myself as I always am, only you haven't seen me lately — you've forgotten what I'm really like."

" As if I could ever forget."

" Darling, that's sweet and probably true."

" All the same, though, I think you're a bit unfair to Greg."

" Greg ? Are we still talking about *him* ? "

How familiar it was, to be arguing with Paul again. She had not seen him for weeks, they had said hello almost as strangers in Randolph's office, they were now by chance thrown together in the same car for a half-hour's drive, and already they were arguing — not quarrelling, for they had never quarrelled . . . just airing their minds in a private tradition of cut and thrust — he with some idea he was leaning towards, but would not yet put into words ; she sensing it already and poised to exert some uncharted manœuvre of checks and balances. The strange thing was that she felt free with him, free even from her own troubles and problems. And the thought came to her : how absurd it was ever to use the word ' reconcile ' about the two of them. It was not in their power any more either to come closer or to move away.

She said, thinking of all this : " Anyhow, Paul, you've had your big chance and it's certainly paid off. Can't you feel a bit joyful about it ? "

" After the way Randolph botched the cutting ? "

" Doesn't seem to have done much harm." (There were a few instances in which, from a commercial angle, she thought Randolph's cutting had done good, but she would not invite the wrong sort of argument by saying so.)

" Harm ? To whom ? To what ? The popcorn sales ? "

" Oh, come now, Paul, you can't talk like that. It's been a critical success too."

He sighed in a bemused way. " Ah, those critics. One of them said that in the street scenes I'd caught the pulse-beat of the American rhythm. That tickled me, not only because I don't know what the hell it means, but because there was once a critic in France who said I was so much in tune with the Gallic spirit it was hard to believe I hadn't been born in Paris. And in Germany when I made *Berliner Tag* they brought up my Pennsylvania Dutch ancestry to explain *that* miracle. . . . All nonsense. People are people. Watch 'em anywhere and you'll see. Great discovery. The Saffron touch — even in a cops and robbers epic."

" You know it isn't really as simple as that."

" *Simple?* Whoever said it was simple ? To see life as it is, plain, not gift-wrapped — why, it's as hard as being note-perfect in the *Hammerklavier*."

She tried to steer him back to her main point, which was that the chance he had taken had come off abundantly, and that from now he would find himself in demand on something like his own terms, if these were at all reasonable. She told him then about her lunch with the other producer. " No need to rush things. Let Michaelson do most of the talking. Just sit back and realize that *Morning Journey* puts you in a market that'll go on rising for some time yet."

" You're a smart gal," he commented absently.

" Am I ? It's the first time I've ever really wanted to be."

" I know how you feel," he responded moodily. " That's why I'm getting out of the place." He said that without any emphasis, as if it were not an important remark.

" *What ?* "

" You heard me, as they say in every damned script I've ever read out here."

" Paul . . . what do you mean ? What's happened ? "

And of course nothing had happened except the worst that could have, for Paul's equanimity ; merely that as a result of *Morning Journey's* success he had been showered with scripts by producers and agents who hoped he might be interested in some property of theirs ; a few of these scripts were averagely good, but many were old stuff dusted off and sent him on the ' how can you lose ? ' principle. Paul should have ignored them, or at least have glanced at only a few pages to convince himself of their quality, but it seemed that out of sheer obtuseness he had read them carefully — as carefully as he had journeyed to small theatres in out-of-the-way suburbs if ever one of Randolph's earlier pictures had been showing there. The fact that he had always returned from these expeditions fuming was no indication that he had not derived a macabre pleasure from them, once he had decided that an indictment against Randolph must be built up with every available piece of material. And now, in a similar but larger sense, an indictment against the whole industrialized picture industry was brewing in his mind, and the pile of scripts he had been sent was just the yeast to make it rise. So it had risen — mountainously. He was in a mood, Carey realized, when he was probably intending to do something he wanted to do and was finding many excellent reasons besides the real one. He kept saying: " There's no mutiny here, Carey," and when she asked what he meant he said one of those things she knew he had either said before or had coined so happily that he would certainly say it again ; he said that to breed art and keep it alive there should be a continual mutiny of ideas. " But there isn't any here. This place is swarming with craftsmen who might have been artists if only they'd stayed away. And everybody's scared — scared of each other, of the future, of gossip columns, of ulcers, of the public, of Washington, of censorship — there's something gets into the blood from being scared of so many things all the time — you can smell it, and I've smelt it lately. . . . These folks are afraid for their lives, they've built themselves a concentration camp that they're all fighting to stay inside — a damned democratic *de luxe* concentration camp where you hold elections by postcard poll of morons and smart alecks, where you bypass the adult intelligence and shoot for the blood pressure of the twelve-year-old ! "

" That reminds me of what Mitchell said," she interposed mischievously.

" Mitchell ? The writer ? Did he ? I don't recall." (But she knew he did ; he would never forget Mitchell, who had answered him back, who had left him hurt, speechless, angry, with ghost-phrases in his mind for ever that he could only exorcise partially by purloining them and adapting them for his own use.)

But he was continuing now, in full flood : " Anyhow, that's the way it is with the people here — they're afraid for their lives and they'll do anything for those lives except run for them — they could if they wanted — the gate's wide open that way — the fence is to keep the crowd *out*, not *in*. Well, *I'm* getting out. I know they'd never really let me do what I want here. They'd hate me, I'd never be one of them, they'd just give me squatter's rights inside the barbed wire . . . Oh dear, now I've upset you, I suppose — I always do, don't I ? "

He hadn't, by what he had said ; it was the recognition of his mood that troubled her, for so often in the past it had been a storm signal in their personal affairs, and though it could hardly be that again, she was disturbed in a way she found hard to explain.

" So you're thinking of going away ? " she said wanly.

" Oh, not immediately. I mean, not tomorrow or the next day. Maybe in a few weeks. Greg's asking for time off too. Hasn't had a real vacation in years, he says. We're going to do something — somewhere — maybe in Europe. Don't know what — yet. And by the way, that's a secret. Not a word or it'll be in all the columns."

" Paul, you know I never gossip. . . . But about *you*, after all you've just said — I don't know quite *what* to answer. . . ."

" Then that's good news, because I thought you'd be mad at me."

" *Mad* at you ? . . . Oh, Paul, I'm too — too *baffled* — to be that. I wish I knew what it is. . . ."

" What *what* is ? "

" The thing that drives you. What *is* it you go for in life ? I know it isn't money — I used to think it was success, but you'd get that here. . . . Is it fame ? Or power ? Or pleasure of a kind — do you *ever* get pleasure ? Or is it something inside yourself that forces you ? "

He gave her the look she knew so well, because it was the most frightening reply of all, as if he had switched off his mind to a care-and-maintenance basis until the subject was changed. He said blandly : " No particular mystery about it, Carey. I just have my work to do and——"

" I know, I know. And that's what you call it — your *work*. But it's more than that. Work's only a word. . . . Oh, words, they're not much use, are they ? Greg can say ' vacation ' and it just means golf, but to you——"

" You don't really like Greg, do you ? " he interrupted, switching on his mind again.

He knew she did, and she knew the question he was asking was a different one. She answered : " It isn't that, Paul. . . . Oh, never mind Greg — he can look after himself — he's established — rich——"

" Sure — nearly as rich as your old man and a damn sight freer with his money."

There was generally in any of his arguments a single explosion, rarely more than one, of sheer vulgarity ; it so often marked a climax that she almost welcomed it. She said quietly : " You may as well tell me just what's in your mind, now you've begun. You think Greg will finance you in some picture of your own, is that it ? "

" Why not ? He's a millionaire — must be. He can't act, as you say, and Majestic probably has him all sewn up anyhow, but there's no law to stop a man from investing in something he's interested in. Maybe I'll make another picture as good as *Erste Freundschaft* or the one they didn't let me finish. He's a likeable fellow, Greg is — I get along with him fine."

Carey half smiled. She did not know whether her main impulse was to warn Paul of Greg or vice versa — to warn Paul that Greg, though rich, was doubtless protected by lawyers and agents and business advisers who would certainly not let him put any substantial stake in a Saffron picture ; to warn Greg also, in case by some miracle of Paul's persuasion he should need it, that Paul was a splendid director who had probably, over a period of years, and balancing fabulous success against equally fabulous failure, won more personal prestige and lost more producers' money than anyone else in the business. . . . And then, in sheer weariness, the thought came : Why should she warn either of them ? Greg could look after himself, and so in his own way could Paul . . . perhaps it had been the mistake of her life ever to think of Paul as helpless — it was like the old problem in *Candida* — who was really the strong man, the poet or the other fellow ?

She said, speaking more in fatigue than in complaint : " So after all this, Paul . . . all the trouble . . . the fighting . . . you're giving it up . . . the thing we came out here for. . . ."

" *We?* Doesn't affect *you*, Carey. Right now you're hot as a firecracker, as they say in these fantastic faubourgs. Didn't you catch Randolph's hint when he said he'd been talking to Michaelson ? I'll bet he wants you for another picture."

Another picture. The thought made a grey shape in her mind. She wondered if she could ever act again ; but she had so often wondered this (sometimes five minutes before the curtain rose on a performance in which she did especially well) that she had come to disregard the misgiving as a mere symptom of mood ; but now it would not be disregarded. And whether it was still foolish, or true for the first time, the fact remained that she was only good enough to satisfy herself when she had also to satisfy Paul. She could ' get by ', of course, without him ; she had done, many times in plays, and doubtless it would be even easier in pictures ; doubtless too there were other directors just as great by any outsider's reckoning. But the grey shape was still in her mind.

Paul was saying something about the Critics' Dinner that night and the possibility that the picture might win a similar award from the New York critics. " If it does it'll mean a trip there for us — Greg, you and me."

" Oh dear, I don't know that I want to go."

" Studio expense. See a few shows." He had no particular care for money, but he was like a child if he could make someone else pay for a jaunt.

She shook her head. " I'm too tired, Paul."

" Tired ? "

" Yes. . . . I don't know how I'll even get through tonight."

He stared at her intently for a moment. " You look tired too." He announced that with an air of discovery. " Come up and have a drink. I don't believe you've ever been in my apartment."

She never had — which might have seemed strange to others, but had not really surprised her. It was a penthouse at the beach, decorated in rather delicate pastel shades — the same standardized charm that you could buy anywhere for enough money, only she guessed Paul had paid far too much. He pulled back the drapes to expose the view of boulevard, harbour, and ocean ; then mixed her a whisky and soda. " You know, Carey, it won't be so bad here for you. You'll be a big success without much trouble, and I'll tell you why — it isn't acting they want, it's a funny kind of personality. You have that — by God you have — you make the camera sing like an instrument."

" I must tell Norris that, because he almost prophesied it."

" Norris ? Oh yes. What's he doing now ? You hear from him ? "

" He's travelling in South America — with Austen."

" Pleasure trip ? "

" Austen will try to make it that. He needs it."

" Austen ? "

" No, Norris. He had a — a sort of breakdown after the strain of the war and the accident. He was *in* the war, not just in uniform. He drove an ambulance for four years."

" Couldn't Austen have kept him out of it ? "

" He could, and would have, but Norris wouldn't let him."

" What is the boy then — a fool or a hero ? "

" Probably neither."

" You miss them, I guess, now the picture's finished ? "

" Yes . . . especially Norris."

" Why especially him ? "

A quite fantastic impulse seized her, so that she said, hearing the words with a certain excitement : " Suppose I said I loved him ? "

" *What?* "

She smiled. Let him misunderstand her ; it would perhaps be revealing, like the play within the play in *Hamlet*. For she could never discuss with him the real predicament without the mask, the protection of an acting part. " You heard me," she said, " as they say in all the damned scripts you ever read out here."

He looked uneasy. " I — I don't get it, Carey. Are you joking ? A boy half your age ? "

" A little more than half."

He snorted. " Good God, I don't believe it. He's practically your son."

" Ah, now, if only he were . . ."

The speaking of the lines eased her, as so often at the opening of a play.

" Perfectly absurd," he mouthed gruffly.

And it was, but the show must go on. " Oh, come now, Paul, use your imagination. You've handled situations like this in pictures, haven't you ? Too censorable to be shown over here, but all right for the Continent. . . . People are people everywhere. The Saffron touch. You see life as it is, don't you, not gift-wrapped ? "

He sat heavily on the couch, his head bowed as in disgust or silent prayer. After a pause he said : " Well, what are you going to do about it ? "

" What do you advise ? "

" Does he think he's in love with you ? "

At this she fluffed ; she could not involve Norris in such a whim. " No," she answered, after hesitation.

" Well, that makes it simple."

" Simple ? "

" Because there's nothing you *can* do."

" And that makes it simple ? " (Back now in full stride.)

" I'm in a blind alley — I can't move forward or backward — I'm just plain stuck, and that's what makes it simple — as simple as being note-perfect in the *Hammerklavier*."

He got up abruptly and glowered down at her. " Carey, what's the matter with you ? Is this a game — a gag of some kind ? I can't remember you in this mood ever before."

" I never have been. Perhaps this is a first time — *Erste Freundschaft*."

" You mean . . ." He weighed an interpretation in his mind and was clearly disconcerted. " You mean — you never were — in love — with *me* ? "

" Does the sun have to be like the moon ? "

" What the devil does that signify ? "

" You were the sun, of course, but the moon, as everyone knows, is for love."

Like all other bad lines he had ever encountered, this maddened him. " For Christ's sake . . . a cue for a song in a fifth-rate musical ! What *is* the matter with you ? Talk sense. You're not on the stage now. . . ."

" But Paul, don't you remember that at moments of intense emotion an actor has to act ? — it's the only way he can come to terms with things . . . it's the consolation he has as an artist . . . you told me all that once. . . ."

Even in his angry bafflement he picked up two words out of her speech and made, so to say, a ring round them. " Intense emotion ? "

" Yes, Paul. Intense emotion — but not yet remembered in tranquillity. Whose definition was that ? Perhaps I'm a fond foolish woman, and to deal plainly, I fear I am not in my perfect mind. . . . Ophelia might have said that too."

" Carey, *stop* it. I don't know what you're driving at. What about Austen in all this ? Of course I'm not surprised if you haven't been hitting it off too well with *him* — he didn't seem to me your kind of man at all——"

" On the contrary, I hit it off with him very well indeed. I find it rather easy to hit it off with men. I'm a sensual woman, I sometimes think."

" Oh, God, Carey, why are you talking like this ? "

" Does it shock you ? I had an idea you might be — at least — amused."

" It — it makes me — it makes me feel — I don't understand you — any more."

He said that so pathetically that she got up and pulled him to the couch beside her. " And you don't, darling, in several little ways. But why bother ? " The absurd little play was over. Perhaps, if he had known it´was a play, he could have put on his mantle of infallibility and understood, but she had caught him with an unfair test — like expecting Paavo Nurmi to sprint for a bus. She did not blame him. She went on with half-chiding affection : " Paul, Paul, don't look so black, I've been acting — as you did when you were rehearsing me in Desdemona and you pretended to suspect me with Harry Foy. . . . Can't I have my own little act too ? "

" But why ? There was a reason for that, but *this* . . . I still don't get it. . . ."

" I know. There's a hair's-breadth of no-man's-land between us. Only a hair's-breadth. Woman's-land, let's call it. Oh boy, what dialogue ! "

He muttered something, but she could see he was relieved, and the look of pathetic puzzlement changed to one of mere glumness. " When are they due back from the South American trip ? " he asked after mopping his forehead.

" I don't know."

" I suppose you'll want to be in New York to meet them ? "

" I don't know."

" But won't they expect you to ? "

" I don't know that either. . . . I don't know anything. I can't see the future at all."

He pondered this for a moment, then suddenly became emphatic. " Got an idea. Why *don't* you do another picture ? "

" *What ?* "

" It's the solution, Carey. Randolph would sign you up

337

tomorrow, I'm certain. You've made a big reputation almost overnight — you've got a ready-made audience for the next thing you do, no matter what it is. And even with someone else directing you'd soon find how work would take your mind off things. . . . Carey, why not? Let me get hold of Randolph right now. . . ."

" No, no, Paul. Please don't. . . . I won't talk to him. . . . Paul, put that phone down. . . ."

" You'd prefer Michaelson to handle it from his end? Well, maybe that's smarter——"

" Paul . . . can't you understand that just now I'd rather die than face another day in a studio? . . . I'm *tired*. Don't you realize that? Things have piled up on me. . . . I'm *tired*."

For the first time he seemed to take her seriously. He said simply : " I wish I could help you."

" You have — a little — just by saying that. But you can't — really. There's not a thing anybody can do. It's in myself. But I can manage. I shall, I know. You don't need to worry about me."

He looked increasingly concerned. " Maybe you should take some time off. Carmel's a good place — Greg likes it there. Six months, maybe. . . . How's your heart, by the way ? "

" 'Tis broke," she answered, so promptly that she startled herself. Then when he stared without smiling she went on : " Don't you remember that — the time we first met — me driving down that hill in Kingstown with my leg under me and you asking what was the matter with it ? "

He smiled then, but she couldn't tell whether he did remember or not. Then she lost all control. She kept crying " 'Tis broke — 'Tis broke—" and Paul was helpless at her side, genuinely distressed but knowing nothing of any way to console her. Presently the tears spent themselves and she shook herself free of grief. " I'm sorry, Paul. That was very silly. I'm really ashamed of myself."

She let him fill up her glass, though she did not drink again, and the conversation after that became casual and

338

unimportant. About three o'clock she left, for she wanted a long rest before the dinner.

. . . . . .

At her apartment an air-mail letter awaited her from Austen's lawyer, Herbert Walsh, in New York. She had met him only once or twice and was surprised to hear from him. The letter said merely:

" DEAR MRS. BOND — I plan to be in your part of the country the 21st to the 25th and should like to discuss with you a certain matter. I hope, therefore, you will not be out of town, or if so, perhaps you would be good enough to let me know where I can contact you. My address will be . . ."

The letter gave her a chill as she read it. She had noticed lately that a great many small matters affected her in this way if they contained any element of uncertainty — a message that someone whose name she did not know had been trying to reach her on the telephone, some anonymous scurrilous letter (such as every movie personality receives occasionally), even the headlights of a car that seemed to be following her at night but was only waiting for a chance to overtake. It was a symptom of her nervous condition, she imagined, due partly to the strain of the picture-making; she was still detached enough in mind to diagnose and smile at her own foolishness. This letter from Mr. Walsh, however, put her in a state of mental spasm. She paced up and down the living-room of the apartment, reading it over and over as if the words themselves were hard to understand, then she crumpled it in sudden reasonless consternation. If someone were trying to torture her, this was the way. A minute later she was at the telephone, the note smoothed out beside the instrument as she read from it Walsh's number. Action had quieted her. But it was too late — six-thirty in New York; Walsh had already left his office and his secretary said she had strict orders not to give anyone his home number.

Carey, still a little distraught, found a groove of relief in the memory of all the stage telephone scenes she had played

339

— controlled emotion in voice, but an utmost betrayal to the eye — how easy it was, and how difficult audiences always thought it ! . . . She said : " Perhaps *you* can help me then. I got a letter today from Mr. Walsh——"

" Yes, Mrs. Bond. I remember sending it. He's going out to visit you."

" You mean — just — just to visit *me* ? "

" I think so."

" But — but if it's so important I — I feel I can't wait to know what it is. . . . I *must* know. . . . It's not fair to have to think of these things for days ahead. . . . Do *you* know what it's about ? I'm sure you must do——"

" I'm sorry, Mrs. Bond — perhaps if you were to telephone Mr. Walsh personally tomorrow . . . well, no, I oughtn't to say that — he probably wouldn't care to talk over the telephone——"

" So you *do* know what it's about ? "

" No, Mrs. Bond, Mr. Walsh doesn't discuss his cases with me."

" *Cases ?* " Her heart felt as if it were being lifted out of her body for a solo exhibition. " *What* case ? I'm not in any case . . . at least I . . . none that I know of. . . ."

" I'm sorry, Mrs. Bond. There's really nothing more I can say. I'm sure when Mr. Walsh gets out to see you——"

" I see, I see. . . . Yes, I understand. . . . I'll wait. . . . Goodbye. . . ."

For a time after that she thought she would be unable to attend the dinner. But that disturbed her even more ; she disliked causing commotion, and had always harboured a slight contempt for last-minute cancellers. Paul had once told her understudy : " You're in a hopeless job. Carey goes on if she can crawl." Somehow the recollection of that tribute gave her power now to face the evening ahead, and once the decision was made she could even raise a mild excitement. It might be fun to have people applauding her again, real live people applauding *her* instead of her photographs.

She rested, changed, then drove downtown where the

dinner was to be held. She was a little late, yet she drove slowly, choosing the quieter residential streets. Suddenly a dog came scampering through a gate and into the roadway in front of her car ; she passed right over. She felt her heart brake sharply with the clenching of feet and hands ; she pulled to the kerb, then looked back. It was true, except that the car, not the wheels, had passed over ; and the dog, a black spaniel, was now back on the sidewalk, scared but unhurt, desperately trying to re-enter the gate. She got out and approached the animal, almightily angry and tender ; in a deep convulsion of deliverance her heart began to hammer again as she stooped to fondle him, but he was unresponsive, merely wanting to be back in his own garden. She unlatched the gate and let him in. Then she resumed the drive. Nobody had seen the incident. How baffling was the alchemy of inches and seconds . . . and she thought of Norris in his jeep with that girl on the Rhineland road. And that other German girl, lovely Wanda Hessely, killed by bombs. There was hazard enough in the lives of those who wanted to live, and for those who wanted to die, was there too much — or not enough ? . . .

At the dinner she received a warm welcome from the five or six hundred guests already congregated. She had met many of them before, casually and at other parties ; some gave her the appraising welcome of those who knew she was on the upgrade in the local hierarchy, but there were others doubtless who were jealous of her success ; she had been in show business long enough to accept that as one of the facts of life, not as any particular proof of evil nature She smiled and shook hands a good deal as she found her place at the high table, next to Calvin Beckford. Greg was on his left, and Paul, to her slight surprise, some way down the table between two pretty girls. Her neighbour on the right was introduced as a Mr. Hare — a small man, sharp-eyed and friendly ; he said he thought he had seen her once in a play in Boston when he was at Harvard, and someone who overheard this laughed because that made her (as she certainly was) at least forty. " I can't remember the play, but I couldn't forget *you*," he said, plugging the hole in his gallantry so promptly that she wondered if he had made both remarks to fix her interest in him. Then Beckford commandeered her and would not let go throughout the first part of the meal. He was a type she had often met and knew how to get along with — showy, glib, eager to impress, to please, to be flattered in return. She much preferred the other man, and at the first chance she turned to him. " I think it must have been *Quality Street* you saw me in, Mr. Hare," she said.

" That's right, so it was."

" Because I don't believe I ever played in Boston in any-thing else. Not in those days."

" Not so very long ago."

" Twenty years."

He smiled. " What does it feel like to be a well-known actress all that time and then have people behave out here as if they'd discovered you ? "

She laughed and was aware of the freemasonry between them of those for whom movie standards were too important to be disregarded but too inept to be taken seriously. " It's funny," she said.

" I hope you'll tell them that in your speech."

" Oh, do I have to make a speech ? " She knew she had, of course, but she had an impulse to act a part — only a small part, just to keep her mind off other things.

" I'm sure we all hope you will," he answered. " But it needn't be a long one. Do speeches make you nervous ? "

" Other people's do occasionally." She was thinking of Paul ; she had caught sight of him down the table ; he seemed to be in the throes of not having a good time ; his two neighbours were talking to each other across him, a thing that would always put him in an ill humour. She added, aware that Mr. Hare was studying her : " Paul's especially. Paul Saffron — the director. He can be so tactless." She wondered why she had said so much. then added hastily : " No, I'm not exactly scared to speak in public, but I find it much harder than acting. Perhaps that only means I find it hard to act the part of myself."

" Ethel Barrymore once told me practically the same thing."

She wondered who he was ; he did not seem the kind that would say a thing like that just to let her know he knew Ethel Barrymore. Probably someone important in the picture world, otherwise he would not have been put next to her. Then a wisp of memory flicked her from somewhere — Hare — Hare — there was a lawyer named Hare who had handled something for somebody she knew . . . she remembered it because she had thought it sensible . . . a clause in a will limiting burial expenses to five hundred dollars. Every celebrity ought to have it, Hare was supposed to have said, like insurance against nuisance suits, and it had been his idea to make it mandatory so that executors and relatives wouldn't be made to look like cheap skates. . . . Yes, a good idea. By then she realized that Mr. Hare was saying nice things about *Morning Journey*. " A real triumph for you, Miss Arundel. I expect you're already bored by people who tell you so."

" No, I enjoy it. Thank you."

" Of course you won't go back to the stage again. I say that because I hope you will."

" I might."

" But first, I suppose, another picture ? "

" No, I've no plans for that. I've no definite plans for anything, except perhaps a vacation in Ireland. . . . By the way, Mr. Hare, you're the lawyer, aren't you ? "

" *The* lawyer ? Let's settle for *a* lawyer."

" I wonder if you could help me."

She had the sudden idea she would ask him about the letter from Walsh. What it could possibly mean. What she ought to do about it. Whether, when she met Walsh, she ought to be alone or to have another lawyer with her. She read in Mr. Hare's attitude such personal friendliness that she felt she could tell him the whole story — if only she herself knew what the whole story was. But of course she didn't. Then how *could* he help her ? How could he possibly judge from Walsh's letter what it meant ? He would probably advise her to see Walsh and find out. It was therefore absurd to bother him about something nebulous. She changed her mind so abruptly that when he answered, " Of course. Trouble of some kind ? " — she had to think fast to find any answer at all. She said : " Oh, nothing very important. I thought of sub-letting my apartment while I go to Ireland, but the lease says I can't."

" Be glad to help you," he answered. " Send — or better still — bring the lease along to my office and I'll see if anything can be done." The chairman had risen and was trying to get silence for his opening remarks. Mr. Hare went on hurriedly : " Any time. Tomorrow morning if you like."

" Thanks. Tomorrow morning, then," she answered, stampeded into another absurdity, as she well realized. For she rented her apartment by the month — there was no question of sub-letting. She wondered what on earth she could say if she did visit him, or alternatively, what he would think if she made some excuse not to go. Then she thought of a better way out ; she would say, when she got to his office : " I've decided not to sub-let, anyhow, but meeting you made me think of something you once did for someone I knew, though I can't remember who it was, but I remember *what* it was . . . a clause in a will limiting burial expenses. . . ." Macabre but reasonable. Then she wondered whether, even with this excuse, she really needed or wanted to visit Mr. Hare at all. . . .

The chairman was speaking. She glanced down the table and watched Paul for a moment, failing to catch his eye. His chin was sunk disconsolately in his chest ; she might have thought he had drunk too much but for knowing that he never did, any more. Yet somehow, looking at him, she was apprehensive ; she wished he had had a neighbour who could have given him some good conversation, instead of the two chattering starlets he had been stuck with. It occurred to her that he would doubtless consider his bad position at the table a slight ; but she was fairly certain it was not, and that he had been put between two pretty girls because someone might have supposed he would enjoy himself there. . . . Meanwhile she was planning what to say when her own turn came. After her remarks to Mr. Hare, he would probably expect her to be not so good; she would surprise him, therefore. Yet it was true; she felt uncovered, vulnerable without the protection of an imagined personality.

The chairman sat down, having said nothing that she had really heard, and during the applause Mr. Hare turned to her again. " Are you by any chance going on to the Fulton-Griffins' when this thing is over ? "

" Oh, I don't think so. I was asked, but I understand there's such a crowd always there, and I hate crowds."

She had never been to a Fulton-Griffin party, though Paul had been once and told her what it was like. She had known then that she wouldn't enjoy it.

" So do I," Mr. Hare said, " but a Fulton-Griffin party is something you ought to see if you haven't been to one before. I thought if you were going I'd have a chance to talk to you without all these interruptions."

" Oh yes, I'd like that, but I really think I ought to go home. I've been rather tired since the picture finished and——"

The chairman was introducing the next speaker, Calvin Beckford. After his first half-dozen words she glanced at Paul with renewed apprehension, sure that he would dislike the man fiercely and progressively. For Beckford had the kind of fruity voice that Paul could not stand, even when an actor assumed it for a part; " Be an undertaker, not an actor," Paul had once said, to a youth whose natural voice had been of that kind, " and change the funeral service to read ' O Passing On, where is Thy Sting ? ' " Now why did she recall that ? . . . She looked at Paul again and noted every sign that he was in a profound gloom. Beckford's voice droned on, the lard-like face falsely radiant as the compliments poured forth. " Unforgettable career fittingly climaxed " was one of them, aimed at herself. Paul would hate that too, and for a number of reasons, one of which was that he hated the word ' unforgettable '. It was a radio word, he always said, meaning ' forgettable '.

At last the orator reached his point, which was the presentation of the plaques; she took hers, bowed to the applause, then made her little speech and forgot to congratulate Mr. Beckford on his approaching seventieth birthday, though she did remember to mention Majestic Studios as the *alma mater* that had nourished *Morning Journey* in its bosom. All very pretty, and over in exactly three and a half minutes.

" Bravo," Mr. Hare whispered, when she sat down. " You did very well."

She smiled and felt that he had been duly impressed.

Then the presentation to Greg, who took even less time to get on his feet and off again.

Then Paul.

She knew from the outset, from the look on his face, from the set of his jaw, from the way he strode to a microphone and focused himself, as it were, into the centre of a silence, that he was going to be impossible. He took the plaque without a smile, and Carey, guessing what was ahead, bit her lip and stared at the table. Then it began . . . practically all the things he had said to her that afternoon. They had either simmered in his mind since then, or in a subconscious way he had been trying them out on her as he so often did . . . a weapon not necessarily to be used, but kept sharpened in readiness. She knew that his decision on such matters was almost always last-minute and capricious — that perhaps if he had been given a better place at the table, if one of his neighbours had been interesting, or if Calvin Beckford had been Jack Benny . . . then he might well have said his thank-you like a gentleman, like the little gentleman he sometimes looked but never actually was.

When it was over she got up from the table and left, slipping out by a side door without a word to anyone. Nobody tried to stop her; she had an impression that Paul's speech had made everything else, for the moment, unnoticed. She ran down the road to the car park, not waiting for the boy to take her ticket. She was full of that curious vacuum of sensation that comes after one has been hurt and before one can really feel anything.

.   .   .   .

Back at the apartment she entered by a tradesmen's side door that bypassed the desk ; she did not want to be told there had been any messages for her. When she reached her rooms the telephone was ringing. The desk usually gave the name of a caller, but this time she lifted the receiver to hear a woman's voice mentioning the name of a newspaper and asking what she thought of Paul Saffron's speech at the Critics' Dinner. She answered, in a flustered way : " Oh, I don't know — I haven't much of an opinion about it."

" But Miss Arundel, what do you think of his remark that *Morning Journey* is the worst picture he ever made ? "

" I — I don't know. I — I——"

" Do *you* think it's the worst picture he ever made ? "

" Well, no — or rather I don't know — I can't say — I haven't seen all the pictures he ever made. . . ."

A laugh at the other end seemed to show that her answer had been considered adequate.

" Just one more question, Miss Arundel, what did you think about Mr. Saffron's statement that——"

" I'm sorry," she interrupted, " that's all I can tell you. I must hang up. I'm very sorry."

She hung up. As she stepped from the instrument she tried to remember what little she had said. Question : " Do you think it's the worst picture he ever made ? " Answer : " I can't say — I haven't seen all the pictures he ever made." — Oh, what a snide remark, the way it would look in print. She felt a heart-constriction, then a surge of anger against Paul for getting into this mess and dragging her into it with him. The telephone rang again. This time she lifted it off the hook and ignored it. She heard the intermittent clicking and wondered how soon the desk clerk would send someone up to see what was the matter. Abruptly, as if challenged to face some issue with every final scrap of strength she had,

she made up her mind to go to the Fulton-Griffins'. She
would startle everyone there, would make a stage entrance,
act the unruffled queen, show everyone that she did not care
for anything that had happened, that Paul could go to the
devil his own way. An impulse of such magnitude demanded
either enthusiasm or quick extinction ; she was able to muster
the former as she chose a new dress, changed quickly, and
left by the same side entrance.

Ten minutes later she was driving along winding uphill
streets. She had put the car-top down, for the feel of the
night and the kind of excitement it might give ; she had
wrapped her head in a scarf that would keep her hair in
shape. Presently the estate of the Fulton-Griffins came into
view. Cars were parked for half a mile along the narrow
drive-way ; retainers, watchful for gate-crashers, scrutinized
first the car, then seemed to recognize her face. The house
was baroque and ugly, even in floodlights, but the gardens
had spaciousness. A heart-shaped swimming-pool glistened
amidst the trees and beside it stood an open-air bar almost
as large. Sounds of frolic came from both.

Nobody quite knew why a rich, respectable, and retired
Middle Western couple lavished such frequent entertainment, or why they did not prefer seclusion to turning their
house into an almost weekly shambles of broken glasses and
cigarette-burned carpets. Presumably they liked to meet
celebrities, old and new ; presumably they liked noise ;
perhaps also they were generous, or bored, or snobbish.
But even all of that could not pierce the final mystery. Their
parties, at least, were not exclusive — or not much more so
than the lobby of the Waldorf. And the one economy they
practised was notorious ; their liquor was never quite
excellent.

Several hundred guests were already mingling outside
and in when Carey arrived, and she made the full sensation
she had planned. She had always been able to act when she
could do nothing else ; it was like starting a motor that left
her with some generated strength in herself. She actually
enjoyed greeting her hostess with : " Believe me, after the

Critics' Dinner coming here is a godsend. I wouldn't have missed it for anything, though. . . . Paul's speech, I mean. The way that man can put his foot in it — with both feet ! "

After that, of course, everyone felt free to comment on the affair as outspokenly as they liked before her, and many did. She let them know how little she cared, how little it all mattered, how happy she was to be at a party where nobody would make serious speeches at all, not even silly ones. She felt waves of sympathy reaching towards her, but also waves of awareness that she was hamming it up, for she could hardly conceal that from professionals. It was the quality of the act that she hoped they would recognize. She talked a lot and was perhaps a little too gay at times. She had even a feeling once or twice that the whole idea of coming to the party had been mistaken, but she rallied herself quickly and switched to another group whose different reaction might reconvince her. In a party of such size and at such a stage of festivity there was always a bewildering series of cross-currents — envies and enmities open or hidden, masquerading sometimes in ways that drink, towards the end of a long evening, would reveal ; it was this sort of thing that often led at Fulton-Griffin parties to the beginnings of scenes that were usually squelched before they made headlines owing to the Fulton-Griffin tactic of planting several reliable house servants to play guests among the guests. Thus there could develop a faintly sinister atmosphere. The strong-jawed man sipping bourbon at the edge of the pool might be getting ready either to push you in or fish you out.

Carey felt exultant as she worked her way through the crowd. For one thing the rooms were cool, air-conditioned, with the windows wide open, an absurdity that yet contrived an enchantment, for pockets of blossom-scented air drifting in from the gardens were deliciously warm. An evening out of a travel folder, with starlit sky and flood-lit lawns to aid the illusion (as Paul had said after his one experience of a Fulton-Griffin party) that the cream of civilization had coagulated here and would make excellent cheese. Half the guests were already a little drunk. The buffet tables were still laden with food that (like the drink) was not quite excellent. On a platform beyond the swimming-pool a seven-piece orchestra played medleys. Some people were dancing.

Suddenly Carey saw Mr. Hare in a corner of the drawing-room all on his own. " Hello, Mr. Hare," she said, smiling.

" Well, Miss Arundel, this *is* a surprise. You changed your mind ? "

" I often do."

" So we *can* finish our talk. That's good."

" Yes, but let's go outside. The gardens are lovely."

They stepped through the French windows to the terrace, avoiding the crowd at the swimming-pool end and discovering a side path that led to a grove of eucalyptus trees.

" I felt I had to come," she said, " just to show I don't feel all the things people are thinking I feel."

" You're very wise." He took her arm and she knew the entire friendliness of the man ; she liked, too, the way he went straight to what must be in both their minds. " What Saffron did say," he said, " as opposed to all the talk of what he said, wasn't really against *you*. Therefore there's nothing for you to be hurt or humiliated about."

" I'm so glad you think that."

" Just stupid of him and in bad taste."

" Oh yes, oh yes, I know it was."

" Rather odd — coming just after you'd told me his speeches sometimes made you feel nervous."

Had she said that ? Oh yes, during the dinner. " Yes, wasn't it odd ? " Because it really was.

" You must have had a lot of experience of him."

" Well, we were married, once."

And it was odd, too, that he hadn't known that, because it obviously gave him a shock. " You *were* ? "

" Didn't you know ? "

" I didn't, and as everybody else here must, it's rather astonishing nobody happened to mention it to me. I suppose they assumed I knew."

" So you've been talking about me to people ? "

" A few people have been talking about you to me."

" What do they say ? "

" They like you — and they don't like him."

Well, that had always been so — almost always. She felt an overwhelming sadness as she answered : " They don't have to couple us together any more."

" Except that you were in the picture together."

" Yes — for a special reason, but that's a long story — I might tell you some time if you're interested."

Some men and girls were approaching.

" Maybe tomorrow ? Don't forget you have a date at my office. Make it eleven-thirty and I'll take you to lunch."

" Fine." She would like that. But her thoughts were on Paul, now that he had been spoken of by both of them. She wondered where he was, what he was doing. She said, as they walked back towards the house : " He didn't show up here tonight, did he ? "

" No. I'm sure I'd have known if he had. Did you think he might ? "

" He's capable of it. If he'd been here I'd have wanted to leave — I couldn't stand any more." And that was true enough.

" I don't blame you."

" I'm just about at the limit of what I can stand, to be frank."

" You probably need that holiday in Ireland you talked about. But why Ireland ? "

" I was born there. Where were you born ? "

" Vermont . . . on a farm."

" So was I. In County Kildare. The greenest fields, and my father rode the wildest and most beautiful horses. . . ." The vision filled her — oh, the lovely country, the white clouds rolling shadows over the fields, the green-blue mountains in the distance. Her eyes could always fill when she thought of it, but now she was embarrassed because she knew Mr. Hare was watching her. She added : " Oh, I guess we all feel like that about where we were born. Vermont is beautiful too."

" Yes, very." And then, telling her there was just time

for one more question, he went on to say something that both amazed and puzzled her. He seemed to think it might, for he cautioned her in advance. " A rather personal question, so don't be startled. . . . Did Saffron ever — in a dressing-room at the studio while the picture was being made — did he ever quarrel with you and threaten you with a gun ? "

She had to laugh. " Good heavens, no. Who on earth made that one up ? "

.   .   .   .

They separated inside the house and she guessed that he left soon afterwards, before she did. She stayed till nearly one, talking and dancing with a few of the sober survivals, but when she was in her car driving downhill towards her apartment the beginnings of panic seized her. Would there have been more messages, newspaper enquiries ? The desk man said : " Did you know you left your phone off the hook, Miss Arundel ? "

She said : " Oh, did I ? Have there been calls ? "

" Quite a number. . . ." He was going to hand her the slips but she said : " I can't do anything about them tonight — send them up tomorrow."

She had hoped the apartment would seem cheerful to relax in after the long strain of the evening ; it was really an elegant apartment, and if only it had been higher, as in New York, she felt it might have worked a miracle on her mood ; she loved height, the look of streets spread out below, a corner window like the prow of a ship in air. She switched on all the lights and lit a cigarette. She did not know whether she could sleep or even whether she wanted to. In a way the evening had been her triumph — she had rallied friends and admirers in droves. Yet was there anyone, anywhere, now, at one in the morning, who would greet her warmly yet incuriously, welcomingly yet without drama, if she telephoned or rang a door-bell ? Greg ? . . . Austen ? . . . Norris ? . . . Even Paul ? . . . It seemed to her that most of those she had talked to so excitedly throughout the evening were by now either drunk or climbing into some little bed, like

Mr. Hare. . . . Then suddenly she thought of Professor Lingard. How incredible that anyone should fill so exactly her precise requirements — Professor Lingard, who had given her a cordial invitation to look through his observatory telescope in the middle of some night! But he had warned her to telephone first, to find if the skies were clear enough. So she telephoned, and soon heard his voice, amiable and distant-sounding: " Why, yes, Miss Arundel . . . of course I remember . . . yes, wonderful . . . no, I'm working as usual. . . . *Tonight?* . . . Why, certainly, you couldn't have chosen a better one. . . . As soon as you like, then. . . . An hour and a half, I should think — there'll be very little traffic . . . you know the way . . . but take it easy now, especially the last stretch. . . ."

The thought of leaving the city and driving into the mile-high mountains lifted her spirits again to a peak of their own; she changed into street clothes and went out. Her car had ample gas; she drove east along Sunset as far as Western, then turned north.

. . . .

There was no doubt of her mental plight. She was in desperate need of reassurance which no one then available could give, and her own name on a darkened theatre marquee did nothing to help — rather the contrary, since it stressed the irony of being alone amidst so many sleeping strangers who knew her by sight and perhaps had warmed to her for a few moments of their waking lives. As she drove she felt the tingling of all her nerves into alternating fear and excitement, so that every car whose lights she saw in the rear-view mirror seemed to be following until it actually overtook; she was used to this illusion by now, and knew how foolish it was, but it made her drive a little faster than usual, though not recklessly. At the corner on Foothill where the climb began, the great eye of the observatory became a symbol in her mind of some ultimate scrutiny, and Professor Lingard himself a human answer to a different problem. For at their one meeting they had established kinship, she had been aware of it ; she also guessed he was not a man to invite her to his mountain-top unless he had rather liked her. As she had said to Paul (the remark that had perhaps most of all shocked him), she found it easy to hit it off with men — Paul's phrase for whatever there was of murk or mystery in his own concept of the relationship. She had an idea she would find it easy to hit it off with Professor Lingard if only his physical eye would leave the heavens for a moment . . . and at that she began to smile, for the quality in her that she freely agreed was sensual was always mixed up with smiling and fun — a comedy role that Paul had disapproved after the first entrancement, and Austen had accepted but never perfectly understood.

The mountains heaved into outlines against the blue-black sky ; it was the smell of *manzanita* that crossed the roadway in gusts ; the eyes of tiny animals blinked out of their secret, populated world . . . and there came to her mind the road over the Sally Gap, the climb so different from this, the car so different from this, herself so different from now, the point where she had left the road once and clambered through high gorse to the summit of Kippure ; there had been tin cans on that summit, not left by picnickers but by gunmen on the run during the time of troubles — tin cans and rotting puttees and an old cartridge belt ; and from the summit where one stood amongst the litter of men's idiocy one could see far over the Gap to the great names of Wicklow — Mullaghcleevaun and Lugnaquilla that lay over the vale of Glenmalure. . . .

And she remembered Paul as he had been for a little time after their marriage ; his ways her own, his discovering joy over what was so natural to her, but partly as spectator even then, and later ceasing to applaud ; his understanding of her that was deep at first, so that they had both felt that life could carry them on its own tide ; but after a while the understanding had fled from the heart to the brain, and then (but only in his moments of greatness) back to a heart that was not hers.

She remembered that year in Los Angeles (for Hollywood

had not yet become the magnetic, polarizing name), the year he had tried to crash the picture industry on the ground floor, and it would have none of him ; the great names — Chaplin, Sennett, Lasky, Griffith. If only, she had often thought, if only someone then had given him a chance he might have become as great as they, and with an easing of so many frustrations that had bedevilled him since — not all, but many. In vain he had written letters, submitted ideas, sought interviews ; his stage success in London had counted for nothing. That was the second year after their marriage, and he had already wooed the New York stage equally in vain. Careers also have currencies, and sometimes a prestige account in one country is not transferable to another ; at any rate nobody in Hollywood was interested in English press clippings about *Othello*. They had rented a frame bungalow between Western and Vermont for twenty dollars a month, Paul assuming that even if he couldn't find a studio job there was always journalism to fall back on. Gradually he had found how that, too, could fail him ; either, after his taste of the stage, he could not write, or else the kind of thing he wrote had lost its small vogue. Merryweather was dead and there was no other editor interested in him. He kept on writing, nevertheless, and the stuff kept on coming back. Then, when they owed a couple of months' rent, she had taken a job as waitress in a restaurant on Pico Boulevard — hard work, but she could earn enough to keep them both till at last his chance came to direct a play in New York — the one that led to the first big success.

And the strange thing was that this year in Los Angeles — the year he later chose to forget (because he thought of it only as the time and place of his failure) — had actually been the happiest in all her life. They had been so close together, and whenever she had returned from the restaurant or he after hours of fruitless job-seeking, the little house had been there to welcome them, its privacies their own and its tasks a pleasure. The first thing she had had to do was to patch the screens because of his phobia about flies ; the second thing was to clip the pepper tree that did not let enough light into the room where he planned to work. And the last thing of all was on the day they left so jubilantly (he with the New York offer in his pocket); she had leaned out of the window as the taxi turned the corner, and something deep in her heart had said goodbye. For she had been able, in that house, to make him happy as never before or since; there he had needed her enough to accept the clearance she could make in the thickets of his emotions — a sunlit clearance before the jungle grew again.

Strange, the moments of pure emotion one remembered. There was a play tried out at New Haven (or was it Philadelphia?) — it had flopped so badly it never reached Broadway, but a curious thing, a very curious thing, happened on the second night. It was a Civil War play, with Lincoln, McClellan, Seward, Pope, and others in it — poor fustian stuff, but Paul had believed he could make it spectacular — one of those mistakes of his that always seemed fewer than they were. Anyhow, there was this play, with authentic scenes and uniforms and guns booming off-stage; and on the second night the press agent had thought to invite local Civil War veterans as guests of the management. About half a dozen came — tottering into the front row and cupping their ears to catch the lines; afterwards Paul asked them on stage to meet the cast and be photographed. So they came, and nobody knew what to say except one old fellow who suddenly hobbled up to General McClellan and shook his gnarled fist in the actor's face while his own became contorted with rage. "For Christ's sake, you ——, why weren't you there to help us at Manassas?" He would have struck the actor had not others led him away. The whole incident was chilling to all who witnessed it, and made the paltry little play seem paltrier than ever. No one had any hopes of success after that; it was as if a curse had been laid.

How odd the mixture when memory sinks its net into the past and makes a random haul, with the mind quiescent and bemused over its find, savouring the items with infinite detachment. For it was indeed a series of other Careys whom Carey saw in all these wayward recollections — a young woman climbing Kippure, a waitress serving pie *à la mode*, an actress in crinolines . . . and now a woman over forty with her name on a thousand marquees, driving an open Cadillac on a summer night to a mountain-top observatory.

.   .   .   .   .   .

Professor Lingard met her at the parking-place, where he had apparently been waiting. Everywhere there was a vast cool silence to which the mind added its own image of height and loneliness. He greeted her warmly but seemed shyer than ever as he guided her by flashlight to the roadway. The stars were brilliant, but it was very dark under the shapes of trees.

" You've chosen a grand night, Miss Arundel."

" I'm glad. I was at a party and when I left I suddenly felt in the mood."

" I'm glad too. I really didn't take you very seriously when you first promised you'd come. And then after I found out who you were . . . you must have thought me terribly stupid for not realizing. . . ."

" Oh no. Why should it matter ? "

" But it really was inexcusable. I felt so embarrassed when someone told me I'd been talking to Carey Arundel, the movie star. . . ."

Movie star. . . . That was evidently all he knew — even now. " But you were very nice and friendly. I enjoyed our conversation."

" So long as you've forgiven me, Miss Arundel. Because before you leave I'm going to take another liberty if I may."

" Oh, please. *Anything*."

" I'd like you to sign an autograph book for a friend of mine . . . a little girl — she's ten — the daughter of the woman who comes in once a day to clean for me. You've no idea what it'll mean to her — and when I tell her Carey Arundel's actually *been* here. . . . I hope it isn't too much to ask ? "

She observed him in the faint glow that reflected back

from the flashlight and wondered how far he was from reading what was in her mind.

" Of course I'll do it . . . and now please stop talking about Carey Arundel. I'm a little bit tired of her and if she doesn't mend her ways I've a good mind to shove her off a cliff. . . . Is there a cliff by the way ? I'm sure there must be."

" Not just here, but you passed some steep ones on the way up. Of course you wouldn't see them at night. Some people find the road rather frightening."

" Not me. I love heights. . . . Tell me what you do here."

" Technically ? I don't think it would interest you very much, though if you really want me to I'll——"

" No, no, I mean the way you live — are you alone all the time ? Do you feel happy ? Is there peace of mind on a mountain-top ? "

They had reached a cabin the door of which he opened. Suddenly she felt : *this is home*. There was actually a small log-fire burning and it was in the firelight that she saw the room first of all. " It gets chilly at nights even in summer," he explained ; and the warmth was indeed a pleasant thing. A couch, chairs, desk, and radio-gramophone were the main furnishings. No pictures, only a strip of matting on the floor, a few books, a map of the area pinned on the log walls, an old-fashioned telephone. " There's also a bedroom, bathroom, and a small kitchen," he said, noticing her interest, but not knowing — how could he know ? — that whenever she entered any room (except decorators' show pieces) her mind made an inventory as if she were looking for something lost from her own life. " Simple, Miss Arundel — primitive, I dare say it seems to you — but good enough for a bachelor . . . Won't you sit down ? I'll tell my assistant to have things ready." He made the call while she watched him. There was a green-shaded lamp he switched on over the desk — it was almost the ugliest lamp she had ever seen, but doubtless in the right position for his work and that was all he cared about.

" So you're not alone ? " she said, when he had hung up.

" He's a student. He likes to help me on good nights. . . .
And you were asking if I'm happy . . . of course I am. I
wouldn't be up here if I weren't. I could probably earn
more money down below."

" Sure. That's where we can all earn more money."

" You say ' sure ' like the Irish, not like the Americans."

" I was born in Ireland."

" I *thought* there was an accent . . . no, not quite an
accent — more a rhythm, a lilt. You can't lose it, can you ?
You shouldn't want to, anyhow. I'm from Wyoming."

" Cowboys," she said absently.

" Now that's odd — because I almost was a cowboy, and
it's still what I'd rather be than anything else — except this.
You like horses ? "

" Love them. Near where I was born there was the
Curragh — that's the great place for horses."

" And music ? You like music too ? "

" Yes. Music and horses and dogs and . . ."

" Classical music ? "

" Yes."

" Bach ? "

Without waiting for a reply he went to the radio-gramophone, saying as he opened it : " We have a few minutes
before he gets everything adjusted." He found a record close
to hand. There was something in the way he let down the
needle on to the outermost groove that seemed to her one of
the most exquisite movements she had ever seen, and the
thought came then that Paul would have seen it like that too,
would have wanted to shoot it slowly and tenderly, and that
Randolph later would have cut the whole scene. " But
nothing happens, Saffron ! A guy starts a record on a turn-
table and you let him use up all that footage ! "

Nothing happens. . . . They would say that too, doubtless, of the Bach Chorale. The music just goes round and
round. . . .

She listened and felt peaceful. The little room, the firelight, Bach . . . the mountain outside, above the world.

Presently the record ended and he switched off the machine. He made no comment, did not even ask if she had liked it. Perhaps he feared she hadn't, perhaps he simply didn't care. He picked up the flashlight, toying with it, as if in hint that they should leave. She looked at him without moving. If only she could stay a while. If only he could grasp how comfortable she was where she was. If only he could guess the kind of reassurance she was seeking.

"Tell me," she said suddenly. "What's going to happen?"

"To happen? Where? How . . . how do you mean?"

"To all of us. . . . That's a terrible thing to ask, isn't it? But I thought you might have some professional ideas. Will the world blow itself up one of these days?"

He smiled. "Some popular science writers have said so. I don't know enough to contradict them."

"But you do know something about atomic energy — Einstein — all that?"

"Not much, and even if I did it wouldn't make me a prophet of world affairs. I'm just an astronomer."

"I wish I knew what you really thought. If people like you don't give us the benefit of an honest opinion, no wonder we're all misled by people who aren't honest."

"But is there much value in an unqualified person's opinion? Of course, if you ask, if I think there'll be a third world war — *that* sort of question — I dare say my guess is no worse than anybody else's."

"*Do* you think there will be?"

"I wouldn't be surprised."

"And if there is, do you think the world will destroy itself?"

"You mean everything go bang all at once? I doubt that. Possibly there'll be a breakdown of what we now call civilization."

"You don't think the invention of all kinds of horrible weapons will prevent the world from daring to go to war?"

"It never has done before, though that's no proof that it couldn't happen."

" But on the whole you'd stick to your first guess that civilization's on its way to suicide ? "

" I don't know that I'd put it quite like that——"

" Suicide's an ugly word, isn't it ? It's something hardly any of us would do individually — and yet collectively, if we take the road we've been warned is fatal, what else can you call it ? "

" I get your point, and it's not the ugliness of the word I'm chary of, it's the melodrama. If nature abhors a vacuum, I should say that science also abhors a catastrophe. In a sense it's too *easy* to contemplate."

" I think I know what you mean. Too Jules-Vernal, my husband once said. My first husband," she corrected herself, and then wondered why it had mattered enough to do so.

He smiled. " Jules-Vernal ? Of course, people still believed in progress in those days, so Jules Verne was just a romantic, but today, when every amateur talks calamity at every cocktail party . . . I'm sorry — I didn't mean to sound superior."

" But you probably are superior — that's why I'm asking you these things. Isn't there anything we can do — any of us — you — or even me ? "

" That again I don't know. The problem seems to be worrying the best minds in the world——"

" If they *are* the best. And you're just an astronomer. So you'll go on with your work — up here — till the whistle blows ? "

" Well, won't movie people go on making pictures——"

" — and bankers go on making money and lawyers go on filing suits and everyone else go on with whatever they do for a living ? "

" Why, yes, I expect they will."

She said, after a rather tense pause : " You know, professor, it all reminds me of a play I was once in — a dreadful thing which we all realized was dreadful, yet we kept on rehearsing in a sort of hypnotic trance as if we were stuck in a groove of disaster and had to go through with it to the end."

" What happened ? "

" It flopped — just as we'd all known it would."

" And what do you think could have been done to prevent that ? "

" Somebody — maybe me, because I was the star — somebody after the first rehearsal should have said : ' Are we all crazy ? ' "

" But if you all were, how would that have helped ? "

During the argument his voice had grown colder and more distant, until this last remark was more like an answer in ice, a final verdict, than a question. Then he got up, as if to change both the temperature and the perspective. She still looked at him without moving. If only she could stay a little longer. . . .

She said : " I'm not crazy any more like that. I think I would know now, and warn the others in time . . . *in time*, of course, is the whole point. *Is* there time in the world today ? Oh, but there must be. If we need a miracle we must have one. Suppose you were lost in a cave in pitch darkness, would you lie down and die or fumble around to try to find a way out ? "

" I'd try to find a way out, because I'd know there was one, since there'd been a way in."

" But maybe the way out today *isn't* the way in. Perhaps that's the mistake we've been making." She broke off with a bemused smile. " I don't know why I suddenly feel so optimistic. Could it be the altitude ? How high is it here ? "

He smiled also. " Five thousand seven hundred feet. And that reminds me of something somebody once said — Chesterton, I think — about the difference between the mathematician and the poet. The mathematician tries to get the heavens into his head, the poet tries to get his head into the heavens. . . . But here, you see, even without being a poet . . ."

" I have a stepson who's neither and yet he tries to do both," she interrupted. The word ' stepson ', which she could not recall using before about Norris, threw her like a

362

fluffed line in a play, so that she went on, less securely:
" He had an idea to study medicine and go out to some
tropical island and doctor the natives. No particular reason
except that he thought he'd rather do it than anything else."

" Then he should. That's one of the best reasons for
doing anything."

" I'm so glad to hear you say that."

He was looking at his watch. " I think everything will be
ready by now. . . . Oh, but before we go — I mustn't
forget." He pulled open the drawer and found the little
girl's autograph book. He was the naïve one now, warmer
and closer. " Her first name's Milly — she left it for me
to write in, but when she finds your name too . . ." He
offered his pen.

" Why, of course." She took the book and wrote in it:
" For Milly from Carey Arundel with love. ' Jesu, Joy of
Man's Desiring.' " And the date.

" It's really most kind of you to take the trouble, Miss
Arundel."

" Oh no. No trouble at all. I wish it were always as
easy to give a little pleasure."

Then he saw what she had written. She could see it
startled him. " That's . . . that's very nice. But I'll have
to explain it to her, won't I ? "

" You can show her the label on the record and say you
played it here tonight and I wanted to do something, somehow, so that it shouldn't ever be forgotten."

" *I* wouldn't have forgotten. . . . Shall we walk over
now ? "

.   .   .   .   .   .

He guided her again by flashlight along the pathway that
led across the rounded hump of the mountain-top to the
Observatory. The huge aluminium structure glistened dimly
as they approached it. He began to talk about what she
would presently see, and after she had met his assistant (a
good-looking youth named Christianson) his manner became
progressively more impersonal. It was doubtless the same

little lecture he had given to countless other visitors — terse, elementary, decked out with a few simple-minded witticisms. He even perpetrated the most obvious of all — " A star come to look at the stars," he told Christianson. It was all Miss Arundel this and Miss Arundel that, but she knew that in a truer sense his politeness and admiration stopped short of real concern ; she was just a charming inhabitant of a lower world who earned as much in a week as he did in a year ; *and he did not care*. Out of sheer kindness he would have done as much for her, perhaps more, had she been Mrs. Anybody from Anywhere.

When they left, after an hour or so, he asked if she would like some coffee, but she felt he hoped she would decline ; she had heard Christianson locking up as they walked away, and it occurred to her that probably they would both go to bed as soon as she had gone.

Christianson caught up with them as they reached the parking lot. It was about a quarter to four. He said : " It's almost dawn. You'll see the sunrise before you're home. Wouldn't you rather have the top up ? It'll be chilly."

" No, I like it open. I'll wear this extra coat."

Lingard helped her on with it. " What a beautiful car ! You should hear my old jalopy wheezing and sputtering when I bring it up here. . . . Mind how you take the curves."

She put out her hand. " It's been so nice, professor. I can't tell you how much I've enjoyed it."

" The firmament or the argument ? "

" Both. And Bach too. Now *there's* a man who had his head in the heavens."

" Yes, and didn't do too badly on earth either. I think he had twenty children." He laughed and turned to Christianson. " I played my favourite record for Miss Arundel while we were waiting. The Chorale."

She laughed back as she answered : " Why, of course, *that's* why I feel optimistic. Bach abhors a catastrophe too. . . . Twenty, did he ? How wonderful ! . . . And please, professor, do give me a ring when you come down to earth — either of you, or both of you — I'm probably going away fairly soon, so don't leave it too long. . . . Oh dear, I'm not in the book — I'd better give you my number."

She began fishing in her purse, but he said : " Just tell it to me. I can always remember numbers."

" You're sure you can ?   It's Excelsior 16641."

" That's easy. Happens to be the square of 129. . . . Good night, Miss Arundel. And thanks again for the autographing."

" Good night. . . . Good morning, rather. Goodbye, Mr. Christianson."

.   .   .   .   .   .

She started the car and drove away. What she intended to do was not even then quite clear in her mind ; final decision, like Paul's, might come by chance or caprice, some lightning alchemy of time or place. The music, like the road, like something in her own head, went round and round — and who would have thought that 16641 was the square of 129 ? That revelation, with all its hint of things hidden before one's own eyes, made some mental link with the look of emptiness as she turned the downhill corners ; it was almost dawn, but the sky seemed blacker, far more abysmal than on the way up. No doubt cars had met with accidents or near-accidents on this road before ; the headlights showed up the scuffs on the guard-rails. No guard-rails on the road over the Sally Gap, where she had driven once with her mother and Fitzpomp in an old-fashioned horse-drawn wagonette — skies cloudy-clear, mountains blue-green in the sun-shadow, no talk of trouble in those days, so it must have been before the Easter Rebellion ; that would make her eleven years old or less. Poor little Fitzpomp with his asthma pills and Gaelic verbs and the muscle-building machine. Those walks with him, her little-girl's hand in his, sometimes through the fields beside the Dodder, or along the Blessington road where the steam tram tooted a greeting as it passed . . . and then the final scene, obliterating all others when she let herself think of it . . . the house in Terenure that Sunday morning, poor little Fitzpomp, leaving her that letter . . . unwilling for her to think (even if she could) that it was all a mishap — unwilling to quit the play without the fullest value of an exit. And the quote from Seneca — the stoic quote — " One cannot complain of life, for it keeps no one against his will ". Perhaps, though, if one had acted professionally in life, one could more easily resist that last temptation — as a good actor will sometimes, for the sheer selflessness of it, take his leave as unmemorably as he can. Or perhaps if one had (to use Paul's phrase) a ready-made audience for the next thing one did, no matter what it was, one could choose that next thing, no matter what it was, with some deep regard for others. . . . Poor Fitzpomp, with no ready-made audience at all. . . . She saw in passing that at one point the guard-rail was broken ; maybe some car had actually gone through. She thought of the crash, the curving fall, the few seconds of being almost airborne . . . she remembered a scene like that in a movie, a car upturned at the foot of a cliff, its occupants dead, but a radio freakishly undamaged, and music — dance music — going round and round. . . . She switched on her own car radio. Sure enough, dance music. Then, after a moment, an early morning news bulletin. . . . Berlin . . . President Truman . . . the Iron Curtain . . . a sentence that made her laugh aloud. " Mother Nature went on a rampage yesterday in our nation's capital." How Paul would enjoy that. *Mother Nature went on a rampage*. She had always had far more time for radio listening than he, and had gathered these flowers whenever she chanced on them and offered them to him like nosegays. She must remember that one, if . . . if, that is, she ever saw him again. Then suddenly she heard his name.

.   .   .   .

As soon as she realized he was at that moment quite probably in jail, she felt cool, rather indignant, and also very slightly amused. Apparently no one had been hurt, just a few fenders dented, it was not a serious case. But she was indignant because she knew he could not have been drunk ; he never did drink too much, he had got over all his excesses in youth, he always said contemptuously, but that of course did not include his central excess of being exactly what he was. She could imagine that this might be what had caused the trouble with the police. It had been the same, once, in New York — and then there had been that more serious trouble in London, when only the judge had finally believed him. He would certainly not have been at his best on his way home from that Critics' Dinner.

She reached the corner where the mountain road joined the main highway ; from there the driving was much safer, with easier curves and fewer cliffs ; the sky, too, was lightening a little. All at once she felt uncontrollably sleepy. She pinched herself to keep her eyes open till she came to a roadside space behind some trees. There she parked and put the top up, intending to take no more than a short nap, but when she woke there was bright sunshine and it was 10 A.M. by her wrist-watch.

Dismayed by having lost so much time she drove on, listening to the radio for more news about Paul. But there was nothing except a mention that the case would come up that morning — might possibly, she surmised, be in progress at that very moment. Some of the more important bulletins ignored the matter altogether, and this reminded her that it was not, after all, an earth-shaking event. That was the trouble with this movie world ; its own belief that it tremendously mattered was more infectious than one realized.

Suddenly she laughed aloud as she had laughed on the way down the mountain in darkness, but this time at something that occurred to her. Mr. Hare had asked about Paul threatening her with a gun, and she had found the question completely mystifying, till now she recalled that studio lunch-hour when, in her dressing-room, Paul had rehearsed the shooting scene from his old German picture, taking the man's part himself and picking up one of the metal tubes that his cigars came in. Someone must have seen and heard all that from a distance . . . how absurd ! She wished she had thought of the explanation in time to tell Mr. Hare. And that reminded her of several appointments that morning —

publicity at the studio, lunch with Mr. Hare . . . of course she could not keep either of them, she must see Paul first. It came to her quite naturally now that she must see him as soon as she could, just to say she was not particularly angry (as everyone would assure him she was). And because everyone would assure her she ought to be, she did not want to see or talk to anyone else before seeing him. She would let him know she had been a little upset at the time, but after all . . . did it matter? What *did* matter? Did *anything* matter? Poor little Fitzpomp had probably taken his own life because he thought that nothing mattered. On the other hand it was possible to think so quite happily if there were only the merest loophole, one's own private *something* tucked away in mind — like Bach, or even the square roots of telephone numbers. . . .

.   .   .   .   .   .

When she reached the streets she stopped at a drug store for coffee and also to telephone Paul at his apartment. She hardly expected him to be back there yet, but it was just possible. She did not leave her name, and the desk clerk (meaningfully, she thought) said he had not been in since the previous day. She drove on through the suburbs. The noon news on the radio told her that the case had ended in a fifty dollar fine. Not so bad. She telephoned his apartment again from quite close; still he was out. Then she parked across the street and waited. If he did not come within an hour or two she would try some other way.

He came within half an hour, driving up in a taxi, alone. She made a U-turn, meeting the kerb behind the taxi; the man saw her manœuvre and was about to drive off again when Paul also saw her and made some wild gesture. " Here — *Here!* " she called out, holding open the door of her car while Paul fumbled with money on the pavement. Why on earth doesn't he give the man a five or a ten quickly? she thought; but that too was like Paul — a big tip, which came from him often, was an expression of his mood, not of any need to get special service. At last he had counted it out and was clambering into the seat next to her. " I thought at first you were someone from a paper," he began breathlessly, with no hello or greeting and no seeming surprise that she was there. " But I guess they've had all they can use."

" Sure," she said, making a fast gear change. " You've given them all they can use."

But then, as she turned the car round the block and headed west along the coast highway, she eyed him sideways and thought he looked rather ill as well as tired and unkempt; and that made her continue, less severely : " The best way to talk is to drive — that is, if you want to talk. I don't know what you want, but I didn't think you'd get much peace today at your apartment. But it'll all die down soon, don't worry. You're not that important."

" You'd have thought so this morning — from the crowd. The judge got mad at them." There was just the faintest twinkle of pride as he said that, and it annoyed her.

" Did you count the house ? " she asked, and that annoyed him. As so often when they met they had to go through this phase of mutual annoyance. She went on : " Tell me what happened."

He gave her what she expected, and had thought she might as well get over, once and for all — a vivid description of an innocent man's martyrdom. She could judge that from the moment the police arrested him he had made things as unpleasant for himself as possible—refusing to call a lawyer or post a bond. " I thought I might as well get the full value of an experience out of it," he said. " And I did, and it was interesting. Quite *horribly* interesting, Carey. It gave me an idea for a modern *Inferno* — the purely visual degradation——"

He went on with the details and she wished she hadn't started the subject ; a modern *Inferno* was just an idea for him to forget, if only because he was always personally influenced by the current enthusiasm of his mind. She interrupted him to say : " You'd like a wash and a shave and a good long rest, I imagine."

" No, don't stop yet. I'm glad you met me like this. And you're right about the apartment — I wouldn't get any peace there. They don't like me. They'd let anybody up to disturb me."

" You don't look very well."

" My God, did you expect me to *bloom* after a night in a tank with a lot of drunks and perverts ? Sorry — I didn't mean to snap at you. To tell you the truth, the whole thing *excited* me — gave me a headache too. One of those bad ones. Of course, not from drinking."

" I know. I knew it couldn't really be that. Why did the police think it was ? "

" Ach . . . those fellows. I couldn't walk in a straight line. And it's a fact, I couldn't. Any more than I could park the car. I never was good at that, anyhow."

" Are you hungry ? "

" No, but I'd like some coffee."

" We'll stop somewhere."

" We'll be recognized."

" I doubt it. And what if we are ? Who cares ? "

" I'll pull my hat down."

" It isn't you they're likely to recognize."

" No ? After all the photographs in the papers ? You know how they do it, Carey ? The man with the camera squats on his heels and shoots upwards through the bars, so that the nostrils gape and the eyebrow shadows reach half-way across the forehead. And then, God help them, they say the camera can't lie. Of course it can lie. Because the Eye can lie. In the beginning was the Eye. Long before the Word. The Eye can tell no more truth than the brain behind it — the Eye lied when the first caveman saw a shape one night and hurled a spear and found he'd killed his wife instead of a sabre-toothed tiger ! "

" Perhaps they were rather hard to tell apart," she said, and then went on : " Oh, Paul, I must tell you something I heard on the radio this morning. Apparently there was a big wind blowing in Washington and the news announcer said ' Mother Nature went on a rampage in our nation's capital '. I thought you'd enjoy that."

He did, as she had guessed, but then seemed abruptly

deflated. " Rampage, rampage," he muttered. " You think that's a good word for something I go on at times ? "

" Yes, I do."

They stopped at a roadside place where there was as good a chance of being unrecognized as anywhere, and she persuaded him to have a bowl of soup as well as coffee. The heat and stuffiness of the place made him instantly drowsy; his eyes kept closing and she noticed that in bringing the spoon to his mouth he often touched his cheek first, as if his hand was not in perfect co-ordination. She remarked on this, as casually as she could. " Do you know you do that, Paul ? "

He replied rather crossly : " No, and what of it ? " Then he smiled in apology. " Reminds me of the only time I tried to play golf. Greg took me round at Carmel. I simply couldn't hit the ball. Not once."

That didn't astonish her so much as the fact that Greg had ever succeeded in putting a club in his hand and getting him on to a course. And then she remembered Interlaken : Paul in shorts, gathering wild flowers in a wood. The things he would do under stress of a personal enthusiasm — for Wanda then, for Greg recently. She said : " Anyhow, I'm glad Greg made you take some physical exercise."

He said gloomily : " He won't again. I'm through with him."

" *What?* With *Greg* ? "

" After last night you bet I am. For him to talk to *me* like that — just because I made a speech he hadn't either the brains or the guts to swallow ! What would he be without me, I'd like to know ? "

" Pretty much what he is now, darling — a successful movie actor."

" But *Morning Journey*'s given him a new reputation — the first picture he's ever got an award for — the nearest he ever came in his life to a real acting performance——"

" And the worst picture you ever made, don't forget. You really are a bit inconsistent, Paul. Does this mean, then, that you're not going abroad with Greg as you planned ? "

" That's all out of the question now."

371

" So what will you do ? "

" I don't know," he answered heavily. " I only know I want to get away some place."

" There's one thing I'd like you to do," she went on, with as much and as little emphasis as she dared. " Have a check-up with a doctor. The one who saw you at the studio said you ought, but you never did. I wish you would, Paul. You're not young any more." She added quickly : " Neither am I."

She paid the bill and they left the restaurant. There had been no mention so far of where they were driving to, or for how long. They were some twenty or thirty miles out, she wasn't quite sure where. She drove on, as the only alter-native to turning back, and after another few miles during which he was silent she saw that his head had slumped forward. This was not unusual when he was being driven, but now for some reason she stopped the car and looked at him intently. That made him wake up.

" You were asleep," she said.

" I guess I didn't sleep at all last night."

" Neither did I — till early this morning. Then I slept in the car by the roadside. I can have adventures too, can't I ? I'll tell you all about it if . . . Or no ; sleep if you'd rather." Then she felt, still watching him, a sudden tightness in her voice. He looked so worn, so shop-soiled ; maybe it was the late sunlight, shining in his face as they drove west—spotlight on Lear in a not too good production. " Oh, Paul, anything you like if only you don't get ill. Will you do what I ask and see a doctor ? "

Weakly, surprisingly, he nodded.

" When, darling ? "

" Any time."

" Now ? "

He half nodded, and she drove on to the next doctor as if it had been to the next gas station. It was beginning to be dusk.

.   .   .   .   .   .

The doctor was intelligent, exact, and considerably interested in his two chance visitors. Also he was clearly not

372

a movie fan. She entered his unpretentious office first, leaving Paul in the waiting-room, dozing off. There were no other patients waiting and she rather gathered she had found him in by chance at such an hour. Paul's general appearance and need of sleep were not unnatural after the kind of night he had spent, but of course she had to think of some other explanation to tell the doctor. " We're touring," she said, " and I think it's been too much for him. He has a bad headache. Perhaps it's the heat . . . but I'm a little worried and I thought . . ."

" And the name ? " he said, pulling a pad towards him.

" Mrs. Bond."

" Well, we'll have a look at him." He left his desk and opened the door to the waiting-room. Carey went past him towards Paul. She touched Paul's shoulder but he did not move; he was breathing heavily, snoring a little, the head sagging on the chest. The doctor walked across. " I guess your father's taking a real nap," he said, stooping over Paul with a smile.

" He's not my father." She had spoken before she could check herself.

" Oh ? "

" He's . . ." She had to say something now. " He's my husband."

The doctor was already shaking Paul more vigorously. At last Paul wakened, blinked to find where he was, then with a sharp shift to gentleness and courtesy, apologized to the doctor. The latter kept on smiling. " That's all right, Mr. Bond." Still only half awake as he staggered into the office on the doctor's arm, Paul did not seem to notice.

.   .   .   .

He went out to the car afterwards, while she talked to the doctor.

" Quite a sick man you've got, Mrs. Bond," he began, and her heart fell through the guard-rail into some abyss of its own.

" He is ? " she stammered foolishly. " He . . . he really *is* ? "

" I'd advise you to call off your holiday and get him home.

373

Then put him in the care of his regular doctor. Maybe you should take the train if you've come a long way."

"Oh no, not far — just from . . . inside the state."

He looked as if he expected her to say more. "Well, don't do any more travelling today. Take him to some hotel — the Bristol up the road isn't so bad — and let him have a good long sleep. He said he didn't get any last night. Were you driving late ? "

"No . . . no. . . ."

"He seems quite exhausted."

"Yes . . . but . . . it's not . . . is it, I mean . . . is it anything *very* serious ? "

"If he doesn't get rest it could be."

"But with rest . . . he'll be all right ? "

"There's a very good chance of it. . . . What does he do for a living ? "

"He's — he's in business."

"For himself ? "

"Oh yes." Even at such a moment she could not help thinking wryly how well the phrase suited all Paul's activities since he was born.

"That's fortunate — he can take things easily, then, if he wants to. Men like him at his age are a problem — if they were working men they'd be glad enough to retire, but because they have their own businesses to run they——"

"He's not so old," she interrupted.

"He told me sixty-three."

It was on her tongue to exclaim : " *What?* Why, he's only *fifty*-three ! " — but then she thought there was little point in developing the issue. She said : " Well, that's not so very old " — and all the time she was wondering why on earth Paul had added ten years to his age. Was it because of some twisted vanity that made him want to hear the comment : " You certainly don't look it " ? But the tragic thing was that he *did* look it ; to be sure of the pleasing answer he should have added twenty years.

"Has he been under any particular strain lately ? " the doctor was asking.

"Well, yes, he . . ." She managed to check herself this time. "His life's more or less all strain — the way he works."

He was clearly puzzled by her reticences, but as they continued to talk she felt that his own were at least as great. She said at last : "You haven't really told me what's the matter with him, have you ? "

"I'd rather your own doctor do that when there's been a chance to make a complete examination."

"That . . . sounds . . . rather frightening. I wish you could give me some idea."

He scrutinized her.

"I'd rather know, whatever it is," she went on. "I'm that kind of person."

"Well . . . if you won't let the word scare you, it looks to me he may have had a slight stroke recently."

"Is that . . . possible ? "

"Without knowing it, you mean ? Yes, if it was only very slight. Certain symptoms . . . but there again, your own doctor . . ."

She paid the fee, thanked him, heard his final words of advice (" take it easy on the trip "), then went out to the car. It was dark by then. Paul was fast asleep and she drove on till she saw the hotel. When she stopped and he wakened she could see he was unaware they had travelled further. He said, as if she had just come out of the doctor's office : "Over-work and high blood pressure. That's all he told me. He tell you anything else ? "

"About the same."

"And how much was the bill for all that ? "

"Ten dollars."

"He must have seen the car." It was always his contention since she had rented a Cadillac that everyone would overcharge her. "Nice fellow, though. I like Mexicans. He told me this town is a third Mexican."

"He told me you must rest, Paul."

"I know, I know."

"Then you start resting . . . now."

He let her take him into the hotel and book rooms and

375

sign the register as she had always done when they had travelled together, and when he entered the bedroom he went straight to the window and pulled the curtains, ready to fulminate if there were no screens. But there were screens. Then he strode through the bathroom to her bedroom and came back and lay on the bed in his own room and lit a cigar. "I asked if I could smoke and he said two a day. I'll bet he didn't know how big these are."

She pulled a chair close to where his arm would swing down, and put an ash-tray on it.

"So this is the Bristol," he said, contemplating the ceiling. "Remember the Bristol in Vienna? No, you weren't with me then. . . . But this is another kind of Bristol. Spittoons in the lobby polished every morning. My ideal of cleanliness. . . . Oh dear, I'm sorry I'm so sleepy. I'll be all right tomorrow. What do we do then?"

"I don't know. We'll settle that when tomorrow comes. This is today."

"And what a day, from start to finish! . . . How kind you are to me, Carey."

"Why wouldn't I be?"

"A hundred reasons if you weren't you."

"But I am, I always am."

He was silent for a few moments, then said: "D'you think I'll ever be able to do any work again?"

"Of course you will."

"I wonder. . . ."

He had spoken so sadly and sincerely, not dramatically at all, that she sat down on the bed and took the hand that did not hold the cigar. She thought with calmness: If he dies, what will *I* do? Will I be free or will freedom be another kind of bondage to all I can remember? Because so long as he's alive, anywhere, with anybody . . . and if that be love, let it flow from me to him whenever he needs it, as now. . . . Oh, Paul, why did I ever meet you if it were not for this, yet why did I ever meet you if it were only for this? So I'm back at last, or you are, it doesn't matter which, but it's late, isn't it? . . . it's so terribly late. . . .

She whispered: "You will work again, when you're rested enough. I'll help you, I'll be with you — you know you can count on me. I can work too — I'll do another picture or a stage play or something. And one of these days, darling, but not yet — because you need that long rest — one of these days, though, you'll make that picture about children you talked of — the one where the camera itself is a child — you were going to tell me about it once when someone came in and interrupted . . . don't you remember?"

He seemed not to at first, but soon he either did so or else began to think about it as if it were a new idea. She did not want to excite him, but the look that came into his face was the look of life itself and it brought life to her. "I think I'd shoot from three feet above the ground," he muttered. "Everything in a child's-eye view — a child's proportion — a smile makes the sun shine twice as bright — we could get a lighting effect for that . . . and the eye widening like a lens — everything big when it loves something — an apple, a toy, the mother's breast, a dog as big as a horse. . . ."

He closed his eyes, sighing contentedly. After a little while she knew he was asleep again, so she took the cigar from his hand and laid it down.